P9-DVT-297

CALGARY PUBLIC LIBRARY

JAN   2018

The Pearl Sister

Also by Lucinda Riley

The Orchid House
The Girl on the Cliff
The Lavender Garden
The Midnight Rose

The Seven Sisters Series

The Seven Sisters
The Storm Sister
The Shadow Sister

THE
PEARL
SISTER

CeCe's Story

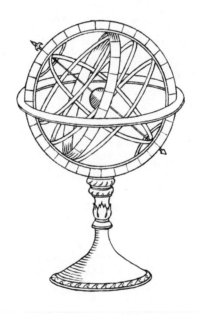

LUCINDA RILEY

ATRIA BOOKS

New York   London   Toronto   Sydney   New Delhi

**ATRIA
BOOKS**

An Imprint of Simon & Schuster, Inc.
1230 Avenue of the Americas
New York, NY 10020

This book is a work of fiction. Any references to historical events, real people, or real places are used fictitiously. Other names, characters, places, and events are products of the author's imagination, and any resemblance to actual events or places or persons, living or dead, is entirely coincidental.

Copyright © 2018 by Lucinda Riley

All rights reserved, including the right to reproduce this book or portions thereof in any form whatsoever. For information address Atria Books Subsidiary Rights Department, 1230 Avenue of the Americas, New York, NY 10020.

First Atria Books hardcover edition January 2018
Originally published in Great Britain in 2017 by Macmillan

ATRIA BOOKS and colophon are trademarks of Simon & Schuster, Inc.

For information about special discounts for bulk purchases,
please contact Simon & Schuster Special Sales
at 1-866-506-1949 or business@simonandschuster.com.

The Simon & Schuster Speakers Bureau can bring authors to your live event. For more information or to book an event contact the Simon & Schuster Speakers Bureau at 1-866-248-3049 or visit our website at www.simonspeakers.com.

Manufactured in the United States of America

10   9   8   7   6   5   4   3   2   1

Library of Congress Cataloging-in-Publication Data

Names: Riley, Lucinda, author.
Title: The pearl sister : Cece's story / Lucinda Riley.
Description: First Atria Books hardcover edition. | New York : Atria Books, 2018. | Series: The seven sisters ; book 4 | "Originally published in Great Britain in 2017 by Macmillan"—Title page verso. | Includes bibliographical references.
Identifiers: LCCN 2017040922 (print) | LCCN 2017046420 (ebook) | ISBN 9781501180057 (eBook) | ISBN 9781501180033 (hardback)
Subjects: LCSH: Sisters—Fiction. | Nineteen twenties—Fiction. | BISAC: FICTION / Literary. | FICTION / Historical. | FICTION / Action & Adventure. | GSAFD: Historical fiction. | Mystery fiction.
Classification: LCC PR6055.D63 (ebook) | LCC PR6055.D63 P43 2018 (print) | DDC 823/.914—dc23
LC record available at https://lccn.loc.gov/2017040922

ISBN 978-1-5011-8003-3
ISBN 978-1-5011-8005-7 (ebook)

For father and daughter,
Richard and Felicity Jemmett

No journey is impossible.
It only takes a single step forward.

LIST OF CHARACTERS

ATLANTIS

Pa Salt—the sisters' adoptive father (deceased)

Marina (Ma)—the sisters' guardian

Claudia—housekeeper at Atlantis

Georg Hoffman—Pa Salt's lawyer

Christian—the skipper

THE D'APLIÈSE SISTERS

Maia

Ally (Alcyone)

Star (Asterope)

CeCe (Celaeno)

Tiggy (Taygete)

Electra

Merope (missing)

CeCe

December 2007

Aboriginal symbol for a human track

I

I remember exactly where I was and what I was doing when I heard that my father had died, I thought to myself as I stared out of the window and saw the complete blackness of night. Intermittently below me, there were small clusters of twinkling lights indicating human habitation, each light containing a life, a family, a set of friends . . .

None of which I felt I had any longer.

It was almost like seeing the world upside down, because the lights below the plane resembled less brilliant facsimiles of the stars above me. This reminded me of the fact that one of my tutors at art college had once told me that I painted as if I couldn't see what was in front of me. He was right. I couldn't. The pictures appeared in my *mind,* not in reality. Often, they didn't take animal, mineral, or even human form, but the images were strong, and I always felt compelled to follow them through.

Like that great pile of junk I'd collected from scrap yards around London and housed in my studio at the apartment. I had spent weeks trying to work out exactly how all the pieces should be placed together. It was like working on a giant Rubik's Cube, though the raw ingredients were comprised of a smelly oil can, an old Guy Fawkes scarecrow, a tire, and a rusting metal pickax. I'd constantly moved the bits into place, happy right up until I added that last vital piece, which always—wherever I put it— seemed to ruin the entire installation.

I laid my hot brow against the cool Perspex of the window, which was all that separated me and everyone else on the plane from asphyxiation and certain death.

We are so vulnerable . . .

No, CeCe, I cautioned myself harshly as panic rose inside me, *you can do this without her, you really can.*

I forced my thoughts back to Pa Salt, because given my ingrained fear of flying, thinking about the moment I heard he'd died was—in a weird way—comforting. If the worst happened and the plane dropped from the sky, killing us all, at least he might be there on the other side, waiting for me. He'd already made the journey up there, after all. And he'd made it alone, as we all did.

I'd been pulling on my jeans when the call had come from my younger sister Tiggy, telling me that Pa Salt was dead. Looking back now, I was pretty sure that none of what she said really sank in. All I could think of was how I'd tell Star, who had adored our father. I knew she would be totally devastated.

You adored him too, CeCe . . .

And I had. Since my role in life was to protect my more vulnerable sister—she was actually three months older than me but she'd found it difficult to speak, so I'd always spoken for her—I'd sealed up my heart, zipped up my jeans, then walked into the sitting room to tell her.

She'd said nothing, just wept in my arms. I'd done everything I could to keep my own tears at bay. For her, for Star. I'd had to be strong because she'd needed me . . .

That was then . . .

"Madam, is there something you need?"

A cloud of musky perfume descended from above me. I looked up and saw the stewardess leaning over me.

"Er, no thanks."

"You pressed the call bell," she said in an exaggerated whisper, indicating the rest of the passengers, who were all asleep. After all, it was four in the morning, London time.

"Sorry," I whispered back, as I removed my offending elbow from the button that had alerted her. Typical. She gave me the kind of nod I remembered one of my teachers had given me when she'd seen me opening my eyes during morning prayer at school. Then, with a rustle of silk, the stewardess disappeared back to her lair. I did my best to make myself comfortable and close my eyes, wanting to be like the four hundred or so random souls who had managed to escape from the horror of hurtling through the air in an aluminum tube by going to sleep. As usual, I felt left out, not part of the crowd.

Of course, I could have booked into business class. I still had some money left from my legacy—but not enough that I wanted to waste it on just another few centimeters of room. Most of my money had gone toward buying the swanky riverside apartment for me and Star in London. I'd thought that a proper home was what she'd wanted, that it would make her happy, but it *so* hadn't . . .

Now here I was, no farther on than this time last year when I'd sat next to my sister in economy class, flying across the world to Thailand. Except this time Star wasn't with me, and I wasn't running *to* something, I was running away . . .

"Would you like breakfast, madam?"

I opened my eyes, feeling groggy and disoriented, and stared up at the same stewardess who had visited me in the middle of the night. I saw that all the cabin lights were on and some of the window blinds were open, revealing the pink hue of dawn.

"No thanks, just coffee. Black, please."

She nodded and retreated, and I wondered why—given I was paying for this entire experience—I felt guilty about asking for anything.

"Where are you headed?"

I turned to face my neighbor, whom I'd only viewed in profile up until now. And even then, it had been a nose, a mouth, and a lock of blond hair hanging out of a black hoodie. Now he was full frontal, staring at me. He was probably no more than eighteen, the traces of adolescent acne still visible on his chin and forehead. I felt ancient next to him.

"Bangkok, then on to Australia."

"Cool," he commented as he tucked into his prison-issue tray of inedible scrambled eggs, over-fried bacon, and a long pink thing that was masquerading as a sausage. "I'll head there eventually, but I'm gonna check out Thailand first. I've been told the Full Moon Parties are something else."

"They are."

"You been?"

"A few times," I replied, his question immediately downloading a selection of memories in my mind.

"Which one do you suggest? Heard Ko Pha Ngan is the best."

"It's been ages since I went there last, but I hear it's huge now—maybe a couple of thousand people. My favorite place is Railay Beach in Krabi. It's very chilled, but I suppose it depends on what you want."

"Heard of Krabi," he said, his jaw working overtime to chew the sausage. "I'm meeting my mates in Bangkok. We've still got a couple of weeks until the full moon to decide anyway. You meeting friends out in Oz?"

"Yeah," I lied.

"Stopping over in Bangkok for a while?"

"Just the night."

I sensed his excitement as the plane began its descent into Suvarnabhumi Airport and the usual set of instructions was issued by the cabin staff for us captives. *It's all a joke, really*, I thought as I closed my eyes and tried to still my banging heart. If the plane crashed, we would all die instantly, whether or not my tray table was in the upright position. I supposed they had to say this stuff to make us feel better.

The plane touched down so gently I hardly knew we were on the ground until they announced it over the PA system. I opened my eyes and felt a surge of triumph. I'd completed a long-haul flight alone and lived to tell the tale. Star would be proud of me . . . if she even cared any longer.

Having gone through immigration, I collected my baggage from the carousel and trooped toward the exit.

"Have a great time in Oz," called my teenage neighbor as he caught up with me. "My mate says the wildlife there is *insane*, spiders the size of dinner plates! See ya!"

With a wave, he disappeared into the mass of humanity. I followed him outside at a much slower pace and a familiar wall of humid heat hit me. I caught the airport shuttle bus to the hotel I'd booked into for my overnight stop, checked in, and took the lift up to my sterile room. Heaving my rucksack off my shoulders, I sat on the white bedsheets and thought that if I owned a hotel, I'd provide my guests with dark sheets that didn't show the stains of other bodies on them the way white does, no matter how hard you scrub.

There were so many things in the world that puzzled me, rules that had been made by someone somewhere, probably a long time ago. I took off my hiking boots and lay down, thinking I could be anywhere in the world, and I hated it. The air-con unit hummed above me and I closed my eyes and tried to sleep, but all I could think about was that if I died right now, not a single human being would know I had.

I understood then what loneliness really was. It felt like a gnawing inside me, yet at the same time, a great hole of emptiness. I blinked away tears—I'd never been a crier—but they kept coming, so that eventually my eyelids were forced to open with the pressure of what felt like a dam about to burst.

It's okay to cry, CeCe, really . . .

I heard Ma's comforting voice in my head and remembered her telling me that when I fell out of a tree at Atlantis and sprained my ankle. I'd bitten my bottom lip so hard in my effort not to be a crybaby that I'd drawn blood.

"She'd care," I murmured hopelessly, then reached for my mobile and thought about turning it on and texting Ma to tell her where I was. But I couldn't hack seeing a message from Star, or, even worse, seeing no message from her at all. I knew *that* would break me, so I threw the phone across the bed and tried to close my eyes again. But then an image of Pa appeared behind my eyelids and wouldn't go away.

It's important that you and Star make your own friends, as well as having each other, CeCe . . .

He'd said that just before we'd gone to the University of Sussex together, and I'd been cross because I didn't *need* anyone else, and neither did Star. Or at least, I hadn't thought she did. Then . . .

"Oh, Pa," I sighed, "is it better up there?"

In the past few weeks, as Star had made it clear she wasn't interested in being with me anymore, I'd found myself talking to Pa a lot. His death just didn't seem real; I still felt him close to me, somehow. Even though outwardly I couldn't have been more opposite to Tiggy, my next sister down, with all her weird spiritual beliefs, there was this odd part of me that knew and felt things too . . . in my gut *and* in my dreams. Often it felt like my dream time was more real and vivid than when I was awake—a bit like watching a series on TV. Those were the good nights, because I had nightmares too. Like the ones with the enormous spiders . . .

I shuddered, remembering my teenage plane companion's parting words . . . They couldn't really be the size of dinner plates in Australia, could they?

"Christ!" I jumped out of bed to halt my thoughts, and washed my face in the bathroom. I looked at my reflection, and with my eyes pink and swollen from crying and my hair slick with grease after the long journey, I decided I looked like a baby wild boar.

It didn't matter how many times Ma had told me how beautiful and unusual the shape and color of my eyes were, or Star had said how much she liked to stroke my skin, which was—in her words—as smooth and soft as cocoa butter. I knew they were just being kind, because I wasn't blind as well as ugly—and I hated being patronized about my looks. Given I had five beautiful sisters, I'd gone out of my way not to compete with them. Electra—who just happened to be a supermodel—was constantly telling me that I wasn't making the best of myself but it was a waste of time and energy, because I was never going to *be* beautiful.

However, I *could* create beauty, and now, at my lowest ebb, I remembered something else that Pa had once said to me when I was younger.

Whatever happens to you in life, darling CeCe, the one thing that can never be taken away from you is your talent.

At the time, I thought it was just another—what's the word Star would use?—*platitude* to make up for the fact that I was basically crap looks-wise, crap academically, and crap with people. And actually, Pa was wrong, because even if other people couldn't take talent away from you, they could destroy your confidence with their negative comments and mess with your brain, so you didn't know who you were anymore or how to please anyone, least of all yourself. That was what had happened to me on my art course. Which was why I'd left.

At least I learned what I wasn't good at, I comforted myself. Which, according to my tutors, was most of the modules I'd taken in the past three months.

Despite the battering my paintings and I had received, even *I* knew that if I lost faith in my talent now, then there wasn't any point in carrying on. It really was all I had left.

I went back into the bedroom and lay down again, just wanting these awful lonely hours to pass, and finally understanding why I saw so many old people sitting on benches whenever I walked through Battersea Park on my way to college. Even if it was freezing outside, they needed to confirm that there were other human beings on the planet, and that they weren't completely alone.

I must have fallen asleep, because I had the spider nightmare and woke myself up screaming, automatically clapping a hand to my mouth to shut myself up in case someone along the corridor thought I was being murdered. I decided I just couldn't stay in this soulless room any longer by myself, so I put on my boots, grabbed my camera, and took the lift down to reception.

Outside, there was a queue of waiting taxis. I climbed into the back of one and directed the driver to the Grand Palace. It had always amused and upset me in equal measure that Bangkok, and what I'd seen of Thailand in general, seemed to be completely overstaffed. In any shop, even if you just went in for a packet of peanuts, there was always one person to guide you around, then another to work the till, and a third to bag your purchase. Labor was so cheap there, it was a joke. I immediately felt bad for thinking that, then reminded myself that this was why I loved traveling: it put things into perspective.

The driver dropped me at the Grand Palace and I followed the hordes of tourists, many of them bearing telltale red shoulders that spoke of a recent arrival from colder climates. Outside the temple, I removed my hiking boots and placed them with the variety of flip-flops and trainers other visitors had left by the steps, then walked inside. The Emerald Buddha was supposed to be over five hundred years old and was the most famous statue in Thailand. Yet he was small compared to the many other Buddhas I'd seen. The brightness of the jade and the way his body was shaped reminded me of a bright green lizard. His limbs were fluid and, to be honest, not very accurate. Not that it mattered—"he" was a beautiful thing.

I sat down cross-legged on one of the mats, enjoying my time out in the sun in this big, peaceful space with other human beings around me, probably contemplating their navels too. I'd never been one for religion, but if I had to pick one, I liked Buddhism best because it seemed to be all about the power of nature, which I felt was a permanent miracle happening right in front of my eyes.

Star often said that I should sign up to become a member of the Green Party when she'd listen to me rant on for ages after watching some TV program on the environment, but what would be the point? My voice didn't count, and I was too stupid to be taken seriously. All I knew was that the plants, animals, and oceans that made up our ecosystem and sustained us were so often ignored.

"If I worship anything, it's that," I murmured to the Buddha. He too was made of earth—of hewn mineral turned to beauty over millennia—and I thought he'd probably understand.

Given this was a temple, I thought I should put in a word to Pa Salt. Maybe churches and temples were rather like telephone exchanges or Internet cafés: They gave you a clearer line up to the heavens . . .

"Hi, Pa, really sorry that you died. I miss you much more than I thought I would. And I'm sorry if I didn't listen to you when you gave me advice, and all your words of wisdom and stuff. I should have because look how I've ended up. Hope you're okay up there," I added. "Sorry again."

I stood up, feeling the uncomfortable lump of tears threatening the back of my throat, and walked toward the door. As I was about to step outside, I turned back.

"Help me, Pa, please," I whispered to him.

Having bought a bottle of water from a street vendor, I wandered down to the Chao Phraya River and stood watching the heavy traffic chugging along it. Tugs, speedboats, and wide barges covered with black tarpaulins continued about their daily business. I decided to get on a passenger ferry and go for a ride—it was cheap and at least better than sitting in my miserable hotel room back at the airport.

As we sped along, I saw glass skyscrapers with golden temples nestled elegantly between them, and along the riverbanks, rickety jetties connected wooden houses to the stream of activity on the water. I took my trusty Nikon camera—Pa had given it to me on my sixteenth birthday, so that I could, as he'd put it, "take pictures of what inspires you, darling"—and snapped away. Star was always nagging me to move to digital photography, but me and technology didn't get on, so I stuck to what I knew.

After getting off the boat just past the Mandarin Oriental Hotel, I walked up the street beside it and remembered how I'd once treated Star to high tea in the famous Authors' Lounge. We'd both felt out of place in our jeans and T-shirts, with everyone else dressed up to the nines. Star had spent hours in the library looking at the signed photographs of all the authors who had stayed at the hotel in the past. I wondered if she ever *would* write her novel, because she was so good at putting sentences together and describing things on paper. Not that it was any of my business anymore. She had a new family now; I'd seen a light in her eyes when I'd arrived home a few weeks ago and a man she called

"Mouse" had been there in our apartment, gazing at her like an adoring puppy.

I sat down at a street café and ordered a bowl of noodles and a beer just for the hell of it. I wasn't good with alcohol, but given I was feeling so awful, it couldn't really make me feel much worse. As I ate, I thought that what hurt the most wasn't the fact that Star had a new boyfriend and job, it was that she'd withdrawn from me, slowly and painfully. Perhaps she thought I'd be jealous, that I wanted her all to myself, which just wasn't true. I loved her more than anything, and only wanted to see her happy. I'd never been so stupid as to think that one day, what with her being so beautiful and clever, a man wouldn't come along.

You were really rude to him when he came to the apartment, my conscience reminded me. And yes, I *had* minded his being there, and, as usual, I hadn't known how to hide it.

The beer did its job and blunted the sharp edges of my pain. I paid, then stood up and walked aimlessly along the road before turning into a narrow alley that had a street market. A few stalls down, I came across an artist painting a watercolor. Watching him sitting at his easel reminded me of the nights I'd sat on Railay Beach in Krabi with my sketch pad and tin of paints, trying to capture the beauty of the sunset. Closing my eyes, I remembered the peace I'd felt when I'd been there with Star, only a year ago. I wanted it back so much it hurt.

I made my way to the riverbank and leaned over the balustrade, thinking. Would it be turning chicken to head for the place I'd felt happiest before going on to Australia? I knew people on Railay Beach. They'd recognize me, wave, and say hello. Most of them were escaping from something too, because Railay was that kind of place. Besides, the only reason I was going to Australia was because of what Georg Hoffman, Pa's lawyer, had told me when I'd been to see him. It was somewhere to head to, far away from London.

So, instead of spending twelve hours flying in a tube to a place where I knew no one, I could be drinking a cold beer on Railay Beach by this time tomorrow night. Surely a couple of weeks or so wouldn't hurt? After all, it was Christmas soon and it might be less awful to spend it in a place that I knew and loved . . .

It was the first time in ages that I'd actually felt anticipation at the thought of doing something. Before the feeling vanished, I hailed the first taxi I saw and directed it back to the airport. Inside the terminal, I went to the Thai Airways ticket desk and explained that I needed to delay my flight to Australia. The woman at the desk did a lot of tapping on her computer and told me it would cost about four thousand baht, which wasn't much in the scheme of things.

"You have flexible ticket. What date you wish to rebook?" she asked.

"Er, maybe for just after Christmas?"

"Everything full. First available flight is eighth of January."

"Okay," I agreed, glad I could now blame fate for having to stay on longer. Then I booked a return flight from Bangkok to Krabi, leaving early the following morning.

Back in my hotel room, I took a shower, brushed my teeth, and climbed into bed feeling calmer. If my sisters heard, I knew they would all say that I was "bumming around" again, but I didn't care.

Like an injured animal, I was going away to hide and lick my wounds.

2

The best thing about Railay Beach is that it's on a peninsula and you can only reach it by boat. Star and I had traveled to many incredible places, but sitting on a wooden bench in a long-tail boat speeding noisily across an aquamarine sea, and that first sight of the incredible limestone pillars rising into a deep blue sky, had to be up there in my top five magical moments.

As we drew closer, I saw ropes attached to the rock, with humans who looked like multicolored ants dressed in bright fluorescent shorts scaling its surface. As I heaved my rucksack onto my shoulders and clambered off the boat, my skin prickled in anticipation. Although my limbs were short, they were strong and agile, and rock climbing was one of the things I was actually good at. Not a useful skill for someone who lived in the center of London and wanted to be an artist, but in a place like this, it meant something. I thought about how, depending where you were on the earth, your particular strengths and weaknesses were either positives or negatives. In school I was a dunce, whereas Star was, *literally*, a superstar. Yet here in Krabi, she'd faded into the shadows and sat on the beach with a book, while I'd reveled in all the outdoor activities the area had to offer. The great outdoors *was* my element, as Ma had once commented, and I had been more well-known in the community here than Star.

The color of the water around me was unique: turquoise one moment as the sun glinted on it, then a deep green in the sheltered shadows beneath the huge rocks. As I waded onto land through the shallows, I saw the beach spread out in front of me: a gentle crescent of white sand edged by the enormous limestone pillars, with palm trees dotted intermittently between the basic wooden shacks that housed the hotels and bars. The calming sound of reggae music emanated from one of them.

I trudged across the burning white sand toward the Railay Beach Hotel, where we'd stayed last year, and leaned on the bar-cum-reception tucked inside the wooden veranda.

"Hi," I said to a young Thai woman I didn't recognize. "Do you have a room available for the next few weeks?"

The woman studied me and got out a large reservations folder. She traced her finger carefully down each page, then shook her head.

"Christmas coming. Very busy. No room after twenty-first."

"Just the next two weeks then?" I suggested.

I felt a hand suddenly slap my back.

"Cee? It is you, isn't it?"

I turned around and saw Jack, an Australian bundle of tall, toned muscle, who owned the hotel and ran the rock-climbing school on the beach around the corner.

"Yeah, hi." I grinned at him. "I'm just checking in, at least for a couple of weeks, anyway, then I get kicked out. Apparently you're fully booked."

"Sure we can find you a cupboard somewhere, darl', don't worry about that. Your sister here with you?"

"Er, no. Just me this time."

"How long are you staying?"

"Until after New Year."

"Well, if you want to give me a hand at the rock, let me know. I could do with it, Cee. Business goes mad this time of year."

"I might. Thanks," I said.

"You fill out details." The Thai receptionist handed me a card.

"Don't worry about that, Nam," Jack told her. "Cee was here with her sister last year so we have them already. Come on. I'll show you to your room."

"Thanks."

As Jack picked up my rucksack, I saw the receptionist giving me the evils.

"Where are you headed after here?" he asked companionably as he led me along a wooden walkway, off which a series of basic rooms lay behind a row of battered doors.

"Australia," I replied as we stood in front of room twenty-two, at the end of the walkway. I saw it was slap-bang next door to the generator, with a view of two big wheelie bins.

"Ah, my home country. Which part?"

"The northwest coast."

"Blistering this time of year, y'know."

"The heat doesn't bother me," I said as I unlocked my door.

"Well, see ya around." Jack gave me a wave and ambled off.

Even though the room was tiny, humid, and smelled strongly of rubbish, I dumped my rucksack on the floor, feeling more chipper than I had in weeks, because it felt so good to be known. I'd loved my occasional days working at the rock-climbing school last year, checking the ropes and fastening clients into their harnesses. At the time, Star and I had been short of cash and Jack had knocked some money off our room in return. I wondered what he'd say if I told him I didn't need to work anymore, because I was now a millionaire. On paper, anyway . . .

I tugged on a frayed piece of cord to switch on the ceiling fan, and eventually, with a lot of clanking and squeaking, it began to turn, stirring up only a whisper of breeze. Discarding my clothes, I put on my bikini and a sarong I'd bought there last year, then left my room and wandered down to the beach. I sat on the sand for a bit, chuckling at the fact that there in "paradise," what with all the long-tail boats motoring in and out of the bay, it was a million times noisier than living on the river in the center of London. I stood up, walked down to the shore, and waded into the sea. When I was far enough out, I lay on my back in the gorgeous water, looked up at the sky, and thanked God, or Buddha, or whomever I was meant to thank, that I'd come back to Krabi. I felt at home for the first time in months.

I slept on the beach that night, as I'd often done in the past, with only a kaftan, a hoodie, and my blow-up pillow for comfort. Star had thought I was nuts—"You'll get bitten to death by mosquitoes," she'd commented whenever I'd trailed out of the room with my bedding. But somehow, with the moon and stars shining down on me, I felt more protected by the roof of the world than I would have done by anything man-made.

I was woken by a tickling on my face, and lifted my head to see a large pair of male feet marching past me toward the sea. Brushing away the sand they'd shed onto me, I saw that the beach was otherwise deserted, and by the look of the light beginning to spread across the horizon, it was just before dawn. Grumpy at being woken so early, I watched as the man—who had a beard and black hair scraped back in a ponytail that straggled out of the back of his baseball cap—reached the shore and sat down, his knees drawn up to his chest, his arms folded around them. I turned over to try to get back to sleep—I got my best rest between four and ten a.m.—but my body and mind weren't interested. So I sat up, assumed the same position as the man in front of me, and watched the sunrise with him.

Given the amount of exotic places I'd visited, I'd actually seen relatively few sunrises in my life, because it wasn't my time of day. The magnificent, subtle hues of dawn breaking reminded me of a Turner painting, but it was far better in real life.

Once the sun's performance was over, the man immediately stood up and walked away along the beach. I heard the faint chug of a long-tail boat in the distance, heralding the start of the human day. I stood up, deciding to retreat to my room to get some more sleep before the beach filled with outgoing and incoming passengers. *Still*, I thought, as I unlocked the door and lay down on my bed, *it was worth being woken up to see that.*

Just as it always seemed to there, time slipped past without my really noticing. I'd agreed to Jack's offer of helping him out at the rock-climbing school. I also went scuba diving, swimming alongside seahorses, tiger fish, and black-tipped reef sharks who barely spared me a glance as they cruised through the corals.

Sunsets were spent chatting on mats on the beach, with the sound of Bob Marley in the background. I was pleasantly surprised by how many Railay residents remembered me from last year, and it was only when darkness fell and they were hanging out at the bar intent on getting drunk that I'd head back to my room. It didn't feel too bad, though, because I was leaving them, not the other way around, and I could always go back and join them if I wanted to.

One thing that had really cheered me up was when I'd finally had the courage to turn on my mobile a day after I'd arrived, and I'd seen that Star had left me loads of texts saying things like, *Where are you?*, *I'm so worried about you!,* and *Please call me!* There had also been a lot of voice mails from her, which mostly said that she was sorry over and over again. It had taken me a while to send a reply—not just because I was dyslexic, but because I didn't know what to say.

In the end, I just said that I was fine, and apologized for not getting in touch sooner, because I'd been in transit. Which I had, from all sorts of stuff. She texted back immediately, saying how relieved she was that I was okay, and asking me where I was, and saying that she was sorry, again. Something stopped me from telling her my location. It was childish, but it was the only secret I had to keep. And she'd kept a lot from me lately.

I only realized I'd been in Railay for two weeks when Nam, the young Thai woman on the reception desk, who acted as though she owned the place, reminded me I had to check out today at noon.

"Bugger," I said under my breath as I walked away, realizing I'd have to spend the morning room-hunting.

I arrived back at the hotel a couple of hours later, having fruitlessly traipsed the length and breadth of Railay Beach in search of a bed for the night—like Mary on her donkey—to find Nam glaring at me again.

"Maid need to clean room. New guest arrive at two p.m."

"I'm on my way," I said, wanting to tell her that actually, I could easily afford to book in at the five-star Rayavadee hotel. *If* they actually had a room, which they didn't, because I'd already checked. I stuffed everything into my rucksack, then dropped off the key to my room. *I'll just have to sleep under the stars for a few days until Christmas is over*, I thought.

Later that evening, having eaten my bowl of pad thai, I saw Jack propping up the bar. He had an arm around Nam, which immediately explained her bad attitude toward me.

"You found a room?" Jack asked me.

"No, not yet, but I'm fine sleeping on the beach for tonight."

"Listen, Cee, take mine, no worries at all. I'm sure I can find a bed for a few nights elsewhere." He nuzzled into Nam's smug little shoulder.

"Okay, thanks, Jack," I agreed swiftly, having spent the afternoon guarding my rucksack on the beach like it was the Holy Grail, and wondering how I could take a shower to wash the sand and salt off my skin. Even *I* needed the basics.

He dug in his pocket for the key and handed it to me, as Nam looked at me with disapproval. Following his directions up a flight of narrow stairs that led from reception, I opened the door, and apart from the smell of sweaty socks laced with a hint of damp towels, I was quite impressed— Jack had the best view in the building. And even better than that, a narrow wooden balcony, built out over the roof of the veranda below.

Locking the door, in case a drunk Jack forgot he'd loaned me his room, I took a shower; his bathroom had a far bigger and more powerful nozzle than the dribbles in the guest rooms below me. I put on a clean T-shirt and shorts and went to sit out on the balcony.

Close to Orion's Belt, I saw the Seven Sisters stars clustered together. When Pa had first shown me my star through his telescope, he had seen that I was disappointed. It was the least bright, which just about said it all, and my mythological story seemed vague at best. Being so young, I'd wanted to be the shiniest, biggest star with the best story of all.

CeCe, he'd said, taking my small hands in his. *You're here on earth to write your own story. And I know you will.*

As I stared at the star cluster, I thought of the letter Pa had written to me, which was given to me by Georg Hoffman, his lawyer, a few days after Pa had died.

Star had refused to open hers, but I'd been desperate to read mine. So I'd taken myself off into the garden and climbed into the branches of a magnificent old beech tree—the same tree I'd once fallen out of when I was small. I'd always felt safe up there, protected from view by its leafy branches. I'd often gone there to think, or to sulk, depending on the situation. Making myself comfortable on the wide bough, I'd torn open the letter.

Atlantis
Lake Geneva
Switzerland

My darling CeCe,
I know reading this letter will be a struggle for you. I beg you to have the patience to finish it. I'll also guess that you will read this without crying, because emotion is a land you keep inside. Yet I'm fully aware of how deeply you feel.

I am certain you will have been strong for Star. You arrived at Atlantis within six months of each other and the way you have always protected her has been a beautiful sight to witness. You love deeply and fiercely, as I have always done. A word of advice from one who knows: Take care that this is not to the detriment of yourself. Don't be afraid of letting go when the time comes—the bond you share with your sister is deep and unbreakable. Trust in it.

As you will already have seen, I have left you girls an armillary sphere in my special garden. Under each of your names is a set of coordinates that will tell you exactly where I found you. There is also a quotation, which I hope you feel is apt. I certainly do.

In addition, I urge you to go and see my dear friend and lawyer Georg Hoffman as soon as you can. Don't worry, what he has to tell you is very good news, and in itself provides a link with your past that will be enough to send you on your way if you want to discover more about your birth family. If you do take the leap, I'd advise you to find out about a woman called Kitty Mercer, who lived in Broome on the northwestern coast of Australia. It was she who began your story.

I realize that you have often felt overshadowed by your sisters. It is vital that you don't lose faith in yourself. Your talent as an artist is unique—you paint as your imagination demands. And once you have found the confidence to trust in it, I am sure you will fly.

Lastly, I want to tell you how much I love you, my strong, determined adventurer. Never stop searching, CeCe, for both inspiration and peace, which I pray will come to you eventually.
Pa Salt x

Pa had been right about one thing—it had taken me almost an hour to read the letter and decipher every single word. Yet he was wrong about something else—I had almost cried. I'd sat up in that tree for a long time, until I'd realized that my backside was numb, and my legs had got pins and needles, so I'd had to climb down.

By the grace of God, I am who I am, had been the quotation he'd had engraved onto the armillary sphere. Given that—both then and now—I actually had no *idea* who I was, it hadn't inspired me, only depressed me further.

When I'd been to see Georg Hoffman in his Geneva office the next morning, he'd said that Star couldn't come in with me, so she'd had to wait outside in reception. He'd then told me about my inheritance and handed me an envelope containing a black and white photograph of an older man standing with a teenage boy by a pickup truck.

"Am I meant to know them?" I'd asked Georg.

"I'm afraid I have no idea, Celaeno. That was the only thing that arrived with the funds. There was no note, just the address of the solicitor who wired the money from Australia."

I'd been planning to show the photograph to Star to see if she had any ideas, but in order to encourage her to open her own letter from Pa, I'd resolved that I wouldn't tell her what Georg Hoffman had said until she did. When she *had* eventually opened hers, she hadn't told me what it said, so she still didn't know about the photograph, or where the money to buy the London apartment had actually come from.

You used to tell me everything . . .

I rested my chin on my hands and leaned over the balcony, hit again by a big dose of the "miseries," as Star and I used to call it when we felt low. Out of the corner of my eye, I noticed a solitary figure standing at the water's edge near the rocks, staring up at the moon. It was the guy from a couple of weeks ago who'd woken me up on the beach. As I hadn't seen him since, and because Railay was such a small community, I'd presumed he'd left. But here he was, alone again in the dark of night. Maybe he didn't want to be seen . . .

I watched him for a while to see where he went, but he didn't move for ages, and I got bored, so I went inside and lay down on the bed to try to sleep. Whoever he was, I just *knew* he was as lonely as me.

3

On Christmas Eve—which just happened to be a full moon to boot—I automatically did what Star and I used to do every year with our sisters, and looked up into the night sky to search for the bright, magical star that Pa always told us was the Star of Bethlehem. I'd once Googled the star he'd pointed to and, with Ally's help, discovered that it was in fact the North Star—Polaris. In Switzerland, it was high in the sky all year round, but tonight I couldn't even find it. Then I remembered that Google also said it was harder to see the farther south you went. I gazed heavenward and thought how sad it was that we weren't kids anymore, and that we could discover the truth by pressing a few keys on a computer.

But tonight, I decided, I *would* believe in magic. I fixed my gaze on the brightest star I could find and thought of Atlantis. Besides, even if Christmas wasn't celebrated in Buddhist culture, Thailand still made an attempt for its international guests by hanging up tinsel and foil banners, which at least put everyone in a good mood.

Just before midnight, I wandered out of the noisy bar and walked down toward the rocks to get the best view of the full moon. And there, already standing in the shadows, was the mystery man—once again in the dark, and once again alone. I felt really irritated because I wanted this moment to be special and to have the space to myself, so I turned tail and walked away from him. Then, when I was far enough away, I looked up and spoke to my sister.

"Merry Christmas, Star. Hope it's a good one, and that you're well and comfortable. I miss you," I whispered to the sky. I sent up a little wish to Pa, and then Ma too, who probably missed Pa just as much as any of us. After that, I sent up a kiss to all of my sisters—even Electra, who didn't really deserve a kiss because she was so selfish and mean and spoiled . . . But it was Christmas, after all. I turned back, my legs feeling a bit wobbly beneath me, due to the extra beer that had been pressed into my hand at the bar earlier.

As I was passing the mystery man, I stumbled slightly and a pair of hands reached out to the tops of my arms to steady me. "Thanks," I muttered. "There was an, er . . . rock in the sand."

"That's okay."

As his hands left my arms, I looked up at him. He'd obviously been in for a swim as his long black hair had been released from its ponytail and hung wet about his shoulders. He had what Star and I had nicknamed a chest beard—although it wasn't a very impressive one—and the line of black hairs traveling from his navel to his shorts formed a shadow in the moonlight. His legs looked quite hairy too.

My eyes traveled back up to his face and I saw that his cheekbones stood out like saws above his dark beard, which made his lips seem very full and pink in comparison. When I actually dared to look him in the eyes, I saw that they were a really amazing blue.

I decided he reminded me of a werewolf. After all, tonight was a full moon. He was so skinny and tall that I felt like a plump pygmy next to him.

"Merry Christmas," he mumbled.

"Yeah, merry Christmas."

"I've seen you before, haven't I?" he said. "You were the girl lying asleep that morning on the beach."

"Probably. I'm there a lot." I shrugged casually as his weird blue eyes swept over me.

"Don't you have a room?"

"Yeah, but I like sleeping outside."

"All those stars, the vastness of the universe . . . it puts things into perspective, doesn't it?" He sighed heavily.

"It does. Where are you staying?"

"Nearby." The Werewolf waved his hand vaguely at the rock behind him. "You?"

"There." I pointed back toward the Railay Beach Hotel. "Or at least, my rucksack is," I added. "Bye then." I turned toward the hotel, doing my best to try to walk in a straight line, which was hard enough on sand, but with two beers inside me, almost impossible. I could feel the Werewolf's eyes upon me as I reached the veranda and allowed myself a quick backward glance. He was *still* staring at me, so I grabbed a couple of bottles of water from the fridge and scurried upstairs to Jack's room. After fumbling to unlock the door, I crept onto the balcony to try to spot him, but he'd disappeared into the shadows.

Perhaps he was waiting for me to go to sleep, and then would numb my senses by sticking two enormous fangs into my neck so I wouldn't scream as he sucked my blood dry . . .

CeCe, that's vampires, not werewolves, I told myself with a giggle, then hiccuped and drank a bottle of water straight down, irritated with myself and my pathetic body for not being able to cope with two small beers. I staggered to the bed, feeling my head spin when I closed my eyes, and eventually passed out into oblivion.

Christmas Day was painfully similar to last year there with Star. The tables on the veranda had all been pushed together, and a parody of a roast lunch had been laid out, as if it was possible to re-create the essence of Christmas in ninety-three-degree heat.

After lunch, feeling bloated from the stodgy European food, I took a swim to work the feeling off. It was almost three o'clock, around the time that England would be waking up. Star was probably spending it in Kent with her new family. I emerged from the sea and shook the water droplets off me like a dog. There were lots of couples lying lazily together on the beach, sleeping off their lunches. It was the first Christmas in twenty-seven years that Star and I had spent apart. Well, if the mystery man was a werewolf, then I was a lone wolf now, and I just had to get used to it.

Later on that evening, I was sitting on the corner of the veranda, listening to music through my iPod. It was of the crashing, banging variety, which always cheered me up when I was feeling low. I felt a tap on my shoulder and turned around to see Jack standing beside me.

"Hi there," I said, taking my earphones out.

"Hi. Can I buy you a beer?"

"No thanks. Had enough last night." I rolled my eyes at him, knowing he'd been far too drunk to notice what I'd had.

"Sure. Look, Cee, the thing is that, well . . ." He pulled up a chair and sat next to me. "Nam and I have . . . fallen out. Can't remember what I did wrong, but she kicked me out of bed at four this morning. She didn't even turn up today to help with the Christmas lunch, so I don't think I'll get a warm welcome back tonight. You know what women are like."

Yeah, I am one, remember? I felt like saying, but didn't.

"So, the problem is, I've got nowhere to kip. D'you mind sharing the bed with me?"

Yes, I do mind! I thought immediately. "Really, Jack, as long as I can leave my rucksack in your room, I'm happy to sleep on the beach," I assured him.

"Seriously?"

"Seriously."

"Sorry, Cee, I'm completely knackered after all the preparations for Christmas and the extra work over the last few days."

"It's fine. I'll just go and get what I need and leave you to it."

"I'm sure we'll be able to find you somewhere tomorrow," he called to me as I walked away, feeling the beach was a much better option than sleeping in the same room as a snoring man I hardly knew. Now, that *would* give me nightmares.

I collected my makeshift bedding, then stuffed the rest of my possessions into my rucksack. Tomorrow, I really needed to find myself a place to stay until I left for Australia in two weeks' time.

On the beach, I made my bed under a bush, and on a whim, I dug my mobile out of my shorts and dialed Atlantis.

"Hello?" The phone was picked up after a couple of rings.

"Hi, Ma, it's CeCe. I just wanted to wish you and Claudia a happy Christmas."

"CeCe! I am so happy to hear from you! Star said you'd gone away. Where are you?"

Ma always spoke to us sisters in French and I had to adjust my brain before I could answer her. "Oh, you know me, Ma, on a beach, doing my thing."

"Yes. I didn't think you'd last long in London."

"Didn't you?"

"You're a free spirit, *chérie*. You have wanderlust."

"Yes, I do." At that moment, I loved Ma just about as much as I'd ever loved her. She never judged or criticized, just supported her girls.

I heard the sound of a deep male cough in the background and my ears pricked up.

"Who's there with you?" I asked suspiciously.

"Just Claudia and Christian," said Ma.

In other words, the Atlantis staff.

"Right. You know, Ma, it was really weird, but when I got to the airport in London three weeks ago, I'm sure I saw Pa. He was walking back the other way and I tried to run and catch him, but he'd gone. I know this sounds stupid, but, like, I was sure it was him."

"Oh *chérie*," I heard Ma sigh deeply down the line. "You are not the first of your sisters to say something like this to me. Both Ally and Star told me that they were convinced they had heard or seen him . . . and perhaps you all did. But not in reality. Or at least, not reality as we know it."

"You think we're all seeing and hearing the ghost of Pa?" I chuckled.

"I think we wish to *believe* we are still seeing him, so perhaps our imaginations conjure him up. I see him all the time here," Ma said, suddenly sounding very sad. "And this is such a difficult time of year for us all. You are well, CeCe?"

"You know me, Ma, never had a day's illness in my life."

"And happy?"

"I'm fine. You?"

"I'm missing your father, of course, and all you girls. Claudia sends her love."

"Same to her. Okay, Ma, it's late here, I'm getting my head down now."

"Keep in touch, won't you, CeCe?"

"Yeah, course I will. Night."

"Good night, *chérie*. And *joyeux Noël*."

I tucked my mobile back into my shorts, then put my arms around my knees and rested my head on them, thinking how hard this Christmas must be for her. Us girls could move on to a future—or at least, we could *try*. We had more life ahead of us than we'd already lived, but Ma had given hers to us girls and Pa. I wondered then if she'd actually loved my father in a "romantic" way, and decided she must have to stay on for all those years and make our family *her* family. And now we had all left her.

I then wondered if my real mum had ever missed me or thought of me, and why she'd given me to Pa. Maybe she'd dumped me in an orphanage somewhere, and he'd collected me from there because he'd felt sorry for me. I was sure I'd been a very ugly baby.

All the answers lay in Australia, another twelve hours' journey from here. It was beyond weird that it was one country in the world I'd refused point-blank to visit, even though Star had quite fancied going. Pathetic that my spider nightmare was the reason, but there it was.

Well, I thought as I settled myself down on the sand, *Pa called me "strong" and an "adventurer."* I knew I'd need every ounce of those qualities to get me onto that plane in two weeks' time.

Again, I was woken by tickling across my face. I brushed the sand away and sat up to see the Werewolf walking to the sea. Wondering briefly how many maidens he'd eaten in the past few hours, I watched his long legs make short work of the sand.

He sat down at the water's edge in the same position as last time, with me directly behind him. We both looked up, waiting for the show to begin, like we were in a cinema. *A cinema of the universe* . . . I liked that phrase, and felt proud of myself for thinking of it. Maybe Star could use it in her novel one day.

The show was spectacular, made even more epic by the fact that there were a few clouds around today, softening the rising sun as it seeped like a golden yolk into the whipped egg whites around it.

"Hi," the Werewolf said to me as he was walking back.

"Hi."

"Good one this morning, wasn't it?" he offered.

"Yeah, great."

"Don't think you'll be sleeping out here tonight, mind you. We're in for a storm."

"Yes," I agreed.

"Well, see ya around." He gave me a wave and wandered off.

Back up on the terrace a few minutes later, I saw Jack was setting up breakfast. Nam normally did this, but she still hadn't been seen since Christmas Eve.

"Morning," I said.

"Morning." He gave me a guilty look before he said, "Sleep well?"

"Not bad, Jack." I beckoned him toward me and pointed to the retreating figure on the beach. "Do you know him?"

"No, but I've seen him a coupla times on the beach late at night. Keeps himself to himself. Why?"

"Just wondered. How long has he been here?"

"I'd reckon at least a few weeks."

"Right. Is it okay if I go up and take a shower in your room?"

"Sure. See ya later."

Having showered, I sat on the floor in Jack's room and sorted through my rucksack. I divided clean and dirty clothes—the dirty pile being the vast majority—and decided I'd drop them off at the laundry on my way to find a room. Then if the worst came to the worst and I ended up outside in a storm tonight, at least I'd have some clean, dry clothes for tomorrow.

Even though there was no such thing as Boxing Day in this part of the world, everyone wandered along the narrow alleyway of shacks that passed for shops, looking as they did in Europe: like they had overdrunk, had overeaten, and were fed up because they'd opened all their presents and the excitement had passed. Even the normally smiley laundry lady looked grim as she separated the darks from the whites and shook out my underwear for all to see.

"Ready tomorrow." She handed me the ticket and I trudged out. Hearing a vague rumble of thunder in the distance, I began my hunt for a room.

I walked back onto the hotel veranda later, hot and sweaty and not having found anywhere that could offer me a room until tomorrow lunchtime. I sat drinking a coconut water and ruminating on whether I should move on—go to Ko Phi Phi perhaps, but there was no guarantee that I'd find anything there either. Well, one night out in the rain wouldn't kill me, and if it got really bad, I could always shelter under one of the restaurant verandas.

"Found a room yet?" Jack asked hopefully as he passed me, carrying a tray of beer to the neighboring table.

"Yeah," I lied, not wanting to put him in a difficult position. "I'll go upstairs and collect my rucksack after lunch."

"Don't fancy giving me a hand behind the bar for a while, do you?" he asked. "What with Nam going AWOL and the hotel full, I haven't been able to get along to the rock. Abi's just called to say they've got a queue as long as a python down there. And about as angry."

"I don't mind, though I wouldn't trust me carrying trays," I joked.

"Any port in a storm, Cee. It'll only be a couple of hours, I swear. Free beer and whatever you want to eat is on the house tonight. Come on, I'll show you the ropes."

"Thanks," I said, and stood up to go with him behind the bar.

Four hours later, there was no sign of Jack and I'd had enough. The bar was heaving and there was a rush on juices—presumably sparked by people using vitamin C or Bloody Marys as a hangover cure. None of the drinks were as simple as just pinging the cap off a beer, and I'd ended up splattered with mango juice when the blender had exploded all over me because I hadn't screwed the top on properly. The previous high spirits of the customers had disappeared overnight with the wrapping paper, and I was fed up with being shouted at for being slow. On top of that, I could hear the rumble of thunder getting closer, which meant that later, probably when me and my rucksack would have to make camp on the beach, the heavens would open.

Jack arrived back eventually, full of apologies for being away for so long. He looked around the now almost empty veranda.

"At least you haven't been too busy. It was heaving down at the rock."

Yeah, right . . . I didn't say anything as I finished my noodles, then went upstairs to collect my rucksack.

"Thanks, Cee. I'll see ya around," he said as I arrived back downstairs, paid the bill for my room, and trudged off.

I walked along the beach as a couple of lightning flashes appeared almost directly above me. I reckoned I had about five minutes before the downpour, so I upped my speed and turned right along an alleyway to a bar I knew, then saw that most of the shack-shops had closed up early because of the impending storm. The bar was also pulling down its shutters as I approached.

"Great," I muttered as the owner gave me a curt nod, and I carried on. "This is totally crazy and ridiculous, CeCe," I groaned. "Just go back to Jack and tell him you'll share his bed . . ."

Yet my legs propelled me forward until I arrived at the beach on the other side of the peninsula. It was called Phra Nang, and aesthetically, it was even more beautiful than Railay. Because of this, it was a huge tourist spot for day-trippers, so I usually avoided it. Also, because the luxury Rayavadee hotel backed onto it, there were scary security guards placed along its perimeter. Star and I had gone down there one night after the last long-tail boat had chugged off, and lain on our backs looking up at the stars. Five minutes later, a torch had been shone on our faces and we'd been told to leave. I tried to argue that all beaches in Thailand were public and the hotel security guards had no right to kick us off, but Star had shushed me as they'd manhandled us toward the path that led back to the plebs' side of the peninsula.

That sort of thing burned in my soul, because the earth and its beauty had been created by nature to be enjoyed for free by everyone, not reserved for the rich.

As a streak of blue and purple lightning lit up the sky, I realized this wasn't the moment to have a philosophical discussion with myself. Looking along the beach, I had a brain wave. The Cave of the Princess was at the far end of it, so I began to leg it across the sand. Two-thirds of the way along, huge drops of water began to fall on me. It felt like being pelted with small pieces of gravel.

I arrived at the entrance to the cave, staggered inside, and threw my rucksack down. I looked up and remembered that for some reason there were actually two versions of the princess, both tiny doll-sized figures who nestled within small wooden temples, half-hidden behind hundreds of assorted colorful garlands. On their altar, there were tea lights burning, which illuminated the inside of the cave with a comforting yellow glow.

I smiled to myself, recalling the first time that Star and I had visited the cave. Thinking it would be like any other Thai place of worship, we'd both expected a gold statue and the ubiquitous garland offerings. Instead, we'd been confronted by hundreds of phalluses of different shapes and sizes. I surveyed them now, poking upward from the sandy floor of the cave like erotic stalagmites, and perched on the rocks all around. Red, green, blue, brown . . . small ones, big ones . . . Apparently, this particular deity was a goddess of fertility. And from the size of the instruments that crowded the cave—some of which towered above my own head—I wasn't surprised.

However, tonight the Cave of the Princess was offering me sanctuary and I was out of the rain that was now streaming down like a curtain at the mouth of the cave. I stood up and walked through the selection of tributes, then knelt at the altar to say thank you. After that, I tucked myself into the side of the cave's entrance and watched the storm.

The sky lit up in spectacular flashes as lightning raged over the sea and the jagged limestone pillars. The rain shone silver in the moonlight as it pounded onto the beach in sheets, as if God were crying buckets from up above.

Eventually, feeling wrung out by the spectacle and the sheer energy the universe possessed, I staggered upright. Moving me and my rucksack deeper into the cave, I laid out my bed for the night and fell asleep behind an enormous scarlet phallus.

4

O_{uch!"}

I sat up swiftly as I felt something hard dig me in the ribs. I looked up into the eyes of a Thai security guard, trying to shake off the deep sleep I'd been in. He hauled me from the floor, speaking fiercely into his radio at the same time.

"Not stay here! Get out!" he barked at me.

"Okay, okay, I'm going." I bent down to pack my bedding into my rucksack. Another security guard, shorter and squatter than the first, arrived inside the cave to help out his mate and between the two of them, they manhandled me outside. I blinked in the light and saw the sun was just about to rise into a cloudless sky. They marched me along the beach, their hands clamped to my arms as though I were a dangerous criminal rather than a tourist who had simply taken shelter from the rain in a cave. The sand still felt damp beneath my feet, the only hint of last night's spectacular downpour.

"You don't have to hold on to me," I said bad-temperedly. "I'm going, I really am."

One of them let out a stream of aggressive-sounding Thai words that I couldn't understand as we walked toward the path at the other end of the beach. I wondered if I was to be thrown into jail like in *Bangkok Hilton*, the Nicole Kidman TV series that had frightened me senseless. If the worst happened, I couldn't even call Pa, who would have been over to Thailand in a shot to get me released.

"Is that you again?"

I turned my head and saw the Werewolf lurking in the bushes at the back of the beach.

"Yeah," I said, knowing my face was red with embarrassment.

"Po, let her go," he ordered, walking toward us.

Immediately, the squat security guard released my arm, then the Werewolf talked in fast Thai to the taller guard, who reluctantly dropped my other arm.

"Sorry, they're very officious," he said in English, raising an eyebrow. He spoke to the two men again, then, his eyes sweeping along the beach, beckoned me to follow him. Both guards saluted him, looking really disappointed as they watched me stumble behind him toward the bushes.

"How did you manage that?" I asked. "I thought I was for the chop."

"I said you were a friend of mine. You'd better come in quickly."

Then he took hold of my arm and dragged me through the foliage. Having had a few seconds' reprieve, my heartbeat began to speed up again and I wondered if I was better off with the two security guards than following a man I didn't know into a Thai jungle. I saw there was a high steel gate hidden among the greenery and watched as the Werewolf pressed some numbers on a keypad to the side of it. It opened smoothly and he ushered me beyond it. More trees followed, but then suddenly a vast and beautiful oasis of a garden came into view. To my right, I saw a large swimming pool, tiled in black and looking like something out of a design magazine. We walked through trees bedecked in a shower of golden blossoms, and onto a wide terrace full of wicker furniture with large, plump cushions being laid out on them by a maid in uniform.

"Want some coffee? Juice?" he asked me as we crossed the terrace.

"Coffee would be great," I said, and he spoke in Thai to the maid as we passed her. We were approaching a number of white pavilions set around a courtyard, each topped by traditional Thai *lanna*-style V-shaped roofs. In the center of the courtyard was a pond filled with pink flowers floating on the water. In the middle of it sat a black onyx Buddha. The whole scene reminded me of one of those exotic spas they were always advertising in magazines. I followed the Werewolf up some wooden steps to the side of one of the pavilions, and found myself on a shady roof terrace which gave the most magnificent view of Phra Nang Beach beyond it.

"Wow," was all I could think of to say. "This is . . . awesome. I've been on this beach loads of times, and never even noticed this place was here."

"Good," he said as he indicated I should sit down on one of the enormous sofas. I eased my rucksack off my shoulders and did so tentatively, worried I might mark the immaculate silk covers. It was the most comfortable thing I'd sat on since I'd arrived in Thailand and I just wanted to lie back on the cushions and fall asleep.

"You live here?" I asked.

"Yes, for now anyway. It's not mine, it's a friend's place," he said as the maid arrived up the steps with a tray of coffee and a selection of pastries laid out in a little basket. "Help yourself."

"Thanks." I poured myself a cup of coffee, then added two peat-brown sugar lumps.

"Can I ask why you were being escorted by the security guards from the beach?"

"I was sheltering from the storm in the Cave of the Princess. I . . . must have fallen asleep while I was waiting for it to stop." Pride prevented me from telling him the truth.

"It was quite some storm," he said. "I like it when nature takes over, shows you who's boss."

"So." I cleared my throat. "What do you do here?"

"Oh . . ." He took a sip of his black coffee. "Not a lot. I'm just taking some time out, you know?"

"Great place to do it."

"You?"

"Same." I reached for one of the buttery croissants. The smell reminded me so much of Claudia's breakfasts at Atlantis, I almost forgot where I was.

"What did you do before?"

"I was at art college in London. It didn't work out, so I left."

"Right. I live in London too . . . or at least, I did. On the river in Battersea."

I looked at him in shock, wondering whether this whole episode was some kind of surreal dream and I was actually still asleep behind the scarlet phallus.

"I live there too! In Battersea View—the new apartments that have just been built near Albert Bridge."

"I know exactly where you mean. Well, hello, neighbor." The Werewolf gave me his first genuine smile as he high-fived me. It lit up his weird blue eyes so he no longer looked like a werewolf, but more like a very skinny Tarzan.

I poured myself another cup of coffee and sat farther back on the sofa so that only my feet dangled over the edge. I wished I didn't have my boots on; then I could have curled them beneath me and tried to look as elegant as the surroundings decreed.

"What a coincidence . . ." He shook his head. "Someone told me once that in any country on earth, there's only six degrees of separation between us and someone we know."

"I don't know you," I pointed out.

"You don't?" He eyed me for a few seconds, his expression suddenly serious.

"Nope, should I?"

"Er, no, I just wondered if maybe we'd bumped into each other on Albert Bridge or something," he mumbled.

"Maybe. I used to cross it every day to walk to college."

"I was on my bike."

"Then I wouldn't have recognized you if you were all done up in Lycra and a helmet."

"True."

We both drained our coffees in awkward silence.

"Are you going back there soon? Like, after New Year or something?" I asked him eventually.

The Werewolf's face darkened. "I don't know. Depends on what happens . . . I'm trying to live for today. You?"

"Same, though I'm meant to be going on to Australia."

"Been there, done that. Mind you, I was working and it's never the same. All you get to see is the inside of hotels and offices, and a load of expensive restaurants. Corporate hospitality, you know?"

I didn't, but I nodded my head in agreement anyway.

"I had thought about going there," he continued. "You know when you just want to get as far away as you can . . . ?"

"I do," I said with feeling.

"You don't sound English, though. Is that a French accent I can hear?"

"Yes. I was born . . . well, I don't actually know where I was born 'cause I'm adopted, but I was brought up in Geneva."

"Another place I've visited and only seen the airport on my way to a ski trip. Do you ski? I mean, stupid question if you live in Switzerland."

"Yes. I love it, but I'm not so keen on the cold, you know?"

"I do."

There was another lull in the conversation, which, given the fact I'd already drunk two large cups of coffee, I couldn't fill with another one.

"How come you speak Thai?" I managed after a bit.

"Thai mother. I was brought up in Bangkok."

"Oh. Does she still live there?"

"No, she died when I was twelve. She was . . . wonderful. I still miss her."

"Oh, sorry," I said quickly, before plowing on. "How about your dad?"

"Never met him," he replied abruptly. "What about you, have you met your birth parents?"

"No." I had no idea how we'd wandered into such an intimate conversation in the space of twenty minutes. "Listen, I should be going. I've put you to enough trouble already." I heaved myself forward until my feet touched the ground.

"So, where are you staying now?"

"Oh," I said airily, "some hotel on the beach, but, as you know, I prefer sleeping outside."

"I thought you said your rucksack had a room. Why have you got it with you?"

I immediately felt like a child who'd been caught hiding sweets under the bed. What did it matter if he knew?

"Because there . . . was a mix-up with my room. I borrowed it and then the . . . person who lived in it fell out with his girlfriend and wanted it back. And everywhere else was full. That's why I headed for the cave when it started to rain."

"Right." He studied me. "Why didn't you tell me that in the first place?"

"I dunno," I said, looking at my feet like a five-year-old would. "I'm not . . . desperate or anything. I can take care of myself—there just wasn't a room available, okay?"

"No need to be so embarrassed, I understand completely."

"I just thought you might think I was a vagrant or something. And I'm not."

"I never thought that, promise. By the way, what's all that yellow stuff in your hair?"

"Christ!" I ran my hand through my hair and found that the ends were matted together. "It's mango. My mate Jack asked me to take care of the bar at the Railay Beach Hotel yesterday afternoon, and there was a run on fruit shakes."

"I see." He tried to keep a straight face but couldn't manage it. "Well, could I at least offer you a shower? And beyond that, a bed for a few nights, until things have calmed down on the beach? The water's piping hot," he added.

Now, that *really* tempted me. The thought of hot water and knowing I looked and smelled disgusting won out over pride. "Yes please."

He led me back downstairs and we crossed the courtyard to another pavilion, on the right of the quadrangle. There was a key in the lock and he turned it, then handed it to me.

"It's all prepared. It always is. Take your time, there's no rush."

"Thanks," I said, and disappeared inside, locking the door firmly behind me.

"Wow!" I said out loud as I looked around. He wasn't wrong about the room's being "prepared." I surveyed the super-king-sized bed made up with big fluffy pillows and a soft duvet—all in white, of course. But clean white, that I just knew didn't have any stains left over from other people. There was a big flat-screen TV behind shutters that you could close if you didn't want to be reminded of the outside world, and seriously tasteful Thai art, and when I touched the walls, I realized they were covered in silk. Dumping my rucksack on the teak-wood floor, I searched inside it for my shower gel, then padded into what I presumed was the bathroom but turned out to be a walk-in wardrobe. Trying another door, I found myself in a room that had a power shower and a massive sunken bath set against a wall of glass, beyond which was a little garden full of bonsai trees and pretty flowering plants that Star would know the names of, but I didn't. The whole thing was shielded by a high wall so that nobody could spy on you as you bathed.

I was *sooo* tempted to run a bath and sink into it, but I felt that would be taking advantage. So I turned on the shower and scrubbed every part of me until my skin was tingling. I needn't have bothered searching for my shower gel, as there was an entire range of luxury body products from some posh eco brand sitting on a marble shelf.

After emerging from the shower—even though I wouldn't have wanted anyone to know it, as I was so anti those lotions and potions that women got conned into buying—I creamed my body to the max with everything on offer. Unwrapping the towel from my head, I shook out my hair and noticed how long it had grown. It was just touching my shoulders and fell around my face in ringlets.

Star had always gone on about how much better I looked with longer hair. Ma had called it my crowning glory, but at sixteen I'd had the lot cut off into a short crop because it was so much easier to maintain. If I was being honest, it had also been an act of rebellion and petulance. As if to show the world I didn't care what I looked like.

I dragged my hair back from my face and held it on the top of my head. It actually made a ponytail for the first time in years, and I wished I had a hair band with which to tie it up.

I padded through to the bedroom and looked longingly at the big bed. After double-checking that the door was still locked, I donned my T-shirt and climbed up onto it. Just ten minutes, I told myself, as I laid my head on the downy white pillows . . .

I was woken abruptly by a loud banging. I sat up, having absolutely no idea where I was. It was pitch-black and I searched blindly for a light. I heard something crash to the floor, and I rolled out of bed in a panic.

"Are you okay?"

I followed the sound of the voice and felt for the door with my palms. My muddled brain finally registered where I was, and who was knocking.

"I can't find the keyhole, and it's very dark in here . . . ," I said.

"Just use your hands to feel for the key. It should be right there in front of you."

The voice calmed me and I searched just below my middle, as that was usually where a door had a lock. My fingers felt for, then grabbed, the key and after a few attempts I managed to turn it, then reached for the handle.

"It's unlocked," I called, "but I still can't open the door."

"Stand back and I'll open it for you."

The room was suddenly awash with light and I managed to breathe again as relief flooded through me.

"Sorry about that," he said as he entered the room. "I'll have to get someone to come and fix the handle. It's just got stiff because it's not been used for a while. You okay?"

"Yeah, sure." I sat down on the bed, taking in deep gulps of air.

The Werewolf studied me silently for a while.

"You're afraid of the dark, aren't you? That's why you like sleeping outdoors."

He was right, but I wasn't going to admit it. "Course not. I just woke up and didn't know where I was."

"Right. Sorry to frighten you, but it's nearly seven o'clock in the evening. You've slept for almost twelve hours. Wow, you must have been tired."

"I was. Sorry."

"That's okay. Are you hungry?"

"I don't know yet."

"If you are, Tam's making supper. You're welcome to join me on the main terrace."

"Tam?"

"The chef. It'll be ready in about half an hour. See you then."

He left the room and I swore loudly. A whole day gone! Which meant I'd almost certainly lost the booking at my new hotel when I hadn't turned up at lunchtime to check in. To add to it, because I'd slept so long, I'd have to go through jet lag all over again, plus my weird werewolf host probably thought I was special needs or something.

Why was he being so nice to me? I wasn't stupid enough to think there wasn't an ulterior motive. After all, he was a man and I was a woman . . . at least to some people. But then, if *that* was what he wanted, it would mean he fancied me, which was beyond ridiculous.

Unless he was desperate and anybody would do.

I dressed in a kaftan I didn't like because it was almost a dress, but it was all I had, given most of my clothes were still at the laundry. Once outside, I surreptitiously locked the door behind me and hid the key in the planter next to it, because my world was in that rucksack.

This place was probably even more beautiful at night than in the day. Lanterns hung from the low roofs, giving out a soft light, and the water around the onyx Buddha was lit from beneath. There was a fabulous scent of jasmine from the massive planters, and even better than that, I could smell food.

"Over here!"

I saw an arm waving at me from the terrace in front of the main pavilion.

"Hi," he said, indicating a chair.

"Hi. Sorry I slept so long today."

"Never apologize for sleeping. I wish I could."

I watched him sigh deeply, and then, as I really didn't think I could carry on calling him the Werewolf, considering he'd been—so far anyway—kind to me, I asked him his name.

"Didn't I tell you the other day?"

"No," I said firmly.

"Oh . . . just call me Ace. What's yours?"

"CeCe."

"Right. A nickname, like mine?"

"Yeah."

"What's yours short for?"

"Celaeno."

"That's unusual."

"Yeah, my pa—the guy who adopted me—had this weird fixation with the Seven Sisters of the Pleiades. Like, the star cluster," I explained, as I usually had to.

"Excuse me, sir, okay to serve now?"

The maid had appeared on the terrace, with a man wearing chef's whites standing behind her.

"Absolutely." Ace led me to the table. "What can I offer you to drink? Wine? Beer?"

"Nothing, thanks. Just water'll be fine."

He poured us both a glass from the bottle on the table. "Cheers."

"Cheers. Thanks for saving me today."

"No problem. As if I don't feel bad enough living in this place all by myself, there's you sleeping on the beach."

"Up until yesterday, it was my choice, but that bed is just fantastic."

"As I said, you're welcome to it for as long as you want. And before you refuse, I'm not just being kind, I'd actually appreciate the company. I've been alone here for nearly two months now."

"Why don't you invite some of your mates from London to come over?"

"That's not an option. Right," he said as a dish of sizzling king prawns was placed in the center of the table. "Let's tuck in."

That dinner was one of the best I'd eaten for a long time—at least since Star had cooked me a roast lunch last November in London. I'd never learned to cook myself because she was so great at it, and I'd almost forgotten what good food tasted like. Course after course made its way into my mouth—fragrant lemongrass soup, tender fried chicken wrapped in pandan leaves, and spicy fish cakes with *nam jim* sauce.

"Oh my God, that was absolutely delicious. I like this restaurant, thanks so much for inviting me. I've got a food baby." I indicated my swollen stomach.

Ace grinned at my description. We hadn't really chatted much over supper, probably because I'd been too busy stuffing my face. "So, has the food convinced you to stay?" Ace took a sip of his water. "I mean, it's not for long, is it? You said you're leaving for Australia after the New Year."

"Yeah, I am." I finally gave in. "If you're sure, it would be great."

"Good. Just one thing I'd ask: I know you're friendly with the crowd on Railay Beach, but I'd really prefer it if you didn't say you were staying here with me, or mention where the house is. I really value my privacy."

His eyes told me everything his casual words hadn't.

"I won't say a word, promise."

"Good. So, tell me about your painting. You must be really talented to have got a place in a London art college."

"Umm . . . I left a few weeks later, 'cause I realized I wasn't. Or not in the way they wanted me to be anyway."

"You mean, they didn't get you?"

"You could say that." I rolled my eyes. "I couldn't do anything right."

"So would you say you're more 'avant-garde' than someone like Monet, for example?"

"You could, but you've got to remember that Monet was avant-garde in his day. It really wasn't my art tutors' fault, I just couldn't learn what they wanted to teach me." I closed my mouth abruptly, wondering why I was telling him about all this. He was probably bored senseless. "What about you? What do you do?"

"Oh, nothing as interesting. I'm just your average City bod. Dull stuff, you know?"

I didn't, but I nodded as if I did. "So you're taking a . . ."—I searched for the word—"sabbatical?"

"Yeah, something like that. Now," he said, stifling a yawn, "can I get you anything else?"

"No thanks, I'm good."

"The staff will come and clear away but I need to try and sleep now. As you know, I'm up before dawn. And by the way, the security guards know you're staying with me, and the key code for the gate from the beach side is seven seven seven seven." He gave me a small smile. "Night, CeCe."

"Night."

As he left, I saw the staff hovering, probably ready for their beds too and wanting to be finished for the day. I decided that, while I was under Ace's protection, I'd chance a wander onto Phra Nang. Walking down the path, I pressed the red button on the pad at the side of the gate. It slid back and I was released onto the deserted beach.

"*Sawadee krap.*"

I jumped as I looked to my left and saw Po, the squat security guard who had manhandled me along the beach at six o'clock this morning. He stood up from his stool, placed discreetly among the foliage that flanked the gate, and saluted me with a false smile.

"*Sawadee ka,*" I said, doing a *wai* with my hands in the traditional Thai greeting.

The tinny noise of Thai pop music blared from a small radio next to his stool, and as I looked at his uneven, yellowing teeth, I saw him—literally—from the other side of the fence, and wondered how many children he had to feed, and how boring and lonely his job was. Except, I thought, as I walked through the foliage, part of me envied his having all *this* to himself. He had beauty and total peace every night. As I walked onto the beach, feeling a freedom that sadly only privilege could buy in this particular neck of the woods, I imagined how one day I would breathe in the world at its amazing best, then paint it onto canvas for *everyone* to see.

I made my way to the sea's edge and dipped my toes in the perfect body-temperature water. I looked up at the sky, chock-full of stars tonight, and wished I had the vocabulary to put into words the things I thought. For I felt things that I couldn't explain, except through the paintings I made or, recently, the installation I'd become obsessed with.

It hadn't been right, of course—it had tried to say too much about too many things—but I'd loved working in my riverside studio. And with Star in the kitchen as she made us supper, I'd felt content.

"Stop it, Cee!" I told myself firmly. I wasn't going to start looking back again. Star had made her move and I was out of her hair, leading my own life. Or at least, trying to.

Then I wondered if Star had ever thought of herself as a burden to *me*. I didn't want to start criticizing her because I loved her, but maybe she'd forgotten the way she'd needed me when she was small and didn't like speaking. She'd also been bad at making decisions and saying what she felt, especially as we'd been trapped in the middle of a bunch of strong-willed sisters. I wasn't trying to make her take the blame or anything, but there were always two sides to a story and maybe she'd forgotten mine.

Surprisingly, though, it seemed I'd found myself a new friend. I wondered what *his* story was, why he was really here; why he only went out at sunrise or after dark and wouldn't invite any friends to stay, despite admitting he was lonely . . .

I walked back slowly across the sand toward the hidden palace in the trees. Even though Po the security guard made to tap in the numbers on the pad, I got there first and pressed "7777" firmly onto the keys so he knew that *I* knew the code.

Having retrieved the key from the planter, I opened the door to my room to find someone had been there before me. The bed was made up with fresh sheets, and the clothes I had discarded earlier were folded neatly on a chair. The invisible cleaning fairy had also left a new set of fluffy towels, and after I'd washed the sand off my feet, I clambered into bed.

The problem was, I mused, that I'd always lived between two worlds. I could happily bunk down on the beach, but equally, I was comfortable in a room like this. And despite all my protests that I could survive with very little, tonight I didn't know which option I preferred.

5

Over the following few days, Ace and I settled into a routine at the palace. He got up really early and me really late, then in the afternoons I made myself scarce, traipsing back to Railay Beach so I wouldn't bother him. I'd told my Railay crowd I was staying in a hotel along the beach and they didn't question it. Consequently, Ace and I only brushed shoulders at suppertime. He seemed to expect me there, and that was fine by me as the food was fantastic. He didn't speak much, but because I was used to Star's quietness, it felt familiar and strangely comforting.

After three days of living a few meters from him, I realized I wasn't in any danger of his jumping me. I knew I just wasn't the kind of girl men fancied, and besides, if I was honest, I'd never really enjoyed sex anyway.

I'd lost my virginity nine years ago right there on Railay Beach. I'd had a couple of beers, which was always dangerous for me, and stayed up way after Star had gone to bed. The guy had been a gap-year student— Will, I think his name was—and we'd gone for a walk on the beach, and the kissing had been quite nice. That had led to our being horizontal and going all the way, which had hurt a bit, but not much. I'd woken up the next morning with a hangover, unable to believe that *that* was what all the fuss was about.

I'd done it since a couple of other times, on different beaches with different bodies, to see if it might get better, but it never did. I was sure that millions of women would tell me I was missing something, but I couldn't miss what I'd never had, so I was fine about it.

It was interesting that even though Star and I had always been pretty much joined at the hip, the one thing we had never confided in each other about was sex. I had no idea whether she was still a virgin or not. At boarding school, the girls used to chatter in intimate detail in bed at night about boys they fancied and how far they'd gone. Yet Star and I had remained silent on the subject, to them and each other.

Perhaps we'd felt that any kind of close physical relationship with a man would have been a betrayal. Well, *I* had anyway.

Leaving my room and not bothering to lock it, as I knew the invisible cleaning fairy would swoop in the moment I left, I wandered down to the terrace, where Ace was waiting for me.

"Hi, CeCe." He stood up briefly as I arrived and sat down. He'd obviously been taught manners and I appreciated the gesture. He poured some fresh water from the jug for us both and surveyed me.

"New top?"

"Yeah. I haggled and got it down to two hundred and fifty baht."

"Ridiculous really, isn't it? When lots of people buy similar in a designer store in London for hundreds of times that price."

"Well, I never would."

"I once had a girlfriend who didn't think twice about spending thousands on a handbag. It wouldn't have been so bad if it was something for life, but then the new-season stuff would come in, and she'd buy another new bag, and the old one would be put in a cupboard with the rest and never used again. Mind you, I once caught her standing there admiring her collection."

"Maybe they were works of art to her. Whatever floats your boat, but it sure doesn't float mine. Anyway, you men are just as bad with your cars," I added as tonight's feast was delivered to the table by the maid.

"You're right," he said, as the maid slid away as silently as she had arrived. "I've owned a series of very flashy cars just because I could."

"Did it make you feel good?"

"It did at the time, yes. I liked the sound of the engines. The more noise it made, the better it was."

"Boys with their toys . . ."

"Girls with their pearls," he countered with a smile. "Now, shall we eat?"

We did so in companionable silence. When I'd had my fill I sat back contentedly. "I'm going to miss this when I'm a simple backpacker again in Australia. It's like a slice of heaven here. You're really lucky."

"I guess you never really appreciate what you've got until you've lost it, do you?"

"Well, you haven't lost this. And *this* is amazing."

"Not yet . . . no." He gave one of his deep sighs. "What are you doing for New Year's Eve tomorrow night?"

"I haven't really thought about it. Jack's invited me to the restaurant to see in the New Year with the rest of the crowd. Want to come?"

"No thank you."

"What are you doing?" I asked out of politeness.

"Nothing. I mean, it's a man-made calendar, and if we lived in, say, China, we'd be celebrating at a different time of year."

"True, but it's still a ritual, isn't it? When you're meant to be celebrating and end up feeling like a real loser if you're sitting there alone, getting texts from your mates at amazing parties." I grinned.

"Last year, I was at an amazing party," Ace admitted. "It was in Saint-Tropez at a club. We'd come in by boat and the hostesses were opening bottles of champagne that cost hundreds of euros each and spraying them all over the place like it was water. At the time, I thought it was great, but I was drunk and most things seem fantastic then, don't they?"

"To be honest, I've not been drunk very often. Alcohol doesn't suit me, so most of the time I steer clear."

"Lucky you. I—and I guess most people—use it to forget. To ease the stress."

"Yeah, it certainly takes the edge off stuff."

"I did some really stupid things when I was boozing," Ace confessed. "So now I don't go there. I haven't had a drink for the past two and a half months, so I'd probably get drunk on a beer. It used to take me at least a couple of bottles of champagne and a few vodka chasers to even begin to feel that edge blunt."

"Wow. Well, I do like the odd glass of champagne on special occasions—birthdays and stuff."

"Tell you what." He leaned forward and stared at me, his blue eyes suddenly alive. "What do you say to opening a bottle of champagne at midnight tomorrow? As you point out, it's for special occasions and it is New Year's Eve, after all. But, we limit ourselves to one glass each."

I frowned and he saw it immediately.

"Don't worry, I was never an alcoholic. I came off completely the minute I realized what I was doing. Equally, I don't want to be the sad person in the corner that refuses a drink and then everyone assumes is a member of AA. I want to enjoy it, but not to need it. Do you understand?"

"I do, but—"

"Trust me; one glass each. Deal?"

What could I say? He was my host, and I couldn't deny him, but I'd have my rucksack packed and at the ready in case things got out of hand.

"Deal," I agreed.

As I sat on Railay Beach the next afternoon, I could feel the pre-Christmas electricity back in the air as all the hotels set up their verandas for the evening's festivities. Fed up with staring at the pathetic charcoal sketch I'd made of the limestone pillars, I stood up and walked across the sand toward the Railay Beach Hotel.

"Hi, Cee, how's it going?"

"Fine," I said to Jack, who was placing glasses on a long trestle table. He looked far perkier than last time I'd seen him a few days ago, propping up the bar with his umpteenth beer. The reason why appeared behind him and put a possessive hand on his shoulder.

"We short of forks," Nam said, glancing at me and giving me her usual death stare.

"Think I got some spare ones in the kitchen."

"Go get them now, Jack. Wanna set up our table for later."

"On my way. You coming tonight?" Jack asked me.

"I might pop down later on, yeah," I replied, knowing that "later on" he wouldn't know if Jesus Christ himself was ordering drinks at the bar.

Jack began to follow Nam into the kitchen, then paused and turned back. "By the way, a mate of mine thinks he knows who your mystery man on the beach is. He's gone off to Ko Phi Phi for the New Year, but he's gonna tell me more when he gets back."

"Right."

"See ya, Cee," he said as he trudged off toward the kitchen, following Nam with his tray like a little lamb behind Bo Peep. That big, butch man who could scale a rock face faster than anyone I'd ever met . . . I just hoped I never treated any future partner of mine like that. But I'd seen so many men being bossed about by demanding females, maybe they liked it.

Did I boss Star around? Is that why she left?

I hated my brain for planting the thought in my head, so I decided to ignore it and get on with a day that was meant to herald new beginnings. I comforted myself that whatever Jack's mate had to tell him about Ace was bound to be nothing. Out here, on a peninsula in the middle of nowhere, the fact that someone had eaten an ice cream instead of a lolly was news. Small communities thrived on gossip and people like Ace who kept to themselves sparked the most rumors. Just because my host hadn't sounded off to anyone and everyone during a drunken conversation didn't make him a bad person. In fact, I thought he was a very interesting person, with intelligent things to say.

As I walked back down the alleyway lined with stalls that led to my other life, I realized I was starting to feel defensive about Ace, just like I'd felt about Star when people had asked me if she was okay, because she was so quiet and didn't say very much.

I arrived back in my room and after showering and creaming—which I was worried was becoming a daily habit I had to lose before it took hold for good—and then dressing in my old kaftan, I wandered out onto the terrace. Ace was already there, wearing a crisp white linen shirt.

"Hi. Good day?" he asked me.

"Yeah, except the art's still going nowhere. I can't draw a square at the moment, let alone anything else."

"It'll come back, CeCe. You just need to get all the negative stuff they said out of your head. That takes time."

"Yeah, it sure seems to. What about your day?"

"The same really. I read a book, then went for a walk and thought about what it said. I've realized that none of these 'self-help' books *can* help, really, because at the end of the day, you've got to help yourself." He gave a wry grin. "There are no easy solutions."

"No, there never are. You've just got to get on with it, haven't you?"

"Yep. Ready for dinner?" he asked me eventually, breaking the silence that hung over the table.

"Bring it on."

An enormous lobster appeared in front of us, accompanied by numerous side dishes.

"Wow! Lobster is my absolute number one favorite seafood," I said happily as I tucked in.

"For a traveler whom I met sleeping on the beach, you seem to have seriously ritzy taste," he teased when we'd both cleaned our plates and moved on to a dessert of fresh fruit and homemade sorbets. "From what you've said, I presume your dad is rich?"

"Was, yeah." I realized I hadn't told Ace about Pa's death, but now was as good a time as any, so I did.

"Sorry to hear that, CeCe. So, this is the first Christmas and New Year without him?"

"It is."

"Is that why you're here?"

"Yes and no . . . I lost someone else close to me too, recently. Like, my soul mate."

"A boyfriend?"

"No, my sister actually. I mean, she's still alive, but she decided to go her own way."

"I see. Well, we are a pair, aren't we?"

"Are we? Have you lost someone too?"

"You could say I've lost just about everything in the past few months. I've got no one to blame but myself." He took a gulp of water. "Unlike you."

"It wasn't my fault Pa died, no, but I think I drove my sister away. By being . . . bossy." I finally voiced the word. "And maybe a bit controlling. I didn't mean to be, but she was really shy as a kid and didn't speak much, so I spoke for her and I guess it never changed."

"So she found her own voice?"

"Something like that, yeah. Broke my heart actually. She was my . . . *person*, if you know what I mean."

"Oh yes, I do," he said with feeling. "When you trust someone implicitly and they let you down, it's very hard."

"Has that happened to you?" I watched as he looked upward and saw real pain in his eyes.

"Yes."

"Do you wanna talk about it?" I asked him, realizing that he was always encouraging me to tell him *my* troubles, but whenever he started to talk about his own, he'd suddenly clam up.

"I can't, I'm afraid. For all sorts of reasons, including legal ones . . . Only Linda knows the truth," he murmured, "and it's best you don't."

There he went again, being the mystery man, and it was really starting to irritate me. I decided it was probably something to do with a woman who was taking him to the cleaners for his millions in a divorce and I wished he wouldn't feel so sorry for himself.

"You know I'm here if you ever want to talk," I offered, thinking that this was turning into a fun evening so far. Not.

"Thanks, CeCe, I appreciate it, and your company tonight. I was dreading spending New Year's Eve alone. As you said, it's just one of those nights, isn't it? Anyway, let's toast to your dad. And to friends old and new." We clinked our glasses of water. Then he glanced down at his watch—a Rolex, and definitely not picked up from one of the fake stalls in Bangkok. "It's ten to midnight. How about I pour us both that glass of champagne we've promised ourselves and we'll take a wander down to the beach to see in the New Year?"

"Sure."

While he was gone, I took a moment to text Star and wish her a happy New Year. I was tempted to tell her about my new friend, but thought she'd probably get the wrong end of the stick, so I didn't. Then I texted Ma and sent a round-robin message to my other sisters, wherever they all were in the world that night.

"Ready?" Ace stood there with a glass sparkling in each hand.

"Ready."

We walked to the gate and Po jumped up to open it for us.

"Five minutes to go . . . Any New Year's resolutions?" Ace asked me, as we stood on the shoreline.

"Blimey, I haven't thought of any. I know! To get back into my art, and to find the balls to go to Australia and discover where I came from."

"You mean, your birth family?"

"Yeah."

"Wow! That's something you haven't told me about."

"And your resolution?" I eyed him in the moonlight.

"To accept what is to come, and to take it with grace," he said, not looking at me, but staring up at the heavens. "*And* to make sure that this is the only glass of champagne I drink tonight," he added with a grin.

A few seconds later we heard the hoots of horns from the fishing boats moored out in the bay, then saw the flash of fireworks from nearby Railay Beach visible over the top of the limestone pillars.

"Oh wow!" I gasped as we saw Chinese lanterns floating gently upward into the sky from the other end of the beach.

"Cheers, CeCe!" he said, clinking his glass of champagne against mine. I watched as he drained the lot in a couple of mouthfuls. "God, that was good! Happy New Year!" Then he threw his arms around me and gave me an enormous bear hug, which sent most of my champagne flying over his shoulder and onto the sand. "You've saved my life in the past few days. I mean it."

"I don't think I have, but thanks anyway."

He pushed me gently back by the shoulders, one hand on each of them. "Oh yes, you have." Then he put his mouth to mine and kissed me.

It was a nice kiss, quite strong, yet soft at the same time. Like a hungry werewolf on Valium. My rational brain—the bit that normally recognized all the warning signs of such a move—did not respond, so the kiss went on for a really long time.

"Come on." Ace eventually dragged his mouth away from mine and began to pull me by the hand back up the beach. As we passed Po, who must have got an eyeful of us kissing, I smiled at him and wished him a happy New Year.

As Ace guided me to his room, his hand still holding mine, I felt like it really might be.

That night . . . well, without going into detail, Ace obviously knew what he was doing. In fact, he seemed to be a bit of an expert, while I definitely wasn't. But it's amazing how quickly you can learn something when you want to.

"CeCe," he said as he stroked my cheek after what must have been a few hours, because I could hear the faint twitter of birds, "you're just so . . . delicious. Thank you."

"That's okay," I said, even if I did feel like he was describing the flavor of an ice cream.

"This is just for now, isn't it? I mean, there can't be any future involved."

"Course not," I replied lightly, worried that I'd given him the impression I was clingy.

"Good, because I don't want to hurt you, or anyone, ever again. Night, sleep tight."

With that, he rolled away from me, in a bed that I reckoned was even larger and comfier than mine, and went to sleep on his side.

Of course it's just for now, I told myself as I too rolled over into my own space, realizing it was the first time I'd ever shared a bed with a man, as all the other previous fumbles had taken place in the great outdoors. I lay staring into the darkness, glad that the shutters on the windows were letting in tiny strips of New Year light, and thinking that this had been just what I needed. It was perfect, I told myself—a morale booster with no strings attached. I'd go off to Oz in a few days' time, and maybe me and Ace would keep in touch occasionally by text. I wasn't a Victorian heroine who had sacrificed her virtue and then got locked into marriage. My generation had been given the freedom to do what we liked with our bodies. And tonight I *had* liked . . .

Very carefully, my fingers moved toward him of their own accord, to find and touch his skin and to make sure he was real and breathing next to me. As he stirred, I drew them away, but he rolled back toward me and enveloped me in his arms.

Warm and safe with the weight of his body against me, I eventually fell asleep.

It transpired that New Year's Eve hadn't been a one-night stand. It became a regular morning, afternoon, and evening stand . . . or more precisely, a lying down. And when we weren't horizontal, we did fun things together. Like Ace dragging me out of bed at the crack of dawn to see the monkeys, who announced their presence with a loud thump on the roof as they invaded the palace in search of leftover food. Once I'd taken photos and one of the security guards had frightened them off with a miniature catapult, I'd skulk back to bed. Later on in the morning he'd wake me with a tray of nice things to eat. During the long, hot afternoons, we'd suck at pieces of pineapple and mango and wade through his collection of DVDs.

One sunrise, a plush speedboat had appeared in the shallows of the sea in front of the palace. Po helped us aboard, then whipped out a camera and offered to take a photo of us, which Ace immediately and vehemently vetoed. As we set off, Ace told me he was taking me somewhere special. Having driven my family's own speedboat up and down Lake Geneva, I soon took over the reins from the captain, steering the boat effortlessly over the waves and doing the odd wheelie just to scare him. When a wall of limestone pillars loomed above us in the middle of the sea, I let the captain take over again. He steered the boat expertly into a hidden lagoon, protected on all sides by vertiginous rocky walls. The water was green and calm, and there were even mangrove trees growing in it. It was called Koh Hong and it was paradise. I was the first to jump into the water, but Ace soon followed and we swam across it as though it were our own private swimming pool, cast away in the middle of the ocean.

Afterward, we sat on the boat deck drinking hot, strong coffee and basking in the peace and tranquility of that incredible place. Then I drove us home and we went to bed and made love. It was a wonderful day and one I knew I'd never forget. The kind of day that happens once in a lifetime, even to someone like me.

On the fifth night that I lay next to Ace in bed, my own room abandoned since New Year's Eve, I wondered if I was in a "relationship." Part of me was terrified, because it wasn't what I had intended, and Ace had made it clear he hadn't either. Yet, another part of me wanted to take a photo of the two of us looking romantically at each other on the beach and send it to all my sisters so that they would realize I wasn't a loser after all. This man, for whatever reason, *liked* me. He laughed at my jokes— which even I knew were really bad—and even seemed to find my funny little body "sexy."

But most of all, he "got" me in a way that only Star had before, and had arrived in my life just when I'd needed him. Both of us were adrift in this world and had washed up together on the same shore, not sure of what was coming next, and it was comforting to hold on to someone, even for a little while.

On the sixth day, I woke up of my own accord, looked at the clock, and saw it was almost one in the afternoon. Ace's usual delivery of fruit, croissants, and coffee was late. I was just about to get up and find him when he opened the door with a tray in his hands. I would have relaxed, except for the look on his face.

"Morning, CeCe. Sleep well?"

"Yeah, from four till now, as you know," I said as he set the tray down.

Normally, he'd come and lie next to me, but today he didn't. Instead, he sat on the edge of the bed.

"I've got some stuff to do. Fancy taking yourself off somewhere for the afternoon?"

"Of course," I said brightly.

"See you for dinner tonight at eight?" He stood up and kissed me on the top of my head.

"Yeah, sure."

He left with a wave and a smile, and being a novice at this whole relationship thing, I couldn't work out whether this was normal. Was it because he had "stuff to do" and the world was finally getting back on its feet after New Year, or should I panic and pack my rucksack? In the end, not wanting to look as though I had nowhere to go and couldn't amuse myself, I walked back down the path to Railay with my sketch pad. As I walked up onto the veranda of the Railay Beach Hotel, I saw the beach was less crowded than it had been at New Year. Nam was serving at the bar, so I ordered a mango shake just so she would have to make it for me. Then I sat on the bar stool, watching her with a smug look that I wasn't proud of.

"You need room?" she asked me as she peeled the mango and dumped it into the blender.

"No, I'm fine, thanks."

"Which hotel you stay at?"

"The Sunrise Resort."

Nam nodded, but I saw a glint in her eye. "Not seen you for a while. Nobody seen you."

"I've been busy."

"Jay say he seen you on Phra Nang getting onto speedboat with man."

"Really? I wish." I rolled my eyes as my heart thumped. Jay was a guy I knew in passing from last year—a friend of Jack's. He'd helped out behind the bar sometimes, but was a full-time drifter who went wherever he could earn a crust. Someone had told me he'd once been a big-shot journalist until the drugs got him. I'd seen him sitting in here bold as brass, smoking a joint. Drugs were not something I approved of and here in Thailand, whether it was a joint or an armful of heroin, possession carried the same harsh penalty.

He'd also had a thing about Star, making a beeline for her every time we'd come in for a quiet drink. She found him as creepy as I did, so I'd made sure she was never alone with him.

"He say he saw you," Nam persisted as she passed over the mango shake. "You got a new boyfriend?"

She said it as if I'd had an old one . . . and then it dawned on me that perhaps she thought that Jack and I had been having a thing, what with me sleeping in his room. Christ, women could be so pathetic sometimes. It was obvious to everyone that Jack was putty in her small, slim hands.

"Nope," I said, then drained my glass as quickly as I could.

"Jay say he know man you were with. Bad man. Famous."

"Then Jay needs a new pair of glasses, 'cause it wasn't me." I counted out sixty baht with a ten-baht tip and put it down on the bar as I stood up.

"Jay in later. He tell you."

I shook my head and rolled my eyes at her again as though I thought she was crazy, then left, trying to act casual. Instead of turning right along the beach back to the palace, I turned left, where I'd told Nam my hotel was, just in case she or Jay, or anyone else for that matter, was watching. I dumped my shoes and towel on the beach in front of the hotel I'd said I was staying at, and walked into the water for a swim and a think.

What had she meant when she'd said that Jay had called Ace a "bad man"? In Nam's book, that probably meant he was a womanizer, nothing more. I knew Ace hadn't been short of girlfriends when he'd lived in London—he was forever mentioning different women he'd shared good times with. As for his being "famous," maybe he was, but I wouldn't know because I never read newspapers or magazines, due to my dyslexia.

I waded out and lay back on the sand to let my skin dry in the sun, and I wondered whether I should tell Ace. It was obvious he was paranoid about his privacy . . . What if he was some famous celebrity? I could always ask Electra—that was the world she lived in every day. And if he was, that would make her shut up for once—the ugly D'Aplièse sister, bagging herself a famous boyfriend. It was almost worth texting to ask her just for her reaction.

But I knew that if I did tell Ace someone was onto him, it would only worry him. And besides, Jay didn't know where he lived—or, at least, I hoped he didn't.

Perhaps I *should* tell Ace . . . but I had only a few days left there before I had to make my way to Australia and I didn't want to spoil our time together. I finally decided that once I was back inside the palace gates, I'd stay put and not come out until it was time for me to leave for the airport. And today, I just had to hope that no one was watching as I went back in.

Choosing a time just before sunset when Phra Nang Beach was

beginning to empty but I could still remain inconspicuous among the throng, I went for another swim, then sat on my towel very near Po, who, when he saw me, immediately tried to press the keypad to let me in. I ignored him and lay down a few meters away. I'd slip inside when all eyes were turned on the sunset in front of me.

Twenty minutes later, the show began and I scurried up to the palace gates like a hunted animal.

I didn't know what to expect when I walked up the path to my room, but at least if Ace had suddenly gone off me and asked me to move out that night, the New Year rush was over and there was plenty of room in the hotels along the beach. Opening the door to my room, I smelled a flowery scent wafting on the air.

"I'm in here, come and join me."

I walked into the bathroom and saw Ace lying in the huge oval bathtub, which was surrounded by numerous tea lights giving off a softly scented glow. On top of the water floated hundreds of white and pink flower petals.

"Join me?"

I giggled.

"What's so funny?"

"You look like a surrealist's version of that famous painting of the dead Ophelia."

"You mean a hairier and uglier version? Cheers," he said with a grin. "And there was me trying to be romantic. Granted, the maid went over the top with the flowers, but never ask a Thai person to run your bath or you end up picking petals off yourself for days afterward. Come on, climb in."

So I did, and lay there with my head resting upon his chest and his arms holding me tight around my middle. It felt fantastic.

"Sorry about earlier," he whispered into my ear, and then gave it a soft kiss. "I just had some stuff to sort out on the phone."

"No need to apologize."

"I missed you," he whispered again. "Shall we eat in tonight?"

"We always do," I replied with a smile.

Much later, when we'd finally made it out of the bath and had tucked into a fresh fish in tamarind sauce, we took a stroll down to the beach and lay there looking up at the stars.

"Show me which one your star is," Ace asked me.

I located the milky cluster and pointed to it. "I'm the third one down from the top, at about two o'clock."

"I can only count six."

"There are seven, but it's really hard to see the last one."

"What's her name?"

"Merope."

"You've not mentioned her before."

"No. She never turned up. Or at least, Pa only brought six sisters home."

"That's weird."

"Yeah, now I think back, my whole childhood was weird."

"Do you know why he adopted all of you?"

"No, but you don't really wonder when you're a child, do you? You just accept it. I loved having Star and my sisters around me. Have you got brothers or sisters?"

"I'm an only child, so I never had to share anything." He gave a sharp laugh, then turned to me. "You don't talk much about your other sisters. What are they like?"

"Maia and Ally are the two oldest. Maia is really sweet, and so clever— she speaks about a million languages—and Ally is amazing, like, really brave and strong. She's had a bad time recently, but she's getting through it. I really admire her, you know? I'd like to be like her."

"So, Ally is your role model in the family?"

"Maybe, yeah, she is. And Tiggy . . ." I thought for a second, wondering how best to describe her. "Other than Star, she's the sister I'm closest to. She's very . . . what's the word for someone who seems to understand things without you saying them out loud?"

"Intuitive?" Ace guessed.

"Yes. She's got this incredibly positive way of looking at the world. If I painted it the way she saw it, it would just be the most beautiful thing. And then there's Electra," I mumbled, "but we don't get on." Then I turned the questioning back on him. "What about your childhood?"

"Like you, I didn't think it was weird at the time. I loved my mum and being brought up in Thailand, then shortly after she died I was sent to school in England."

"That must have been hard, being away from everything you knew."

"It was . . . fine."

"What about your dad?" I asked.

"I told you, I don't know him."

The tone of his voice was terse, and I sensed not to ask him more, even though I was seriously curious.

"Have you ever wondered if Pa Salt was your real father?" he asked eventually out of the darkness.

"I've never even thought about it," I said, even though suddenly I *was* thinking about it. "That would mean he traveled the world collecting his six illegitimate daughters."

"That would be strange," Ace agreed, "but surely there must be a reason?"

"Who knows? And actually, who cares? He's dead now, so I'm never going to find out."

"You're right. No point dwelling on the past, is there?"

"No, but we all do. We all think of mistakes we've made and wish we could change them."

"You haven't made any mistakes to change, have you? It was your parents who did that by giving you up."

I turned to look at Ace then, and maybe it was the moonlight, but his eyes seemed too bright, like he was holding back tears.

"Is that what your dad did? Gave you up?"

"No. So, are you going to search for your birth parents in Australia then?"

It was the patented Ace method of question-tennis and the ball had been expertly returned to me. I let him have this one because I knew he was upset.

"Maybe," I said with a shrug.

"How did you find out that's where you were born?"

"When Pa died last June, he left all us girls something called an armillary sphere, which had the coordinates of where he'd found us engraved on it."

"Where was yours?"

"A place called Broome. It's on the northwest coast of Australia."

"Right. What else?"

"He told me I should go there and find out about a woman called Kitty Mercer."

"Is that all?"

"Yes, from him anyway, but I also found out a few days later that I'd been left an inheritance."

"'Curiouser and curiouser,' as Alice once said. Did you ever try to look up this Kitty Mercer on the Internet?" he asked.

"Er, no." I was glad that it was dark so he couldn't see me blush. I was beginning to feel like I was being interrogated. "It's not really fair that you're asking me all these questions when you won't answer any of mine."

He chuckled then. "You're great, CeCe. You just tell it how it is." Then he rolled me on top of him and kissed me.

Two days later, I woke up realizing I had no idea what the date was and knowing I'd completely lost track of time. I climbed out of bed and rifled through my rucksack to find the printout of my tickets back to Bangkok and on to Sydney. Then I checked my mobile for today's date.

"Oh shit! I leave tomorrow," I groaned, feeling horrified at the prospect. I slumped onto the bed just as Ace came through the door with the habitual tray. Perched among the croissants was a book.

"I got you something," he said as he set the tray down.

I stared at the book. On the front cover was a black-and-white photograph of a beautiful woman. She was wearing an old-fashioned dress with a very high neckline, fastened with rows of tiny pearl buttons. It took me a good few seconds to work out the name on the cover.

"*Kitty Mercer, the Pearling Pioneer,*" I read out loud.

"Yes!" Ace said triumphantly, jumping under the covers with me, then handing me a cup of coffee. "I looked her up on Google—she has her own Wikipedia page, CeCe!"

"Really?" I nodded dumbly.

"She sounds incredible. From what I read, she achieved a lot in an age when women struggled to be in charge. So I ordered her biography and had it express delivered by speedboat from a bookshop in Phuket."

"You did what?" I eyed him.

"I've already skimmed through it and it's such an interesting story. You'll love it, really." He picked up the book and pushed it toward me and it was all I could do to stop myself recoiling from both him and it. I set the coffee down on the side table and climbed off the bed.

"Why have you gone to all this trouble?" I asked him as I pulled on my T-shirt. "It's none of your business. If I'd wanted to find all this out, I'd have done it myself."

"Christ! I was only trying to help! Why are you cross?"

"I'm not cross," I snapped, even though we both knew I was. "I haven't even decided yet if I want to find out anything about my original family!"

"Well, you don't have to read it now, you can keep it for when you're ready."

Ace tried to hand me the book again and I pushed it away.

"Maybe you should have asked me first," I said as I put on my shorts and immediately lost my balance, which didn't look as dignified as I'd needed it to.

"Yeah, maybe I should have."

I stomped out of the room and went upstairs to sit on the roof terrace, needing to cool down alone for a while.

Ten minutes later, he came to sit next to me on the silk sofa, one hand still clutching the book.

"What's really wrong, CeCe? Tell me."

I chewed on my lip for a bit, staring out at the people swimming in the ocean below us. "Look, it's really cool of you to go to the effort of getting that book. It can't have been easy to get it so quickly. I just . . . I'm not good with books. I never have been. That's why I haven't looked up anything about Kitty Mercer. I've got . . . dyslexia, really bad dyslexia actually, and I find it hard to read."

Ace put his arm around my shoulders. "Why didn't you just say so?"

"I dunno," I mumbled. "I'm embarrassed, okay?"

"Well, you shouldn't be. Some of the brightest people I know are dyslexic. Hey, I know, I'll read it out loud to you." He pulled me to him so I was nestling into his shoulder. "Right," he said, and began turning the pages before I could stop him.

"'*Chapter one. Edinburgh, Scotland, 1906 . . .*'"

KITTY

Edinburgh, Scotland

October 1906

6

Kitty McBride lay in her bed and watched the tiny house spider weaving its web around a hapless bluebottle that had flown into its trap in a corner of the ceiling. She'd seen the bluebottle buzzing across her ceiling last night before she turned out the gas lamp—a hardy last remnant of a warm autumn turning to winter. She mused that the spider must have been busy all night to mummify the bluebottle within its silken threads.

"That will surely be a month's supper for you and your family," she told the spider before drawing in a determined breath and throwing off her covers. Shivering her way across the freezing room to the washstand, she gave herself a far briefer lick and spit than her mother would have approved of. Through the small window, she saw a thick early morning mist was shrouding the terraced houses on the other side of the narrow street. She pulled on her woolen undershirt and fastened the buttons of her dress across her long, white throat, then scraped her mane of auburn hair off her face and into a coil on the top of her head.

"I look like a veritable ghost," she told her reflection in the looking glass as she moved to the undergarment drawer to retrieve her rouge. She dabbed a little on her cheeks, rubbed it in, then pinched them. She had purchased the compact at Jenners on Princes Street two days ago, having saved all her shillings from the twice-weekly piano lessons she gave.

Father, of course, would say that vanity was a sin. But then, Father thought most things were sinful; he spent his time writing sermons and then preaching his thoughts to his flock. Profanity, vanity, the demon drink . . . and his favorite of all: the pleasures of the flesh. Kitty often wondered how she and her three sisters had arrived on the planet; surely he would have had to indulge in those "pleasures" himself to make their births possible? And now her mother was expecting another baby, which meant that they must have done the *thing* together quite recently . . .

Kitty balked as a sudden image of her parents naked flew into her head. She doubted she would *ever* be able to remove her vest and bloomers in front of anyone—least of all a man. Shuddering, she replaced her precious rouge in the drawer so Martha, one of her younger sisters, wouldn't be tempted to steal it. Then she opened her bedroom door and hastened down the three flights of wooden stairs for breakfast.

"Good morning, Katherine." Ralph, her father, sitting at the head of the table with his three younger daughters sitting quietly along one side of it, looked up and gave her a warm smile. Everyone always said she resembled her father in looks, with his full head of curly auburn hair, blue eyes, and high cheekbones. His pale skin had barely a line on it, even though Kitty knew he was in his midforties. All his female parishioners were deeply in love with him and hung on every word he spoke from the pulpit. *And at the same time*, she thought, *probably dreaming of doing all the things with him that he told them they shouldn't.*

"Good morning, Father. Did you sleep well?"

"I did, but your poor mother did not. She is plagued by nausea, as she always is in the early stages of her pregnancies. I've had Aylsa take up a tray to her."

Kitty knew this must mean her mother was most unwell. The breakfast routine in the McBride household was usually strictly adhered to.

"Poor Mother," Kitty said as she sat down, one chair along from her father. "I shall go up and see her after breakfast."

"Perhaps, Katherine, you would be kind enough to visit your mother's parishioners today and run any errands she needs?"

"Of course."

Ralph said grace, picked up his spoon, and began to eat the thick oat porridge, which was the signal for Kitty and her sisters to begin too.

This morning, being a Thursday, breakfast was punctuated by Ralph testing his daughters on their addition and subtraction skills. The weekly timetable was sacred: Monday was spelling, Tuesday, capital cities of the world. On Wednesday, it was the dates of when the kings and queens of England had ascended the throne, with a potted biography of her father's choosing on one of them. Friday was the easiest as it covered the Scottish monarchy, and there hadn't been many Scottish kings and queens after England had taken over. Saturday was used for each child to recite a poem from memory, and on Sunday Ralph fasted to prepare for his busiest day and went to his church before anyone else in the household was up.

Kitty loved Sunday breakfasts.

She watched her sisters struggling to combine the numbers and then swallowing the porridge quickly to give the answer without their mouths being full, which would have elicited a disapproving frown from Father.

"Seventeen!" shouted Mary, the youngest sister at eight, who was bored of waiting for Miriam, her older sister by three years, to answer.

"Well done, my dear!" Ralph said proudly.

Kitty thought this was extremely unfair on poor Miriam, who had always struggled with her numbers and whose nervous personality was overshadowed by her more confident sister. Miriam was Kitty's secret favorite.

"So, Mary, as you have beaten your sisters to the answer, you may choose which parable I will tell."

"The Prodigal Son!" Mary said immediately.

As Ralph began to speak in his low, resonant voice, Kitty only wished he had taught them more parables from the Bible. In truth, she was very weary of the few he favored. Besides, no matter how hard she tried, she couldn't understand the moral behind the tale of the son who disappeared for years from his family's table, leaving another son to take on the burden of his parents. And then, when he came back . . .

". . . bring the fatted calf and kill it. Let us feast and celebrate!" Ralph decreed for her.

Kitty longed to ask her father if this meant that anyone could behave just as they liked and still return home to a joyous welcome, because that was how it sounded. She knew Ralph would tell her that their Father in heaven would forgive anyone who repented of their sins, but in reality, it didn't sound quite fair on the other son, who'd stayed and been good all along, but didn't get the fatted calf killed for him. Then Ralph would say that good people got their reward in the kingdom of heaven, but that seemed an awfully long time to wait when others got it on earth.

"Katherine!" Her father broke into her thoughts. "You're daydreaming again. I said, would you please take your sisters up to the nursery and organize their morning studies? As your mother is too unwell to give them lessons, I shall come up to the nursery at eleven and we shall have an

hour of Bible study." Ralph smiled benignly at his daughters, then stood
up. "Until then, I will be in my study."

When Ralph appeared in the nursery at eleven, Kitty ran to her bedroom
to retrieve the books she intended to return to the public library before
she embarked on visiting her mother's parishioners. Descending the stairs
to the entrance hall, she hastily pulled her thick shawl and cape from a
peg, eager to escape the oppressive atmosphere of the manse. As she
tied the ribbons of her bonnet beneath her chin, she entered the drawing
room and saw her mother sitting beside the fire, her pretty face gray and
exhausted.

"Dearest Mother, you look so tired."

"I confess that I am feeling more fatigued than usual today."

"Rest, Mother, and I shall see you later."

"Thank you, my dear." Her mother smiled wanly as Kitty kissed her
and left the drawing room.

Stepping out into the bracing morning air, she made her way through
the narrow streets of Leith and was greeted by numerous parishioners,
some of whom had known her since she was no more than a "squalling
bairn," as they often liked to remind her. She passed Mrs. Dubhach, who,
as usual, asked after the reverend and gushed over last Sunday's sermon,
to the point where Kitty began to feel quite nauseous.

After bidding farewell to the woman, Kitty boarded the electric tram
heading for central Edinburgh. After changing trams on Leith Walk, she
alighted near George IV Bridge and headed for the Central Library. She
glanced at the students who were chatting and laughing as they walked up
the steps to the vast gray-brick building, lights shining out from the many
mullioned windows into the drab winter sky. Inside the high-ceilinged
main hall it was barely warmer than outside, and as she set her books
down at the returns desk, she hugged her shawl tighter to her as the
librarian dealt with the paperwork.

Kitty stood patiently, thinking about one particular book she had
recently borrowed: Charles Darwin's *On the Origin of Species*, first published
over forty years ago. It had proved to be a revelation for her. In fact, it
had been the catalyst that had caused her to question her religious faith

and the teachings that her father had instilled in her since childhood. She knew he would be horrified to think she had even read such blasphemous words, let alone given them any credence.

As it was, the reverend only grudgingly condoned her regular visits to the library, but for Kitty, it was her haven—the place that had provided the bulk of her education in subjects that went far beyond what she learned from Bible study or her mother's basic English and arithmetic lessons. Her introduction to Darwin had come about by chance, after her father had mentioned that Mrs. McCrombie, his church's wealthiest benefactor, was considering a visit to her relatives in Australia. Kitty's interest had been piqued, and knowing next to nothing about the distant continent, she had browsed the library shelves and had stumbled upon *The Voyage of the "Beagle"*, which chronicled the young Darwin's adventures during a five-year journey around the globe, including two months spent in Australia. One of his books had led to another, and Kitty had found herself both fascinated and disturbed by the revolutionary theories Mr. Darwin espoused.

She wished that she had someone she could discuss these ideas with, but could only imagine her father's apoplexy if she ever dared to mention the word "evolution." The very idea that the creatures which populated the earth were not of God's design, but instead the outcome of millennia spent adapting to their environment, would be anathema to him. Let alone the notion that birth and death were not His to bestow, because "natural selection" determined that only the strongest of any species survived and bred. The theory of evolution made prayer seem rather arbitrary because, according to Darwin, there was no master beyond *nature*, the most powerful force in the world.

Kitty checked the clock on the wall, and having completed her business with the librarian, she did not linger among the shelves as she normally would, but made her way outside and caught a tram back to Leith.

Later that afternoon, she hurried toward home through the bitterly cold streets. Tall, austere buildings lined either side of the road, all made of the same dull sandstone that blended into the constant grayness of the sky. She could see by the layered light of the gas lamps that a heavy fog was descending on the city. She was weary, having spent the afternoon visiting sick parishioners—both those on her own list and those on her mother's. To her dismay, when she'd arrived at the front door of a tenement block on Queen Charlotte Street, she'd found that Mrs. Monkton, a dear old lady who Father swore had fornicated and drunk herself into poverty, had died the day before. Despite her father's comments, Kitty had always looked forward to her weekly visits with Mrs. Monkton, although trying to decipher what the woman said, due to the combination of a lack of teeth and an accent one could cut with a knife, was a task that took considerable concentration. The good humor with which Mrs. Monkton had taken her slide into penury, never once complaining about the squalor she lived in after her fall from grace—*Aye, I was a lady's maid once, ye know. Lived in a reet grand house until the mistress saw the master had set his sights o' me,* she'd cackled once—had provided Kitty with a benchmark. After all, even if the rest of her own life continued along the same narrow track, at least she had a roof over her head and food on her table, when so many others hereabouts did not.

"I hope you are in heaven, where you belong," whispered Kitty into the thick night air as she crossed Henderson Street to the manse on the other side of the road. As she neared the front door, a shadow crossed her path and Kitty stopped abruptly to avoid colliding with its owner. She saw that the shadow belonged to a young woman who had frozen in her tracks and was staring at her. Her tattered scarf had slipped from around her head to reveal a gaunt face with huge haunted eyes and pallid skin framed by coarse brown hair. Kitty thought the poor creature could only be about her own age.

"Do excuse me," she said, as she stepped awkwardly aside to let the girl pass. But the girl did not move, just continued to stare at her unwaveringly, until Kitty broke her gaze and opened the front door. As she entered the house, she felt the girl's eyes boring into her back and she slammed the door hurriedly.

Kitty removed her cape and bonnet, doing her best to divest herself of that pair of haunted eyes at the same time. Then she pondered the Jane Austen novels she'd read and the descriptions of picturesque rectories sitting in the middle of delightful gardens in the English countryside, their inhabitants surrounded by genteel neighbors leading similarly privileged lives. She decided that Miss Austen could never have traveled so far up north and witnessed how *city* clergymen lived on the outskirts of Edinburgh.

Just like the rest of the buildings along the street, the manse was a sturdy Victorian four-floor building, designed for practicality, not prettiness. Poverty was only a heartbeat away in the tenement buildings near the docks. Father often said that no one could ever criticize him for living in a manner above his flock, but at least, thought Kitty as she walked into the drawing room to toast her hands by the fire, unlike others in the neighborhood, the manse's inhabitants were warm and dry.

"Good evening, Mother," she greeted Adele, who was sitting in her chair by the fireside darning socks, resting them and the pincushion on her small bump.

"Good evening, Kitty. How was your day?" Adele's soft accent was that of Scottish gentility, her father having been a laird in Dumfriesshire. Kitty and her sisters had loved traveling south each summer to see their grandparents, and she had especially delighted in being able to ride horses across the sweeping countryside. She had always been perplexed, however, that her father had never accompanied them on their summer sojourns. He cited the need to remain with his flock, but Kitty had begun to suspect that it was because her grandparents disapproved of him. The McBrides, although wealthy, had come from what Kitty had heard termed "trade," whereas her mother's parents were descendants of the noble Clan Douglas, and frequently voiced their concern that their daughter lived in such reduced circumstances as a minister's wife.

"Mrs. McFarlane and her children send their best wishes, and Mr. Cuthbertson's leg abscess seems to have healed. Although I have some sad news too, Mother. I'm afraid Mrs. Monkton died yesterday."

"God rest her soul." Adele immediately crossed herself. "But perhaps it was a blessed relief, living like she did . . ."

"Her neighbor said they'd taken her body to the mortuary, but as there are no relatives and Mrs. Monkton hadn't a farthing to her name, there's nothing for a funeral or a decent burial plot. Unless . . ."

"I'll speak to your father," Adele comforted her daughter. "Although I know church funds are running low at the moment."

"Please do, Mother. Whatever Father said about her descent into sin, she had definitely repented by the end."

"And she was delightful company. Oh, I do so hate the onset of winter. The season of death . . . certainly around these parts." Adele gave a small shudder and put a hand protectively across her belly. "Your father's at a parish committee meeting this evening, then out to take supper with Mrs. McCrombie. He's hoping she will once more see her way clear to giving our church a donation. Heaven knows, it needs it. It cannot run on eternal salvation alone."

Or on the promise of something we cannot even see, or hear, or touch . . .

"Yes, Mother."

"Perhaps you would go upstairs to your sisters, Kitty dear? Bring them down to see me when they're in their nightgowns. I feel so weary tonight, I simply cannot climb the stairs to the nursery floor."

A surge of panic ran through Kitty. "You are still unwell, Mother?"

"One day, my dear, you will understand how draining pregnancy can be, especially at my age. We two shall eat at eight, and there is no need to dress for dinner, as your father is out," she added.

Kitty climbed the interminable stairs, cursing the double blight of being a minister's daughter and the eldest of a brood of four, soon to be five. She walked into the nursery and found Martha, Miriam, and Mary squabbling over a game of marbles.

"I won!" said Martha, who was fourteen and possessed a temperament as stubborn as Father's religious beliefs.

"It was me!" Mary retorted with a pout.

"Actually, I think it was me," put in Miriam gently. And Kitty knew it *had* been her.

"Well, whoever it was, Mother wants you to complete your ablutions, dress in your nightgowns, and go and kiss her good night in the drawing room."

"Go to the drawing room in our nightgowns?" Mary looked shocked. "What will Father say?"

"Father is out having supper with Mrs. McCrombie. Now," Kitty said as Aylsa arrived in the nursery with a washbasin. "Let's see the state of your faces and necks."

"D'ye mind sorting them out, Miss Kitty? I must see to the supper downstairs," Aylsa pleaded with her.

"Of course not, Aylsa." Kitty knew the girl, as their only housemaid, was utterly exhausted by this time of night.

"Thank you, Miss Kitty." Giving her a grateful nod, Aylsa scurried out of the nursery.

When all three of her sisters were in their white muslin nightgowns, Kitty marched them downstairs to the drawing room. As her mother kissed them good night one by one, Kitty decided that at least her early experience of childcare would stand her in good stead when she had children of her own. Then, looking at her mother's burgeoning stomach and the fatigue plain on her face, she thought that perhaps she wouldn't have any at all.

Once her sisters had been dispatched off to bed, Kitty and her mother sat down in the dining room to eat a supper of tough broiled beef, potatoes, and cabbage. They discussed church business and the coming festive season, which, for the McBride family, was the busiest time of the year. Adele smiled at her.

"You're such a good girl, Kitty, and I am so very glad of your help, both inside the house and out while I am . . . encumbered. Of course, soon it will be time for you to have a husband and a family of your own. You'll turn eighteen next week. Goodness, I can't quite believe it."

"I'm in no rush, Mother," said Kitty, remembering the last time the minister of the North Leith parish had come to tea with his wife and pointedly introduced her to his son, Angus. The young man had blushed every time he'd spoken through thick, wet lips about how he was to follow his father into the ministry. She was sure that he was perfectly nice, but although she still didn't quite know what she wanted, it certainly wasn't to be the wife of a minister. *Or* Angus.

"And I will be lost without you here," Adele continued, "but one day it will be so."

Kitty decided to grasp the moment, for it was not often she and her mother were alone. "I wanted to ask you something."

"What is it?"

"I have been wondering whether Father would consider letting me train as a teacher. I would so very much like to have a profession. And, as you know, I enjoy teaching my sisters."

"I am not sure that your father would approve of you having a 'profession,' as you put it," Adele said with a frown.

"Surely, he would see it as God's work? Helping the less fortunate to learn to read and write," Kitty persevered. "It would mean I was no longer a burden to you if I was earning my own keep."

"Kitty dear, that is what a husband is for," Adele said gently. "We must remember that even though your father has selflessly given himself to the Lord and his path has led us here to Leith, you are a descendant of the Douglas clan. No woman from my family has ever worked for a living. Only for charity, as we both do now."

"I cannot see how anyone—either my grandparents or the Lord above—would think it shameful for a woman to work. I saw an advertisement in the *Scotsman* for young women to train as teachers and—"

"By all means, ask your father, but I am sure that he will wish for you to carry on doing your good works in the parish until you find a suitable husband. Now, my back is aching on this hard chair. Let us go and sit in the drawing room where it is warmer and more comfortable."

Frustrated by her mother's lack of support for the idea she'd been harboring for the past few weeks, Kitty did as she'd been bidden. She sat by the fire as her mother took up her knitting for the forthcoming baby and pretended to read a book.

Twenty minutes later, they heard the front door open, heralding the return of the Reverend McBride.

"I think I will retire to bed, Mother," said Kitty, not in the mood to make conversation with her father. Crossing him in the hallway, she dipped a curtsy. "Good evening, Father. I trust you had a pleasant supper with Mrs. McCrombie?"

"Indeed I did."

"Well then, good night." Kitty made for the stairs.

"Good night, my dear."

A few minutes later Kitty climbed into bed, noticing how the spider had wrapped its web so thoroughly around the bluebottle that it was hardly to be seen, and praying that her father had not set his daughter in a similar trap of the marriage variety.

"Please, Lord, anybody but Angus," she groaned.

The following morning, Kitty sat at the desk in her father's study. She had offered to take over the task of completing the parish accounts while her mother was indisposed, which included totting up the amounts from the collection plate at church, along with any other charitable donations, and balancing them against what seemed like frighteningly large outgoings. As she worked through this week's columns of figures, she heard a loud knocking on the front door and ran to answer it before it woke her mother, who was resting upstairs.

She opened the door to a young woman whom she recognized immediately as the girl who had appeared outside the manse the night before.

"Good morning. May I help you?"

"I need tae see Ralph," the young woman said, urgency apparent in her voice.

"The Reverend McBride is out visiting parishioners," Kitty said. "Might I pass on a message?"

"You're no' lyin', are ye? I reckon he's bin hidin' from me. I need tae speak to him. Now."

"As I said, he is not at home. May I pass on a message?" Kitty repeated firmly.

"Ye tell him Annie needs a word. Ye tell him it can't wait."

Before Kitty could reply, the young woman turned swiftly and ran off down the street.

As she closed the front door, Kitty wondered why the woman had used her father's Christian name . . .

When Ralph arrived home two hours later, she tapped tentatively on the door of his study.

"Come."

"Sorry to disturb you, Father, but a young lady came by the house this morning."

"Really?" Ralph looked up, put down his pen, and removed his reading glasses. "And what did she want? A few ha'pennies, no doubt. They all do."

"No. She specifically asked me to tell you that 'Annie needs a word.' And it can't wait. Apparently," Kitty added lamely. There was a pause before Ralph put his reading glasses back on his nose and picked up his pen once more. He began to write as Kitty hovered in the doorway.

"I think I know the girl," he responded eventually. "She waits outside the church on Sundays. I took pity on her once and threw her some coins from the collection. I'll deal with her."

"Yes, Father. I'll be off to run some errands now." Kitty withdrew from the study and hurried to retrieve her bonnet, shawl, and cape, relieved to escape from a sudden tension she felt but couldn't begin to describe.

On the way back home with a heavy basket of eggs, milk, vegetables, and a waxed wrapper full of the haggis her father loved and the rest of the family tolerated, the cold wind stiffened. Kitty pressed her shawl tighter around her shoulders as she walked down a narrow alley that was a shortcut to Henderson Street. The sight of a familiar figure just ahead of her in the deepening gloom made her freeze where she was. Her father was standing on a doorstep with the poor creature— Annie—who had knocked on the manse door earlier that day. Kitty shrank back into the shadows, instinct telling her she should not reveal herself.

The woman's features were contorted in what could have been pain or anger as she whispered hoarsely to him. Kitty watched as Ralph reached out and gripped Annie's hands tightly, before leaning in close to whisper something in her ear and planting a tender kiss on her forehead. Then, with a wave, he turned and walked away. Annie stood alone, her hands clasping and unclasping over what Kitty saw was a markedly distended belly. A second later, she disappeared inside and the door was firmly shut.

After waiting a good five minutes Kitty walked home, her legs unsteady beneath her. Mechanically, she went through her chores, but her mind was continually spinning with possible answers to what she had seen. Perhaps it hadn't been what it had seemed; perhaps her father had simply been comforting the poor woman in her distress . . .

Yet, in the darkest corner of her mind, Kitty already knew.

Over the following few days, she avoided her father as much as she could, the situation made easier by the fact her eighteenth birthday was fast approaching. The house positively buzzed with secrets and excitement at the prospect of a celebration, her sisters shushing her out of the room to whisper conspiratorially together, and her parents spending time together in the drawing room with the door firmly closed.

On the eve of her birthday, Ralph caught her as she headed upstairs to bed.

"My dearest Katherine, tomorrow you will no longer be a child."

"Yes, Father." Kitty could not bring herself to meet his gaze.

"You are a credit to both myself and your mother." Ralph bent down and kissed her on the cheek. "Good night, and God bless you."

Kitty nodded her thanks and continued up the stairs.

In bed, she pulled the covers over her head, shivering in the late autumn chill.

"Lord, forgive me," she sighed, "for I'm no longer sure who my father is."

Aylsa was already up to lay the fires when Kitty descended the stairs the next morning. Needing some fresh air to clear the fog of confusion and the exhaustion of another restless night, she slipped out of the house and walked in the direction of the docks.

She stopped to sit on a low wall, watching the sky's slow awakening, which sent hues of purple and pink across its miraculous breadth. Then she saw a figure emerge from the street that she had just walked down. It was Annie, who Kitty realized must have seen her passing along the alley and followed her.

Their gazes locked as the woman approached her.

"He came tae see me," said Annie gruffly, dark smudges of exhaustion evident beneath her eyes. "He cannae hide no more behind God. Aye, he knows the truth!"

"I . . ." Kitty moved away from her.

"What'm I meant to do?" Annie demanded. "He gave me a few coins and told me to go get rid o' it. I cannae, I'm too far gone."

"I don't know, I'm sorry, I—"

"Och, you're sorry! Fat lot of good that does me! It's your daddy that needs to be sorry."

"I have to go. I really do apologize," Kitty repeated as she rose to her feet, picked up her skirts, then walked swiftly away in the direction of home.

"He's the devil!" Annie shouted after her. "*That's* the truth!"

Somehow, Kitty got through the rest of the day—she opened the thoughtful homemade presents from her sisters and blew out the candles on the cake that Aylsa had made especially for her. She suppressed a shudder as Ralph kissed and embraced her—a natural act that, up until a few days ago, she had delighted in. Now it somehow felt unclean.

"My dear, you have grown into a fine young woman," Adele said proudly. "I pray that one day soon you will have a family of your own and be the lady of your own household."

"Thank you, Mother," Kitty replied quietly.

"Dearest Katherine, my special girl. Happy birthday, and may the Lord bless you in your future. I believe He has something special in mind for you, my dear."

Later that evening, Kitty was called into her father's bare cell of a study that lay at the back of the house facing a brick wall. He always said that the lack of a view helped him focus on his sermons.

"Katherine, do come and sit down." Ralph indicated the hard-backed wooden chair in the corner of the room. "Now then, you are aware that I had supper with Mrs. McCrombie recently?"

"Yes, Father." Whenever Kitty had glanced at her father's patron across the aisle in church, she had seen an extravagantly dressed, plump middle-aged woman who looked out of place in the far poorer crowd. Mrs. McCrombie never visited them at home. Instead, her father went to see her in her grand house just off Princes Street. Therefore, the sum total of their shared conversation amounted to a polite "good morning" if their paths crossed outside church after the service.

"As you know, Katherine, Mrs. McCrombie has always been a generous benefactress of our church and our community," said Ralph. "Her eldest son went into the clergy but was killed in the first Boer War. I fancy she rather sees me as his replacement, and, of course, gives to the church in his memory. She's a good woman, a Christian woman who wants to help those less fortunate than herself, and I'm eternally grateful that she has chosen my church as her charity."

"Yes, Father." Kitty wondered where this was leading and hoped the conversation would be over soon. It was her eighteenth birthday, after all, and just now, she could hardly bear to breathe the same air as him.

"The point is that, as you know, Mrs. McCrombie has family in Australia, whom she hasn't seen for many years, namely her youngest sister, her brother-in-law, and two nephews who live in a town called Adelaide on the south coast. She has decided that while she is still in good health, she should go to visit them."

"Yes, Father."

"And . . . she is looking for a companion to accompany her on the long journey. Obviously, the girl must come from a good Christian home and also be able to assist her in the care of her wardrobe, dressing her, and the like. So . . . I have suggested you, Katherine. You will be away for nine months or so, and having discussed it with your mother, I feel it's a wonderful opportunity for you to go and see some of the world, and at the same time, settle that restless spirit of yours."

Kitty was so shocked at his suggestion, she had no idea how to answer him. "Father, really, I am quite content here. I—"

"It is in you, Kitty, just as it was once in me before I found the Lord . . ."

Kitty watched his eyes leave her face and travel to somewhere far distant in his past. Eventually, they came to focus back on her. "I know you are searching for a purpose, and let us pray you will find it through being a good wife and mother one day. But for now, what do you say?"

"In truth, I hardly know what to say," she replied honestly.

"I will show you Australia in the atlas. You may have heard that it is a dangerous and uncharted country and it is certainly full of heathen natives, although Mrs. McCrombie assures me that the town of Adelaide is as civilized a society as Edinburgh. Many of our faith sailed there in the 1830s to escape from persecution. She tells me there are several beautiful Lutheran and Presbyterian churches already built. It is a God-fearing place and under Mrs. McCrombie's wing, I have no hesitation in sending you there."

"Will I . . . will I be paid for my services?"

"Of course not, Katherine! Mrs. McCrombie is funding a berth for you and covering all other expenses. Do you have any idea how much such a trip costs? Besides, I think it's the least our family can do, given what she has so generously donated to our church over the years."

So I am to be offered as a living, breathing sacrifice in return . . .

"So, my dear. What do you think of that then?"

"Whatever you believe is best for me, Father," she managed, lowering her eyes so that he couldn't see the anger contained within them. "But what about Mother when the baby arrives? Surely she will need my help?"

"We have discussed that, and I have assured your mother that when the time comes, I will see that funds are available to hire extra help."

In all her eighteen years at the manse, there had never been "funds" to "hire extra help."

"Katherine, speak to me," Ralph implored her. "Are you unhappy about this arrangement?"

"I . . . don't know. It . . . has all come as a surprise."

"I understand." Ralph leaned down and took her hands in his, his mesmeric eyes boring into hers. "Naturally you must be confused. Now, you must listen to me. When I met your mother, I was a captain with the Ninety-Second Highlanders and our futures looked set. Then I was sent to fight in the Boer War. I saw many of my friends—and enemies— extinguished by the fire of other men's rifles. And then I myself was shot at the Battle of Majuba Hill. In hospital afterward, I had an epiphany. I prayed that night that if I were saved, I would dedicate my life to God, give every breath to try to halt the injustice and the bloody murder that I'd seen. The following morning, with the doctors not expecting me to last the night, I woke up. My temperature was down and my chest wound healed within days. It was then I knew and understood what my future path would be. Your mother understood too; she is full of God's love herself, but in doing what I felt I must, she has suffered, and so have you and your sisters. Do you see, Katherine?"

"Yes, Father," Kitty answered automatically, although she didn't.

"This journey to Australia with Mrs. McCrombie is an opening to the kind of society that your mother's family is part of. Just because I feel a need to save souls does not mean that the future of my daughters should be curtailed. I am sure that if you acquit yourself well on this trip, Mrs. McCrombie would be happy to introduce you to a wider circle of young gentlemen both here and in Australia that might make a more suitable match for you than I ever could, given our humble financial status. She knows of my sacrifice to further the Lord's work and of the aspirations of your mother's family in Dumfriesshire. She wishes to do her best for you, Katherine. And so do I. Now then, do you understand?"

Kitty looked at her father, then at the soft hands that were clutching hers, and an unbidden memory of a moment similar to this made her withdraw them. Finally, she understood all too well the machinations of her father's mind and his plan to rid himself of her.

"Yes, Father, if you think it best, I will go with Mrs. McCrombie to Australia."

"Wonderful! Of course, you will need to meet with Mrs. McCrombie so that she can see for herself what a good girl you are. And you are, aren't you, dear Katherine?"

"Yes, Father." Kitty knew she must leave the room before her anger overflowed and she spat in his face. "May I go now?" she asked coldly, rising from her chair.

"Of course."

"Good night." Kitty dipped a curtsy, then turned tail and almost ran out of the study and upstairs to her bedroom.

Closing the door and locking it behind her, she threw herself onto her bed.

"Hypocrite! Liar! Cheat! And my poor mother—your *wife*—expecting a child too!" She spat the words into her pillow. Then she cried long, stifled sobs of despair. Eventually, she stood up, put on her nightgown, and brushed her hair in front of the mirror. Her reflection glowed pale in the gaslight.

You know that I see through you, Father. And that is why you are sending me away.

7

Y our father is such an inspiration to me, Miss McBride, and I'm sure to you too."

"Of course," lied Kitty as she sipped the Earl Grey tea from a delicate china cup. They were sitting in the large overheated drawing room of a grand house in St. Andrew Square, one of the most sought-after addresses in Edinburgh. The room was stuffed with more elegant objects than she'd seen in Miss Anderson's fancy-goods emporium. A display cabinet lined one wall, cluttered with statuettes of cherubs, Chinese vases, and decorative plates. A chandelier dripping with crystals bathed everything in a soft light which gleamed off the polished mahogany furniture. Mrs. McCrombie was obviously not one to hide her wealth.

"So devoted to his flock and denying both himself and his family all the advantages that your mother's birthright could have given him."

"Yes," Kitty replied automatically. Then, looking at the glazed eyes of her soon-to-be employer, she decided that the older woman looked like a young girl in love. She also noticed the large amount of face powder Mrs. McCrombie had caked on her skin and thought about how much it must have cost to cover the many lines that wriggled their way across her face. The high color of her cheeks and her nose spoke of too many drams of whiskey.

"Miss McBride?" Kitty realized Mrs. McCrombie was still speaking to her.

"I do beg your forgiveness. I was just looking at that rather marvelous painting," Kitty improvised, pointing out a drab and miserable depiction of Jesus carrying the cross on his shoulders to Calvary.

"That was painted by Rupert, my beloved son, God rest his soul. Just before he went off to the Boer War and ended up in Jesus's arms. Almost as if he knew . . ." Then she beamed warmly at Kitty. "You obviously have an eye for art."

"I certainly enjoy things of beauty," Kitty responded, only relieved she'd managed to say the right thing.

"Then that is to your credit, my dear, given there have been so few of them around you during your childhood, due to your dear father's sacrifice. At least it will have prepared you for what we may find in Adelaide. Even though my sister assures me they have every modern convenience I myself enjoy here in Edinburgh, I can hardly believe that such a new country can compete with a culture of centuries."

"I will indeed be interested to see Adelaide."

"And I will not," Mrs. McCrombie said firmly. "However, I feel it is my duty to visit my sister and my young nephews at least once before I die. And as they seem disinclined to come here, I must journey there." Mrs. McCrombie gave a mournful sigh as Kitty sipped her tea. "The journey will take at least a month aboard the *Orient*, a ship which my sister Edith assures me provides every comfort. However . . ."

"Yes, Mrs. McCrombie?"

"If you accompany me, there will be no fraternizing with young men aboard ship. No carousing, or attending any of the dances in the lower-class lounges. You will share a berth with one other young lady and you will be available to me at all times. Is that understood?"

"Completely."

"My sister has also warned me that even though it is winter here, it will be summer there. I have a seamstress sewing me a number of muslin and cotton gowns and I suggest you source similar attire for yourself. In essence, the weather will be hot."

"Yes, Mrs. McCrombie."

"I am sure you know that you are awfully pretty, my dear. I hope you won't be one of those gels who swoons at the mere glance of a man."

"I have never thought of myself as such," said Kitty, seeing her freckled complexion in her mind's eye, "but I assure you that I will not. After all, my father is a minister in the church and I have been taught modesty."

"Your father tells me that you can sew and mend? And know how to pin up hair?"

"I fashion my mother's and my sisters'," Kitty lied, thinking she might as well be hung for a sheep as a lamb. She was going to Australia, and that was that.

"Do you get sick often?" Mrs. McCrombie raised her eyeglass to study Kitty more closely.

"My mother tells me I survived diphtheria and measles, and I rarely get a cold."

"I hardly think that that will be our greatest concern in Australia, although of course I will pack some camphor oil for my chest. Well now, there is little more to discuss. We shall meet again on the thirteenth of November." Mrs. McCrombie rose and offered her hand. "Good day to you, Miss McBride. We shall cross the oceans together with a sense of adventure."

"We will. Good-bye, Mrs. McCrombie."

Kitty spent the following two weeks preparing the small trunk that had been bought for her by her father. The fact she was following in Darwin's footsteps so soon after reading his books seemed positively surreal. Perhaps she should have been frightened: After all, she had read enough in his books to know that the natives in Australia were extremely hostile toward the white man and cannibalism had even been rumored. She doubted Mrs. McCrombie would venture anywhere near where that kind of thing would happen, especially as any native who cooked her in his pot would have a decent meal for his extended family.

The house grew quiet as she worked into the night on her sewing machine, fashioning simple gowns which she hoped would be suitable in the heat. And at least the activity gave her a focus that blunted the gnawing in her stomach every time she thought about Annie and her father. She knew she had one last thing to do before she left.

The morning of her departure, Kitty woke before dawn and hurried out of the house before anyone saw her. Walking down the alley that led toward the docks, she tried to calm herself by taking in the sights and sounds of Leith for the last time. It was the only home she had ever known in all of her eighteen years and it would be what seemed like a lifetime before she saw it again.

She arrived at Annie's door, drew in a deep breath, and knocked cautiously. Eventually, the door was opened and Annie appeared, dressed in a threadbare smock and apron. Her eyes traveled briefly over Kitty's face, before she silently stood aside to let her pass.

The small room within was sparsely furnished and bitterly cold. The stained horsehair mattress on the floor looked uninviting, but at least the floor was swept and the rough wooden table in the center of the room looked well scrubbed.

"I . . . came to see how you were," Kitty began tentatively.

Annie nodded. "Aye, I'm well. And so's the bairn."

Kitty forced her eyes down to look at the neat bump that contained what was soon to be her half brother or sister.

"I promise you, I'm nae a sinner," Annie said hoarsely. Kitty looked up to see tears in her eyes. "I only . . . I was only with the reverend twice. I trusted in God's love, in your father's love, that he . . . Ralph would guide me. I . . ." She broke her gaze from Kitty's and went to a dresser in the corner, searching for something in a drawer.

She returned with a pair of reading glasses, which Kitty recognized immediately. They were identical to those her father wore to write his sermons.

"Ralph left them here last time he came tae see me. I promised him I'd keep what happened tae m'self. And I made a promise tae God an' all. Ye give him these back. I want nothing of his under my roof any longer."

Kitty took the glasses from Annie, wondering if she might be sick all over the floor. Then she reached into her skirts and drew out a small drawstring pouch.

"I have something for you too." Kitty handed the pouch to Annie.

Annie opened it, looked inside, and gasped. "Miss, I cannae take this from you, I cannae."

"You can," Kitty insisted. For the past two weeks, she had secreted away coins from the parish donations, and last night had taken a bundle of notes from the tin her father kept locked in a drawer. It was an amount large enough to provide future sustenance for Annie and the baby, at least until she could work again. By the time Ralph discovered it was missing, Kitty would be on her way to the other side of the world.

"Then thank you." Annie pulled out the other item in the bag—a small silver cross on a chain. She ran her fingers over it uncertainly.

"It was given to me at my christening by my grandparents," Kitty explained. "I want you to keep it for the . . . the child."

"It's kind of ye, Miss McBride. Very kind. Thank you." Annie's eyes glistened with unshed tears.

"I'm leaving for Australia today . . . I'll be gone for some months, but when I return, may I come again to see how you're getting on?"

"Of course, miss."

"In the meantime, I'd like you to have the address of where I'll be staying. In case of an emergency," Kitty added, holding out an envelope and then feeling foolish—she had no idea if the woman could even read or write, let alone whether she would know how to post a letter to another country. But Annie merely nodded and took it.

"We'll never forget your kindness," she said as Kitty moved toward the door. "G'bye, miss. And may the Lord keep ye safe on your travels."

Kitty left the dwelling, then walked toward the docks and stood on the edge beside the seawall, watching the seagulls hover over the mast of a ship chugging into port. She took the reading glasses from her skirt pocket, then threw them as far as she could into the gray water below her.

"Even Satan disguises himself as an angel of light," she muttered. "God help my father, and my poor, deluded mother."

"All ready?" Adele appeared at Kitty's bedroom door.

"Yes, Mother," she replied as she snapped the locks down on her trunk and reached for her bonnet.

"I will miss you desperately, dearest Kitty." Adele came toward her and enveloped her in a hug.

"And I you, Mother, especially as the baby will be born without its big sister being present. Please take care of yourself while I am not here to make sure you do."

"You mustn't worry, Kitty. I have your father, Aylsa, and your sisters with me. I will send you a telegram as soon as he or she has made their appearance in the world. Kitty, please don't cry." Adele brushed a tear from her daughter's cheek. "Just think of the stories you'll have to tell us when you arrive home. It's only nine months, the same time it takes for a little one to be born."

"Forgive me, it is simply that I will miss you so very much," Kitty sobbed onto her mother's comforting shoulder.

Shortly afterward, standing at the front door with her trunk being loaded onto Mrs. McCrombie's carriage, Kitty proceeded to hug her sisters. Miriam in particular was crying inconsolably.

"My dearest Katherine, how I will miss you."

Then Ralph took her into his arms. She stood, tense and taut, inside them. "Remember to say your prayers every day, and may the Lord be with you."

"Good-bye, Father," she managed. Then, pulling herself free of him and with one last wave at her beloved family, she climbed into the carriage, and the driver shut the door behind her.

As the RMS *Orient* hooted and began to make her way out to sea, Kitty stood on the deck watching her fellow shipmates screaming good-byes to their relatives below them. The quay was packed with well-wishers waving Union Jacks and the occasional Australian flag. There was no one to wave her off, but at least, unlike many of the people around her, she knew she would be returning to England's shores.

As the well-wishers became indistinguishable figures and the ship steamed down the Thames Estuary, a silence fell on those around her as each of the passengers realized the enormity of the decision they had made. As they dispersed, she heard the odd sob—and knew they were wondering if they would ever see their loved ones again.

Although she had seen the big vessels that docked in Leith Harbor many times, it now seemed a daunting task for this steamship to carry them across the seas safely to the other side of the world, despite the impressive height of the two funnels and the masts that held swaths of sails.

Walking down the narrow stairs to the second-class corridor that contained her berth, Kitty felt rather like this entire experience was happening to someone else. Opening the door and wondering how she would ever sleep with the rumble of the huge engines below her, she made a forty-five-degree turn in order to close the door behind her. The room—if one could call it that, its dimensions being akin to a short, thin corridor—contained two coffinlike bunks and a small storage cupboard in which to put clothes. A washbasin sat in the corner and Kitty noticed that it and all the other fittings were bolted to the floor.

"'Ello. You me new roommate?"

A pair of bright hazel eyes framed by a shock of dark curly hair appeared over the wooden rail of the top bunk.

"Yes."

"My name's Clara Dugan. 'Ow d'you do?"

"Very well, thank you. I'm Kitty McBride."

"From Scotland, eh?"

"Yes."

"Me, I'm from the good ol' East End o' London. Where you 'eaded?"

"To Adelaide."

"Never 'eard of it. I'm going to Sydney meself. You're dressed smart. You a lady's maid?"

"No. I mean . . . I'm a companion."

"Oooh! Get you," said Clara, but not unkindly. "Well, if I knows anything about the gentry, unless your lady 'as brought a maid as well, it's you who'll do all the fetching and carrying on board. And who'll mop up 'er puke when we're on rough seas. Me brother Alfie told me the ole ship stank for days when there was a storm. 'E's there already, making a right good life for 'imself, 'e says. 'E told me to save up me money so I wouldn't have to go steerage. Five souls died on 'is crossing," Clara added for good measure. "I worked night and day for two years in a factory to pay for me berth. It'll be worth it, though, if we get there."

"Goodness! Then let's hope our journey goes more smoothly."

"I can be anyone I want to be when I get there. I'll be free! Ain't that just the best?" Clara's bright eyes danced with happiness.

There was a sudden rap on the door and Kitty went to open it. A young steward was grinning at her.

"Are you Miss McBride?"

"Yes."

"Mrs. McCrombie has requested you go to her cabin. She needs help unpacking her trunk."

"Of course."

As Kitty followed the steward out of the cabin, Clara lay back with a wry smile.

"Well, at least *some* of us are free," she shouted after Kitty.

After an initial night tossing and turning in her bunk, enduring feverish half dreams of storms, shipwrecks, and being eaten alive by natives, all punctuated by loud snores from the bunk above her, Kitty's days soon fell into a routine and passed quickly. While Clara slept on, Kitty was up at seven to wash, dress, and tidy her hair. Then she'd walk along the gently rolling corridor and take the stairs to the first-class section on the deck above her.

She'd found her sea legs almost immediately, and even though both Clara and Mrs. McCrombie had taken to their beds as they'd encountered what the crew had called a "gentle swell," Kitty was surprised to find herself feeling very well indeed. This had earned her much praise from the crew, especially from George, Mrs. McCrombie's personal steward, who Clara said had the "eye" for her.

Compared to the sparse decor of the second-class berths, the first-class accommodation was positively sumptuous. Underfoot were plush carpets with intricate William Morris designs, the brass furnishings were polished to a high shine, and exquisitely carved wooden paneling adorned the walls. Mrs. McCrombie was in her element, dressing every evening for dinner in an array of extravagant gowns.

Kitty spent most of her mornings attending to Mrs. McCrombie's personal needs, which included an awful lot of mending. She sighed at the torn seams of corsets and bodices, eventually surmising that Mrs. McCrombie must have refused to reveal her true size to her seamstress out of vanity. At lunchtime Kitty would go to the second-class dining room and eat with Clara. She was amazed at how fresh the food was and by the dexterity of the waiters as they carried trays of drinks and plates across the sometimes heaving floors. In the afternoons, she would take a bracing walk on the promenade deck, then retire with Mrs. McCrombie to the first-class saloon to play bezique or cribbage.

As the steamer progressed south through the Mediterranean, stopping briefly in Naples before continuing to Port Said and then easing through the Suez Canal, the weather became warmer. Even though Mrs. McCrombie refused to leave the ship when it docked, citing how they might pick up some "deadly plague from one of the natives," looking out onto these impossibly exotic foreign shores, Kitty began to feel the feverish grip of adventure.

For the first time in her life, she flouted the rules and danced at rousing ceilidhs, held in the smoky, gas-lit third-class saloon. Clara had practically dragged her to the first one and Kitty had sat primly on the sidelines as she watched her friend enjoy dance after dance to the lively Celtic band. She was soon persuaded to join in, and found herself whirled from one young man to another, all of whom behaved like perfect gentlemen.

She'd also warmed toward Mrs. McCrombie, who, after a whiskey or three at cocktail hour, displayed a wicked sense of humor as she told raucous jokes that would surely have given her father a heart attack. It was during one of these evenings that Mrs. McCrombie confided her nerves at seeing her younger sister again.

"I haven't seen Edith since she was eighteen, not much older than you, my dear, when she left for Australia to marry dear Stefan. She's almost fifteen years younger than me—her arrival was rather a shock to Papa." Mrs. McCrombie gave a smirk and then burped discreetly. "She looks nothing at all like me either," Mrs. McCrombie added as she gestured for a waiter to top up her glass. "And I suppose you know that your father was quite the ladies' man when my family knew him in those days."

"Really? Goodness," Kitty replied neutrally, hoping Mrs. McCrombie would elaborate, but her patron's attention had already been claimed by the ship's band starting up and the conversation was not pursued.

As they approached Port Colombo in Ceylon, the good ship *Orient* was tossed about in heavy seas. Kitty remained upright, tending to both Mrs. McCrombie and Clara, as they turned green and took to their beds. She mused that seasickness was indeed the greatest social leveler as no amount of wealth could prevent it. Passengers of all classes were at the mercy of the choppy waves, and the ship's stewards were kept busy handing out ginger infusions, which supposedly settled the stomach. Kitty could not stop Mrs. McCrombie pouring generous measures of whiskey into her medicinal drinks, claiming, "Nothing will stop the awful spinning, so I might as well run with it, my dear."

As they crossed the vast Indian Ocean, the continent of Australia like a promised land before them, Kitty experienced a heat stronger than she could ever have imagined. She sat with Mrs. McCrombie on the promenade deck—the best place to catch a breeze—with a book from the ship's library and pondered how she had acquired an identity all of her own. No longer was she just the Reverend McBride's daughter, but a capable woman who had the best sea legs George the steward had ever known on a woman, and was quite able to stand on them without the protection of her mother and father.

As she looked up at the cloudless skies, the horror of what she had discovered before she had left was thankfully receding farther into the distance along with Scotland. When Mrs. McCrombie announced they were only a week away from their destination, Kitty experienced a stomach roll that had nothing to do with the movement of the ship. This was Darwin's land—the land of a man who did not hide behind God to explain his own motives or beliefs, but celebrated the power and creativity of nature. The best and worst of it in all its beauty, rawness, and cruelty, laid bare for all to see. Nature was honest, without bigotry or hypocrisy.

If she could find an accurate metaphor for how she currently felt, Kitty decided it would be akin to Mrs. McCrombie shrugging off her too-tight corsets and deciding to breathe again.

Most of the passengers were on deck the morning that the *Orient* was close to a first sighting of Australia's coastline. Excitement and trepidation were palpable as everyone craned their necks to see what, for so many on board, would be their home and the start of a new life.

As the coastline came into view, a strange hush descended on deck. Sandwiched between the blue of the sea and the shimmering sky lay a thin, red-colored strip of earth.

"Quite flat, ain't it?" Clara said with a shrug. "No 'ills I can see."

"Yes, it is," said Kitty dreamily, hardly able to believe she was actually seeing with her own eyes what had previously appeared as an unreachable blob in an atlas.

As the ship drew into the port of Fremantle and berthed in the harbor, cheering broke out. It appeared to Kitty even larger than the Port of London, where they had originally embarked, and she marveled at the impossibly tall passenger and cargo ships that lobbied for space at the quayside, and the crowds of all creeds and colors going about their business beneath her.

"Golly-gosh!" Clara threw her arms around Kitty. "We've actually gone and made it to Australia! 'Ow's that then?"

Kitty watched the disembarking passengers walk down the gangplank clutching their worldly goods and their children to them. A few were met by friends or relatives, but most stood on the dock looking dazed and confused in the bright sunshine, until they were rounded up and led off by an official. Kitty admired each and every one of them for their courage to leave a life in the country of their birth to make a new and better one here.

"A rough old crowd, from what I could see," said Mrs. McCrombie over a luncheon of lamb chops in the dining room. "But then, Australia was initially populated by the dregs of society, shipped from England. Convicts and criminals, the lot of them. Except for Adelaide, of course, which was built to a plan to encourage the more . . . genteel among us to make a life there. Edith tells me it's a good, God-fearing town." She cocked her ear nervously as the unfamiliar twang of Australian voices floated up through the open windows, fanning herself violently as beads of perspiration appeared on her forehead. "One can only hope that the temperature in Adelaide will be cooler than it is here," she continued. "Good Lord, no wonder the natives run about with no clothes on. The heat is quite unbearable."

After lunch, Mrs. McCrombie went to her cabin for a nap and Kitty wandered back onto the deck, fascinated by the cattle still being led off the boat. Most of them looked emaciated and bewildered as they stumbled down the gangplank. "So far from the fresh green fields of home," she whispered to herself.

The following morning, the ship set off again, with Adelaide as its next stop. The two days before their arrival were spent packing Mrs. McCrombie's extensive wardrobe back into her trunks.

"Perhaps you can come and visit me in Sydney when I'm settled in? It can't be that far between the towns, can it? It looked close on the map," Clara commented over their last lunch together on board.

Kitty asked George the steward later that night whether this might be possible, and he chuckled at her ignorance.

"I'd reckon that in a straight line, it's over seven hundred miles between

Adelaide and Sydney. And even then, you'd have to see off tribes of blacks carrying spears, let alone the 'roos, and snakes and spiders that can kill you with one bite. Did you look on the map, Miss McBride, and wonder why there's no towns in the interior of Australia? No white human can survive for long in the outback."

When Kitty settled down to sleep for her last night on board, she sent up a prayer.

"Please, Lord, I don't mind snakes or kangaroos, or even savages, but please don't have me cooked alive in a pot!"

As the *Orient* sailed into Adelaide port, Kitty bade farewell to a tearful Clara.

"So, this is good-bye then. Been nice knowin' ya, Kitty. Promise to write to me?"

The two girls hugged each other tightly.

"Of course I will. Keep safe, Clara, and I hope all your dreams come true."

As Kitty helped Mrs. McCrombie down the gangplank, she felt on the verge of tears herself. Only now, at the point of disembarkation, did she realize how she would miss her shipboard friends.

"Florence!" Kitty watched as a slim, elegant woman with a head of rich mahogany hair waved and walked toward them.

"Edith!" The two sisters gave each other a restrained peck on both cheeks.

Kitty walked behind them as a liveried driver led them to a carriage. She glanced at Edith's attire—a brocade dress buttoned up to her neck, not to mention the corset and bloomers that would lie beneath it—and wondered how she stood the heat. Kitty longed to plunge stark naked into the cool waters lapping at the dock.

When they reached the carriage, a young boy with the blackest skin Kitty had ever seen was heaving the trunks onto the rack at the back of it.

"Goodness!" Mrs. McCrombie turned to her suddenly. "In my excitement at seeing you, dear sister, I have forgotten to introduce you to Miss Kitty McBride, the eldest daughter of one of our dear family friends, the Reverend McBride. She has been my helpmeet and savior during the voyage," Mrs. McCrombie added fondly, with a glance at Kitty.

"Then I am pleased to make your acquaintance," replied Edith, sweeping a cool gaze over Kitty. "Welcome to Australia and I hope you will enjoy your stay with us here in Adelaide."

"Thank you, Mrs. Mercer."

As Kitty waited for the two sisters to climb into the carriage, she had the strongest feeling that Edith's welcome was as hollow as it had sounded.

8

The dusty journey from the port through the stifling heat had begun with tin-roofed shacks near the docks, graduating to rows of bungalows and, finally, to a wide street lined with gracious houses.

Alicia Hall, named after Edith's mother-in-law, was a grand white colonial mansion, sitting on Victoria Avenue. Built to withstand the heat of the day, the house was surrounded on all sides by cool, shady verandas and terraces fenced with delicate latticework. At sunset, a chorus of insects that Kitty could not yet name produced a cacophony of sound.

Since arriving three days ago, Mrs. McCrombie—or Florence, as Edith called her—had spent her time either sleeping off the arduous voyage in her room, or sitting with Edith on the veranda as they caught up with each other's lives.

Currently, the three of them were the only residents in the hall: Mr. Stefan Mercer, Edith's husband and the master of the house, was apparently away seeing to one of his many business interests, and the couple's two sons were also absent. Apart from breakfast, lunch, and dinner—when neither sister included her in conversation beyond an initial greeting and a "good day" when she left—Kitty had kept to her airy pastel-painted room on the upper floor of the house.

So far, the solitude had been no hardship. Kitty had been content to take a book from the downstairs library and read it on the terrace that led from her bedroom. But as the days continued to drag on in the same routine and Christmas approached, Kitty's thoughts turned to home. As she wrote a letter to her family, she could almost breathe in the freezing foggy air, and see in her mind's eye the huge Christmas tree on Princes Street, festooned with tiny lights that bobbed and danced in the breeze.

"I miss you all," she whispered as she folded the notepaper in two, her eyes wet with tears.

After breakfast, she normally took a perambulation around the vast and lush garden. It was laid out in sections, with clear paths cut into the grass, some of them shaded by frames filled with wisteria. Dark green topiary bushes were perfectly pruned, as were the herbaceous borders that contained bright specimens she had never seen before—fiery pink and orange flowers, glossy green leaves, honey-scented purple blooms into which large blue butterflies dipped to drink the sweet nectar.

The boundaries of the garden were lined by huge trees with unusual ghost-white bark. Whenever she drew close to them, she smelled a gorgeously fresh herbal scent wafting on the breeze, and promised herself she'd remember to ask Edith what they were.

Yet, however beautifully maintained it was, Kitty was beginning to feel as if Alicia Hall were a luxury prison. Never before in her life had she been so devoid of activity; an army of servants took care of the occupants' every need and with Australia waiting for her behind the garden walls and little to keep her busy, time began to hang heavy upon her.

As Christmas grew nearer, Kitty was walking back from the garden after her morning stroll when she saw a man appearing through the back gates. She stopped in her tracks, taking in the red dust that covered his shock of indeterminate-colored hair, his filthy clothes and boots. Her first instinct was to dash inside and tell the servants there was an itinerant lurking on the property.

She slid behind a pillar on the veranda and watched him surreptitiously from behind it as he moved toward the servants' entrance.

"G'day," he called out, and Kitty wondered how he could see her as she was extremely well hidden. "I can see your shadow, whoever you are. Why are you hiding?"

She knew that the man could easily grab her as she ran across the veranda to safety, but reminded herself that she'd been in far worse situations with drunken Scotsmen on the docks. So she took a deep breath and revealed herself.

"I wasn't hiding. I was merely sheltering from the sun."

"It's pretty strong this time of year, but nothing compared to the heat up in the north."

"I wouldn't know. I've only just arrived."

"Have you indeed? From where?"

"Scotland. Do you have business at this house?" she demanded.

He appeared amused at the question. "Well, I hope I do, yes."

"Then I will tell Mrs. Mercer that she has a visitor when she returns."

"Mrs. Mercer isn't at home at present?"

"I am assured that she will return soon," Kitty replied, realizing her mistake. "But there are many servants in the house."

"Then I shall go and speak with them about my business," he stated, striding toward the rear entrance that led to the kitchen. "Good day to you."

After hurrying inside and climbing the stairs up to her room, then walking out onto her terrace, she saw a horse and cart clopping out of the back gates a few minutes later. Relieved that the servants must have seen him off, she collapsed onto her bed, fanning herself violently.

That evening, Kitty readied herself to go down for dinner. She still marveled at the fact that on the other side of the world in a land of heathen natives, there was electric light *and* a bathtub that could be filled any day she chose. Kitty took a long refreshing dip, pinned up her hair, cursed her freckles, then walked down the elegant curved staircase. She came to an abrupt halt, for below her was the most exquisite and unexpected sight: a Christmas tree bedecked with tiny glistening ornaments that glimmered in the soft light of the chandelier overhead. The familiar scent of pine reminded her so much of Christmas Eve with her family, it brought a tear to her eye.

"God bless you all," she whispered, as she continued downward, comforting herself that this time next year, she'd be back at home. As she reached the bottom of the stairs she saw a man, dressed formally for dinner, hanging the last bauble on the tree.

"Good evening," said the man, emerging from the branches.

"Good evening." As she stared at him, Kitty realized there was something familiar about the timbre of his voice.

"Do you like the tree?" he asked, walking toward her, his arms crossed as he looked up at his handiwork.

"It's beautiful."

"It's a present for my . . . Mrs. Mercer."

"Is it? How kind."

"Yes."

Kitty looked at him again, his dark hair gleaming under the light and . . .

"I believe we have met already, Miss . . . ?"

"McBride," Kitty managed, realizing exactly who he was and why she recognized him.

"I am Drummond Mercer, Mrs. Mercer's son. Or at least, her number two son," he added.

"But . . ."

"Yes?"

"You . . ."

Kitty watched his eyes fill with amusement and felt her face flush with embarrassment.

"I'm so sorry. I thought—"

"That I was an itinerant, come to rob the house?"

"Yes. Please do accept my apologies."

"And you must accept mine for not introducing myself earlier. I came overland from Alice Springs by camel, which is why I looked so . . . *déshabillé.*"

"You came by camel?"

"Yes, camel. We have thousands of them here in Australia, and contrary to what people may tell you, they are the most reliable form of transport across our treacherous terrain."

"I see," said Kitty, trying to take all this in. "Then no wonder you looked filthy. I mean, if you'd been riding across Australia. I came here by boat, and it took me a number of weeks and . . ." Kitty knew she was "wittering on," as her father always used to say.

"You are forgiven, Miss McBride. It is quite incredible how the dirtiest vagrant can scrub up well, is it not? I took a pony and cart when I arrived here to go and collect our tree for Mother from the docks. We have one shipped over every year from Germany and I wanted to make sure I got the pick of the crop. Last year, the needles dropped off within a day. Well now, shall we go through to the drawing room for drinks?"

Kitty pulled herself up to her full height and squared her shoulders as she took his proffered hand. "I'd be delighted."

That night at dinner, with Drummond at the table, Kitty felt that the atmosphere had lightened. He teased her mercilessly over her earlier mistake, with Mrs. McCrombie having to wipe the tears of laughter from her cheeks. Only Edith sat there with a look of distaste on her face at the hilarity.

Why is she so cold toward me? Kitty wondered. *I have done nothing wrong . . .*

"So, Miss McBride, have you ventured into our quality little town yet?" Drummond asked her over pudding.

"No, but I would certainly love to as I am yet to buy Christmas tokens for your family," she confided to him in a whisper.

"Well, I must go tomorrow to see to some . . . business. I can offer you a lift on the pony and cart if you wish."

"I would be most grateful, Mr. Mercer. Thank you."

After their unfortunate initial meeting, Kitty had to admit that Drummond had proved to be delightful company. He had an easygoing way about him and a lack of formality that Kitty found hugely appealing. He was also quite the most handsome man she had ever laid eyes on, what with his height and broad shoulders, bright blue eyes, and thick, wavy dark hair. Not that that was relevant, of course, Kitty thought as she slipped into bed later. He'd hardly be looking at her—the daughter of a poor clergyman and strewn with hundreds of freckles. Besides, the thought of any man coming anywhere near her made her shudder. When it came to physical intimacy, all she could think of presently was the hypocrisy of her father.

Drummond handed her up onto the cart the next morning and Kitty settled herself next to him.

"Ready?" he asked.

"Yes," she replied. "Thank you."

The horse clopped out of the gates and along the wide avenue. Kitty breathed in the glorious smell that she couldn't quite place.

"What is that scent?" she asked him.

"Eucalyptus trees. Koalas love them. My grandmother tells me that when they built Alicia Hall in 1860 there were a number of koala families living in the trees."

"Goodness! I have only ever read about them in books."

"They look very much like living, breathing teddy bears. If I see one, I'll show you. And if you hear a strange bellow at night that sounds akin to something between a snore and a growl, you'll know there's a male koala in the grounds foraging for leaves or on the prowl for a mate."

"I see." Kitty was slowly getting used to Drummond's odd accent—it was a mixture of German intonation and the odd soft Scottish burr on a word, all mixed in with an occasional Australian expression for good measure. The sun was burning down on her, and she pulled her bonnet lower to shield her face.

"Struggling with the temperature, are you?"

"A little, yes," she admitted, "and the sun burns my skin in an instant."

"It will toughen up soon enough, and I must say you have the most adorable freckles."

She shot Drummond a glance to see if he was making fun of her again, but his expression was steady as he concentrated on steering the horse down the increasingly busy road. Kitty sat quietly as they entered the town, noticing that the streets were far wider than in Edinburgh, and the buildings sturdy and elegant. Well-dressed residents were strolling along the paths, the women holding parasols to ward off the sun's strong rays.

"So, what do you make of Adelaide so far?" Drummond asked her.

"I haven't seen enough of it to judge."

"Something tells me you keep your thoughts to yourself, Miss McBride. Is that true?"

"Mostly. Simply because I doubt other people would be interested in them."

"Some of us would," he offered. "Quite the enigma, aren't you?"

Again, Kitty did not reply, unsure whether it was a compliment or an insult.

"I went to Germany once," he said, breaking another silence. "So far, it's my only trip to Europe. I found it cold, dark, and rather dull. Australia may have its problems, but at least the sun shines here and everything about it is dramatic. Can you cope with a little drama, Miss McBride?"

"Perhaps," she replied neutrally.

"Then you will do well in Australia, because it isn't for the fainthearted. Or at least, outside the city boundaries it isn't," he added as he pulled the pony and cart to a halt. "This is King William Street." He indicated a street lined with shops, their frontages painted in bright colors, with gleaming signs advertising their wares. "It's as civilized as it gets. I will drop you here on Beehive Corner, and collect you in two hours at one o'clock prompt. Does that suit you?"

"It suits me very well, thank you."

Drummond dismounted from the cart and offered Kitty his hand to help her down. "Now, go and do what you ladies seem to enjoy best, and if you're a good girl, I'll take you off to see Father Christmas on Rundle Street later. G'day." Drummond winked at her as he climbed back onto the cart.

Kitty stood there in the dusty street watching the carriages, the horse-drawn carts, and the ponies which bore men with wide-brimmed hats. Looking up, she saw what Drummond had referred to as "Beehive Corner"—a beautiful red and white building with arches and finials, topped off with a delicately painted bee. Confident she would find it again, she walked along the street, peering through the windows. Now perspiring profusely in the heat, she came across a haberdashery shop and entered to peruse the surprisingly large selection of ribbons and laces on offer. It was, if that was possible, even hotter inside the shop than out. Feeling the sweat dripping down the back of her neck, she bought a yard of lace for both Mrs. McCrombie and Mrs. Mercer, and some white cotton fabric for the men, thinking that she could fashion it into handkerchiefs and stitch Scottish thistles into the corners.

She paid and left the oppressive fug of the shop before she disgraced herself and fainted right then and there. Hurrying along the road, desperately in search of shelter from the sun and a cooling glass of water, she staggered onward until she spied a sign in the distance: THE EDINBURGH CASTLE HOTEL.

She burst through the doors into a crowded, smoky room with enormous fans stirring the air above her head. Pushing her way through to the bar and hardly noticing that the entire room had gone silent at her presence, she sank onto a stool and mouthed, "Water, please," to a barmaid, whose bodice seemed fittingly low-cut for the intense heat. The girl nodded and scooped some water from a barrel into a mug. Kitty grabbed it and drank the lot down, then asked for another. Once that was drained and her senses began to return to her, she raised her head and looked up to find forty or so pairs of male eyes studying her.

"Thank you," she said to the barmaid. And, gathering her dignity, she stood up and began to walk toward the door.

"Miss McBride!" An arm caught hers just as her hand reached for the brass doorknob. "What a coincidence to see you here."

She looked up into the amused eyes of Drummond Mercer and felt the heat rising once again to her cheeks.

"I was thirsty," she replied defensively. "It's very hot out there."

"Yes, it is. In retrospect, I should never have left you alone on the street, being a newcomer to these climes."

"I am perfectly fine now, thank you."

"Then I am glad. Is your shopping complete?"

"Complete as it will ever be. How anyone can shop in this heat, I really don't know," she said, fanning herself.

"A wee measure o' whiskey for you, miss?" said a voice from behind her.

"I—"

"Medicinal purposes only," Drummond reassured her. "I'll keep her company, Lachlan," he added as they threaded their way back to the bar. "And by the way, this young lady hails from Edinburgh."

"Then any dram the lassie wants is on the house. 'Tis a shock when you first arrive here, miss," the man continued as he slid behind the counter and opened a bottle. "Aye, I remember that first week when I believed I'd arrived in hell. An' dreamed o' the foggy, bitter nights back home. There, get that down yae and we'll toast to the old country."

Even though she had never partaken of alcohol, having watched Mrs. McCrombie knock back huge whiskies night after night on board the *Orient*, Kitty assured herself that one small glass wouldn't harm her.

"To the homeland," Lachlan toasted.

"To the homeland," Kitty replied. As the two men threw the golden liquid back in one, she took a small sip of her own and swallowed. It trickled down her throat, burning her tender insides. The assembled company were watching her with interest, and feeling the whiskey settle quite nicely in her stomach, she tipped the glass back and drained it. Then, as her new companions had done, she slammed it down on the bar.

"Aye, a true Scots lass." Lachlan gave her a mock bow, and the onlookers cheered and clapped appreciatively. "Another dram for us all!"

"Well, well," said Drummond, as he handed her a fresh glass, "most impressive, Miss McBride. We might make an Aussie of you yet."

"I am no coward, Mr. Mercer, you should know that now," Kitty said as she tipped the second whiskey down her throat, then sat down abruptly on her stool, feeling far better than she had a few minutes earlier.

"I can see that, Miss McBride." Drummond nodded sagely.

"Now, how about a chorus of 'Over the Sea to Skye' for the bonnie wee lass who's homesick for our land," cried Lachlan.

The entire bar burst into song, and really, Kitty thought, having spent her life as part of a quavery female church choir, there were some quite tuneful male voices. After that, she accepted another dram of whiskey and joined in with a rousing chorus of "Loch Lomond." She was led to a table, and sat down with Drummond and Lachlan.

"So, where did you live, missy?"

"Leith."

"Aye!" Lachlan banged the table and poured himself another whiskey from the bottle. "I was born in the south. The commoners' parts, o' course. But enough of the old country, let's see more of that famous Scottish bravery then!" He poured another dram into Kitty's glass and raised an eyebrow at her.

Without a word of retort, she lifted the glass to her mouth and drained it, her eyes fixed on Drummond's.

An hour later, having demonstrated various Scottish dances with Lachlan to cheers from the onlookers, Kitty was just about to drain another dram when Drummond covered it with his hand. "Enough now, Miss McBride. I think it's time we took you home."

"But . . . my friends . . ."

"I promise I will bring you back here another day, but we really must return home, or Mother may think I've abducted you."

"Aye, if I were a few years younger," Lachlan chimed in, "I'd be doing the same myself. Our Kitty is a beauty, she is. And don't yae worry, wee lassie. Ye'll do very well here in Australia."

As Kitty tried but failed to stand, Drummond hauled her upright. Lachlan planted affectionate kisses on both her cheeks. "Merry Christmas! And just remember, if ye're ever in any trouble, Lachlan's always at your service."

Kitty did not remember much of the walk to the horse and cart, although she most certainly remembered the feeling of Drummond's arm supporting her about her waist. After that, she must have fallen asleep, for the next thing she knew, she was in his arms being carried through the entrance to Alicia Hall and up the stairs, and lowered gently onto her bed.

"Thank you kindly," she murmured, then hiccuped. "You're a very kind man."

9

Kitty awoke groggily in darkness with what felt like a herd of elephants stampeding inside her head. She sat up and then winced, because the elephants were pounding her brain to mush with their enormous feet and the contents of her stomach were rising to her throat . . .

Kitty leaned over the side of the bed and vomited onto the floor. Groaning, she reached for the bottle of water that sat beside her bed and drank its contents swiftly, then sank down onto the pillows, trying to clear her addled mind. And when she had, wishing fervently she hadn't.

"Oh Lord, what have I done?" she whispered, horrified at the thought of Mrs. McCrombie's face—she may well have been partial to the odd dram herself, but would certainly not approve of her "companion" knocking back whiskey in bars and singing rousing choruses of old Scottish ballads . . .

It was all just too dreadful . . . Kitty closed her eyes and decided it was best to slip back into unconsciousness.

She was woken again by the sound of voices and the putrid smell of vomit that filled the room.

Was she on board the ship still? Had there been a storm?

She sat up, and was at least relieved that the herd of elephants seemed to have moved on from her head to pastures new. The room was pitch-black, and Kitty reached to turn on the gas lamp by her bed, immediately seeing the pool of vomit on the floor below her.

"Oh Lord," she whispered, as she stood up on jellylike legs. Her head throbbed as she forced it to be vertical, but she managed to wobble toward the washstand and retrieve some muslin cloths and the enamel washbasin to try to clean up the mess. She dumped the soiled cloths in the basin, wondering what on earth she should do with them. The door creaked open and she turned to see Drummond standing on the threshold.

"Good evening, Miss McBride. Or should I call you Kitty, the pride of Scotland and the Edinburgh Castle Hotel?"

"Please . . ."

"Only teasing, Miss McBride. We do a lot of that here in Australia, as you've no doubt discovered. How are you feeling?"

"I think you can see very well for yourself." She looked down at the bowl of her own sick that was resting on her knees.

"Then I will come no further, partly because of the smell in here—I suggest that when you make your way downstairs, you open the doors to your terrace—but mostly because it would be highly unseemly to be found in a lady's bedroom. I have told both my mother and my aunt that, due to my lack of care for you, you suffered a bout of sunstroke while out shopping in town and are therefore too unwell to join us for dinner."

Her eyes lowered in embarrassment. "Thank you."

"Don't thank me, Kitty. In truth I should apologize to you. I should never have encouraged you to drink that first whiskey, let alone the second and third, especially in the heat, when I knew you were unused to both."

"I had never drunk a drop before in my life," Kitty whispered. "And I am thoroughly ashamed of my behavior. If my parents could have seen me . . ."

"But they didn't, and no one shall ever hear of it from my lips. Take it from me, Kitty, when one is away from one's family, it is sometimes pleasant to be able to be oneself. Now, Agnes will be up shortly with some broth and also to remove that basin you are holding toward me like a Dickensian orphan."

"I shall never drink another drop for as long as I live."

"Well, even though today was the best entertainment I've had in a long time, I must hold myself responsible for your suffering now. Try to rest and get some broth down you. It is Christmas Eve tomorrow, and it would be a shame for you to miss that. Good night."

Drummond closed the door and Kitty put the stinking basin down onto the floor, horror and humiliation suffusing her.

What was it that Father always said about situations like this? Perhaps not *this* particular situation, Kitty acknowledged with a grimace, but he'd always taught her that having made a mistake, one should hold one's head up high and learn from it. So, she decided, tonight she would not lie up here and allow Drummond to believe she was a flimsy wallflower. Instead, she would join the assembled company downstairs for dinner.

That will show him, she thought as she took a deep breath and teetered over to her wardrobe. By the time Agnes the maid knocked on the door, she was dressed and combing her sweat-matted hair up into a neat knot on the top of her head.

"How are you feeling, Miss McBride?" Agnes asked her. The girl was even younger than Kitty herself and spoke with a strong Irish lilt.

"I am recovered now, thank you, Agnes. When you return downstairs, please tell Mrs. Mercer that I will be joining the table for dinner."

"Are you sure, miss? Pardon for sayin' so, but ye've still got that green color on ye and it wouldn't be doing at all to be ill at the table," Agnes said as she wrinkled her nose at the stinking basin and covered it with a clean muslin cloth.

"I am perfectly well, thank you. And I do apologize for that." Kitty indicated the basin.

"Oh, don't be bothering yourself, I've had much worse before they installed a privy here," Agnes said with a roll of her eyes.

Ten minutes later, Kitty was making her way gingerly down the staircase, hoping she wasn't making a terrible mistake, as even the fresh scent of pine made her feel nauseous. She saw Drummond standing below her, arms folded, admiring the Christmas tree.

"Good evening," she said as she reached the bottom of the stairs. "I decided I was well enough to join you for dinner after all."

"Really? And who might you be?"

"I . . . please don't tease," she begged him. "You know very well who I am."

"I assure you that we have never been formally introduced, although I have to presume that you are Miss Kitty McBride, my aunt's companion."

"You know I am, sir, so please stop playing games. If this is some new joke, a punishment for earlier . . . I—"

"Miss McBride, how wonderful to see you up and about after your terrible bout of sunstroke!"

Now Kitty knew how ill she must be, as another Drummond appeared from the drawing room, a glint of amusement and warning in his eyes.

"Pray, let me introduce my brother, Andrew," he continued. "As you may have just realized, we are twins, although Andrew was born two hours earlier than I."

"Oh," Kitty said, thanking the Lord that Drummond had arrived when he did, or she might have revealed all to Andrew. "Forgive me, sir, I did not realize."

"Please don't worry at all, Miss McBride. I can assure you, it's a very common mistake." Andrew walked toward her and held out his hand. "I am very pleased to finally make your acquaintance and delighted that you are well enough to join us this evening. Now, shall I escort you into the dining room? We must introduce you to our father."

Kitty took Andrew's proffered elbow gratefully, her legs still feeling unsteady beneath her. She caught Drummond giving her a sly wink but turned her head away and ignored it.

The dining table was bedecked with festive decorations: Elegant gold napkin holders and sprigs of fir tree with red baubles nestled inside them shimmered in the glow from the candles. Kitty watched in fascination as the Mercers said a prayer in German, before Andrew lit the fourth candle in the intricate wreath that sat in the center of the table.

As everyone sat down, Andrew caught Kitty's look of curiosity.

"They are Advent candles," he explained. "My parents were kind enough to wait for me to return home so I could light the last one before Christmas Eve—it was always my favorite thing to do as a child. It is an old German Lutheran tradition, Miss McBride," he added.

Over a dinner of beef, which she managed to swallow if she took very small bites and chewed each one thoroughly, Kitty studied the twins surreptitiously. Even though identical in looks, with their dark hair and blue eyes, their personalities were anything but. Andrew seemed much the more serious and thoughtful of the two, sitting next to her and asking her polite questions about her life back in Edinburgh.

"I must apologize on behalf of my brother. He should have known that the midday sun was far too strong for any young lady, especially one so newly arrived to these shores." Andrew frowned across the table at Drummond, who responded with a nonchalant shrug.

"You know me, brother dear. I'm totally irresponsible. Good job you now have Andrew around to protect you, Miss McBride," he added.

At the head of the table sat Stefan Mercer, the twins' father. He had the same blue eyes as his sons, but was rather on the portly side, with a large bald patch covered in freckles atop his head. He told her of how his family had arrived on Australia's shores seventy years ago.

"You may already know that many of our forefathers originally came to Adelaide because it allowed them to worship the Lord in any religion they chose. My grandmother was German and joined a small settlement named Hahndorf up in the Adelaide Hills. My grandfather was a Presbyterian from England, and they met here and fell in love. Australia is a freethinking country, Miss McBride, and I no longer subscribe to any particular man-made doctrine. As a family, we worship at the Anglican cathedral in the town. Tomorrow night we will go there for Midnight Mass. I do hope you will feel able to accompany us."

"It will be a pleasure," said Kitty, touched that Stefan was obviously concerned that it was not a Presbyterian church.

Struggling over pudding—a delicious trifle with real cream on the top of it—Kitty listened to the three men talk about the family's business interests, which seemed to have a lot to do with something called "shell," and how many tons of it the crews had brought back on something they called "luggers." Drummond talked of "mustering," which she surmised was somehow linked with "heads" of cattle. His best "drover" had not returned and Drummond announced without irony that he'd been "cut up into pieces by the blacks and put in a pot for supper."

Sitting here in this elegant, comfortable house, Kitty thought it extraordinary that such things could take place outside the boundaries of a town which, compared to the rough streets of Leith, was positively genteel.

"You must find the conversation quite shocking," said Drummond, mirroring her thoughts.

"I have read a book by Darw—" Kitty stopped herself, not knowing if Drummond would approve ". . . an author who spent time on these shores and who made mention of it. Do the natives really spear people?"

"Sadly, yes." Drummond lowered his voice. "In my opinion, only due to severe provocation from their unwanted invaders. The Aboriginal tribes have been on their land for many thousands of years—they are perhaps the oldest indigenous population in the world. Their land and their way of life was taken by force from right under their noses. But—" Drummond checked himself. "Such a subject is perhaps for another time."

"Of course," said Kitty, warming to Drummond a little. Then she turned her attention back to Andrew. "Where do you live?"

"Up on the northwest coast in a settlement called Broome. I have recently taken over the running of Father's pearling business. It is an . . . interesting part of the country, with a long history. There is even a dinosaur footprint stamped into a rock, which can be seen at very low tide."

"Goodness! How I would love to see that. Is Broome far away? Perhaps I could take a trip there by train."

"Sadly not, Miss McBride." Andrew suppressed a smile. "By sea it would take you several days at least and by camel, many more than that."

"Of course," said Kitty, embarrassed by her geographical naïveté. "Even though I know the dimensions of the country in theory, it's difficult to believe that traveling across it could actually take so long. I hope I may have a chance to advance beyond the town here, even if just to touch a rock that has been there since the dawn of time. I hear there are interesting carvings and paintings adorning many of them."

"Indeed there are, although knowledge of the interior—especially the area surrounding Ayers Rock—is my brother's province. It is close, in Australian terms at least, to where he runs our cattle station."

"One day I would love to visit the rock. I have read about it," Kitty enthused.

"I gather that you are interested in ancient history and geology, Miss McBride?"

"I am most interested in how we—" Kitty checked herself for a second time. ". . . God came to put us here in the first place, Mr. Mercer."

"Please, call me Andrew. And yes, it is all indeed fascinating. And perhaps, during their time here," Andrew said, raising his voice and directing his question to Mrs. McCrombie, "Aunt Florence and Miss McBride would enjoy a cruise up the northwest coast? After the wet season has ended in March, of course."

"Florence dear, don't even consider it," Edith interjected suddenly. "The last time I made the journey to Broome, there was a cyclone and the ship ran aground just beyond Albany. My eldest son lives in a completely uncivilized town full of blacks, yellows, and the Lord only knows what other nationalities—thieves and vagabonds the lot! I have sworn that I shall never set foot in the place again."

"Now, now, my dear." Stefan Mercer laid a hand on his wife's forearm. "We must not be unchristian, especially at this time of year. Broome is certainly unusual, Miss McBride, a melting pot of all creeds and colors.

I personally find it fascinating, and lived there for ten years when I was setting up my pearling business."

"It is a godforsaken morally corrupt town, dominated by the pursuit of wealth and full of greedy men wishing to pursue their lust for it!" Edith interrupted again.

"Yet is that not what Australia is all about, Mother?" Drummond drawled loudly. "And"—he indicated the enormous dining room and the contents of the table—"we too?"

"At least we behave in a civilized manner and have good Christian values," Edith countered. "Go there if you must, sister dear, but I shall not accompany you. Now, shall we ladies retire to the drawing room and leave the men to their smokes and talk of the unsavory side of life in Australia?"

"If you would forgive me," Kitty said a few seconds later as she stood with Edith and Florence in the entrance hall, "I am still not feeling quite myself, and I wish to be well for Christmas Eve tomorrow."

"Of course. Good night, Miss McBride," said Edith curtly, looking somewhat relieved.

"Sleep well, dear Kitty," called Mrs. McCrombie, following her sister across the hall to the drawing room.

Upstairs, Kitty walked out onto the terrace, looked up to the stars, and searched for the special Star of Bethlehem that she and her sisters had always watched for in the skies on Christmas Eve. She couldn't see it here in the night sky, perhaps because they were so far ahead of the British clock in Adelaide.

Walking back inside, she left the doors leading to the terrace ajar, as the bedroom still smelled of her earlier illness. Daringly, as the night was so very hot, Kitty ignored her nightgown and crept beneath the sheets in her chemise.

A glaring sun woke her the following morning. Sitting up and realizing that today was Christmas Eve, she was about to step out of bed when something enormous and brown dropped from the ceiling onto the bedsheet covering her thighs. The thing immediately started crawling at pace toward her stomach, and Kitty let out a piercing shriek as she realized it was a giant hairy spider. Rooted to the spot as it made its way toward her breasts, she screamed again, not caring who heard her.

"What the hell is it?!" said Drummond as he appeared in the room, looked at her, then immediately saw the problem. With a practiced swipe of his hand, the offending spider was lifted from her by one of its many legs, wriggling as Drummond walked outside with it onto the terrace. She watched as he tossed the creature over the balustrade, then returned inside, shutting the doors firmly behind him.

"That's what comes of leaving them open," he admonished her with a wag of his finger, which had so recently held a predator between it and his thumb.

"It was you who told me to open them!" Kitty retaliated, her voice coming out as a high-pitched squeak.

"I meant for a short while, not the entire night. Well, that's rich." He glared at her. "I'm roused from my slumber at the crack of dawn on Christmas Eve to aid a lady in distress, and rather than a thank-you, I get an earful for my troubles."

"Was it . . . poisonous?"

"The huntsman spider? No. They occasionally give you the odd nip, but mostly they're as friendly as you like. Just great, ugly things who do a good job of keeping the insect population under control. Those are nothing compared to what you come across in the Northern Territory, where I live. The outside 'dunny'—a privy, as you would know it—teems with them, and some of them *are* dangerous. I've had to suck the poison out of a couple of my drovers before now. Nasty creatures, those redbacks."

Kitty, her heart still pounding, but her senses returning to her at last, decided that Drummond took great pleasure in shocking her.

"It's a different life out there," he said, as if he were reading her thoughts. "A matter of survival. It toughens you up."

"I'm sure it does."

"Well, I'll leave you to get some further rest, given it's only five thirty in the morning." He nodded to her and walked toward the door. "And by the way, Miss McBride, may I ask if you always sleep in your chemise? Mother would be horrified." With a grin, Drummond left the bedroom.

Three hours later, over a breakfast of freshly baked bread and delicious strawberry jam, Mrs. McCrombie produced a large package and passed it to Kitty.

"For you, my dear," she said with a smile. "Your mother asked me to keep this until Christmas. I know how homesick you have been, and I hope this may ease your longing for Scotland."

"Oh . . ." Kitty held the heavy package in her hands. Tears pricked the corners of her eyes, but she blinked them back.

"Go on, open it, child! I have been traveling with it for weeks now, wondering what is in it!"

"Shouldn't I wait until tomorrow?" Kitty asked.

"The German tradition is to open our gifts on Christmas Eve," replied Edith. "Even though we save ours for eventide. Please, my dear, go ahead."

Kitty tore open the brown paper and pulled out various items, delight bubbling inside her. There was a tin of her mother's famous homemade shortbread, ribbons from her sisters along with drawings and cards. Her father had sent a leather-bound prayer book, which Kitty returned to the box without even reading the inscription inside.

She spent the rest of the morning offering her domestic services, showing the black kitchen maid how to roll pastry, then dole out the mincemeat that Mrs. McCrombie had brought with her into the small pastry shells. Goose was on the menu tonight apparently, and a turkey sat in the cool room for tomorrow's Christmas Day feast. In the burning heat of the afternoon, Kitty sent up messages of love to her family waking on the eve of Christmas, and thought of her sisters, who would be so excited for the events of the next two days. As her body was still exhausted from its alcoholic battering yesterday, she took an afternoon nap and woke to a knocking on the door.

"Come," she said drowsily, and watched as Agnes entered the room, bringing folds of turquoise silk hung carefully over her arms.

"'Tis from Mrs. McCrombie, miss. 'Tis a Christmas present and she said you're to wear it tonight for dinner."

Kitty watched Agnes hang the garment on the outside of her wardrobe. It was the most beautiful dress she had ever seen, but she worried that she would not be able to raise her arms in it for fear of patches of perspiration appearing beneath her armpits.

The family gathered in the drawing room at five, where Kitty was introduced to the famous Mercer matriarch, Grandmother Alicia herself. Alicia was not at all what Kitty had been expecting—rather than having the perpetual look of disapproval that defined Edith, Alicia's plump face was wrinkled into congenial folds, within which her blue eyes twinkled with mirth. It was sad, Kitty thought, that she was unable to conduct much of a conversation with her as Alicia spoke mainly German, despite having lived in Adelaide for many years. Andrew translated Alicia's apologies for her limited English, but the warm touch of her hands was enough to tell Kitty that she was welcome in what was originally Alicia's own home.

She marveled at how the twins switched so confidently between languages, as they conversed with the assembled company in both German and English. She was also touched that everyone had sweetly included her in the present giving. There was an ivory comb from Edith and Stefan, tiny seed-pearl earrings from Andrew, and from Drummond a handwritten note tied up in a package.

Dear Miss McBride,

This note is to tell you that your real Christmas present is stowed at the bottom of the wardrobe in your bedroom. I promise it is not a live spider.
Drummond

She watched his amused expression as she read it, then pulled out a sky-blue ribbon and smiled. "Thank you, Drummond. The color is quite beautiful, and I will use it to trim my hair for dinner later."

"It's to match your eyes," he whispered as any attention on their conversation was diverted by the presentation of Edith's Christmas gift from her husband.

"My dear, merry Christmas." Stefan kissed his wife on both cheeks. "I hope it is something you will like."

Inside the box was a truly glorious pearl, strung on a delicate silver chain. Its smooth opalescent surface gleamed richly in the last rays of the fast-sinking sun.

"Goodness," said Edith, as she let her sister fasten it around her neck. "More pearls."

"But this one is special, my dear. The best of this year's haul. Is it not, Andrew?"

"Yes, Father. T. B. Ellies himself declared it so, Mother. None larger has been found in the seas off Broome this year."

Kitty's eyes were transfixed by the gleaming, dancing bead sitting above Edith's considerable bosom. She marveled both at the size of such a precious jewel, and the indifference with which Edith had seemed to greet it.

"You like pearls?" Andrew, who was sitting next to her on a velvet-covered chaise longue, asked her.

"I love them," she replied. "I was forever opening clams on the beach back in Leith to find one, but, of course, I never did."

"No, and I doubt you ever would have done. They need a particular climate and breed of oyster, not to mention many, many years to come to fruition."

After the present opening, everyone retired to their rooms to change before dinner, and Kitty took the opportunity to see what exactly it was that Drummond had decided to give her for Christmas. Knowing him, a bottle of whiskey or a dead huntsman spider in a frame . . . The package was so tiny that it took her some time to root about in the bottom of her wardrobe to find it. It was an unremarkable box, tied with a simple ribbon. She opened it eagerly, and found a small gray stone nestled inside.

She picked it up and felt its coolness on her hot palm, feeling perplexed at why he had given this to her. Just like any pebble she could find on a beach in Leith, it was a plain slate gray, and even when she held it to the light she could not see any interesting striations in it.

But when she turned it over, she saw it was carved on the other side. Fascinated, she ran her fingers over the ridges and valleys, the edges of which had been rounded with age and much handling, but she was unable to make out a shape or a word.

Stowing it in the cabinet next to her bed, and feeling mean-hearted for her earlier harsh thoughts on Drummond's gift, she called Agnes in to help her into her new dress and fasten the tiny mother-of-pearl buttons that ran from the bottom of her back up to her neck. She already felt far too hot, and trussed up like the proverbial Christmas turkey, but her reflection in the mirror made up for it. The color of the silk complemented her eyes perfectly, making them shine turquoise. As Agnes fastened Drummond's ribbon into her curls, Kitty dabbed some rouge onto her cheeks, then stood up and went downstairs to join the party.

"Well, well, you look quite lovely tonight, Miss McBride," said Mrs. McCrombie with the proud air of a mother hen. "I knew that color would suit you the minute I saw it."

"Thank you very much, Mrs. McCrombie. It's the best Christmas present I've ever had," Kitty replied fervently as the doorbell rang to announce more Christmas Eve guests and they walked through to the drawing room to join those who had recently arrived.

"The best present, eh?" said a low voice from behind her. "Charmed, I'm sure."

It was Drummond, looking smart in full evening dress.

"I was simply being polite. Thank you for the ribbon . . . and the stone, but I have to confess, I have no idea what it is."

"That, my dear Miss McBride, is a very rare and precious thing. It's called a *tjurunga* stone, and it once belonged to a native of the Arrernte Aboriginal tribe. It would have been his most precious possession, presented to him at his initiation into manhood as a symbol of his special responsibilities."

"Goodness," breathed Kitty. Then her eyes narrowed. "You didn't steal it, did you?"

"What on earth do you take me for? As a matter of fact, I found it a few weeks ago when I was crossing the outback on my way here from the cattle station. I slept in a cave and there it was."

"I hope the person to whom it belongs hasn't missed it."

"I'm sure he is long dead, and won't complain. Now, Miss McBride"— Drummond reached out to a passing drinks tray and took two glasses from it—"may I offer you a little sherry?"

Kitty saw the twinkle in his eye and refused. "No, thank you."

"I must admit, you've scrubbed up rather well tonight," he said as he gulped down the dainty amount of sherry in one, then proceeded to drain the one she had refused too. "Merry Christmas, Kitty," he said softly. "So far, it's been an utter . . . adventure, to make your acquaintance."

"Miss McBride . . ."

Kitty turned and found Andrew at her side. And thought that it really was most disconcerting having a pair of identical twins in the same room; one felt as though one was seeing double.

"Good evening, Andrew, and thank you for my beautiful earrings. I'm wearing them tonight."

"I'm happy to see they go well with your lovely dress. May I offer you a small sherry to toast the Yuletide?"

"Miss McBride is teetotal. Never touches a drop, do you?" Drummond murmured next to her.

As he ambled off across the room, Kitty wondered how long it would be before she was moved to slap him just to remove the smug smile from his face. The guests soon assembled in the dining room, where a sumptuous feast awaited them: roast goose, traditional roast potatoes, and even a haggis that Mrs. McCrombie had stored in the ship's cold room on the voyage over. From their fine clothes and the women's jewels, Kitty knew she was sharing a Christmas feast with the crème de la crème of Adelaide society. A pleasant German gentleman who spoke perfect English sat to her right, and told her of his brewing business and his vineyards, which apparently flourished in the Adelaide Hills.

"The climate is similar to that of southern France, and the grapes grow well. Mark my words, in a few years' time, the world will be buying Australian wine. This"—he reached for a bottle and showed it to her—"is one of ours. Can I entice you to try a drop?"

"No thank you, sir," she said in a hushed voice, not able to stand another knowing look from Drummond, sitting across the table from her.

Once the dinner was over, a crowd gathered around the piano and sang "Stille Nacht" in German, followed by traditional British Christmas carols. When the repertoire was exhausted, Edith, who had already displayed a surprising talent on the piano, turned to her eldest son.

"Andrew, will you sing for us?"

The assembled company clapped him politely to the piano.

"Forgive me, ladies and gentlemen, for I am rusty. As you can imagine, I do not get much of an opportunity to perform in Broome," said Andrew. "I shall sing 'Ev'ry Valley' from Handel's *Messiah*."

"And I shall do my best to accompany him," said Edith.

"My goodness, what a voice," whispered her wine-making neighbor after Andrew had finished and the drawing room rang with applause. "Perhaps he could have been a professional opera singer, but life—and his father—had other plans. That's Australia for you," he added under his breath. "High on sheep, cattle, and ill-begotten riches, but low on culture. Our country will change one day, you mark my words."

By then, it was almost eleven in the evening, and the guests were escorted into carriages by their grooms to trot off into the center of Adelaide for Midnight Mass.

St. Peter's Cathedral was an imposing sight, with its intricate Gothic spirals reaching up into the sky, and warm candlelight spilling out through its stained-glass windows. Drummond escorted his mother and aunt into the cathedral, while Andrew helped Kitty down from her carriage.

"You have a beautiful voice," she said to him.

"Thank you. Everyone tells me that, but perhaps you never value what comes easily to you. And also, apart from entertaining Mama and Papa's guests on high days and holidays, it serves no purpose," Andrew commented as they followed the crowd up the steps to the cathedral.

The inside of the church was just as impressive, with tall, vaulted arches framing the pews. The service, which was what Kitty's father would have called "high church," was full of wafted incense and clergy with the kind of gold-threaded robes which Ralph would have derided. Kitty went up for Holy Communion, kneeling at the altar between Drummond and Andrew. At least, she thought, her toes weren't curling from the biting cold, as they usually did in Father's church in Leith on Christmas Eve.

"Did you enjoy that? I know it's not what you're used to," asked Andrew as they filed out.

"I am of the belief that the Lord almost certainly doesn't mind where you worship, or how, as long as you are glorifying His name," Kitty answered tactfully.

"If there is a God at all. Which, personally, I doubt," came Drummond's voice out of the darkness behind her.

As she retired to her room later, having checked the terrace doors were tightly shut and then scrutinizing the ceiling and the corners for any sign of eight-legged hairy monsters that might decide to join her in bed, Kitty decided that it had been a very interesting day.

10

Between Christmas and Hogmanay—or, as people called it here, New Year's Eve—there were outings to keep the residents of Alicia Hall entertained. They took a picnic to Elder Park and listened to an orchestra playing on the bandstand, then the following day found them at Adelaide Zoo. While Kitty delighted at the various furry inmates, such as the wide-eyed possums and the adorable koalas, Drummond found more pleasure in pulling her toward the reptile house and showing her an array of snakes. He was at pains to point out which ones were benign and those that could kill.

"The pythons are mainly harmless, although they do give you a hell of a nip if you tread on them by accident. It's those Australian browns which are difficult to see on the earth that are the most venomous. And"— he pointed at the glass—"that stripy one coiled around the twig in the corner. That's a tiger snake and equally nasty if you get bitten. Snakes will only bother you if you bother them, mind you," he added.

Drummond suggested Kitty take a ride on an elephant, the crowning glory of Adelaide Zoo. Kitty was hoisted up inelegantly onto the aging gray back of her steed. She sat atop, feeling just like the Indian maharani she had seen pictures of in a book.

"You should wait until you try a camel—now, that is a bumpy ride," Drummond shouted up at her.

That night, she arrived home and immediately wrote to her family to tell them that she'd ridden on an elephant—in the most unlikely of places.

Hogmanay arrived and Kitty was told that a big evening party was always hosted by Edith.

"She puts us through this every year," Drummond groaned at breakfast that morning. "She insists we wear our tartan."

"That's normal in Edinburgh all year round," Kitty retorted.

"And that is the point, Miss McBride. I am a born and bred Australian who has never set foot in Scotland, and actually, more to the point, never intends to. If the boys back at Kilgarra station ever knew that I hopped around in a skirt for the night looking like a girl, I'd never hear the last of it."

"Surely it's not much to ask to please Mother?" Andrew put into the conversation. "Remember, she was born there and misses the old country. And I'm sure Miss McBride will enjoy it too."

"I didn't think to bring my clan tartan . . ." Kitty bit her lip.

"I'm sure Mother can lend you one of hers. She has a wardrobe positively bursting with plaid. Excuse me." Drummond stood up. "I have some things to do in town before I leave for Europe."

"Your brother's going to Europe?" Kitty asked Andrew after Drummond had left the room.

"Yes. Tomorrow, with Father," he replied. "Drummond wants to purchase some heads of cattle—his stock dwindled this year due to a drought and the blacks' spears, and Father has some magnificent pearls to sell from his haul this year and trusts no one to do it for him. Besides, it's the wet season up in the north, and not a comfortable place to be. Our luggers in Broome are mostly in harbor due to the cyclone season. I will return soon to man the ship, so to speak. I've spent the past three years up there learning the ropes from Father and will take over managing it for him from now on, before Mother divorces him for desertion." Andrew gave Kitty a rueful smile.

"I remember her saying that she did not enjoy her time in Broome."

"When my mother lived there ten years ago, it was hard for a woman, but as the pearling industry grows, so does the town. And with such a mixed society, it is certainly never dull. An acquired taste, but speaking for myself, I find it exciting. I think you would too, because you have an adventurous spirit."

"Do I?"

"In my opinion, yes. And you seem to take people at face value."

"My father—and the Bible," she added hastily, "say never to judge by creed or color, but only by a person's soul."

"Yes, Miss McBride. It's rather interesting, isn't it, that those who would consider themselves true Christians can behave like the opposite? Ah well . . . ," he said, then lapsed into an embarrassed silence.

"Now"—Kitty rose to her feet—"I must seek out your mother and offer my help with the preparations for tonight's party."

"That is kind of you, but I doubt she will need it. Like everything she manages, it will be run like a well-oiled machine."

As Kitty put on her turquoise dress that evening, which Agnes had skillfully steamed to remove any sweat patches, there was a rap on her door. Mrs. McCrombie came in bearing a length of plaid.

"Good evening, my dear Miss McBride. Here is your sash for this evening's festivities. Courtesy of myself, and my poor departed husband. I shall be proud to see you wearing the McCrombie tartan. In these past few weeks, you have become nothing less than a daughter to me."

"I . . . thank you, Mrs. McCrombie." Kitty was deeply touched by her words. "You have been so very kind to me."

"May I have the honor of fastening it on for you?"

"Of course. Thank you."

"You know," said Mrs. McCrombie as she draped the tartan across Kitty's right shoulder, "it has been a pleasure to watch you blossom in the weeks since we left Edinburgh. You were rather a mouse when I first met you. But now look at you!" Mrs. McCrombie fastened a delicate thistle brooch at Kitty's shoulder. "Why, you are a beauty and a credit to your family. You will make any man a wife to be proud of."

"Will I . . . ?" Kitty replied as she allowed herself to be propelled toward the mirror.

"Look at yourself, Miss Katherine McBride, with your proud Scottish heritage, your clever brain, and your pretty physique. Oh, it has amused me so watching my two nephews vie for your attentions in their different ways." Mrs. McCrombie giggled girlishly and Kitty knew she'd already been at the whiskey.

"So," she continued, "I have asked myself, which one will she choose? They are both so different. My dear, have you decided which twin it will be?"

Given that Kitty had never even presumed to think that either of the wealthy twins considered her anything other than sport (Drummond) or a younger sister (Andrew), Kitty answered honestly.

"Really, Mrs. McCrombie, I am sure that you are wrong. The Mercers are quite clearly one of the most powerful families in Adelaide . . ."

"If not Australia," Mrs. McCrombie added.

"Yes, and I, as the poor daughter of a minister from Leith, could never consider myself good enough for either of them. Or their family—"

The sound of the doorbell clanging came to her rescue.

"Well now, my dear." Mrs. McCrombie took her in a warm, bosomy embrace. "Let us just see what happens, shall we? And in case I don't get the chance to wish you a happy 1907 later tonight, I shall do so now. I just *know* it will be a happy one."

Kitty watched as Mrs. McCrombie swept from the room, a veritable ship in full sail. Once the door was closed, she collapsed onto her bed in relief and confusion.

If there was one thing Kitty knew she was good at, it was dancing reels. She and her siblings had been taught by their mother, partly because Adele loved to dance, but mainly because there wasn't much else with which to while away a long winter's evening in Leith. *And* it had the benefit of keeping them all warm.

And goodness, thought Kitty, as she danced "The Duke of Perth," it was certainly doing that tonight. She envied the men, who at least had the luxury of bare legs in their kilts, while she in her corseted silk dress and heavy tartan sash sweated away like the proverbial pig. Yet tonight, she didn't care, dancing reel after reel with numerous partners until finally, shortly before midnight, she sat down to rest and Andrew brought her a large glass of fruit punch to quench her thirst.

"My, my, Miss McBride, we have seen yet another facet of your personality tonight. You are a most accomplished dancer."

"Thank you," she said, still panting and praying Andrew did not step too close to her, because she was sure she smelled awful.

Minutes later, he led her into the entrance hall with the rest of the guests, so that the old Scottish tradition of welcoming the first person across the threshold at the stroke of midnight could be observed. Gathering around the Christmas tree, which looked forlorn with its shed pine needles pooling into green puddles on the floor, Kitty stood next to Andrew.

"Ten seconds to go!" roared Stefan from the crowd, and they began to count down the numbers until the crowd cheered and wished one another affectionate New Year's greetings.

Kitty suddenly found herself in Andrew's embrace.

"Happy New Year, Miss McBride. I wanted to ask . . ."

Kitty saw the anxiety on his face. "Yes?"

"Would it be all right if I called you Kitty from now on?"

"Why yes, of course."

"Well, I do hope that in 1907 we can continue our . . . friendship. I . . . that is, Kitty . . ."

"Happy New Year, my boy!" Stefan interrupted their conversation as he slapped his son on the back. "I have no doubt at all that you will do me proud in Broome."

"I will do my best to, sir," Andrew replied.

"And happy New Year to you too, Miss McBride. You have been a delightful adornment to our family Christmas." He leaned forward and kissed Kitty warmly, his handlebar mustache tickling her cheek. "And I'm sure we both hope that you may decide to extend your time with us in Australia, eh, boy?" Stefan gave his son an obvious wink before moving on to offer his other guests New Year felicitations.

Andrew swiftly excused himself to go in search of his mother and Kitty wandered onto the veranda in search of some cool air.

Instantly, she was swept up from behind by a strong pair of arms and twirled around in circles, then finally lowered back to the ground.

"Happy New Year, Miss McBride, Kitty . . . *Kat* . . . yes, that nickname suits you perfectly, for you are feline, light on your feet, and far cleverer, I suspect, than most people give you credit for. In short, you are a survivor."

"Am I?" Kitty's head was spinning and she steadied herself. She looked up at Drummond. "Are you drunk?"

"Hah! That's rich coming from you, Miss Kitty-Kat. Perhaps a little, but people tell me I'm an affectionate drunk. Now, I have something to say to you."

"And what might that be?"

"You must know as well as I do that plans are afoot to make sure you join our family on a more permanent basis."

"I . . ."

"Don't pretend you have no idea what I mean. It is quite obvious to everybody that Andrew is in love with you. I have even heard my parents discussing it. Father is all for it; Mother—for whatever churlish female reason—less so. But given that my father's word goes in this house, I'm sure it won't be too long before a proposal is forthcoming."

"I can assure you that no such thought has crossed my mind."

"Then you are either full of false modesty, or more stupid than I took you for. Naturally, as the eldest, he gets the first shot at you, but before you decide, I wanted to throw my hat into the ring and tell you that, for a woman, you have a number of qualities which I admire. And . . ."

For the first time since Kitty had known him, she saw uncertainty in Drummond's eyes.

"The thing is this." Then he took her in his arms and kissed her hard upon the lips. Whether from shock or sheer pleasure, Kitty did not immediately pull away, and her entire body proceeded to melt like a knob of butter left out in the Australian sun.

"There now," he said as he finally let her go. Then he leaned down to whisper in her ear. "Remember this: My brother can offer you security, but with me, you'll have adventure. Just swear to me that you won't make a decision until I'm back from Europe. Now, I'm off to the Edinburgh Castle to celebrate until dawn with my friends. Good night, Miss McBride."

With a wave, Drummond left her on the veranda and headed to the back of the house. As she heard the pony and cart trotting out of the gate, Kitty moved her fingers tentatively to her lips. And relived every second of the pleasure she had felt at his touch.

Kitty did not see Drummond the next morning—he'd gone early to the steamer to supervise the loading of the trunks. Kitty handed over the letters that Stefan Mercer had kindly said he would post to her family when he reached Europe.

"Or in fact," he said with a wink, "I may even go and deliver them personally. Good-bye, my dear." He kissed her on both cheeks. Then, with the household waving him off, he climbed into the carriage.

Kitty ate breakfast alone with Andrew, as Mrs. McCrombie was taking hers in her room and Edith had gone to the dock to wave her husband and son good-bye. Given the various conversations that had taken place yesterday, she felt uncomfortable sitting there with him. He seemed unusually subdued.

"Miss McBride . . . ," he said eventually.

"Please, Andrew, we agreed you must call me Kitty."

"Of course, of course. Kitty, do you ride?"

"I do indeed, or rather, I *did*. I learned as a child when we went down to stay with my grandparents in Dumfriesshire. Some of the ponies were rather wild, coming from the moors, and I spent quite a lot of my time being thrown off. Why do you ask?"

"I was just thinking how there's nothing like a gallop to clear out the cobwebs. We keep a bungalow up in the Adelaide Hills with a small stable attached to it. How say you we go up there today? The air is clearer and cooler, and I think you would like it. Mama has given her full permission for me to chaperone you, by the way."

They arrived up at the Mercer family bungalow two hours later. Having expected little more than a cottage, Kitty was amazed to see the low-lying house was nothing less than a one-story mansion, set in lush gardens and surrounded by vineyards. She made a three-hundred-and-sixty-degree turn, seeing the way the green hills dipped and rose around them. It reminded her a little of the Scottish Lowlands.

"It's beautiful," she breathed, meaning it.

"I'm glad you like it. Now, let me show you the stables."

Half an hour later, the two of them set out for a ride. As they trotted down the valley and onto a plain, Kitty chanced a canter. Taking the lead from her, Andrew kept pace, and Kitty laughed out loud in delight at the fresh air on her skin and the verdant green all about her.

When they returned to the bungalow, she saw a light lunch had been laid out on a table on the veranda.

"This looks delicious," Kitty said, still panting from exertion as she flopped into a chair, and without further ado took a slice of bread, still warm from the oven.

"There's fresh lemon cordial for you too," Andrew offered.

"Who made all this?"

"The housekeeper here. She lives in all year round."

"Even though you told me on the way here you rarely visit?"

"Yes. Father is very rich, and I intend to be too."

"I am sure you will be," Kitty said after a pause.

"Of course," Andrew continued hastily, realizing he had made an error, "it is not my main goal, but especially here in Australia, money can help."

"It can help anywhere, but I truly believe it cannot buy happiness."

"I couldn't agree more, Kitty. Family and . . . love, is all."

They ate the rest of their lunch in virtual silence, Kitty simply concentrating on enjoying her surroundings. And trying not to think of the probable reason for this outing.

"Kitty . . ." Andrew eventually broke the silence. "Perhaps you know why I've brought you up here?"

"To show me the view?" she answered, sounding disingenuous even to her own ears.

"That, and . . . it cannot come as a complete surprise to you to know how . . . fond I've become of you in the last ten days."

"Oh, I am sure you would tire of me if you knew me for longer, Andrew."

"I doubt it, Kitty. As usual, you are just being modest. I have spoken to my aunt at length, a woman who has known of you for most of your life, and she could not find a bad word to say about you. In her eyes, as well as mine, you seem to be perfect. And, having already told my father and mother of my intentions, and them both agreeing . . ."

At this, Andrew stood up abruptly and came to kneel in front of her. "Katherine McBride, I would like to ask you to do me the honor of becoming my wife."

"Goodness!" Kitty said after a suitable pause, which she hoped denoted ignorance of such a proposal. "I am shocked. I never thought . . ."

"That is because you are who you are, Kitty. A girl . . . woman, in fact, who does not recognize her own beauty, either inside or out. You *are* beautiful, Kitty, and I knew the first moment I saw you that I wished for you to be my wife."

"Did you?"

"Yes. I would not say that I am of a romantic nature, but . . ." Andrew blushed. "It was truly a case of love at first sight. And then"—he chuckled to himself—"I knew that it had to be right when you showed such enthusiasm for the dinosaur footprint in Broome. Most girls wouldn't even know what a dinosaur was, let alone be interested in its fossilized footprint. So, what do you say?"

Kitty looked down at Andrew, at his undoubtedly handsome face, then raised her head and surveyed the beautiful estate that this man would presumably inherit. Her thoughts traveled back to Leith and her father, who had professed to adore her, but then, because of what she knew, had banished her to the other side of the world.

"I . . ."

Her demon mind issued a vivid picture of Drummond, and

subsequently began to play a selection of memories across a frame in her head. The way he teased her, treated her less like a china doll than an equal, how he made her laugh despite herself . . . and, most of all, how she'd felt when he'd kissed her only a few hours ago.

The question was, did he bring out the best or the worst in her? Whichever it was, she was certainly a different person when she was with him.

"Please, I understand that this is a shock, coming so soon after we've met," Andrew persisted into her silence. "But I must return to Broome in February or March, and as Mama pointed out, that leaves little time to prepare for any wedding. That is, not that I want to rush you into a decision, but . . ."

Andrew's voice trailed off and she thought what a sweet soul he was.

"May I take a little time to think about it? I had planned to go home to Scotland and my family. And this would mean . . . well, staying here. For the rest of my life. With you."

"Dearest Kitty, I understand completely. You must take all the time you need. Aunt Florence has told me what a close family you come from and I know the sacrifice you would be making if you were to marry me. And of course, at least for the next few years, you would be living in Broome."

"A place that your mother loathes."

"And one that I believe you would grow to love. It has changed much since she last deigned to visit. Broome is thriving, Kitty; the ships that arrive daily from all over the world bring luxuries and precious things that you would not believe. But yes," Andrew agreed, "it is still an unformed society, where many rules of normal social behavior don't exist. Yet I feel that you would embrace it as strongly as my mother derided it, simply because of your egalitarian and generous nature. Now, I must stand up before my kneecap breaks in two." Andrew stood, then grasped Kitty's hands in his. "How much time do you need?"

"A few days?"

"Of course. From now on," he said, kissing one of her hands softly, "I shall leave you be."

During the ensuing three days, Kitty discussed the situation with herself, a magnificent parakeet in the garden, and, of course, God. None of whom were able to give her any further insight on the subject. She longed for her mother's wisdom, which would be given purely out of love and her daughter's best interests.

Although would it? Kitty pondered, as she paced up and down her bedroom, realizing there was every chance that Adele would urge her daughter to jump at the opportunity to marry such a handsome man from a fine, wealthy family, given the frugal life they lived in Leith.

The bald truth was that even though Kitty had known marriage was the next stage of her life once she turned eighteen, it had always seemed far away in the future. Yet now, here it was. The question she asked herself over and over was whether one must *love* one's future husband from the first moment one set eyes on him. Or whether initially, the excitement of an engagement came from a far more pragmatic angle: that of knowing one had been plucked from the tree of single young ladies—especially being as poor as she was—and that one was secure for the rest of one's life. Maybe love would grow through the sharing of an existence together, which would one day include a family.

Kitty was also sure that if the Mercers had seen the straitened circumstances in which her own family lived and realized she was less than a "catch," they may have viewed the union very differently. Yet this was not Edinburgh but Australia, where she and everyone else who reached its dusty red soil could reinvent themselves and be anyone they chose.

What *was* in Scotland in the future for her anyway? If she was lucky, marriage to Angus and a life as a clergyman's wife that would be little different from her first eighteen years, except perhaps harder.

Despite Drummond's words about having "adventure" with him, Kitty realized that marrying *either* twin and following them up to the north of this vast landmass would provide that.

Yet . . . the way that her body had dissolved when Drummond kissed her. When Andrew had taken her hand and kissed it, it hadn't been unpleasant, but . . .

Finally, completely exhausted from equivocating with herself, Kitty decided to go to Mrs. McCrombie. Biased though she may have been, she was the nearest thing Kitty had to family here.

She chose a moment when Edith had gone out to pay some house calls. They took tea together and Mrs. McCrombie listened while Kitty poured out her mind's machinations.

"Well, well." Mrs. McCrombie raised an eyebrow, to Kitty's surprise showing neither pleasure nor distaste. "You already know that I expected this to happen, but, my dear, I do feel for you. Neither of us can be as naive as to believe that your decision won't have an irrevocable effect on the rest of your life."

"Yes."

"How much have you missed Edinburgh since you've been here?"

"I've missed my family."

"But not the place itself?"

"When the sun burns down, I long for the chill, but I like what I have seen of Australia so far. It's a land of possibility where anything might happen."

"For better or worse," Mrs. McCrombie interjected. "Young lady, from my perspective, I will repeat what I said on New Year's Eve. I can only say that you have blossomed since you have been here. I do believe Australia suits you and you suit it."

"I have definitely felt more free here, yes," Kitty ventured.

"However, if you marry Andrew, you must resign yourself to not seeing your family again for perhaps many years. Although, my dear, no doubt you will start a family of your own. It is a natural progression, whether it be in Edinburgh or Australia. One way or another, once a woman marries, her life changes. And Andrew himself? Do you like him?"

"Very much indeed. He is thoughtful, kind, and clever. And from what he has told me, hardworking too."

"He is that indeed," Mrs. McCrombie acknowledged. "However it may look to an outsider, being the son of an extraordinarily rich father has its drawbacks. He must prove to both Stefan and himself that he can be just as successful. Unlike Drummond, who by accident of birth does not carry that same sense of responsibility. The heir and the spare to the Mercer throne," Mrs. McCrombie chuckled. "May I ask you, Kitty, did Drummond . . . speak to you before he left for Europe?"

"Yes." Kitty decided it was no time to spare her blushes. "He asked me to wait for him."

"I thought as much. He could hardly take his eyes off you from the first moment he met you. All that silly teasing . . . a juvenile way of seeking your attention. And what did you say to him?"

"I said . . . nothing. He left then and I didn't see him again before he got on the boat to Europe."

"How very dramatic. Well, I don't wish to patronize you by pointing out the advantages of each of my nephews, but, Kitty my dear, what I can tell you is that when a young lady decides to commit herself to marriage, what she needs from her intended is very different from what she may dream of as a young girl. By that I mean security, safety—especially in a country such as this; a steady, reliable type, whom one can depend upon for protection. Someone you respect, and yes, before you ask, love does grow. And I have no doubt that Andrew loves *you* already."

"Thank you, Mrs. McCrombie, for your very wise counsel. I shall think on what you have said. And I must do so quickly, as I know we have so little time."

"It's my pleasure, Kitty. As I'm sure you are aware, I would like nothing better than to become officially related to you, but the decision is yours to make. Just remember, Andrew is not only offering you his love, but an entire new life, which you alone can make of what you will."

Later that day, when she saw Andrew arrive home on the pony and trap, she walked swiftly downstairs to meet him at the door and tell him of her decision before she changed her mind.

"Andrew, may I speak with you?"

He turned toward her, and she knew he was studying her face to see if he could discover the answer in her eyes.

"Of course. Let us go through to the drawing room."

Kitty noted the tension in his body as they entered the room and sat down.

"Andrew, forgive me for taking some time to think about your proposal. As you know, it is a momentous decision for me. However, I *have* decided, and I would be honored to become your wife, on the understanding that my father agrees to the match." Kitty fell silent, breathless from saying the words, and looked at Andrew. He did not look as happy as she had thought he might.

"Andrew, have you changed your mind?"

"I . . . no. That is . . . are you absolutely sure?"

"I am absolutely sure."

"And no one has pressured you into this?"

"No!" Now that she had given him the answer, he seemed to be grilling her on the reasons for her assent to his request.

"I . . . well, I believed that you were steeling yourself to refuse me. That perhaps there was someone else. I . . ."

"I swear, there is no one."

"Right, well, so . . ."

Kitty watched as the clouds visibly lifted from Andrew's eyes.

"Good grief! That makes me the happiest man in the world! I must write immediately to your father to request his permission, but . . . would you take exception to me doing so by telegram? As you know, letters take so long to arrive and time is of the essence. And of course, I shall send one to Father too, asking him to make haste to your parents' front door while he is Europe." The words were tumbling out of Andrew as he paced exultantly up and down the drawing room. "I hope that your father will be prepared to entrust his beloved daughter to me. He knows of our family through my aunt, of course." Andrew paused in his pacing to take her hands in his. "I swear to you now, Katherine McBride, that I will love you and give you the best of everything for the rest of your life."

Kitty nodded and closed her eyes as he kissed her lightly on the lips.

Two days later, Andrew showed Kitty the telegram that had just arrived.

ANDREW STOP DELIGHTED TO GIVE MY BLESSING ON YOUR MARRIAGE TO MY DAUGHTER STOP MUCH LOVE TO YOU AND KATHERINE STOP MOTHER AND FAMILY SEND CONGRATULATIONS TO BOTH OF YOU STOP RALPH STOP

"The final hurdle!" Andrew exclaimed jubilantly. "Now we can announce it to the world and set about preparations for the wedding. It may not be as grand an affair as you might wish for, given the time constraints, but Mother knows everyone there is to know in Adelaide and she can pull strings to make sure you have a beautiful gown at least."

"Really, Andrew, such things are not important to me."

"That might be so, but this wedding is important to Mother. So, we shall tell her and Aunt Florence this very evening."

Kitty nodded, then turned away from him and walked upstairs, knowing her eyes were brimming with tears. When she arrived in her room, she threw herself on the bed and sobbed, because everything she had believed about her father's wishing to get rid of her for good had just been proved right.

On the morning of her wedding to Andrew a month later, Kitty stood in front of the long mirror in her wedding dress. Edith had indeed pulled strings, and she was wearing a white gown fit for a princess. Her waist had been cinched into a whisper of itself, and the high neck set off her auburn hair, which Agnes had piled fetchingly on top of her head. The rich Alençon lace was bedecked in hundreds of small pearls that gleamed and sparkled with the slightest move.

"Ye look beautiful, Miss Kitty. I'm wanting to cry . . . ," said Agnes as she straightened the tulle veil over Kitty's shoulders.

"Good morning, Kitty."

Kitty saw the reflection of Edith walking into the room behind her.

"Good morning."

"Doesn't she look a picture, m'um?" said Agnes, wiping her nose.

"She does indeed," Edith replied stiffly, as if it hurt her to say the words. "May I have a word with Katherine alone?"

"O' course, m'um."

Agnes scuttled out of the room.

"I came to wish you good luck, Katherine," said Edith, walking around her daughter-in-law-to-be, checking the dress was perfect.

"Thank you."

"I once knew your father when I was much younger. I met him at a ball in the Highlands. I believed that he was as smitten with me as I was with him. But then, your father always was a charmer, as I'm sure you're aware."

Kitty's heart began to beat faster. She did not reply, knowing Edith had more to say.

"Of course, I was wrong. It transpired that he was not only a charmer, but a chancer. A cad who enjoyed seducing women, and once he had done with them, he would move on to the next. To put it bluntly, I was left high and dry by him. I will not go into detail, but along with breaking my heart, he almost ruined my reputation. I . . . well, suffice to say that if it hadn't been for Stefan arriving from Australia and us meeting by chance in London—and him having no knowledge of any . . . 'notoriety' I had acquired—my future prospects would have been ruined."

Deep breaths, Kitty ordered herself as she felt the heat of both embarrassment and shock prickling on the skin beneath her dress.

"I can assure you, what I am telling you is true. I hope you can understand why I was less than pleased when my sister wrote to me telling me you were accompanying her and that I had to welcome you into my home. For of course, the truth of the matter was brushed under the carpet and my sister had no idea of what her sainted Ralph had done to me. And now . . ." Edith came to stand in front of her. "You—his daughter—are to marry my eldest son, and we are to be related. The irony is not lost on me, as I'm sure it isn't on your father."

Kitty looked down at the yards of white lace pooling about her elegantly slippered feet. "Why are you telling me this?" she whispered.

"Because you are joining our family and I want no further secrets between us. And also to warn you that if you ever hurt my son the way your father hurt me, I will hunt you down and destroy you. Do you understand?"

"I do."

"Well, that is all I have to say. I can only hope that you have your mother's nature. My sister tells me she is such a sweet woman and very stoic. In retrospect, I have realized I had a lucky escape, for I am sure that your mother has suffered during her marriage to that man, just as I did. *Him!* A minister?!" Edith chuckled hoarsely, but then, seeing Kitty's obvious distress, regained her composure. "Now then, Kitty, we will never mention the subject again." Edith moved closer and kissed her tentatively on both cheeks. "You look beautiful, my dear. Welcome to the Mercer family."

CeCe

Phra Nang Beach, Krabi, Thailand

January 2008

Aboriginal symbol for a honey ant site

11

Ace stretched his arms wide and yawned, dropping the book onto the sofa. I sat up, mulling over the story I had just heard.

"Wow," I murmured. "Kitty Mercer sounds amazing! Moving to the other side of the world, marrying a man she hardly knew, and inheriting what sounds like a mother-in-law from hell."

"I suppose that's what a lot of women did in those days, especially those who had a life they didn't want to go back to." Ace looked off into the distance. "Like Kitty's," he added eventually.

"Yeah, her father sounds like a real jerk. Do you think she made the right choice, marrying Andrew over Drummond?"

Ace studied Kitty's picture on the front cover. "Who knows? We make so many choices every single day . . ."

His face closed off then, so I didn't push him on what decisions *he'd* made that had led to his hiding out here in the palace. "The question is," I said, "what's she got to do with me? I don't think we're related—we look nothing alike." To illustrate the point, I held up the book to my head and tried to put on the same stern expression as her. Ace gave a chuckle, then brushed a finger over my cheek.

"You don't have to look alike to be related. Take me—my father is European, and I'd bet you're mixed race too. Haven't you ever wondered?"

"Course I have. To be honest, I always just accepted it—people would try to guess where I was from if I told them I was adopted. They'd say all sorts—South Asian, South American, African . . . It's like everyone wants to put you in a box and stick a label on you, but I just wanted to be me."

Ace nodded. "Yeah, I get that too. Here in Thailand they call us *luk kreung*—literally 'half child.' But even though I know where my blood comes from, it doesn't mean I understand who I am or where I belong. I feel out of place wherever I am. I wonder if you'll feel like you belong in Australia."

"I . . . I don't know." I was beginning to feel flushed and hot, all the questions he was asking me making my head spin. I stood up. "I'm going for a last swim and sunset," I said as I walked across the terrace to the stairs. "I want to take some photos."

"What do you mean, a 'last' swim?"

"I'm leaving tomorrow. I'm going to get my bikini."

Arriving at the gate a few minutes later with my camera, I found Ace already hovering beside it in his swimming trunks, shades, and baseball cap.

"I'll come with you," he said.

"Okay." I tried not to show my surprise when he pressed the red button, and I handed my camera to Po as Ace legged it at top speed toward the sea with me trailing behind him. We swam out a long way, much farther than anyone else, and he held me in his arms and kissed me.

"Why didn't you tell me you were leaving before?"

"To be honest, I'd lost track of the days. It was only when I looked at the plane ticket in my rucksack this morning that I realized."

"It'll be strange without you, CeCe."

"I'm sure you'll manage. C'mon," I said as we waded out, "I need to get my camera and take some pics of the sunset before it's gone."

I collected my camera from Po and went back onto the beach to capture the sunset, as Ace lurked in the foliage watching me.

"You want photo? I take it," Po offered.

"Would you mind being in it?" I asked Ace. "With the sunset and stuff behind us? Just for the memory?"

"I . . ." There was a flicker of fear in his eyes before he reluctantly agreed.

I instructed Po on which button to press, and with our backs facing the beach, Ace put his arm around me and we posed in front of the setting sun on Phra Nang. Po snapped away eagerly until Ace put up a hand to stop him before pressing the code on the gate and disappearing through it. I followed in his wake, stopping to collect my camera.

"Madam, I take to shop and print for you? My cousin, he run good place in Krabi town. I go there now, pictures back tomorrow morning," Po offered.

"Okay, thanks," I agreed as I ejected the roll of film from the unit. "Make two sets of prints, yes?" I gesticulated with my fingers, thinking it would be a good memento to leave for Ace.

"No problem, madam." Po smiled at me. "My pleasure. Three hundred baht for two set?"

"Deal." I walked away wondering why he was being so helpful and thought that maybe his guilty conscience was still plaguing him. Perhaps, just occasionally, human beings wanted to make up for past misdemeanors.

That evening, I wondered if it was me who was not myself, but the conversation that usually flowed over dinner was now stilted and unnatural. Ace was weirdly quiet and didn't even laugh at my jokes, which he normally did no matter how bad they were. As soon as I put down my knife and fork, he yawned and said we should get an early night, and I agreed. In bed, he reached for me silently in the darkness and made love to me.

"Night, CeCe," he said as we settled down for him to sleep and for me to lie awake.

"Night."

I listened for the change in breathing pattern to let me know that he was asleep, but I didn't hear it. Eventually, I heard him sigh and a tentative hand reached out in the darkness to find me.

"You asleep?" he whispered.

"You know I rarely am."

"Come here, I need a hug."

He drew me to him and held me so tight that my nose was pressed against his chest and I could barely breathe.

"I really meant what I said earlier. I'll miss you," he murmured in the darkness. "Maybe I will come out to Australia. I'll give you my mobile number. Promise to text me a forwarding address?"

"Yeah, of course."

"We are a pair, aren't we?"

"Are we?"

"Yes, both at a crossroads, not knowing where we go next."

"I s'pose."

"Well, it's true for you at least. Sadly, I know exactly where I'll be going. Eventually . . ."

"Where?"

"It doesn't matter, but I just want to tell you that if things were different . . ." I felt his lips gently caress the top of my head. "You're the most real person I've ever met, Celaeno D'Aplièse. Never change, will you?"

"I don't think I can."

"No," he chuckled. "Probably not. I just want you to promise me one more thing."

"What's that?"

"If you . . . *hear* things about me in the future, please try not to judge me. You know that things are never quite what they seem. And . . ." I knew he was struggling to find the words. "Sometimes, you have to do stuff to protect those you love."

"Yeah, like I did for Star."

"Yes, sweetheart, like you did for Star."

With that, he kissed me again and rolled over.

Of course, I didn't sleep a wink that night. All sorts of emotions—some of them new—were racing around my head. I only wished I could confide in someone, ask their opinion about what Ace had said to me. But the fact was, Ace had become my "someone" . . . my friend. I turned the word over in my mind. I'd never had a proper friend before who wasn't my sister, and perhaps I didn't know how friendship even worked. Was I *his* friend too? Or had he simply been using me to ease his loneliness . . . and had I been doing the same? Or were we more than just friends?

I gave up lying sleepless in the bed and crept out to the beach, though it was even too early for sunrise. My heart started to pound as I thought of leaving the security of the little universe Ace and I had created together. I'd miss him—and this paradise—a lot.

Po was just returning to his post for the daytime shift as I walked back to the gate to enter the palace for the final time.

"Got your pictures, madam." He reached into his nylon rucksack to retrieve some brightly colored photo envelopes. He leafed through four of them, checking the contents, and I wondered if this was a service he offered on the side to other residents of Phra Nang Beach to make a few extra baht.

"These yours," he confirmed, tucking the other two packs back into his rucksack.

"Thanks," I said, reminding myself to pay him and give him a decent tip when I left, then I walked up the path to my room to pack.

An hour later, I hoisted my rucksack onto my back and shut the door behind me. I stomped miserably down to the terrace, where Ace was pacing up and down. I was chuffed to see that he looked as depressed and agitated as I did.

"You off?"

"Yeah." I drew the envelope of photos out of my back pocket and put it on the table. "They're for you."

"And here's my mobile number," he said, handing me a piece of paper in return.

We stood there awkwardly, staring at each other. And I just wanted the moment to be over.

"Thanks so much for . . . everything."

"No need to thank me, CeCe. It's been a pleasure."

"Right then." I made to heave the rucksack onto my shoulders again, but then he opened his arms.

"Come here." He pulled me to him and gave me an enormous hug, his chin resting on the top of my head. "Promise to keep in touch?"

"Yeah, course."

"And you never know, I just might make it to Australia," he said as he carried my rucksack to the gate.

"That would be great. Bye then."

"Bye, CeCe."

Po pressed the red button to let me out, and I gave him the cash for the photos, then offered him the tip. Surprisingly he refused it, shaking his head and looking at me with that guilty expression of his.

"Bye-bye, madam."

I walked down Plebs' Path to Railay, feeling too upset to go and say good-bye to Jack and the gang. Not that I expected they'd miss me. As I passed the bar, I saw Jay loitering on the edge of the veranda with a Singha beer, an accessory that seemed to be glued permanently to his fingers. I made to walk straight past him—I wasn't in the mood for small talk.

"Hiya, CeCe," he intercepted me. "You off?"

"Yeah."

"Not taking your new boyfriend with you?" I saw a glint in his booze-soaked eyes and a smile that managed to be more like a sneer on his lips.

"You got it wrong, Jay. I don't have a boyfriend."

"Nah, course you don't."

"I've got to go, or I'll miss my flight. Bye."

"How's that sister of yours?" he called after me.

"Fine," I shouted back, as I continued to walk.

"Send her my best, won't you?"

I pretended not to hear and marched on across the sand toward the long-tail boats waiting to ferry passengers back to Krabi town.

As the plane left the runway at Suvarnabhumi airport heading for Sydney, I thought that the upside of my head's having been so full of Ace in the last few hours was that at least I hadn't dwelled on either the twelve-hour plane journey *or* what I might find when I got there. I had also managed to buy what the airport pharmacist had called "sleepy pills" to aid my journey. I'd taken two for good measure just as boarding was announced—but if anything, I now felt more awake and alert than I normally did and wondered if those pills contained caffeine rather than a sleeping potion.

Thankfully, the plane was relatively empty and I had two spare seats next to me, so as soon as the seat belt sign was switched off, I stretched across them and made myself comfortable, telling my brain that I was exhausted and drugged and would it please do me a favor and go to sleep.

It obviously wasn't listening and after some restless tossing and turning, I sat up and accepted the plane food offered by the Thai stewardess. I even had a beer to calm my thoughts. That didn't work either. So as the cabin lights dimmed, I lay back down and forced myself to think of what lay ahead.

After landing in Sydney in the early morning, I was headed for a town called Darwin right up on the northern tip of Australia. From there, I had to take another plane to the town of Broome. What had really irritated me about this when I'd booked my flights was that I had to fly straight over both places down to near the bottom of Australia, then all the way back up again. This meant extra hours in the air, never mind the time spent in transit at the Sydney airport.

I'd looked up Broome on the Internet at the airport, and from the photos, it looked like it had a really cool beach. These days it was a tourist spot more than anything else, but long ago, due to what I'd learned from Kitty Mercer's biography, I knew it had been the center of the pearling industry. I wondered if that was where my legacy had come from . . .

If there was one thing that the past few weeks had taught me, it was that the cliché of money not buying happiness was absolutely true. I thought of Ace, who was obviously super rich, but lonely and miserable. I wondered if he was missing me. Tonight, I was really missing him . . . Not in a soppy way, like I couldn't live without him or anything, or longed for the touch of his hand on mine. I mean, the sex had been fine, and much better than any I'd had before, but the bit I'd enjoyed the most was the closeness, just like I'd had with Star.

Ace had filled the yawning gap she had left behind. He'd been my friend, and even my confidant up to a point. *That's how I miss him*, I thought, *just the fact that he was there beside me.* I knew that in the real world outside the palace, our paths would never have crossed. He was a rich City boy, used to blond female twigs who bought designer handbags and wore five-inch stilettos.

It had been a moment in time: two lonely people cast adrift on a beach, helping each other through. He would move on, and so would I, but I really hoped we'd always be friends.

At this point either the beer or the "sleepy pills" kicked in, because I was conscious of nothing more until the stewardess woke me up to tell me we were landing in Sydney in forty-five minutes.

Two hours later, I took off again on a far smaller plane to retrace my earlier flight path back up across Australia. As we left Sydney behind, I looked down and saw emptiness. Nothing, literally *nothing*, except for red. Yet it was a red that wasn't really red . . . the closest I could come to describing the color of the earth beneath me was that it looked like the paprika spice that Star sometimes used in her cooking.

Immediately I wondered how I could replicate the color in a painting. After a while I realized I had ages to think about this, because the paprika earth went on and on and on beneath me. It was mostly flat, the landscape reminding me of a gone-off tomato soup: browning at the edges, with the odd thin dribble of cream that had been poured on the top of it to indicate a road or a river.

Yet as we neared Darwin, with my final destination close by, I felt a sudden clutch at my heart that sent it beating faster. I felt oddly exhilarated and tearful, in the way I did when I watched a moving but uplifting film. It was like I wanted to slam my fist through the Perspex window, jump out, and land on that hard, unforgiving red earth that I felt instinctively was somehow a part of me. Or, more accurately, I was a part of *it*.

After we'd landed, the elation I'd felt was soon replaced by abject fear as I boarded what looked like some kind of plastic toy plane, it was so tiny. No one else around me looked worried as we bumped and bounced in the air currents and then descended into somewhere called Kununurra, a town I'd never heard of and which certainly wasn't Broome. When I made to get off, I was told that this was just a stop and Broome would be the next port of call, as if we were on a bus or a train. The scary flying bus took off again and I took another sleepy pill to calm my nerves. When we finally touched down on an airstrip that looked not much longer than the average Geneva driveway, I actually crossed myself.

Out on the concourse of the tiny airport, I looked for the information center and saw a desk, behind which sat a girl who had skin just about the same color as mine. Even her hair—a mass of ebony curls—looked similar.

"G'day, can I help you?" She smiled at me warmly.

"Yeah, I'm looking for somewhere to stay in town for a couple of nights."

"Then you've come to the right place," she said, handing me a heap of leaflets.

"Which one do you recommend?"

"My favorite is the Pearl House on Carnarvon Street, but I'm not meant to give personal preferences," she added with a grin. "Shall I find out if they have a room?"

"That would be great," I replied, feeling my legs twitching beneath me—they'd obviously had enough of carrying me thousands of miles across the globe. "Could it be on the second floor? Or the third? Just not on the ground."

"No worries."

While she made a call, I told myself that I was being ridiculous; spiders could climb upward, couldn't they? Or along drainpipes into showers . . .

"Yeah, Mrs. Cousins has got a spare room," she said as she put the phone down, wrote out the details, and handed them to me. "The taxi rank is just out front."

"Thanks."

"You French?" she asked.

"Swiss, actually."

"Come here to see your relatives?"

"Maybe," I said with a shrug, wondering how she knew.

"Well, my name's Chrissie and here's my card. Call me if you need some help and maybe I'll see you around."

"Yeah, thanks," I said as I walked off toward the exit, amazed at both her friendliness and her perception.

I was already sweating by the time I climbed into a taxi and the driver told me it was only a short journey into town. We stopped in front of a low building overlooking a large green, the wide road lined with a mixture of small shops and houses.

The hotel was basic, but as I entered my room, I was glad to see it was spotless *and*, having done a thorough inspection, spider-free.

I went to check the time on my mobile, but the battery was obviously completely dead. All I could go by was that dusk was falling, which probably meant it was around six o'clock at night. My body was telling me it was time for sleep, even if my mobile couldn't.

I stripped off my plane clothes, climbed between the sheets, and eventually fell asleep.

I woke up to see a really bright sun glaring in from the naked window. I showered, dressed, and hurried downstairs to see if there was anything to eat.

"Can I get some breakfast?" I asked the lady on reception.

"That was cleared away hours ago. It's almost two in the afternoon, love."

"Right. Is there anywhere local I can get something to eat?"

"There's the Runway Bar down the road that does pizza and what have you. Best you can do this time of day. There's more places open later."

"Thanks."

I went and stood outside the hotel. Even for me, the sun felt searingly hot, as if it had moved a few thousand miles closer to the earth during the night. Everyone else who had a brain was obviously inside hiding from it, because the street was deserted. Farther down, I saw four bronze statues next to a car park and went to take a look. Three were of men in suits, all old judging by the wrinkles, and the fourth—wearing a jumpsuit, heavy boots, and a round helmet that covered his entire face—looked like an astronaut. There were plaques with tiny writing on them, probably describing what made these men so special, but I was beginning to feel sick in the sun and I knew I needed food. By the time I arrived at the Runway Bar, sweat was pouring off me from the humidity.

I went to the counter and immediately ordered water, gulping back the whole bottle as soon as it was handed to me. I decided on a burger, and took one of the free maps detailing the attractions in the town before finding a seat at a faded plastic table.

"Youse a tourist?" asked the young guy who brought the burger over to me.

"Yeah."

"You're brave, love. We don't get many of you here at this time of year. It's the Big Wet, ya see. My advice is don't go far without an umbrella. Or a fan," he added. "Though both are pretty useless in the wet season."

I ate my burger in about four mouthfuls, then studied the map of the town again. As usual, the letters in the words jumbled before my eyes, but I soldiered on and eventually found the place I was looking for. Going back to the counter to pay and grab some more water, I pointed out the spot on the map to the waiter.

"How far away is this?"

"The museum? From here, it's about a twenty-minute walk."

"Okay, thanks." I turned around to leave but he stopped me.

"It's closed this arvo, though. Try tomorrow."

"I will. Bye."

It felt like everything in Broome was closed in the afternoon. Back in my room, I remembered my dead mobile and plugged it in next to the bed to charge. While I was in the bathroom, I was surprised to hear it pinging again and again and I scurried back to look at it.

"Wow!" I grunted under my breath as the screen displayed messages from Star and my other sisters. I opened the text page on my phone and scrolled down, and the messages kept on coming. I saw there were a number of missed calls too.

I started on the texts first.

STAR: Cee! OMG! Call me. Xx
MAIA: CeCe, where are you? What's going on? Call me! X
ALLY: It is YOU, isn't it? Call me. X
TIGGY: Are u okay? Thinking of you. Call me. Xx

Electra . . .

Electra had texted me . . .

In a total panic as to why all my sisters were suddenly contacting me, I concentrated on deciphering Electra's text.

You dark horse, you!

There was no kiss or a "call me" at the end of her text, but neither did I expect it.

"Something's up," I muttered to myself as I scrolled down and saw a text from a number I didn't know.

I trusted you. Hope you're happy.

I leapt to my rucksack and got out the scrap of paper on which Ace had written down his mobile number and saw it matched the number on my screen.

"Oh God, Cee . . ." I scraped the palms of my hands distractedly up and down my cheeks. "What have you done? Christ!" I mentally retraced my footsteps since leaving Thailand, searching for clues as to what it could have been.

You've been on a plane for most of the time . . .

Nope, there was nothing. Nothing I'd said, or even *thought*, about Ace that was bad. Quite the opposite, in fact. I stood up and paced across the small, tiled room, then I went back to my mobile and dialed the voice mail number, to be told in a strong Australian accent that it wasn't the right one, but without telling me what the right one *was*. I threw the phone onto the bed in irritation.

Even though it would cost a fortune, I had to find out what had happened. The best way was to go straight to the horse's mouth, which was Ace.

Wishing for once I was a drinker—a few shots of whiskey chased down by a tequila slammer or four might have calmed the trembling in my fingers—I tapped in Ace's number. Squaring up my body as though I were about to have a physical fight, I waited for it to connect.

A different Australian voice informed me, "This number is unavailable." Thinking that maybe I'd got it wrong, I tried another ten or even fifteen times, but still the answer was the same.

"Shit! So, what do I do now . . . ?" I asked myself.

Phone Star . . . she'll know.

I paced some more, because it would mean breaking the silence, and I knew that hearing her voice for the first time in weeks might break *me* too. Still, I knew I had no choice. There was no way I was going to be able to sleep tonight without knowing what I'd done.

I dialed Star's number and it rang eventually, which was something. Then I heard my sister's voice, and did my best to swallow a gulp of emotion as she said hello.

"It's me, Sia . . . ," I said, reverting automatically to the pet name I used when I spoke to her.

"Cee! Are you okay? Where *are* you?"

"In Australia . . . in the middle of nowhere." I managed a chuckle.

"Australia? But you always refused to go there!"

"I know, but here I am. Listen, do you know why I've got all these texts from everyone?"

There was a silence on the other end. Finally, she said, "Yes. Don't you?"

"No. I really don't."

Another pause, but I was used to those from her and I waited for her to choose her words. The result was disappointing.

"Oh," she said. "I see."

"See what? Seriously, Sia, I really don't know. Can you tell me?"

"I . . . yes. It's to do with the man you were photographed with."

"Photographed with? Who?"

"Anand Changrok, the rogue trader who broke Berners Bank and then disappeared off the face of the earth."

"Who? *What?!* I don't even *know* an 'Anand Changrok.'"

"A tall, dark-haired man who looks oriental?"

"Oh. God. *Shit . . .* it's Ace!"

"You do know him then?" said Star.

"Yes, but not what he's done. What *has* he done?"

"He didn't tell you?"

"Of course he didn't! Otherwise I wouldn't be calling you to find out, would I? And what do you mean, he 'broke' a bank?"

"I don't know the details, but it's to do with illegal trading. Anyway, by the time his fraud was discovered, he'd already left the UK. From what I read in the *Times* yesterday, intelligence services all over the world have been looking for him."

"Jesus Christ, Sia! He never said a word."

"How on earth did you meet him?"

"He was just some guy on Phra Nang Beach—you remember, the really"—I stopped myself from saying "ace"—"beautiful one with the limestone pillars."

"Of course I remember."

I thought I heard a slight catch in her voice as she said this.

"But how come everyone in the world seems to know that *I* knew him?" I continued.

"Because there's a photograph of the two of you on a beach with your arms around each other on the front of every single newspaper in England. I saw it this morning at the newsagent's next to the bookshop. You're famous, Cee."

I paused to think, and an entire stream of memories downloaded in my brain: Ace's refusal to come out in public by day, his insistence that I never tell anyone where I was living . . . and, most of all, Po, the security guard who'd taken the photograph . . .

"Cee? Are you still there?"

"Yeah," I said eventually, as I thought how Po had been keen to take photos of me and Ace together. By handing him my camera on our last night, I'd also handed him the perfect opportunity. No wonder he'd been so eager to take my roll of film to his "cousin" in Krabi town . . . He'd obviously made copies too, which would explain the extra photograph wallets I'd seen in his rucksack. Then I remembered Jay, the ex-journalist, and wondered if the two of them had been in cahoots.

"Are you okay?" Star asked me.

"Not really, no. It was all a mistake," I added limply as I also remembered the envelope of photos I'd left for Ace on the table. If there was ever an act that had come from the best part of my soul that could be interpreted as having come from the worst, that was it.

"Cee, tell me where you are. Seriously, I can get on a plane tonight and be there for you by tomorrow. Or at least the day after."

"No, it's okay. I'll be fine. You okay?" I managed.

"Yes, apart from the fact that I miss you. Really, anything I can do to help, just tell me."

"Thanks. Gotta go now," I said before I broke down completely. "Bye, Sia."

I pressed the button to end the call, then switched off my mobile. I lay down flat on my bed, staring up at the ceiling. I couldn't even cry—I was way past tears. Once again, it looked like I'd managed to mess up a beautiful friendship.

12

I woke up the next day feeling a bit like I had the morning after I'd heard the news about Pa Salt's death. The first few seconds of consciousness were okay, before the deluge of reality poured down on my head. I rolled over and buried my face in the cheap foam pillow. I didn't want to be awake, didn't want to face the truth. It was almost—but not quite—funny, because even if I *had* known Ace was a wanted criminal, I was far too much of a dunce to have made something out of it. Others had been clever enough to do it, though, and I'd got the blame.

Ace must have hated me. And he had every right to.

Just imagining what he must have been thinking of me right then was enough to turn my stomach. For real, I realized as I dashed to the toilet and retched. Standing up, I washed my mouth out and drank some water, deciding that all I could do was to go and confront the evidence. "Face your fears," I told myself as I dressed and went downstairs to reception.

"Is there an Internet café around here?" I asked the woman behind the desk.

"Yeah, sure. Turn right and walk about two hundred meters. There's an alleyway, and you'll see it there."

"Thanks."

I stepped outside into massive paprika-colored puddles that pooled on the uneven pavements and realized it must have poured down last night. As I walked, I felt floaty, like I was drunk, which was probably caused by a lethal cocktail of misery and fear at what the computer screen might show me.

Once I'd paid my few dollars to the woman at the front of the café, she indicated a booth and I went into it and sat down, feeling sick again. I logged on with the code she'd given me, then stared at the web browser wondering what I should tap in. Star had told me Ace's real name, but for the life of me, I couldn't remember what it was. And even if I could have, I wouldn't have been able to spell it.

"*Bank crash.*"

I pressed enter, but it brought up something about Wall Street in 1929.

"*Wanted cremenal bank man.*"

That brought up a page about John Wayne in some cowboy movie.

In the end I tapped in "*bank man hiding in thailand*" and pressed "enter." A whole screen of headlines ranging from the *Times* to the *New York Times* to a Chinese paper flickered up. I clicked on "Images" first, as I needed to see what everybody else had seen.

And there it was: the photo of the two of us at sunset on Phra Nang Beach—*me!* Staring back at me in full Technicolor, for all the world to see, including this—as John Wayne might say—one-horse town.

"Christ." I swore under my breath, studying the picture more closely. I saw I was actually smiling, which I didn't often do in photos. Encircled in Ace's arms, I looked happy, so happy that I almost didn't recognize myself. *And actually, I don't look that bad*, I thought, instinctively patting the hair that currently massed in tight ringlets around my shoulders. I understood now why Star liked it better long; at least I looked like a girl in the photo, not an ugly boy.

Stop it, I told myself, because this really wasn't the moment to be vain. Yet as I clicked on the endless reproductions of the photo—including those in a load of Australian papers—I allowed myself a grim chuckle. Of all the D'Aplièse sisters to end up on the front page of a shedload of national newspapers, I had to be the most unlikely. Even Electra had never managed such a full house.

Then I got real, clicked onto the articles, and began trying to decipher what they were saying. The good news was that at least I was "an unnamed woman," so I wasn't bringing shame on my family. But Ace . . .

Two hours later, I left the café. Though my legs had let me puddle-jump earlier, now it was all I could do to make them put one foot in front of the other. Turning into the hotel lobby, I asked the receptionist how I could get to the beach. I needed some air and some space, big-time.

"I'll call you a taxi," she said.

"I really can't walk?"

"No, darl', it's too far in this heat."

"Okay." I did as I was told and sat down on a hard, cheap sofa in the lobby until the taxi arrived. I climbed inside and we set off with me sitting numbly in the back. The view out of the window seemed to be devoid of human life—there was only the red earth alongside the wide road, and loads of empty building lots where clouds of white birds sat in the tall shady trees, their heads turning as one as the taxi went by.

"Here you go, love. That'll be seven dollars," the driver said. "Stop into the Sunset Bar over there when you need a lift back and they'll give me a holler."

"Sure, thanks," I said, giving him a ten-dollar bill and not waiting for the change.

I plunged my feet into the soft sand and ran toward the big blue mass, knowing that if anyone needed to drown their sorrows, it was me. Arriving on the shoreline, my toes felt the coolness of the water and even though I was still in my shorts and a T-shirt, I dived straight in. I swam and swam in the gorgeous water, so clear that I could see the shadows of seabirds flying above flickering on the underwater sand. After a while I waded back to shore, totally exhausted, and lay flat on my back in this deserted piece of heaven in the middle of nowhere. To the left and right of me, the beach seemed to stretch on for miles and the heat that had felt so oppressive in town was swept away by the ocean breeze. There wasn't another person in sight, and I wondered why the locals weren't queuing up to swim in this perfect pool on their very doorstep.

"Ace . . . ," I whispered, feeling I should say something meaningful to the sky to express my distress. But as usual, the right words wouldn't come, so I let the feelings run through me instead.

What I had eventually puzzled together from all the online articles was that Ace was "notorious." I'd had to look up the word in an online dictionary, like Star had taught me to: *widely and unfavorably known* . . .

My Ace, the man I had trusted and befriended, was all things bad. No one in the world had a good word to say about him. Yet, unless he was the most brilliant actor on the planet, I couldn't believe that the guy they were describing was the same one I had lived and laughed with up until only a few days ago.

Apparently he'd done a load of fraudulent trading. The sum he'd "gambled away" was so astronomical that at first I thought they'd got the number of zeros wrong. That anyone could lose that much money was just outrageous—I mean, where exactly did it go? Certainly not down the back of the sofa, anyway.

The reason everyone was doubly up in arms was because he'd run away the minute it had all been discovered and no one had seen hide nor hair of him since November. Until now, of course.

Thanks to me, his cover had been blown. Yet, having seen all the photographs of him a year or so ago in his sharp Savile Row suits, clean-shaven, with hair far shorter than mine usually was, it seemed unlikely that anyone in Krabi would have recognized the skinny werewolf guy on the beach as the most wanted man in the banking world. Now I thought about it, his borrowed Thai paradise had been the perfect place to hide: There, among the thousands of young backpackers, he'd had the perfect smokescreen.

Today's *Bangkok Post* said that the British authorities were now in talks with the Thai authorities to have him "extradited." Again, I'd gone back to the online dictionary, and found out this meant that they were basically going to drag him back to England to face the music.

I felt a couple of sharp pinpricks on my face and looked up to see the storm clouds that had gathered into angry gray clumps overhead. I legged it up to the beach bar just in time, and sat with a pineapple shake to watch the natural light show. It reminded me so much of the storm I'd seen from the Cave of the Princess before I'd been semi-arrested, and now it looked like Ace was going to be arrested for real when he got back to England.

If only things were different . . .

At the time, I thought Ace's problems had something to do with an-other woman, but it couldn't have been farther from the truth. If our paths ever crossed again, I was sure he'd want to knife me rather than hug me.

What made that stupid lump come back to my throat was the fact that he *had* trusted me. He'd even given me his precious mobile number, which I knew from countless films could be traced to find the location of the owner. He must have really wanted to keep in touch with me if he'd been willing to take that risk.

I knew, just *knew*, that that lowlife Jay was part of this. He'd probably recognized Ace through his seedy journalist's eyes, then followed him to the palace and bribed Po to get pictures as proof. I didn't doubt he'd sold the photo and Ace's whereabouts to the highest bidder and was now celebrating that he had enough dosh to keep himself in Singha beer for the next fifty years.

Not that it mattered now. Ace would never believe it hadn't been me and nor would I, if I were him. Especially as I'd purposely not told him about Jay's recognizing him, albeit only so he wouldn't worry. It would sound like a bunch of pathetic excuses. I couldn't even contact him now anyway; I'd have bet my life that his SIM card was swimming with the fishes on Phra Nang Beach.

"Oh, Cee," I berated myself as desolation engulfed me. "You've totally mucked it up again. You're just useless!"

I want to go home . . .

"G'day," a voice said from behind me. "How ya doing?"

I turned around and saw the girl from the tourist information desk standing behind me.

"Okay."

"You waiting for someone?" she asked me.

"No, I don't know anybody here yet."

"Then mind if I join you?"

"Course not," I said, thinking it would be rude to say otherwise, even if I wasn't exactly in the mood for small talk.

"Did you just go swimming?" She frowned at me. "Your hair's wet."

"Erm, yeah," I said, patting it nervously, wondering if it was sticking up or something.

"Strewth! Has no one warned you about the jellyfish? They're brutal this time of year—we don't go into the sea here until March, after the coast is clear. You got lucky then. One sting off an irukandji and you coulda carked it. Like, died," she translated.

"Thanks for telling me. Any other dangerous things I should know about?"

"Aside from the crocs in the creeks and the poisonous snakes that roam around this time of year, no. So, have you managed to contact yer rellies yet?"

"You mean my relatives?" I double-checked, trying to keep up with the Aussie slang. "No, not yet. I mean, I don't think I actually have any alive here. I'm tracing my family history and Broome is where I was told to start."

"Yeah, it fits." The girl—whose name I was struggling to remember—flashed her lovely amber eyes at me. "You've got all the hallmarks of being from around these parts."

"Have I?"

"Yeah. Your hair, the color of your skin, and your eyes . . . bet I could tell you where they came from."

"Really? Where?"

"I'd reckon you've got Aboriginal blood with some whitefella mixed in, and maybe those eyes came from Japtown, like mine." She gestured vaguely inland. "Broome was heaving with Japanese a few generations ago, and there are lots of mixed kids like us around."

"You're part Aboriginal?" I asked, wishing now I'd taken some time to do more research on Australia, because I really was sounding like a dunce. At least I suddenly recalled her name. It was Chrissie.

"I have Aboriginal grandparents. They're Yawuru—that's the main Aboriginal tribe in this neck of the woods. What's CeCe short for?" she asked me.

"Celaeno. I know, it's a weird name."

"That's beaut!" It was Chrissie's turn to look amazed.

"Is it?"

"Yeah, course it is! You're named after one of the Seven Sisters of the Pleiades—the Gumanyba. They're like goddesses in our culture."

I was speechless. No one had ever—*ever*—known where my name came from.

"You really don't know a lot about your ancestors, do you?" she said.

"Nope. Nothing." Then feeling rude as well as stupid, I added, "But I'd really like to learn more."

"My grandma is the real expert on all that stuff. Reckon she'd be stoked to tell you her Dreamtime stories—stuff that's been passed down through the generations. Give me a call whenever and I'll take you to meet her."

"Yeah, that would be great." I glanced out at the beach and saw the rain was now a memory, replaced by a golden-purple sun sinking fast toward the horizon. My attention was caught by a man and a camel strolling along the beach in front of the bar.

Chrissie turned to look at them too. "Hey, that's my mate Ollie—he works for the camel tour company," she said, waving enthusiastically at the man.

Ollie came up to the café to say hello, leaving his camel waiting on the beach, its face sleepy and docile. Ollie was darker skinned than us, his long face handsome, and he had to stoop to embrace Chrissie. I sat there awkwardly as they began chatting, realizing that they weren't speaking English to each other, but a language I'd never heard before.

"Ollie, this is CeCe—it's her first time in Broome."

"G'day," he said, and shook my hand with his callused one. "Ever been on a camel?"

"No," I said.

"D'ya fancy having a go now? I was taking Gobbie out for a stroll to teach him some manners—he's new and wild, so we haven't tied him to the others yet. But I'm sure you sheilas can keep him in check." He winked at us.

"Really?" I said nervously.

"Sure, any mate of Chrissie's and all that," he said warmly.

We followed Ollie to Gobbie the camel, who turned his head away like a spoiled toddler as Ollie ordered him to kneel. After the umpteenth time, Gobbie finally agreed.

"You ever done this before?" I whispered to Chrissie as we both clambered onto his back. The scent coming off him was overpowering; in essence, he stank.

"Yeah," she whispered, her breath tickling my ear. "Get ready for a bumpy ride."

With a lurch, Gobbie suddenly stood up, and I felt one of Chrissie's hands close around my waist to steady me as we were propelled upward into the sky. The sun was beginning to dip toward the ocean, and the camel's body cast a long shadow on the golden sand, his legs spindly, like something from a Dalí painting.

"You okay?"

"Yeah, I'm good," I replied.

The ride was certainly not smooth, as Gobbie seemed to be doing his very best to run away. As we jolted over the sand, the two of us screamed as Gobbie began to canter and I realized just how fast camels could move.

"Come back, ya drongo!" Ollie shouted, panting to keep pace, but Gobbie took no notice. Eventually, Ollie managed to slow the camel down, and Chrissie rested her chin on my shoulder, panting in relief.

"Strewth! That was quite a ride!" she said as we then walked more sedately along the beach. The setting sun had set the sky alight with pinks, purples, and deep reds which were perfectly reflected in the ocean below. I felt as if I were gliding through a painting, the clouds like pools of oils on a palette.

Gobbie carried us back to the Sunset Bar, where he tipped us off inelegantly onto the sand. We waved good-bye to Ollie, and then went up the veranda steps.

"Reckon we could use something cold after all that excitement," Chrissie said as she flopped into a chair. "What d'ya want to drink?"

I asked for an orange juice and so did she, then we sat together at the bar, recovering.

"So how you gonna find your family?" she asked. "Got any clues?"

"A couple," I said, fiddling with my straw, "and I don't really know what to do with them. Apart from the name of a woman who led me here, I've got a black-and-white photograph of two men—one old and one much younger—but I've no idea who they are, or what they've got to do with me."

"Have you shown it to anyone here yet? Maybe someone would recognize them," Chrissie suggested.

"No. I'm going to the museum tomorrow. I thought I might get some answers from there."

"D'ya mind if I take a look? If they're from around these parts, I might know 'em."

"Why not? The photo is back in my room at the hotel."

"No worries. I'll give you a lift, then we can take a look together."

We walked outside to the street, where dusk had brought with it the sounds of thousands of insects buzzing through the air, only to be snatched up by bats swooping to catch their prey. A shadow crossed the empty road, and at first I thought it was a cat, but when it froze and stared at me, I saw it had big wide eyes and a pink pointed snout.

"That's a possum, Cee," Chrissie commented. "They're like vermin here. My grandma used to put them in her pot and cook 'em for supper."

"Oh," I said as I followed her through the car park to a battered, rusting moped.

"You okay on the back of the bike?" she asked.

"After that camel ride, it sounds like heaven," I joked.

"Jump aboard then." She handed me an old helmet, and I put it on before looping my hands around her middle. After a wobbly start, we set off. There was a welcome breeze on my face—a respite from what was another incredibly humid evening, with not a breath of wind to stir the heavy air.

We came to a halt in front of the hotel and as Chrissie parked the moped, I ran inside to fetch the photograph. When I returned to reception, Chrissie was chatting with the woman behind the counter.

"I've got it," I said, waving it at her. We settled in the tiny residents' lounge off reception, sitting together on the sticky leatherette sofa. Chrissie bent her head to study it.

"It's a really bad picture, 'cause the sun's directly behind them and it's in black and white," I said.

"You mean you can't tell what color the people in it are?" Chrissie queried. "I'd say the older man is black and the boy is lighter skinned." She held the photograph under the light of a lamp. "I'd reckon it was taken in the 1940s or '50s. There's some writing on the side of the pickup truck behind them. Can you see?" She passed the photo back to me.

"Yeah, looks like it says 'JIRA.'"

"Holy dooley!" Chrissie pointed at the taller figure standing in front of the car. "I think I know who that man is."

There was a pause as she gaped at me with excitement and I stared back at her blankly.

"Who?"

"Albert Namatjira, the artist—he's just about the most famous Aboriginal man in Australia. He was born in and worked out of a mission in Hermannsburg, a couple of hours outside Alice Springs. Y'don't think he was related to you, do you?"

A shiver ran through me. "How would I know? Is he dead?"

"Yeah, he died a fair while back, in the late 1950s. He was the first Aboriginal man to have the same rights as the whites. He could own land, vote, drink alcohol, and he even met the queen of England. He was an amazing painter—I've gotta print of *Mount Hermannsburg* on my bedroom wall."

Clearly, Chrissie was a fan of this guy. "So, before that time, Aboriginal people didn't have those rights?"

"Nah, not until the late sixties," she explained. "But Namatjira got his rights early 'cause of his artistic talent. What a bloke. Even if he isn't a rellie of yours, it's a big clue to where y'might have come from. How old are you?"

"Twenty-seven."

"So . . ." I watched Chrissie do some mental arithmetic. "That means you were born in 1980, which means he might be your granddad! Y'know what this means, right?" she said, beaming at me. "You gotta go to Alice Springs next. Wow, CeCe, I can't believe it's him in the pic!" Chrissie threw her arms around me and squeezed me tight.

"Okay," I gulped. "I'd actually been planning on heading to Adelaide to speak to the solicitor who passed on a legacy to me. Where is Alice Springs?"

"It's right in the middle of the country—what we call the Never Never. I've always wanted to go there—it's near Uluru." When she saw my confused expression, she rolled her eyes. "Ayers Rock to you, idiot."

"So what kind of stuff did this guy paint?"

"He totally revolutionized Aboriginal art. He did these incredible watercolor landscapes, and started a whole new school of painting. It takes serious skill to paint a good watercolor, rather than just blobbing paint onto a canvas. He gave his landscapes luminosity—he really knew how to layer the watercolors to get the play of light just right."

"Wow. How do you know all this?"

"I've always loved art," Chrissie said. "I did Aussie culture as part of my tourism degree and spent a semester at uni studying Aboriginal artists."

I wasn't ready to admit that I'd studied art at college too but had dropped out. "So, did this guy ever paint other stuff, like portraits?" I asked, curious to know more.

"Portraits are complicated in our culture. Like, it's a big taboo because you're replicating someone's essence; it would grieve the spirits up there 'cause they've done their job down here and want to be left in peace. When one of us dies, we're not supposed to speak their name again."

"Really?" I thought about how often me and Star had mentioned Pa Salt since he'd died. "Isn't it good to remember those you love and miss?"

"Course, but speaking their name calls them back, and they're happy to help us from up there."

I nodded, trying to take it all in, but it had been a long day already and I couldn't hide a huge yawn.

"I'm not boring you, am I?" she teased me.

"Sorry, I'm just super tired from traveling."

"No worries, I'll let you get your beauty sleep." She stood up. "Oh, and give me a call tomorrow if you're up for meeting my grandma."

"I will. Thanks, Chrissie."

With a wave, she walked out of the hotel and I climbed the stairs, too exhausted to process what I'd just discovered, but feeling a shiver of excitement at the fact that the man in the photograph had been an artist, just like me . . .

13

I was awake weirdly early the next morning. Maybe because I'd had a dream—which had been so real and vivid that I struggled to bring myself back to reality.

I'd been a little girl sitting on the knee of an older woman, who for some reason was naked, at least up top. She'd led me by the hand across a red desert to a plant under which was some kind of insect nest. She pointed to it and said it was my job to look after them. I was pretty sure it had something to do with honey, but the *really* strange thing was that, despite my hatred of anything with far more legs than I had, I'd actually held one of the insects like it was a pet hamster or something. I'd stroked it with my small fingers as it had crawled across my palm. I even remembered feeling the tickling sensation of its legs. Whatever it was, I knew it had been my friend, not my enemy.

Galvanized by all that I had learned yesterday, I picked up the hotel phone and dialed the number of the solicitor's office in Adelaide. Even if I wasn't going there, I thought I might as well get some answers. After several rings, a crisp female voice came on the line.

"Angus and Tine, how can I help you?"

"Hi, can I speak to Mr. Angus Junior, please?"

"He retired a few months ago, I'm afraid," the woman said. "But Talitha Myers has taken on his casework. Shall I make an appointment for you?"

"I'm actually in Broome, and I just wanted to ask a few quick questions. Should I call back when she's free or—"

"Hold on, please."

"Talitha Myers speaking," said a different voice. "How can I help you?"

"Hi, I received an inheritance last year that was sent from Mr. Angus to my father's lawyer in Switzerland. My name is Celaeno D'Aplièse."

"Okay. Do you know the exact date when the inheritance was sent to your father's lawyer?"

"I got it in June last year when my dad died, but I'm not sure how long before that his lawyer had actually received it."

"And what was the name of the lawyer?"

"Hoffman and Associates in Geneva."

"Right, here it is." There was a pause. "So what can I do for you?"

"I'm trying to trace my family and I was hoping you had a record of who the inheritance was from?"

"Let me look at the notes on the computer, though sadly they won't tell me much, as Mr. Angus preferred to write everything down, like all the oldies do . . . Nope, nothing. Hang on, I'll just check if there's anything written in the ledgers."

There was a clatter, and then I heard the sound of pages turning.

"Here it is. So . . . from what I can gather—it says to refer to notes for January 1964—'trust set up by deceased Katherine Mercer.'"

Katherine, Kitty . . . I almost dropped the phone in shock. "Kitty Mercer?"

"You know of her?"

"A bit," I mumbled. "Do you have any idea who she set the trust up for?"

"Can't make it out from these notes, I'm afraid, but I can go down into the vaults to take a look at the 1964 ledger. Should I give you a call once I've found out?"

"That would be brilliant, thanks." I gave her my mobile number, then ended the call, my heart in my throat. Was I somehow related to Kitty after all?

I left the hotel to walk down the road back to the Internet café, wanting to spend some time looking into Albert Namatjira. I halted in front of a newsagent's on seeing a familiar face on the front of the *Australian*.

CHANGROK GIVES HIMSELF UP AND FLIES HOME

"Shit!" I gasped as I studied the photo more closely: Ace was in handcuffs, being led down the steps of a plane and surrounded by a load of men in uniform.

I bought the paper, knowing it would take me a long time to decipher what the paragraph beneath it said. It was also "continued on page 4." I turned tail and walked back to the hotel. It was pointless to carry on to the Internet café—my brain was incapable of multitasking at the best of times, and this really wasn't the moment to investigate Albert Namatjira as well.

Back upstairs in my room, I realized how much I'd depended on Star to translate the gobbledygook of newsprint, e-mails, and books for me. And even though she had texted me a couple of times overnight to check I was okay, and I was sure she'd be happy to help, I felt it was important that I proved to myself that I could cope alone. So I sat cross-legged on my bed and did my best to decode what the newspaper said about my Ace.

Anand Changrok, the rogue trader who broke Berners investment bank last November, flew home today from his Thai hideout and gave himself up at Heathrow. Changrok refused to comment as he was led away by police. Berners Bank, one of the oldest banks in the UK, was recently bought for £1 by Jinqian, a Chinese investment bank.

With news of Changrok's arrest, crowds of angry investors surrounded the entrance to the bank on the Strand in London to protest at their lost funds. Many had their pensions invested in funds run by Berners and have lost their life savings. David Rutter, Berners's chief executive officer, has declined to comment on what level of compensation investors will be offered, but the board of directors announced that a full investigation into how the situation was allowed to develop unnoticed is being carried out.

Changrok has meanwhile been remanded to Wormwood Scrubs prison and will appear in court next Tuesday on charges of fraud and document forgery. Sources say it is unlikely he will receive bail.

So, Ace was currently locked up in a cell in a London prison. I chewed my lip in agitation, thinking that if I'd never asked Po to take that picture, maybe he would have joined me in Australia and the two of us could have become outlaws in the outback together. Maybe I should go and visit him, try to explain the truth in person . . . like, he could hardly run away, given where he was. But it was a long way to go if he refused to see me.

I checked my watch and saw it was past eleven o'clock and the Broome Historical Museum should be open.

I set off with the tourist map of Broome in my hands. As I walked along the wide avenue, I peered through the shop windows and saw trays of pearls—not just white ones, but black and pink pearls strung together on necklaces, or fashioned as delicate earrings. An almighty racket struck up in one of the trees as I passed it.

To my left, across a strip of dense mangroves, was the vast ocean that seamlessly joined the sky at the horizon. Eventually, I spotted the Historical Museum. It looked like a lot of the other buildings in Broome: single story with a corrugated roof and a veranda running along the front.

Once inside, I felt immediately conspicuous as I was the only visitor. A woman sat behind a desk at a computer and popped her freckled face up to give me a tight smile.

I wandered around and saw that everything in there seemed to be about the pearling industry. There were a lot of model boats featured and black-and-white pictures of people sailing on them. My eyes glazed over reading the plaques with descriptions written on them in tiny letters, and I headed for a corner full of ancient-looking equipment. There was another suit identical to the one that was featured in the bronze astronaut sculpture, the round holes in the metal helmet staring at me like empty eyes. I squinted at the card below it, and finally twigged that this was a pearl-diving suit, long before the days of neoprene.

On the next display, pearls sat on red velvet cushions in little wooden boxes. A lot of them looked misshapen, like glistening teardrops that had just splashed to the ground. I had never been a jewelry girl, but there was something about these creamy orbs that made you want to reach out and touch them.

"Can I help you?"

I jumped back from the display guiltily, even though I'd done nothing wrong.

"I was just wondering if you'd ever heard of someone called Kitty Mercer."

"Kitty Mercer? Course I have, love. Doubt there's a Broome local that hasn't. She's one of the most famous people to ever live here."

"Oh, that's good then," I said. "Do you have any information on her?"

"For sure, darl'. Are you doing a school project or something?"

"Uni, actually," I improvised, insulted she thought I was so young.

"I have a lot of female students who come in here to research Kitty

Mercer. She was one of Australia's great female pioneers. She more or less ran this town during the early twentieth century. There's a biography of her up there on the rack—it was only written a while back by a local historian. I read it and found out all sorts of things about her I didn't know. I'd recommend it."

"Oh yeah, I think I've got that one already," I said hastily as I saw the biography Ace had bought for me. I wondered if this was the only source of information about Kitty; maybe I'd ask if there was a TV documentary on her I could watch because it would literally take me years to finish the book by myself. Then my eyes fell on a table next to the rack, which offered a small selection of audiobooks. I recognized the cover on the front of one of them.

"Is this a CD of the biography?"

"Yes."

"Great, thanks, I'll take it," I said, relief flooding through me.

"That'll be twenty-nine dollars, love. You're not from around here, are you?" she said as I counted out three ten-dollar bills.

"No."

"Come back to research your own history?" she probed.

"Yeah. That and the uni essay."

"Well, any further help you need, you just let me know."

"I will. Bye, then."

"Bye, love. Glad to see one of you got to uni."

I left the museum gratefully, because there was something about the way the woman looked at me with a mixture of sympathy and discomfort that I didn't like. I tried to push it from my mind as I nipped into a discount store I'd seen on the way and managed to buy a portable CD player and a pair of cheap headphones, as I was pretty sure the other residents of the hotel wouldn't be interested in hearing endless hours of Kitty Mercer's life story being played through the thin bedroom walls.

I grabbed another burger from the café for lunch, and as I walked back to the hotel, I noticed a few black-skinned kids squatting on the green. In fact, one was lying down flat and seemed to be asleep. One who was awake gave me a nod, and I watched another take a slurp out of a beer bottle.

I saw a woman walking around them in a big loop, like they were going to attack her in broad daylight or something. They seemed okay to me—

just a bunch of youths like you'd find on any street corner in a city, town, or village.

I had just arrived back in my hotel room when my mobile rang and I saw it was Ma. Feeling bad because I hadn't replied to her messages, I picked up my phone.

"Hello?"

There was a long pause, which was probably the sketchy connection from Switzerland.

"CeCe?"

"Yes. Hi, Ma."

"*Chérie!* How are you?"

"Good. Well, okay anyway."

"Star tells me you are in Australia."

"Yes, I am."

"You left Thailand?"

"Yup."

There was another pause, which was definitely made by Ma. I could virtually hear her brain whirring as she decided whether or not to ask me about Ace.

"And you are well?" she said eventually.

"I always am, Ma," I said, wondering when she'd cut to the chase.

"*Chérie,* you know I am here for you if you ever need me."

"I know. Thanks."

"How long will you be in Australia?"

"I'm not sure, to be honest."

"Well, I am just glad to hear your voice."

"And me," I said.

"So, I will say good-bye."

"Ma . . ." As she obviously didn't want to bring it up, I knew I had to.

"Yes, *chérie?*"

"Do you think Pa would have been cross about that photograph?"

"No. I am sure you did nothing wrong."

"I didn't. I really didn't know about Ace and what he'd done. Has anyone contacted you? I mean, like the newspapers?"

"No, but I will say nothing, even if they do."

"I know you won't. Thanks, Ma. Good night."

"Good night, *chérie.*"

I ended the call, thinking how much I loved that woman. Even if my trip to Australia ended with my finding out who my biological mother had been, I couldn't imagine anyone being more kind, understanding, and supportive than Ma. She had loved us girls with all her heart—which was more than my birth mother had obviously done, because unless Pa had grabbed me out of her arms, she had given me away. There was probably an explanation; maybe she'd been sick, or poor, and thought I was going to a better life with Pa Salt.

But . . . shouldn't the bond between mother and child be stronger than any of that?

I sat back down on the bed, wondering whether I even wanted to continue on this bizarre journey to actually *find* the people who had given me away. Like, maybe they didn't *want* me back. Yet Maia, Ally, and Star all seemed to have found new and happier lives because they'd followed their trails . . .

My mobile rang again and I saw it was Chrissie. As I answered, I wondered how she always seemed to be there just when I was feeling low.

"Hi, CeCe? Did you go to the museum today?"

"Yeah."

"Find out anything?"

"Quite a bit, but I'm not sure what it's got to do with me yet."

"Like to meet up later? I spoke to my grandma and she'd really like to meet you."

"Sure."

"So how about I swing past your hotel at three, and take you off to see her?"

"That sounds good, Chrissie, as long as it's no bother."

"No bother at all. Bye, CeCe."

I was just tucking my mobile into my shorts pocket when it rang again and I saw it was Star.

"Hi." Star sounded a bit breathless. "You okay?"

"Yup. Fine. You?"

"Yes, good. Listen, Cee, I thought I should warn you that I had a phone call today. From a newspaper."

"What?"

"I'm not sure how they got my number, but they asked me if I knew where you were. I said I didn't, of course."

"Jesus," I muttered, suddenly feeling as hunted as Ace had. "I really don't know anything, Sia."

"I believe you, darling Cee, of course I do. I just wanted you to know that they have your full name. Do you know how?"

"I bet it's that Jay bloke on Railay—the one who fancied you, remember? He's an ex-journalist and I reckon it was him who sold the photo to the papers. He's mates with Jack at the Railay Beach Hotel and they have all our details—phone numbers, addresses, and stuff—from when we checked in. And it was Jack's girlfriend who told me Jay had recognized Ace. She's the receptionist there. Jay probably bribed her to have a look through her paperwork."

I heard a sudden chuckle from the other end of the line.

"What's so funny?"

"Nothing. I mean, there has to be a funny side to all this, doesn't there? Only *you* could end up on the front page of every newspaper with the most wanted man in the banking world and not even know who he was!"

I heard her giggle again, and suddenly she sounded like the old Star. "Yeah, I bet Electra's really jealous," I chuckled.

"I'm sure she is. She's probably on the phone to her PR people right now. It's hard to get one front page, let alone all of them. Oh, Cee . . ."

Star continued to laugh and in the end I joined her, because the whole situation was so crazy and ridiculous; I ended up clutching my sides while I had an attack of the "terrics," as we used to call it in our shared baby language.

Eventually, we both calmed down and I drew in some deep breaths before I could speak again.

"I really liked him," I wailed. "He was a genuinely nice guy."

"I could see from the picture that you did. It was in your eyes. You looked really happy. I love your hair, by the way, and that top you were wearing."

"Thanks, but none of it matters now because he hates me. He thinks I was the one who told the media where he was, because the photo was on my camera roll. The security guard had it developed for me and I even gave Ace a set as a leaving present. Like I was rubbing his nose in it or something."

"Oh, that's terrible, Cee. You must be devastated."

"Yeah, I am, but what can I do?"

"Tell him it wasn't you?"

"He'd never believe me. Really, Sia, he wasn't at all like the papers describe him."

"Do you think he did it?"

"Maybe, but something doesn't add up."

"Well, if it makes you feel any better, Mouse says he's convinced that Ace is just a fall guy. Someone else at the bank must have known what was going on."

"Right," I said, not knowing whether to be happy or sad that her boyfriend "Mouse" was on my side, given he'd played a big part in the trouble between me and Star in the first place.

"Look, if there's anything we can do this end to help, please call."

Her use of the word "we" grated on me further. "Thanks. I will."

"Keep safe, darling Cee. I love you."

"I love you too. Bye."

I ended the call, and having felt so much better when the two of us had been laughing like the old days, I now felt depressed by the fact that one word had reminded me how much had changed. Star had her Mouse, whose arms held her tightly every night. She had ended her journey into the past and begun her future, while I was nowhere near doing either.

At three o'clock on the dot, Chrissie arrived in reception. Despite the heat, she was wearing a pair of faded jeans and a tight-fitting T-shirt, with a red bandana holding her curls back from her face.

"G'day, CeCe, ready to hit the frog—I mean, hit the road?"

I got on the back of her moped, and we set off. I recognized the airport as we drove parallel with the runway and then turned some sharp corners until we reached a dusty road that had tin-roofed shacks set back from the track. It wasn't a shantytown, but it was obvious that the people who lived inside the huts didn't have any spare cash to beautify their homes.

"This is it." Chrissie drew the bike to a halt and held it steady for me as I climbed off. "I'm warning you that my grandma might seem a bit weird to you, but I promise that she's not crazy. Ready?"

"Ready."

Chrissie led me up a path through what was technically a front garden but looked more like a sitting room. There was a worn brown sofa, various wooden chairs, and a lounger that had a pillow and a sheet on it, like someone had been sleeping there.

"Hi, Mimi," Chrissie called to a spot behind the sofa. As I followed her around it, I saw a tiny woman sitting cross-legged on the ground. Her skin was the color of dark chocolate and her face was crisscrossed with hundreds of lines. She was the oldest person I'd ever seen, yet around her forehead she wore a trendy bandana just like her granddaughter.

"Mimi, *ngaji mingan*? This is Celaeno, the girl I was telling you about," Chrissie said to her.

The old woman looked up at me and I saw her eyes were amazingly bright and clear, like a young girl had been put inside an ancient person's skin by mistake. They reminded me of two hazelnuts sitting in pools of white milk.

"*Mijala juyu*," she said, and I stood there awkwardly, having no idea what she'd just said. She patted the ground beside her and I sat down next to her, confused by the empty sofa and the chairs.

"Why is she sitting on the ground?" I asked Chrissie.

"Because she wants to feel the earth beneath her."

"Right."

I could feel the old woman's eyes still on me as if she were scanning my soul. She reached out a gnarled hand to stroke my cheek, her skin on mine feeling surprisingly soft. Then she pulled on one of my curls and smiled. I saw she had a big gap between her two front teeth.

"You knowum Dreamtime story of the Gumanyba?" she said in halting English.

"No . . ." I looked back at her blankly.

"She's talking about the Seven Sisters, Cee. That's what they're called in our language," Chrissie interpreted.

"Oh. Yeah, I do. My dad told me all about them."

"They our *kantrimen*, Celaeno."

"That means our relatives," Chrissie put in.

"We family, one people from same *kantri*."

"Right."

"I'll explain what she means another time," whispered Chrissie.

"All begin in the Dreamtime," the old lady began.

"What did?"

"The Seven Sisters story," said Chrissie. "She'll tell it to you now."

And, with Chrissie translating, I listened to the story.

Apparently, the Seven Sisters would fly down from their place in the sky and land on a high hill, which was hollow inside, like a cave. There was a secret passageway that led inside it, and it meant that the sisters could come and go between the heavens and the earth without being seen. While they were down here with us, they'd live in the cave. One day, when they were out hunting for food, an old man saw them, but they were too busy with their hunting and didn't notice him. He decided to follow them, because he wanted a young woman as his wife. When they rested by a creek, he jumped out and grabbed the youngest sister. The others ran back to their cave in a panic, then went along the secret passage and flew back up to the top of the hill and into the sky, leaving the poor youngest sister trying to escape from the old man.

When I heard this, I thought it was really mean of the others to leave her behind.

Anyway, the youngest sister did manage to escape and ran back to the cave. Realizing the rest had already flown away and knowing the old man was still chasing her, she too climbed up the secret passageway and flew off after the rest of her sisters. Apparently this was why the youngest sister—who I'd thought was called Merope, but the old woman called something else—couldn't often be seen, because she had lost her way back to her "country."

When the old woman had finished talking, she sank into a deep silence, her eyes still on me.

"What's really weird," I said to Chrissie eventually, "is that there are only six of us sisters, as Pa never brought home a seventh."

"In our culture, everything is a mirror of up there," Chrissie replied.

"I think the old man your granny talked about must be Orion, who Pa told us about in the Greek stories."

"Probably," she said. "There's a heap of legends about the sisters from different traditions, but this is ours."

How can these stories from all over the world be so similar? I thought suddenly. I mean, when they were originally told all those thousands of years ago, it wasn't like the Greeks could send an e-mail to the Aboriginal people, or the Mayans in Mexico could talk on the phone to the Japanese. Could there actually be a bigger link between heaven and earth than I'd thought?

Maybe there was something *mystical*, as Tiggy would say, about us sisters being named after the famous ones in the sky, and the seventh being missing . . .

"Where you-um from?" the old woman asked me, and I switched back to reality.

"I don't know. I was adopted."

"You-um from here." She picked up what looked like a long pole with markings on it and banged it onto the hard dusty earth. "You *kantrimen*."

"Family," Chrissie reminded me, then turned to her granny. "I knew the second I saw her that a part of her was."

"Most important part: heart. Soul." The old woman thumped her chest, her hazelnut eyes full of warmth. She reached out her hand and squeezed mine with unexpected strength. "You come home. Belong here."

As she continued to hold my hand, I suddenly felt dizzy and on the verge of tears. Maybe Chrissie noticed, because she stood up and gently helped me to standing.

"We have to go now, Mimi, 'cause CeCe's got an appointment."

I nodded at Chrissie gratefully, holding on to her arm for support far more than I wanted to. "Yeah, I have. Thanks so much for telling me the story."

"Tellum you much more. Come back," the woman encouraged me.

"I will," I promised, thinking her accent was the strangest I'd ever heard—she said her few English words in a broad Australian way, but rounded them off with extra consonants, which softened them. "Bye."

"*Galiya*, Celaeno." She waved at me as Chrissie led me off along the garden/sitting room toward her moped.

"Wanna go grab a drink? There's a servo just around the corner."

"Yeah, that would be great," I replied, having no idea what a "servo" was, but not ready to get back on the wobbly moped just yet.

It turned out to be a petrol station with a small general store attached. We both bought a Coke and went to sit on a bench outside.

"Sorry about my grandma. She's really . . . intense."

"Don't be sorry. It was so interesting. It just made me feel odd, that's all. Hearing all about this"—I searched for the word—"*culture* that I might belong to. I knew very little about it before I came here."

"No need to feel bad. Why would you know, Cee? You were adopted and taken to Europe when you were a baby. Besides, the oldies want to make sure their stories are told, especially in our culture. It's all passed on by word of mouth, see? From generation to generation. Nothing's ever written down."

"You're saying that there's no . . . Bible, or Qur'an, with all the stories and rules and stuff written in it?"

"Nothing. In fact, we get really hacked off if people do write it down. It's all spoken, *and* painted a lot too. Cee." She glanced at my stunned expression. "You look really fazed, what's up?"

"It's just that, well . . ." I gulped, feeling everything was getting weirder by the second. "I'm really dyslexic, so I can't read properly even though I've had the best education my father could give me. The letters just jump around in front of my eyes, but I'm, well, an artist."

"You are?" It was Chrissie's turn to look stunned.

"Yeah."

"Then why didn't you tell me before? That's just ripper! 'Specially as you might be related to Namatjira!"

"I'm nothing special, Chrissie . . ."

"All artists are special. And don't worry, I'm more aural and visual as well. Maybe it's just in our genes."

"Maybe. Chrissie, can I ask you something?"

"Course you can, anything."

"I know I'm gonna sound like an idiot as usual, but is there . . . prejudice against the Aboriginal people in Australia?"

Chrissie turned her pretty face toward me and nodded slowly. "Too right, mate, but that's not for now, sitting outside a servo drinking a Coke. I mean, you talk to any whitefella and they'll tell you there isn't. At least they're not murdering us by the thousands and stealing our land—they stole that a couple of hundred years ago and still haven't given most of it back. Every January, the whitefellas celebrate 'Australia Day,' the day a fleet of British ships arrived to 'claim' our country. We call it 'Invasion Day,' 'cause it's the day that the genocide of our people began. We've been here for fifty thousand years, and they did their best to destroy us and our way of life. Anyway," she added with a shrug, "it's old news, but I'll tell you more another time."

"Okay," I said. I didn't want to ask what "genocide" meant, but it sounded really bad.

"Does it freak you out?" she asked me after a pause. "Like, realizing that you're one of us, or that part of you is, anyway?"

"No. I've always been different. An outsider, you know?"

"I do." She put a warm hand on my arm. "Right, let's get you back to your hotel."

After Chrissie had dropped me off and told me to call if I needed anything, I went into my room and fell onto the bed. For the first time I could ever remember, I went to sleep immediately where I lay.

When I woke up, I cracked open one eye to look at the time on my mobile. It was past eight o'clock in the evening, which meant that I'd slept for three hours straight. Maybe the info overload of the past two days had had the same effect as a sleeping pill: My brain knew I couldn't cope, so it switched me off. Or maybe, just maybe . . . it was some kind of deep relief that already, by gathering the guts to come here, I was finding out who I really was.

You come home . . .

Even if I believed I had, did I want to be labeled by what had been my gene pool but no part of my upbringing? I stood up and went for a pee, then looked at my flat nose in the mirror, and knew it was the nose of both the old woman and my new friend Chrissie. They certainly had a deep sense of themselves and pride in their culture, and maybe that was what I needed: some pride. I might not have belonged to Star anymore—I'd learned the hard way that you could never *own* anyone. But just maybe, I could belong to both myself *and* a culture that defined me.

In the wider world, I was a loser, but today, sitting with Chrissie and her granny, they had seen my heritage as a strength. In other words, I had people in my corner who understood, because they were like me too. My . . . *kantrimen.* Family.

I went back to the bedroom feeling energized. I decided I'd call Chrissie and see if she could tell me more about Aboriginal culture. When I picked up my mobile, I saw I had twelve new text messages and several voice mails.

The first two texts were from Star:

So great to speak and laugh last night. You know where I am if you need me. Love you, S xxx

Me again, more newspapers called! DON'T ANSWER YOUR PHONE!!

Then . . .

This is a message for CeCe D'Aplièse. Hi. My name's Katie Coombe. I'm a journalist at the *Daily Mail*. I'd like to interview you about your relationship with Anand Changrok. Call me on my mobile anytime to give your side of the story.

And another . . .

This is a text for CeCe D'Aplièse from the BBC1 news desk in London. We'd like to talk to you about Anand Changrok. Please call Matt at the number below. Thanks.

And another . . .

Hi, is this CeCe's mobile number? I'm Angie from the *News of the World*. Let's talk terms for a full interview with you.

And so on, and so on . . .

"Shit!" The journos were obviously on my tail. With Ace locked up and under police and court protection, there was nothing they could get from him, so they were coming to me. For one moment, I considered calling Wormwood Scrubs to ask if I could speak to Ace and ask him if there was anything he wanted me to say to the media on his behalf.

Stop being an idiot, Cee, I told myself. *He wouldn't trust you to get him a mango shake from a beach café . . .*

Linda knows the truth, he'd said to me once.

So, who was Linda? A girlfriend? Or maybe a wife, although in the papers, there hadn't been any mention of his having a partner. Apart from me, of course, but as one of the tabloids had called me his "girlfriend du jour," they were obviously labeling me as one of a heap that had gone before.

Still, some gut instinct told me I should be doing something for him. After all, he'd helped me when I'd needed it. The question was, what? And how?

There was one thing I could do . . .

I pulled the SIM card from my mobile, then checked on the handset address book that all the numbers I needed were stored there. I took the SIM card to the toilet, wrapped it in a piece of toilet paper, and threw it into the bowl. Then I flushed it, hard. Feeling satisfied that no one could trace me now, I left the room, walked down the road to a corner shop, and bought a local SIM card. I texted Star and Ma with the new number. My mobile rang thirty seconds later.

"Hi, Sia," I said.

"I was just checking it was working."

"It is, but it's pay-as-you-go and the lady in the shop says I have to pay for calls coming in from abroad, so I've probably got about thirty seconds left on my twenty dollars."

"It was a good idea to bin your SIM card. I've had another load of calls today. Mouse said that if they're clever, they can probably trace you through the airline record too, so—"

Star was abruptly cut off and I saw a text banner appear across the top of my phone telling me my credit had run out.

"This is getting ridiculous," I groaned as I walked back down the street to the hotel. I wasn't James Bond, or even Pussy Galore, or whatever she'd been called.

"Hi, Miss D'Aplièse," the receptionist greeted me. "Have you decided how much longer you'll be staying yet?"

"No."

"Well, just let me know when you have." I noticed the receptionist studying me intensely. "You haven't stayed here before, have you? Your face looks familiar."

"No, never," I replied, trying to keep my voice steady. "Thanks, bye," I said, and plodded back upstairs to my room.

The frogs were still giving their evening chorus beyond my open window. I switched on the overhead light in my room and saw the CD player sitting on the nightstand, reminding me that I should listen to some more of Kitty's story, as I needed distraction. I lay down on the bed, loaded new batteries into the machine, and stuck in the second disc. Putting on my headphones, I lay back, pressed "play," and closed my eyes to find out what happened to Kitty Mercer next.

KITTY

Broome, Western Australia

October 1907

14

Kitty stirred as Andrew kissed her on the forehead.

"I'm off down to the quay," he said. "A lugger is due in the next hour or so, and I want to look at the haul and make sure that none of those damned Koepangers have any pearls hidden about their sly and devious persons. Rest well today, won't you, my dear?"

"I will." Kitty looked at her husband, dressed as always in his smart pearling master's uniform: a gleaming white suit with a mandarin collar and mother-of-pearl buttons, topped with a white pith helmet. She knew that when he returned home for lunch, the suit would inevitably be covered in red dust and he would have to change before he went out again. Here in Broome it was constantly laundry day, but rather than having to sweat over pots of hot water herself, the suits were folded up by her maid and sent off to Singapore to be laundered when the biweekly steamer next returned.

It was only one of the many eccentricities in Broome that she had quickly been forced to accept now that she was no longer a minister's daughter, but the wife of a wealthy pearling master.

She had boarded the coastal steamer *Paroo* in Fremantle with Andrew soon after their marriage and after some rough days at sea, the shoreline had finally emerged in the distance. Kitty had seen a flat, yellow beach and a collection of tin-roofed houses tightly packed together. The ship had moored at a jetty almost a mile long, the dark brown water lapping up its wooden supports. Dense mangrove forest hugged the shore, behind which was a row of corrugated-iron sheds. The infamous pearling luggers sat forefront in the bay, their masts clustered together against the broad, bright blue sky.

Having left the ship, she and Andrew had been driven by pony and trap through the tiny enclave of the town and Kitty had been less than encouraged. With the arrival of the steamships and luggers came a raucous influx of people filling the bars and hotels along Dampier Terrace—the town's main street—with piano music, rough voices, and cigar smoke. Kitty had been reminded of the Wild West of America that she had read about. It was as hot as she could possibly imagine, and the smell of unwashed bodies permeated the humid, windless air.

The tin-roofed bungalow, which her father-in-law had built without any thought other than providing a temporary roof over his and Edith's heads while he established his pearling business, had been less than enticing. Andrew had promised to provide Kitty with a more comfortable home, and building works had been completed only a couple of months ago.

Seven months after her arrival, Kitty was slowly becoming accustomed to this strange, isolated town, hemmed in on one side by the sea, and the vast red desert on the other. The few houses along the dusty and often flooded Robinson Street, where the wealthy white population mostly resided, stood only a few minutes from the overcrowded shantytown. Broome had not one elegant or gracious bone in its vibrant multicultural mix, yet it was the epicenter of the world's pearling industry. If she was driven into town by Fred, her Aboriginal groom, she would encounter a mishmash of different races who had come off the day's ships and were looking for ways to find entertainment. Money flowed like water here, and there were plenty of establishments that were happy to lap it up. Yamasaki and Mise stocked a selection of wonderful Japanese treasures, as well as soft silks that could be transformed into beautiful ball gowns to be flaunted by the pearling masters' wives during the ball season.

Kitty struggled upright in bed, her back aching from the weight of her engorged belly, and only thanked the Lord that the baby would be here in less than three months. Dr. Blick, whom Kitty had watched drink the whiskey bottle dry when she had met him at various social engagements, had assured her of the best of care when the time came. After all, Andrew—or, at least, his father—owned the largest pearling business in Broome, with a fleet of thirty-six luggers that carried hundreds of tons of shell into harbor each year.

When she'd first arrived, the phrases that Andrew often used, such as "luggers," "lay-ups," and "shell grades," had all been foreign to her, but as he spoke of little else when they were having dinner together in the evenings, her mind had slowly assimilated the workings of the business.

The Mercer Pearling Company had endured a difficult start to the season, when a lugger and all the crew upon it had been lost to a cyclone. She had quickly learned that out here, human life was fragile and eminently replaceable. It was a fact she was still struggling to come to terms with. The cruelty and harshness of life in Broome—especially the treatment of the local Aboriginal population—was something she knew she could never fully accept.

She had been horrified the first time she had seen a group of Aboriginal men in chains, shackled together at their necks and overseen by a guard with a rifle as they cleared debris from a house that had recently been destroyed by a cyclone. Andrew had pulled her away as she had begun to weep in horror.

"You don't understand the ways of Broome yet, my dear," Andrew had comforted her. "It is for their own good. In this way, they can be productive to society."

"In chains?" Kitty had been shaking with latent fury. "Denied their freedom?"

"It is a humane method. They can still walk a good way in them. Please, darling, calm down."

Kitty had listened helplessly as Andrew had explained that those in charge believed that the "blacks" would run back to the desert the minute they had the chance. So they chained them to each other, and attached them to a tree overnight.

"It is cruel, Andrew. Can you not see that?"

"At least if they work, they are given tobacco or sacks of flour to take home to their families."

"Yet not a living wage?" she'd entreated him.

"That isn't what they need, my dear. These people would sell their own wives and children at the drop of a hat. They are like wild animals, and sadly, they have to be treated as such."

After weeks of dispute between them on the subject, Kitty and Andrew had simply agreed to disagree. She was convinced that, with kindness and understanding and some respect for the fact that these people had been in Australia for far longer than the white settlers, some more gentle accord could surely be reached. Andrew assured her it had been tried before and had failed miserably.

Yet the knowledge that this inequality was wrong gnawed away at her conscience. She had even had to ask for special dispensation from the police constable to keep Fred on the premises at night, as he would otherwise be rounded up with the rest and herded back to a camp outside of town, away from his white "masters."

That situation, plus the sickeningly regular loss of life in the overcrowded shantytown and upon the ocean, was the price every person in Broome had to pay for the far-higher-than-average wages. And, for a scant few, there was the ultimate prize: that of finding the perfect pearl.

Naively, Kitty had presumed that every shell would contain one, but she had been wrong. The industry mainly survived on the mother-of-pearl linings. Hidden inside the ugly mottled brown shells that blended into the seabed was a lustrous material that sold by the ton around the world, to be used as decoration for combs, boxes, and buttons.

Only rarely would a triumphant captain present the pearl box to the pearling master with a rattle. And inside the box—which could not be opened once the pearl had been dropped inside it, as only the pearling master himself held the key—there would be a treasure of possibly huge value. Kitty knew that Andrew dreamed every night of finding the most magnificent pearl which would make him not only rich, but famous too. A pearl that would establish *him*—rather than his father—as the chief pearling master of Broome. And, therefore, the world.

There had been a number of occasions when he had arrived home with a pearl the size of a large marble, his eyes shining with excitement as he had shown her the often oddly shaped jewel. Then it had been off to T. B. Ellies's shop on Carnarvon Street to see if Andrew's find was good. T. B. was renowned as the most skilled pearl skinner in the world.

Like diamonds, pearls had to be crafted and polished to reveal their true beauty. Kitty had been intrigued when she'd learned that pearls were made up of thin layers, like those of an onion. T. B.'s skill lay in his ability to file away each imperfect layer without damaging the sheen on the one below it. She had watched T. B. hold a pearl to the light, as if his keen brown eyes could look through to its very core. His sensitive fingers then felt for minuscule ridges as he used his files and knives to erase them, squinting through his jeweler's eyeglass.

"It is merely oyster spit," he had said matter-of-factly as Kitty had watched him work. "The animal feels an irritation—a grain of sand perhaps—and builds up layers of spit around it to cushion itself. And behold, the most beautiful mineral is created. But sometimes . . ." Here he had frowned before shaving away another sliver. "Sometimes the layers protect nothing but a pocket of mud." He'd held up the pearl for Kitty and Andrew to see, and indeed, a small spot of brown was seeping out of a hole. Andrew had barely withheld a groan as T. B. continued working. "A blister pearl. Shame. Will make a nice hat pin, perhaps." The corner of his mouth lifted into a wry smile under his mustache as he resumed his work.

Kitty privately wondered if the quiet Singalese man knew that he wielded more power than anyone in Broome. He was the dream-maker—in his unassuming wood-fronted shop, he could carefully skin fine layers of pearl to reveal a majestic life-changing jewel, or turn hope to a pile of pearl dust on his workbench.

Broome was a unique and intense microuniverse all of its own, one that encompassed every soul that lived there. And Kitty herself was now another cog in the machine, playing the role of a dutiful pearling master's wife.

"One day, my dear," Andrew had said as he held her in his arms after another disappointment in T. B.'s shop, "I will bring you the most magnificent pearl. And you will wear it for all to see."

Kitty fingered the rope of small delicate pearls Andrew had chosen and had strung together for her. Apart from his obsession with finding such a special treasure, nothing was too much trouble to please her; Kitty had learned not to voice her dreams, otherwise Andrew would go to the greatest lengths to fulfill them. He had filled the house with beautiful antique furniture bought from the boats that docked in Broome from all over Asia. She had once expressed a love of roses, and a week later, he had taken her hand and led her to the veranda to show her the rosebushes that had been planted around it before she woke.

On their wedding night, he had been gentle and courteous with her. While the act itself was something that Kitty subjugated herself to rather than actively enjoyed, it had certainly not been unbearable. Andrew had perhaps been more thrilled than she the moment she'd announced her pregnancy to him five months ago, when the child had been little more than the size of a pearl inside her. Andrew had already told her how his "son" would follow in his father's footsteps to Immanuel College in Adelaide, and then on to the university there. A week later, Kitty had taken delivery of a beautifully carved mahogany bassinet and countless toys.

"What a dichotomy Broome is," she sighed as she heaved herself from the bed and reached for her silk robe. Ninety-nine percent of the town lived in appalling conditions, yet anything the richer residents wished for could be delivered to this tiny isolated outpost in the space of a few weeks.

Kitty picked up and shook out her house slippers thoroughly, having learned that spiders and cockroaches liked to hide in their cozy interiors. She threw them down on the floor and squeezed her swollen feet inside them. Used to being active, as her belly grew she'd refused to confine herself to the house, knowing she would go mad with boredom if she did so.

Over breakfast, she made a list of all the things she needed to buy in town. Before her pregnancy, she would always walk the ten minutes to Dampier Terrace and its array of stores, which sold everything from caviar brought in from Russia to succulent beef freshly slaughtered at the Hylands Star butchery. They ate well and plentifully, with a choice and quality far superior to what was available in Leith. Tarik, their Malay cook, had introduced her to curries, which, to her surprise, Kitty had found wonderfully tasty.

After pinning on her sunbonnet, she picked up her basket and parasol, then walked around the side of the house to the stables, where Fred lay sleeping on the straw. She clapped her hands and he was alert and upright within seconds. He smiled at her, one of his front teeth missing, which Kitty had learned was common in Aboriginal males and had something to do with a ritual.

"Town?" She pointed toward it, as Fred's grasp of English was basic at best. He spoke the language of the Yawuru tribe that was indigenous to Broome.

"Go alonga town," he agreed as Kitty watched him hitch the pony to the cart, relieved that he was actually here. Fred was apt to disappear to, as he put it, "go walkabout, Missus Boss." As with the missing tooth, Kitty had learned that most Aboriginals did this, disappearing for weeks into the untamed and dangerous hinterland beyond the town. Initially she had been horrified when she had realized that Fred slept on a pallet of straw in the stables.

"Darling, the blacks don't want to live inside. Even if we built him a shelter, he'd sleep outside it. The moon and the stars are the roof over the Aboriginal's head."

Nevertheless, Kitty had felt uncomfortable about the arrangement and while their own house was being renovated, she had insisted Andrew build some basic accommodation with washing facilities, a bed, and a small kitchen area which Fred could use as he chose. So far, Fred had not chosen to avail himself of the facilities. Even though she made sure his uniform was freshly laundered, she could still smell him at a few paces.

Kitty accepted Fred's help to climb up onto the cart and sat next to him, enjoying the slight breeze on her face as the pony clopped along into town. She only wished she could speak with Fred, *understand* him and the ways of his people, but even though she had tried to help him improve his English, Fred remained distinctly uninterested.

Once they had reached Dampier Terrace, Kitty raised her hand and said, "Stop!" Fred helped her climb down.

"I stayum here?"

"Yes." Kitty gave him a smile and walked off in the direction of the butcher's.

Having completed her shopping for supper that night, then stopped to chat with Mrs. Norman, the wife of another pearling master, she emerged into the bright sunlight. Feeling rather faint in the cloying heat, she turned up a narrow alley that offered comparative shade as she fanned herself. She was just about to walk back to the pony and cart when she heard a low keening coming from the opposite side of the alley.

Walking toward a pile of discarded rubbish, thinking that perhaps it was shrouding an injured animal, she removed a stinking crate and saw a human curled up into a ball behind it. The skin color told her it was an Aboriginal, and the outline of the figure said it was female.

"Hello?"

There was no response, so Kitty bent down and reached out a hand to touch the ebony skin. The human ball flinched and unraveled itself to reveal a young woman staring at her with terror in her eyes.

"I do-a nothing wrong, missus . . ."

The girl shrank farther back into the pile of stinking rubbish. As she did so, Kitty noticed the large bulge of her stomach.

"I know. I'm not here to hurt you. Do you speak English?"

"Yessum, missus. Speaka bit."

"What has happened to you? I can see that we're in the same . . . condition." Kitty indicated her own bump.

"You an' me have baby, but best I die. Will go away. Life here no-a good for us, missus."

With great effort, Kitty knelt down. "Don't be afraid. I want to help you." She risked reaching out a hand again to touch the girl and this time, she didn't flinch. "Where are you from?"

"Come-a from big house. Big fella boss, he saw"—the girl patted her stomach—"no home for me no more."

"Well now, you are to stay here. I have a pony and cart along the road. I will take you to my home to help you. Do you understand?"

"Leavum me, missus. Me bad news."

"No. I am taking you to my home. I have somewhere you can stay. You are not in danger."

"Best I die," the girl repeated, as tears squeezed out of her closed eyes.

Kitty raised herself to standing, wondering what on earth she could do to persuade the girl she spoke true. She unclipped the pearl necklace that nestled at her throat, then bent down and put it into the girl's hands, thinking that if she was a "bad un," the girl would be long gone by the time she returned, but if not . . .

"Look after this for me while I go and get the cart. I trust you, as you must trust me."

Kitty walked at pace to find Fred and have him move the cart to the entrance of the narrow alley. She indicated that he should climb down and follow her. To her relief, the girl was still there, sitting upright with the string of pearls clasped tightly in her hands.

"Now then, Fred, can you help this girl into the cart?" Kitty both spoke and mimed the words.

Fred looked at his mistress in disbelief. She watched as he eyed the girl and she eyed him back.

"Do as I say, Fred, please!"

There then began a conversation in Yawuru, as Fred took it upon himself to grill the girl who was sitting in the rubbish and holding

Missus Boss's pearls. At times it became quite heated, but in the end Fred nodded.

"She okay, Missus Boss."

"Then hurry up and help her into the cart."

Fred tentatively reached out his hand, but the girl refused it. Slowly and proudly she staggered to her feet by herself.

"I do-a the walkin'," she said as she passed Kitty, her head held high.

"Where puttum her?" Fred asked.

"It's best if she lies in the back, and we put the tarpaulin over her."

Once Kitty had organized this arrangement, Fred helped her to climb onto the front of the cart with him.

"Now then, take us home, Fred."

When they arrived, Kitty fetched clean sheets for the hut that Fred never used and helped the girl—who by this time could hardly stand—onto the mattress. Fetching some witch hazel, she bathed a swelling around the girl's eye, spotting more bruises on her cheek and her chin as she did so.

Leaving a pitcher of water beside the bed, Kitty smiled down at her.

"Sleep now. You're safe here," she enunciated.

"No one come-a beat me?"

"No one." Kitty showed her the big iron key in the lock. "I go out," she said, gesticulating, "then you lock the door. You are safe. Understand?"

"Yessum, understand."

"I will bring you some soup later," she said as she opened the door.

"Why-a you so kind, missus?"

"Because you are a human being. Sleep now." Kitty closed the door gently behind her.

That evening, having given Camira—for that was what the girl had said her name was—some broth, Kitty had opened a good bottle of red wine to accompany Andrew's supper. Once he had drunk two large glasses, she broached the subject of the young girl currently residing in their hut.

"She told me she was a maid at a house on Herbert Street. When her condition became obvious, they threw her out. She was also very badly beaten."

"Do you know who her master is?" asked Andrew.

"No, she wouldn't tell me."

"I'm not surprised," he said, taking another slug of his wine. "She damn well knows we could go to him and find out the real story."

"Andrew, I believe she *is* telling us the real story. No one wants a pregnant maid. The chances are, she was raped." Kitty said the word without a second thought. Such incidents here in Broome were commonplace, with drunken sailors hungry for "black velvet," as Aboriginal women were termed.

"You can't know that."

"No, I can't, but I can tell you that the girl told me she'd been educated at the Christian mission in Beagle Bay and she can speak relatively good English. She is certainly no whore."

Andrew sat back in his chair and looked at her in disbelief. "Are we to house and feed a pregnant Aboriginal girl on our property? Good God! When we are out she could creep into the house and steal everything we own!"

"And if she does, we have the money to replace it. Besides, I don't believe she will. Andrew, for God's sake, the girl is pregnant! She is expecting new life. Was I, as a Christian woman, meant to leave her there in the gutter?"

"No, of course not, but you must understand that—"

"I have been here now for seven months, and there is nothing about this town that I don't understand. Please, Andrew, you must trust me. I do not believe the girl will steal from us, and if she does, I take full responsibility for it. She is almost certainly nearer to her time than I. Shall we have the death of two souls on our conscience?"

"And I can tell you that the minute she has given birth, she'll be on her way."

"Andrew, please." Kitty put her fingers to her brow. "I understand your reticence, but I also know how easy it is in a place like this to become hardened to the plight of others. Imagine if I were in her shoes . . ."

"All right," he said eventually, nodding. "Your condition has made you vulnerable to seeing others less fortunate than yourself in the same position. She can stay, at least for the night," he added.

"Thank you! Thank you, my darling." Kitty rose and went to him, placing her arms about his shoulders.

"But don't say I didn't warn you. She'll be gone tomorrow with everything she can carry," he said, always needing to have the last word.

The following morning, Kitty knocked on the door of the hut and found Camira pacing the room like a claustrophobic dingo.

"Good morning, I have brought you some breakfast."

"You keepa me here?" Camira pointed at the door.

"No, I told you that the key is in the lock. You are free to leave whenever you wish."

The girl stared at her, studying her expression.

"I free-a go now?"

"Yes, if you wish." Kitty opened the door wide and used her hand to indicate the path.

Silently, Camira walked through it. Kitty watched as she hesitated on the threshold, looking left and right, and at Fred, who was chewing tobacco as he made an attempt at grooming the pony. She stepped outside and walked tentatively across the red earth, her senses alert for sudden attack. When none came, she continued, walking toward the drive that led onto the road. Kitty left the hut and made her way back into the house.

Watching from the drawing room window, she saw Camira's small figure recede into the distance. A sigh escaped her as she realized that Andrew had probably been right. Her baby kicked suddenly inside her, and she walked into the drawing room to sit down. The heat today was oppressive.

An hour passed, but just as she was about to give up hope, she saw Camira walking toward the house, then hesitating for a second before making her way back up the drive. After waiting for another ten minutes, Kitty walked over to the hut, taking with her a glass of cool lemonade that Tarik had just made, with ice shaved from the newly delivered block.

The door to the hut was ajar, but still, she knocked on it.

Camira opened it and Kitty noticed that everything on the breakfast tray she'd taken in earlier had been eaten.

"I brought you this. It's full of goodness for the baby."

"Thank you, missus." Camira took the lemonade from Kitty and sipped it tentatively, as if it might be poisoned. Then she drank the lot down in one. "No keepa me prisoner?"

"Of course not," Kitty said briskly. "I want to help you."

"Why you wanta help me, missus? No whitefellas wanta."

"Because . . ." Kitty searched for the simplest answer. "We are both the same." She indicated her stomach. "How long were you at the mission?"

"Ten years. Teacha fella say I good student." A small expression of pride passed through Camira's dark eyes. "I knowa German too."

"Do you now? My husband speaks it, but I do not."

"Whattum you want, missus?"

Kitty was about to say "nothing," but then realized that Camira currently could not grasp the concept of kindness from a "whitefella."

"Well, for a start, if you stay here, perhaps you could teach Fred some English."

Camira wrinkled her nose. "He-a smell. No wash."

"Maybe you can teach him to do that too."

"Me be-a teacha, boss?"

"Yes. And also"—Kitty thought on her feet—"I am looking for a nursemaid to help when the baby comes."

"I knowa 'bout babies. I takem care in mission."

"That's settled then. You stay here"—she indicated the hut—"and we give you food in return for help."

Camira's serious face studied Kitty's. "No locka the door."

"No locka the door. Here." Kitty handed her the key. "Deal?"

Finally, a glimmer of a smile came to Camira's face. "Deal."

"So, did your little black bolt off with everything she could steal when your back was turned?" asked Andrew when he returned for lunch.

"No, she went for a walk and then came back. Can you believe that she speaks some German, as well as English? And she has been brought up a Christian."

"I doubt it goes any farther than skin-deep. So what will you do with her?"

"She tells me she took care of the babies brought to the mission.

I have suggested that in return for helping me with the new baby and teaching Fred some basic English, she can stay in the hut."

"But, Kitty, my dear, the girl is pregnant! Chances are, it's a white man's child. And you know the rules on half castes."

"Andrew!" Kitty slammed her knife and fork onto her plate. "Camira can be no older than me! What would you have me do with her? Toss her back out into the rubbish where I found her? And as for the rules . . . they are cruel and barbaric. Tearing a mother away from her baby . . ."

"It's for their own protection, darling. The government is doing their best to make sure these children do not die in the gutter. They wish to round them up and teach them Christian ways."

"I cannot begin to imagine how I would feel if *our* child was physically snatched from my grasp." Kitty was shaking now. "And why, when we can at least help one of them, would we refuse to do so? It is nothing less than our Christian duty. Excuse me, I find myself . . . unwell." Kitty rose, then walked to the bedroom and lay down, her heart pounding.

She knew all about the rules for half-caste children, had seen the henchmen of the local Protectorate doing the rounds of Broome in a cart, seeking out any baby or child whose lighter skin would give the game away immediately. Then she'd hear the sound of keening mothers as the babies and children were dumped on the cart to be taken away to a mission orphanage, where their Aboriginal heritage would be drummed out of them, and replaced by a God who apparently believed it was better to have Him than to grow up with a mother's love.

Some minutes later, there was a knock at the door and Andrew walked in. He came to sit beside her on the bed and took her hand.

"How are you feeling?"

"I am a little faint, that is all. It is very close today."

Andrew took a muslin cloth from the pile on the nightstand and dipped it in the pitcher of water. He folded it across her brow. "You are nearing your time too, darling. If it pleases you to help a mother in similar circumstances, then who am I to deny you? She can stay, at least until she has had the child. Then we shall . . . take a view."

Kitty knew he meant "see what color the baby is," but this was no time to be churlish.

"Thank you, my darling. You are so kind to me."

"No, you are the one who is kind. I've been in Broome for too long.

And perhaps I *have* become inured to the suffering around us. It takes a fresh pair of eyes to see it anew. However, I have a position and a reputation to uphold. I—and you—cannot be seen to flout the law. Do you understand, Kitty?"

"I do."

"So, when do I meet your little black?"

Kitty gritted her teeth at his words. "Her name is Camira. I shall have a couple of dresses made up for her. She has only the clothes she stands up in, and they are filthy."

"I'd burn them if I were you. God knows where they've been, but we shall no doubt find out soon enough anyway. If she was working as a maid, we will know her former employers. Now." Andrew kissed her gently on the forehead and stood up. "I must go into town. I have an appointment with T. B. The *Edith* has brought in a particularly good haul and there are a couple of pearls I want him to skin. One of them may be very special." Andrew's eyes glinted with pleasure and avarice.

Do we not have enough already? Kitty thought with a sigh as Andrew left the room.

She knew the real god in *this* town—and his name was Money.

15

In January, as the barometer on the drawing room wall plummeted, indicating the start of the wet season, Kitty woke up with sweat dripping from her brow. She was due any day and she prayed to the Lord it would happen soon. The humidity hung like a soupy, airless blanket and she dug deep to breathe. Too exhausted to rise, she lay there wishing for both a storm and her water to break. She rang the bell to indicate to the kitchen that she wanted breakfast. These past few days she had been in bed, unable to countenance the thought of putting on her corset—albeit one specially made for her condition—plus the numerous petticoats, plus a dress on top of that. It was easier to lie here in her nightgown, her belly unrestricted and her skin comparatively cool.

Her thoughts turned again to Camira, and Kitty bit her lip hard in frustration. It had all been going so well; even Andrew had said what a bright little thing she was after he'd asked her a few questions in German. Since the "deal" had been wrought between the two women, and as Camira had realized she would be neither locked up nor taken away in the night to the local prison for misdemeanors unknown, she had proved herself willing and eager to help in any way she could. Whoever had formerly employed her had taught her well. Soon she was busy about the house, tutting at what she obviously thought was the tardiness of the maid, a sloe-eyed Singalese girl called Medha, who spent more time looking at her face in the mirror than actually cleaning it.

Kitty concealed her amusement as Camira took control, issuing orders for the floors to be swept at least three times a day to remove the interminable dust, and scrubbed every other. The mahogany furniture gleamed from layers of beeswax, and the cobwebs that had ingratiated themselves into high corners were swept away along with their inhabitants. As Camira bobbed about the drawing room as lightly as a butterfly, Kitty watched from her writing bureau, where she could hardly raise the energy to pick up her fountain pen. Even though Camira was almost certainly farther on in her pregnancy than she, it did not seem to affect her.

Ten days ago, Kitty had even discussed with Andrew the idea of getting rid of Medha and having Camira take over.

"Let's just wait and see what happens after her baby is born. No point in doing anything hasty. If she ups and leaves, we're high and dry at a moment when you will need all the help you can get."

And then the following day, as if Camira had heard Andrew's words, Kitty had gone to the hut and found it deserted.

"Fred, where is Camira?" she'd asked him as she stepped outside.

"She gone."

"Did she say where?"

"No, Missus Boss. Gone," Fred had informed her.

"I did warn you, darling. These blacks just don't play by the same set of rules as we do," Andrew had said later. "Good job we didn't sack Medha."

Kitty had felt intense irritation at Andrew's obvious satisfaction that he'd been right all along. Every day since Camira's disappearance, Kitty had gone to the hut and found it as deserted as the day before. And given the fact she had promised Andrew not to advertise Camira's presence in their home, Kitty could not ask around the town to find out if anyone had seen her.

"She go walkabout, missus," was all Fred would say.

Apart from her anger that Camira had left without so much as a by-your-leave, especially after her kindness to the girl, Kitty missed her. She had discovered that Camira had a very good grasp of English and a wicked sense of humor. She had found herself chuckling over small things for the first time since she had arrived in Broome, and had almost felt that Camira—despite their vast cultural differences—was a kindred spirit. As Kitty's time had drawn nearer, she had felt comforted by the girl's calm, capable manner.

"Don' ya be worryin', Missus Boss, I singa your baby into the world, no problem."

And Kitty *had* believed her, and had relaxed and smiled until even Andrew had noticed the difference and been glad that Camira was there.

A tear dribbled out of one of Kitty's eyes. She would not make the same mistake again.

There was a short knock on the door. Kitty roused herself into a sitting position as it opened.

"Mornin', Missus Boss, I bringa you breakfast. Medha, she still sleepin' on the job."

Kitty watched in total shock as Camira—a newly slim Camira—dressed immaculately in her white uniform, with a headband holding back her glossy raven curls, danced toward her with the tray. "Tarik tellum me you bin naughty girl an' not eatin' your food good. I make-a you egg and bringa you milk for baby," she chirped as she placed the breakfast tray across Kitty's thighs.

"Where . . . ?" Kitty swallowed, trying to find the words. "Where have you *been*?"

"I go walkabout, havem baby." She shrugged as though she'd just been down to the bakery to buy a loaf of bread. "She come good an' easy. Women sayum she pretty an' healthy. Eat a lot, though." Camira rolled her eyes and indicated her breasts. "No sleepa for me."

"Why on earth didn't you tell me where you were going, Camira?" Anger was beginning to replace relief at the sight of her. "I've been worried sick!"

"No worry, Missus Boss. Easy. She poppum out like snail from shell!"

"That is not what I meant, Camira. Although of course I am happy that you and your baby are well and healthy."

"You come alonga hut after breakfast and I showa baby to you. Me helpum you eat?" Camira proffered the spoon after she'd expertly sliced the top off the boiled egg with a knife.

"No, thank you. I'm quite capable of feeding myself."

As Kitty ate the egg, Camira bustled around the room, putting things straight and complaining about the layer of red dust that had gathered on the floor since she was last there. Kitty realized that she would probably never know where the girl had gone. She felt only relief that Camira's labor was over and envied her incredible recovery from it.

Later that morning Kitty followed Camira to the hut, where the girl carefully unlocked the door. There on the floor, in a drawer that Camira had taken out of the chest, was a tiny infant, squalling with all its might.

"Tolda you she a hungry one," said Camira as she plucked the child up, sat down on the bed, and promptly undid the loops that held the buttons on the front of her blouse. Kitty saw the huge engorged breast, the nipple now dripping with milky fluid as Camira arranged the baby upon it. The squawking stopped instantly as the baby suckled, and Kitty's eyes were glued to the process. She had never seen another woman's breasts—her own baby would be bottle-fed by a nurse as breastfeeding was considered only for savages. And yet, as Kitty watched mother and baby joined in such a natural ritual, she decided it had a beauty all of its own.

When the baby's lips finally released the nipple and its head lolled back against Camira's chest, the girl swiftly arranged it over her shoulder and began to rub its back vigorously. The baby burped and Camira gave a nod of approval.

"Holdum her?" She proffered the baby toward Kitty.

"It's a little girl, you said?"

"Her name is Alkina—it meanum 'moon.'"

Kitty took the naked baby in her arms and caressed the soft, perfect skin. There was no doubt that, in comparison to her mother, Alkina was of a lighter hue. The baby suddenly opened its eyes and stared right at her.

"Goodness! They are . . ."

"Women saya yella," said Camira as she fastened up her blouse. "From a yella man in Japtown. He bad fella."

Kitty stared down at the telltale signs of a heritage that had blessed this baby girl with the most gorgeous pair of eyes she had ever seen. They were an arresting amber shade that was almost gold, and their almond shape made them appear even larger in the tiny face.

"Welcome to the world, Alkina, and God bless you," Kitty whispered into a miniature ear.

Perhaps it was her fancy, but the baby seemed to smile at her words. Then she closed her incredible eyes and slept peacefully in Kitty's arms.

"She is beautiful, Camira," Kitty breathed eventually. "Her eyes remind me of a cat."

"Women saya that too. So I callum 'Cat' as nickname," she giggled as she gently took the child from Kitty and tucked a piece of cloth around its bottom before tying it at both sides.

Someone once called me that too . . . , Kitty thought. Placing the baby back in her makeshift cradle, Camira brushed her daughter's forehead and whispered some unintelligible words against her skin. Then her eyes darkened and she put a finger to her lips. "Cat secret, yessum? Or bad baby fellas come take her. You understand?"

"I promise, Camira, Cat will be safe here with us. I will tell Fred to guard her when you are working in the house."

"He still smellum bad, but Fred good fella."

"Yes, Fred's a good fella," Kitty agreed.

Two weeks later, still no storm had broken and no baby of her own had appeared to ease Kitty's mounting discomfort. Andrew was not helping matters by sulking about the two pearls he'd entrusted to T. B. Ellies's skilled hands, only to watch them be whittled away to dust in front of him.

"It's simply not fair. Father is always asking me why the luggers never discover the treasures he used to when he was commanding them. Good grief, Kitty, when he first came to Broome, one could walk along Cable Beach and pluck them up by hand in the shallows! Does he not understand that the entire world has moved here since and is fishing for them? We are pushing into deeper and more dangerous waters every day. We lost another diver only last week due to the bends."

Kitty now knew the condition and the symptoms as thoroughly as she knew the common cold. She had been intrigued to catch a glimpse of a diver for the first time, a young Japanese man who was being fitted into a new diving suit that Andrew had ordered from England. The slight man had climbed into the enormous beige canvas suit and a heavy spherical bronze helmet had been lowered over his head and screwed on tightly at his collar. His feet were weighed down by leaden boots and his crewmates supported him as they checked that the airflow through the slim pipe was working correctly.

She'd shuddered at the thought of all those tons of water pressing down on the man's frame as he dived twenty fathoms below, protected only by flimsy canvas and the precious air that flowed through his lifeline. The intense pressure could severely damage the ears and joints, and if a diver persevered, it could lead to paralysis and death, a condition known as the bends.

"God rest his soul." Kitty crossed herself. "They are brave men."

"Who are paid a fortune to *be* brave," Andrew pointed out. "I've had another request to up their wages, and still I hear talk of this ridiculous 'no blacks' policy actually being implemented in Broome. Can you imagine whites ever signing up to do the job?"

"No," she replied, "but then no matter what their skin color, I cannot imagine anyone risking death every day simply to earn money."

"My dear, you have never known starvation, or the responsibility these men feel to earn as much for their families as they possibly can."

"You are right," she said quietly, irritated at how Andrew could encompass both avarice and morality in a few short sentences. She stood up. "I think I'll retire for a nap."

"Of course. Shall I send for Dr. Blick to call on you this evening?"

"I doubt he can tell me more than that the baby is not yet ready to make its entrance into the world, and I know that all too well."

"Mother told me that most first babies are late."

But most of their mothers are not living in Broome, with the wet season approaching, Kitty thought to herself as she nodded at him and left the room.

Camira woke her later that evening and placed a cup of something noxious smelling on her nightstand.

"Missus Boss, baby nottum come. Not good. We helpa little fella, yes?" She proffered the cup to Kitty. "My women drinkum this. Missus Boss, it is time."

"What's in it?"

"Natural. From the earth. No harm. Drinkum now."

And Kitty, desperate as she was, did as she was told.

The pains started a few hours later, and as Kitty rose to use the privy, a splash heralded the breaking of her water. Calling for Andrew, who was currently sleeping next door in his dressing room, Kitty walked back to the bedroom and lay down.

"The baby is coming," she told him as he arrived at the door.

"I will send for Dr. Blick immediately."

"And Camira," Kitty said, as a contraction surged through her. "I want Camira with me."

"I will get her now," Andrew promised as he dressed hurriedly and shot off.

Throughout that long feverish night, as the thunderclouds gathered above Broome, Kitty could remember little, apart from the pain and the soothing voice of Camira.

Dr. Blick had arrived—from the look of his rolling countenance, straight from a drinking den on Sheba Lane.

"What is a black doing in the birthing room?" he'd slurred to Andrew.

"Leave her!" Kitty had shouted as Camira hummed under her breath and rubbed Kitty's back.

Andrew shrugged his shoulders at the doctor and nodded. After a fast examination, Dr. Blick told her there was plenty of time to go and that she was to call if she needed him. Then he left the room. So it was Camira who encouraged her to stand up, to pace the floor "and walka the baby outta there, as I singa it here."

At four in the morning, the clouds finally burst and the rain started to pelt on the tin roof.

"He's-a coming, he's-a coming, Missus Boss, very soon now . . . dunna you worry."

And as the lightning flashed above them, illuminating the garden outside and Camira's trancelike expression, with a huge push and a crash of thunder, Kitty's baby arrived into the world.

Kitty lay there, unable to do anything but pant with relief that the pain was over. She raised her head to see her baby, but instead saw Camira between her legs, biting on something.

"What are you doing?" she whispered hoarsely.

"I'm-a settin' him free, Missus Boss. Here." She swept the baby up in her arms, turned it upside down on her palm, and slapped its bottom hard. At this indignity, the baby gave out a loud shriek and started to cry.

"Here now, Missus Boss. Holdum your baby. I get docta fella." Then she stroked Kitty's forehead. "He big strong boy. You clever woman."

And with that, she left the room.

Dr. Blick, who had obviously been sleeping off last night's entertainment in the drawing room, staggered through the door.

"Good Lord! That was a fast labor," he commented, as he tried to wrestle the baby out of Kitty's arms.

"He is well, doctor, and I wish him to stay with me."

"But I must check him over. It is a 'he'?"

"Yes, and he is perfect."

"Then I shall tidy you up down below."

She watched as Dr. Blick lifted the clean sheet that Camira had placed over her.

"Well now, I see there's no need." Dr. Blick had the grace to blush as he realized he'd slept through the entire event.

"Would you ask my husband to come in to see his son?"

"Of course, dear lady. I am glad for all that it was such a smooth and fast process."

Yes, it was, because Camira was here and you were not, thought Kitty.

As Andrew entered the bedroom, Kitty thanked all of the stars in the sky that Camira had returned to her.

Broome, Western Australia

December *1911*

16

"My dear, I need to discuss something with you," said Andrew, folding his copy of the *Northern Times* and putting it neatly by his breakfast plate.

"And what might that be?"

"Father wants me to sail to Singapore in the new year, and from there travel with him to Europe. He wishes me to meet his contacts in Germany, France, and London, because he has finally had enough of traveling and wants me to take over the sales side of the pearls too. We will be away for nearly three months. I had thought of asking you to accompany me, but it will be an arduous trip at that time of year when the seas are so rough. Especially for a child not yet four years old. I presume you wouldn't be prepared to leave Charlie behind with Camira?"

"Good Lord, no!" replied Kitty. Charlie was the sun in her morning and her moon at night. She missed him after an hour, let alone three months. "Are you sure he couldn't come with us?"

"As you know yourself, life onboard ship can be dull and unpleasant. We shall not be stopping at any port for longer than a day or two. I must be back by the end of March for the start of the new season."

"Then perhaps I could sail on from London with Charlie and travel up to Edinburgh? I would very much like my mother, and the rest of my family, to meet him. My new brother, Matthew, is almost five, and has never yet met his big sister."

"Darling, I promise that next year, when I am finally master of my own timetable, we shall travel back to Scotland together. Perhaps for Christmas?"

"Oh yes!" Kitty closed her eyes in pleasure.

"Then I could leave you both for a few weeks in Edinburgh while I conduct my business. But this year, with Father in tow, that is just not possible."

Kitty knew that Andrew meant his father did not want a young child tagging along with them. Equally, she knew from experience that Andrew would not stand up to him and insist. "Well, I cannot leave Charlie, and that is that."

"Then would you consider traveling to Adelaide with Charlie while I am gone? At least you would have the company—and security—of my mother and Alicia Hall?" Andrew suggested.

"No. I shall stay here. I have Camira and Fred to guard me, and three months is not that long."

"I don't like to think of you alone here, Kitty, especially during the wet season."

"Really, Andrew, we will be fine. I have all our friends to watch over me too. And now Dr. Suzuki has come to town and set up his new hospital, my health and Charlie's is assured," she added.

"Perhaps I should postpone the trip until next year, when we can travel together, but I am so eager to become autonomous, without feeling that Father is constantly looking over my shoulder."

"Darling, even though we will miss you, we are safe here, aren't we?" Kitty turned to Charlie, who was sitting between them, eating his egg and toast.

"Yes, Mama!" Charlie—a little blond angel with egg yolk and crumbs smeared on his face—banged his spoon on his plate.

"Hush, Charlie." Andrew took the spoon away from him. "Now, I must leave for the office. I will see you both at luncheon."

As he left, Camira arrived in the dining room to clean Charlie up and take him off to play in the garden with Cat. Fred had proved himself a useful carpenter and had erected a baby swing out of wood, which he had hung by two strong ropes to a boab tree. In fact, thought Kitty contentedly, Fred had changed almost beyond recognition. No longer did he smell, and due to Camira's tireless tutelage, he had slowly begun to grasp English.

The breakthrough in Fred and Camira's relationship had happened almost four years ago, just after Charlie's birth. Mrs. Jefford, the wife of one of the most powerful pearling masters in town, had decided to come calling to the house unannounced—an unusual event in itself, as these things were normally arranged at least a week before.

"I was just passing, Kitty dear, and realized that I had not yet paid my respects to you since your son was born. I was away in England, you see, visiting my family."

"It is most kind of you to think of us." Kitty had ushered her into the drawing room. "May I get you a glass of something cool to drink?" she'd asked as she watched Mrs. Jefford's beady eyes travel around the room.

"Yes, thank you. What a dear little place this is," she'd commented as Kitty signaled for Medha to bring in a jug of lemonade. "So . . . homey."

As Kitty had sat down, she'd glanced out of the window and seen Camira, her eyes full of fear, her hand signaling a cut throat. Mrs. Jefford had proceeded to tell Kitty about the treasures she'd recently acquired in her own home. "We believe that the vase may well be Ming," she'd tittered.

Kitty was used to the one-upmanship of the pearling masters' wives, who vied, it seemed, even harder than their husbands to claim the crown for the most successful pearler in Broome.

"Mr. Jefford was so lucky last year finding eight exquisite pearls, one of which he sold recently in Paris for a king's ransom. I'm sure that one day your husband will be equally successful, but of course he is still young and inexperienced. Mr. Jefford has learned the hard way that many of the valuable pearls never make it into his hands. And has devised ways and means to make sure that they do."

Kitty had wondered how long this eulogy to self and husband would last. When Mrs. Jefford had finally exhausted her list of recent extravagances, Kitty had asked her if she'd like to see baby Charlie.

"He's napping now, but I am sure I can wake him early. Just for once," she'd added.

"My dear, having had three of my own, I know how precious a sleeping baby is, so please do not do so on my account. Besides, Mrs. Donaldson told me recently that you have employed a black nursemaid to care for him?"

"I have, yes."

"Then I must warn you never to leave her alone with the child. The blacks have a price on white babies' heads, no less!"

"Really? Do they wish to put them in a pot and cook them?" Kitty had asked, straight-faced.

"Who knows, my dear!" Mrs. Jefford had shuddered. "But I repeat, they cannot be trusted. Only a few months ago, I had to sack my last maid, once it came to my attention that she was supplementing her income by whoring in the brothels in Japtown. And when I say it came to my attention, I mean that the girl was a good few months gone. She did her best to hide it from myself and Mr. Jefford, of course, but in the end, one could hardly fail to notice. When I said that her services were no longer required, she literally attacked me, begging me to forgive her and have her stay. I had to fight her off. Then she disappeared into the shantytown, never to be seen again."

"Really? How dreadful."

"It was." Mrs. Jefford studied Kitty's expression. "The child she was carrying is almost certainly a half caste, and as it will surely have been born now, it must be found and taken by the Protectorate to a mission."

"Goodness! What a tragic story." By now, Kitty had realized exactly why Mrs. Jefford had come to pay a visit.

"I will say that she was a good worker and I have missed her since, but as a Christian woman, I could not countenance an illegitimate child under my roof." Mrs. Jefford had thrown her a beady look.

"I am sure you could not. Oh, I believe I have just heard Charlie crying. Will you excuse me?" Rising from her chair, Kitty had walked as sedately as she could to the door. Closing it behind her, she had dashed into the kitchen, telling Medha to rouse Charlie for her, then grabbed the blacking from beside the range and hurried outside to the backyard. Entering the hut without knocking, Kitty had found Camira hiding under the bedstead, her baby girl clutched to her chest.

"Make baby black." Kitty had pushed the blacking toward her. "Fred your *husband*, understand?"

In the gloom, all Kitty could see was Camira's terrified eyes. "Understand," she'd whispered.

Then she had raced back to the kitchen, where Medha was holding a screaming Charlie. "Please bring a bottle through to the drawing room," Kitty had ordered as she'd grabbed the baby and walked back to Mrs. Jefford.

"Forgive me for taking so long. He had a full napkin," she'd said as Medha arrived with the bottle.

"Surely your nursemaid sees to that kind of thing?" Mrs. Jefford had probed.

"Of course, but Camira went to fetch some more muslin from the haberdashery, while her husband collected the ice from town on the cart. They have only just returned."

"What a handsome little chap," Mrs. Jefford commented as Charlie sucked away heartily on his bottle. "Did you say that the name of your nursemaid was Camira?"

"I did, and I feel very fortunate to have her. She was educated at Beagle Bay mission, where she cared for the babies in the nursery."

"Do you know," said Mrs. Jefford after a pause, "I am almost certain that Camira was the given name of the pregnant maid I had to let go. We called her 'Alice,' of course."

"Of course," Kitty had said. "I am still learning the way of these things."

"You say she is married?"

"Why, yes, to Fred, who has worked for both my father-in-law and my husband for years. He drives the trap, tends the ponies, and keeps the grounds under control. And oh, he is so very proud of his new baby daughter. Alkina arrived into the world just two weeks before Charlie. They are a devoted family, and study the Bible regularly," Kitty had thrown in for good measure.

"Well, well, I had no idea Alice had a husband."

"Then perhaps you would like to meet the happy family?"

"Yes, of course I would be . . . pleased to see Alice and her new child."

"Then come with me." Kitty had led Mrs. Jefford to the backyard.

"Fred? Camira?" Kitty's heart had pounded in her chest as she rapped on the door of the hut, having no idea whether Camira would have understood her instructions. To her utter relief, the "happy family"—Fred, Camira, and the baby, swaddled in her mother's arms—had appeared at the door of the hut.

"My dear friend Mrs. Jefford wanted to meet your husband and see your new baby," Kitty enunciated, trying to calm the fear in Camira's eyes. "Isn't the baby beautiful? I think she looks just like her father."

Camira nudged Fred and whispered something to him. To his credit, Fred folded his arms and nodded, just like a proud daddy.

"Now," Kitty had said, noticing the blacking smears on the baby's face were starting to smudge in the heat, "Fred, why don't you take Alkina while I pass Charlie to Camira to feed? I confess, I am quite exhausted!"

"Yessum, missus," Camira had squeaked. The exchange of babies ensued and Fred disappeared back inside the hut.

"Bless my soul!" Mrs. Jefford had said, fanning herself violently in the heat as they followed Camira back toward the house. "I had no idea that Alice was wed. They usually aren't, you see, and . . ."

"I understand completely, Mrs. Jefford." Kitty had placed a comforting arm upon hers, enjoying every moment of the woman's discomfort. "And it's so very thoughtful of you to take the trouble to visit me and Charlie."

"It was nothing, my dear. Now, I am afraid I must leave immediately as I have a game of bridge with Mrs. Donaldson. We must have you and Andrew to dine very soon. Good-bye."

Kitty had watched Mrs. Jefford hurrying along the front path toward her carriage. Then she'd walked into the kitchen, where Camira was sitting, visibly shaking, while she fed Charlie the rest of his bottle.

"She believed it! I . . ." Kitty had started to giggle, and then as Fred's desperate face had appeared at the kitchen door, holding out baby Cat like a ritual sacrifice, Kitty had let him in and taken the blackened baby from him.

"Missus Jefford thinkum Fred my husband?" The look of disgust on Camira's face made Kitty laugh even harder. "I notta marry a man who smellum bad like him."

Fred had beaten his chest. "I-a husband!"

And the three of them had laughed until their sides ached.

From that moment on, Fred had taken his fictitious duties seriously. When Camira was working inside the house looking after Charlie, Fred stood guard over Cat, as though the day Mrs. Jefford had visited had joined the three of them as a real family. He had started to wash and had smartened up considerably, and nowadays he and Camira bickered like an old married couple. It was obvious that Fred adored her, but Camira would have none of it.

"Notta right skins for each other, Missus Kitty." It had taken months of persuasion for Camira to call her mistress by her Christian name, rather than "boss."

Kitty had no idea what that meant or where Camira's religious allegiance actually lay: One moment she would be whispering to her "ancestors" up in the skies, and singing strange songs in her high, sweet voice if one of the children caught a fever. The next, she was sitting with Fred in the stable, reading him the Bible.

Since Mrs. Jefford's visit, there had been no threats from the local Protectorate. Camira was free to walk wherever she wished to in Broome, with Cat and Charlie nestled together in the perambulator. To the whites, she was now a married woman, under the protective banner of her "husband."

Kitty sat down to write a letter to her mother, and included a recent picture of herself with Andrew and Charlie that had been taken by the photographer in town. So far from her family, she found Christmas the most difficult time of year, especially as it came at the start of the "Big Wet," as Camira called it. She pondered the thought of Andrew going to Europe in January, and only wished she and Charlie could travel with him to visit her mother and sisters in Edinburgh, but she knew from experience that it was pointless to beg him again.

In the past four years, her husband had become further wedded to his business. Kitty read the tension on his face when a haul was coming in on a lugger, and the stress of disappointment later the same day when it revealed no treasure. Yet the business was doing well, he said, and his father was pleased with the way things were going. Only last month another lugger and crew had been added to their fleet. Kitty was just glad that she had Charlie to occupy her, for her husband's attention was constantly elsewhere. There was one thing he craved above all—the discovery of a perfect pearl.

"He is so driven," she said to herself as she sealed the envelope and put it on a pile for Camira to post later. "I only wish he could be content with what he has."

"I have written to Drummond," Andrew said over dinner that night, "and explained to him that you have insisted on staying in Broome while I am

in Europe. He's usually in Darwin in January, supervising the shipment
of his cattle to the overseas markets. I suggested that if that's the case, he
might look in on you once his business is completed."

Kitty's stomach did an immediate somersault at the mention of
Drummond's name. "As I have assured you, we will be fine. There's no
need to trouble your brother."

"It would do him good. He is yet to meet his nephew and living on
that godforsaken cattle station of his, I worry he is turning native, so
lacking is he for any civilized company."

"He is not yet married?"

"Chance would be a fine thing," Andrew snorted. "He's far too smitten
with his heads of cattle to find a wife."

"I am sure he is not," said Kitty, wondering why she was defending her
brother-in-law. She had neither seen him nor heard a word from him in
nigh on five years—not even a telegram to congratulate the two of them
on the birth of Charlie.

This, however, did not stop her from remembering how he'd kissed
her that New Year's Eve, especially as marital relations with her husband
had dwindled considerably. Often, Andrew would retire before she did,
and when she arrived in the bedroom he was already fast asleep, exhausted
from the stress of the day. Since Charlie's birth almost four years ago,
Kitty could count on the fingers of one hand the number of times he'd
reached for her and they'd made love.

The lack of a second child had been duly commented on by the
gossipy circle of pearling masters' wives. Kitty replied that she was
enjoying Charlie far too much to put herself through another pregnancy,
and besides, she was still young. The truth was that she longed for another
baby, yearned for the big family that she herself had been brought up in.
And also, if she was honest, the loving touch of a man . . .

"You are absolutely set on staying here rather than going to Alicia
Hall?" Andrew was asking her as Camira cleared the dinner plates from
the table.

"For the last time, darling, yes."

"Then I will confirm the trip with Father. And I promise you, Kitty,
that next year I will take you and Charlie back to visit your family." Andrew
rose and patted his wife's shoulder.

On the deck of the *Koombana* a month later, guilt and regret filled Andrew's eyes as he embraced his wife and child.

"*Auf wiedersehen, mein Kleiner. Pass auf deine Mutter auf, ja?*" Andrew set Charlie down as the *Koombana*'s bell rang out to warn all nonpassengers to leave the ship.

"Good-bye, Kitty. I'll send a telegram when we reach Fremantle. And I promise to arrive home with something extraordinary for you." He winked at her, then tapped his nose, as Kitty swept Charlie up into her arms.

"Take care of yourself, Andrew. Now, Charlie, say good-bye to your father."

"*Auf wiedersehen*, Papa," Charlie chirped. On Andrew's insistence, he had been spoken to in both English and German and switched between the two languages with ease.

After walking down the gangplank, Kitty and Charlie waited on the quay with a horde of well-wishers. The *Koombana*'s presence in Broome always saw its residents in festive mood. The ship was the pride of the Adelaide Steamship Company—the height of luxury and a feat of engineering, built with a flat bottom so that it could glide into Roebuck Bay even at low tide. The horn blew and the residents waved the *Koombana* on her way.

As Kitty and Charlie took the open-topped train along the mile-long pier back to the town, Kitty looked at the sparkling water beneath her. The day was so unbearably humid, she had an overwhelming urge to take off all her clothes and dive in.

Once again she thought how ridiculous the social rules on behavior were; as a white woman, the idea of swimming in the sea was one that could simply not be countenanced. She knew Camira often took Cat down to the gloriously soft sand and shallow waters of Cable Beach when the jellyfish weren't in, and had offered to take Charlie too. When Kitty had suggested it to Andrew, he had refused point-blank.

"Really, darling, sometimes you do have the most ridiculous notions! Our child, swimming with the blacks?"

"Please don't call them that! You know both their names very well. And given our child lives by the sea as both you and I did, surely he should be taught to swim? I'm sure you did at Glenelg."

"That was . . . different," Andrew had said, although Kitty had no idea why it was. "I'm sorry, Kitty, but on this one, I'm putting my foot down."

As Charlie slumbered against her shoulder, worn out from the heat and excitement, Kitty gave a small smile.

While the husband's away, the "Kat" can play . . .

The following day, Kitty asked Camira if there was perhaps a hidden cove where Charlie could splash in the water. Camira's eyebrows rose at her mistress's request, but she nodded.

"I knowa good place with no stingers."

That afternoon, Fred drove the pony and cart to the other side of the peninsula. For the first time since she'd arrived in Australia, Kitty felt the sheer bliss of dipping her feet into the gloriously cool waters of the Indian Ocean. Riddell Beach was not the vast sandy stretch that Cable Beach boasted, but it was infinitely more interesting, with its large red rock formations and tiny pools full of fish. With gentle encouragement from Camira, who had removed her blouse and skirt as innocently as a child, Charlie was soon screeching and splashing happily in the water with Cat. As Kitty paddled in the shallows, holding up her petticoats, she was sorely tempted to do the same.

Then Camira pointed up to the heavens and sniffed the air. "Storm a-coming. Time to go home."

Even though the sky looked perfectly clear to Kitty, she had learned to trust Camira's instincts. And sure enough, just as Fred steered the pony and cart into their drive, a rumble of thunder was heard, and the first raindrops of the approaching Big Wet began to fall. Kitty sighed as she took Charlie into the house, for as much as she'd longed for the blissful coolness of the air that would arrive with the storm, in less than a few minutes' time, the garden would be a river of red sludge.

The rain lasted all night and well into the next day, and Kitty did her best to amuse Charlie inside the house with books, paper, and coloring pencils.

"Play with Cat, Mama?" He looked up at her mournfully.

"Cat is with her own mama, Charlie. You can go and see her later."

Charlie pouted and his eyes filled with tears. "Wanna go now."

"Later!" she snapped at him.

Recently, Kitty had noticed how, no matter what exciting things she suggested the two of them do together, all Charlie wanted was to be with Cat. Certainly, Camira's daughter was an extraordinarily lovely little girl, with a gentle nature that calmed Kitty's more hyperactive son. There was no doubt that she was already a beauty, with her gorgeously soft skin the color of gleaming mahogany and her mesmeric amber eyes. She'd also realized in the past few months that Charlie was not just bilingual, but trilingual. Sometimes, she would hear the children playing together in the garden and talking in Cat's native Yawuru.

Kitty had said nothing about this to Andrew, but the fact that Charlie was clever enough to understand and speak three languages, when she herself sometimes struggled to find the right word in one, made her proud. Yet, as she watched Charlie peering out of the kitchen window, looking desperately for Cat, she wondered if she'd allowed Charlie to spend more time in her company than he should.

The rain finally stopped, although the red sludge had overwhelmed her precious roses, and, with Fred's help, she spent the next morning clearing the beds as best she could. That afternoon, knowing it was low tide and feeling it important to spend some time alone with her son, she drove Charlie on the cart to Gantheaume Point to show him the dinosaur footprint.

"Monsters!" said Charlie, as Kitty tried to explain that the enormous gouges in the rocks far beneath them were made by a giant foot. "Did God make 'em?"

"Did God make *them*, Charlie," she reprimanded him, realizing Cat and Camira's pidgin English was having an effect. "Yes, he did."

"When he makum the baby Jesus."

"Before he *made* the baby Jesus," said Kitty, knowing Charlie was far too young to try to grapple with such philosophical questions. As they headed back home, she mused that life only became more confusing when one viewed it through the eyes of an innocent child.

That evening, Kitty put Charlie to bed and read him a story, then, as Andrew wasn't there, she took her supper on a tray in the drawing room.

Picking up a book from the shelf, she heard another rumble of thunder outside and knew further rain was on its way and the Big Wet had begun in earnest. Settling down to read *Bleak House*, which served on all levels to cool her senses, she heard the rain begin to pour onto the tin roof. Andrew had promised that next year he would have it tiled, which would lessen the almighty clatter above them.

"Good evening, Mrs. Mercer."

Kitty almost jumped out of her skin. She turned around and saw Andrew, or at least, a half-drowned and red-sludge-spattered version of him, standing at the drawing room door.

"Darling!" she said as she rose and hurried toward him. "What on earth are you doing here?"

"I was desperate to see you, of course." He embraced her and she felt his soggy clothes dampening her own.

"But what about the voyage to Singapore? The trip to Europe? When did you decide to turn back?"

"Kitty, how good it feels to hold you in my arms once more. How I have missed you, my love."

It was something about the smell of him—musky, sensuous—that finally alerted her.

"Good grief! It's *you*!"

"You are right, Mrs. Mercer, it is indeed *me*. My brother asked me to come to see if you were well in his absence. And as I was passing by . . ."

"For pity's sake!" Kitty wrenched her body away from his. "Do you take pleasure in your joke? I believed you were Andrew!"

"And it was very lovely . . ."

"You should have announced yourself properly. Is it my fault that you look identical?!" Moved beyond rational thought at his impudence, Kitty slapped him sharply across the face. "I . . ." Then she sank into a chair, horrified at her actions. "Forgive me, Drummond, that was totally uncalled for," she apologized as she watched him rub his reddening cheek.

"Well, I've had worse, and I *will* forgive you. Although even I don't believe that Andrew calls you 'Mrs. Mercer' when he walks through the door, seeking his supper and his wife's company. But you are of course correct," he conceded. "I should have announced myself the minute I walked through the door, but—forgive my vanity—I thought that you would know me."

"I was hardly expecting you—"

"Surely Andrew told you that he'd invited me to pay a visit?"

"Yes, but not so soon after he'd left."

"I was already in Darwin when the telegram was sent on to me in December. I decided there was little point in going back to the cattle station, only to return and do as my brother had bidden me. Do you by any chance have any brandy? It sounds odd given the heat, but I actually find myself shivering."

Kitty saw the red rivulets dripping off him and forming a puddle on the floor. "Goodness, forgive me for having you stand there when you are soaked through and probably exhausted. I shall call my maid and have her fill the bathtub for you. Meanwhile, I shall find the brandy. Andrew keeps a bottle for guests somewhere."

"You are still teetotal then?"

He gave her a lopsided grin, and despite herself, Kitty smiled. "Of course." She took a glass and a bottle from a cupboard and did as Drummond had asked. "Now, I will get your bath filled."

"There is no need to call your maid. Just point me in the direction of the water and tub." He tossed the brandy back in one mouthful and then proffered the glass to her to be filled again.

"Are you hungry?" she asked him.

"I'm famished, and will gladly eat any fatted calf you have to hand. But first, I need to get out of these wet clothes."

Having led Drummond to Andrew's dressing room and shown him the pitchers with which to fill the tub, she went to the kitchen to put together a tray of bread, cheese, and soup left over from lunchtime.

Drummond entered the kitchen twenty minutes later with a towel wrapped around his waist. "All the clothes I have with me are filthy. May I borrow something of my brother's to wear?"

"Of course, take what you wish." Kitty could not help stealing a glance at his bare chest—the sinews taut across it, and the muscles lying beneath the deep tan of his shoulders that spoke of hard manual labor.

He arrived in the drawing room in Andrew's silk robe and slippers. He ate the soup silently and hungrily, then poured himself further brandy.

"Did you travel by boat between Darwin and Broome?" she asked politely.

"I traveled overland, part of the way on horseback. Then I happened upon the Ghan cameleers as they made camp on the banks of the Ord River. The river was swollen, so they were waiting until the water subsided enough for the camels to be safely hauled across on a line. Poor blighters, they're not keen on swimming. I continued my journey with them, which was far more entertaining than traveling alone. The stories those cameleers have to tell . . . and all the time in the world to tell them. It took many days to get here."

"I have heard that the desert beyond Broome is a dangerous place to be."

"It is indeed, but I'd imagine not nearly as deadly as the viperlike tongues of some of your female neighbors. Give me a black's spear or a snake any day, above the stultifying conversation of the colonial middle classes."

"You make our lives here sound very dull and pedestrian," Kitty said irritably. "Why do you always wish to patronize me?"

"Forgive me, Kitty. I understand that everything is relative. The fact that you sit here now, a woman alone and unprotected in a town thousands of miles from civilization, where murder and rape are commonplace, is a credit to your strength and bravery. Especially with a young child."

"I am not unprotected. I have Camira and Fred."

"And who might Camira and Fred be?"

"Fred takes care of the grounds and the horses, and Camira helps me in the house and with Charlie. She has a daughter of her own, of similar age to my son."

"I presume they are blacks?"

"I prefer not to use that term. They are Yawuru."

"Good for you. It is unusual to have such a family unit working for you."

"I wouldn't call them that, exactly. It's complicated."

"It always is," Drummond agreed, "but I am glad for you. Once such people are committed, they make the most loyal of servants and protectors. To be honest, I am astounded that my brother allowed you to employ such a couple."

"They aren't a couple."

"Whatever arrangement they have is unimportant. What *is* important is that Andrew overrode his prejudice and allowed them close. Now I am no longer so concerned about you being here in Broome alone. I admit to being horrified when I received the telegram. Why did my brother not take you with him?"

"He said it was a business trip and that Charlie would become restless aboard ship. He wanted me to go to Adelaide to stay with your mother, but I refused."

"You thought that option a fate worse than death, no doubt." Drummond raised an eyebrow and refilled his brandy glass. "I am sure that you have realized by now that the only thing that matters to Andrew is proving himself to Father. And, of course, becoming richer than him."

"These things matter to him, of course they do, as they matter to any man—"

"Not to me."

"To every other man, then." Kitty stifled her irritation as she watched Drummond drain his brandy glass yet again.

"Perhaps I have never known the pressure of being the eldest son of a rich man. I've often mused on the fact that those two short hours it took me to follow Andrew into the world were a godsend. I am happy to have him take the Mercer crown. As you may have realized, I am a lost cause, unfit for civilized society. Unlike Andrew, who is—and has always been—a stoic pillar of it."

"He is certainly a good husband to me and a caring father to Charlie. We want for nothing, I have no complaints."

"Well, I do." Drummond suddenly slammed his glass down onto the table. "I asked you to wait until I'd returned from Europe before you said yes to Andrew. And you didn't."

Kitty stared at him, outraged at his vanity. "Do you really believe I thought you were being serious? I didn't hear another word from you!"

"I was on a boat when my brother proposed. I hardly felt it appropriate to send a telegram asking him why his fiancée hadn't adhered to my wishes!"

"Drummond, you were drunk that night, as you are now!"

"Drunk or sober, what the hell is the difference?! You *knew* that I wanted you!"

"I knew nothing! Enough!" Kitty stood up, now shaking with anger. "I will not listen to this rubbish any longer. I am Andrew's wife. We have a child and a life together, and that is the end of it."

Silence fell between them; the only sound in the room was the rain rattling down on the roof above them.

"My apologies, Kitty. I have traveled a long way. I am exhausted and not used to civilized company. Perhaps I should go to bed."

"Perhaps you should."

Drummond stood up, swaying slightly. "Good night." He walked to the door, then turned around to look at her. "That New Year kiss is what I remember most of all. Don't you?"

With that, he left the room.

17

Kitty hardly slept that night, Drummond's words racing around her head like a swarm of flies feasting on a carcass.

"Please ignore anything I said, I was delirious from exhaustion and drink," he said at breakfast the next morning. Then he took Charlie into his arms and threw him high into the air, catching the laughing child and placing his chubby legs about his own broad shoulders.

"So, nephew of mine, we men must stick together. Show me what needs to be shown around here."

They promptly disappeared out of the drive, and were gone so long that Kitty was quite beside herself with worry when they eventually returned.

"Charlie has shown me the town," Drummond said, setting him onto his feet. Kitty noticed her son's face was filthy from chocolate and ice cream and God knew what else.

"I did, Mama, and everyone thought he was Papa! He lookum the same!"

"He does *look* the same, yes, Charlie."

"We fooled a few people, didn't we, Charlie?" Drummond laughed as he set about wiping the child's dirty mouth.

"We did, Uncle Drum."

"We might well be receiving some house calls from confused neighbors who believe that your husband has returned early from his travels. Personally, I can hardly wait." Drummond winked at Kitty.

Sure enough, in the days that followed, there was a stream of townsfolk beating a path to her door. Each time, Drummond greeted them politely, behaving like the perfect host. He was far more ebullient than his brother, joking with them gently about their mistake and charming all who met him. The end result was a flood of dinner invitations arriving through the letter box.

"Yet another one," Kitty said as she opened it. "And it's from the Jeffords! Truly, Drummond, we must refuse them all."

"Why? Am I not your brother-in-law? Let alone Charlie's uncle and my father's son? Have I not been invited here at the specific request of my twin brother?"

"You said only recently that a snakebite was less deadly than the viper tongue of a female neighbor. You will see such an event as sport, and however dull you may find our 'colonial middle-class' acquaintances, I do not wish you to offend them," Kitty retorted.

"I told you that I was drunk that evening. I remember nothing," he called after her as she stalked along the hallway and into the drawing room.

"What the matter, Missus Kitty? You lookum sad." Feather duster in hand, Camira surveyed her.

"Nothing, I think I must be tired."

"Mister Drum upset you?"

"No." Kitty sighed. "It's too complicated to explain."

"He likem light in sky; Mister Andrew dark, likem earth. Both good, jus' different."

Kitty thought how accurate Camira's assessment of the twins was.

"Charlie likem him, me an' Fred likem him. He good here now for us."

But not for me . . .

"Yes, it is good he is here. And you're right, Charlie seems to adore him."

"Mister Drum makem the life better for you, Missus Kitty. He funny fella."

Kitty stood up. "I think I'll take a nap, Camira. Could you mind Charlie whilst I do?"

Camira studied her suspiciously. "Yessum. I in charge of little fella."

Kitty went to lie down and wondered if she was sick. She certainly felt feverish, and despite her best intentions, the mere thought of Drummond's presence only a few feet away through a paper-thin wall had set her senses on fire. He hadn't said a single intimate word to her since the first night, and he'd confessed to being drunk then anyway . . .

Kitty rolled over to try to get comfortable and allow her tired mind some rest. Perhaps he really was here out of best intentions: minding his sister-in-law as his brother had asked him to do.

.

IN SINGAPORE STOP HEAR DRUMMOND WITH YOU STOP GLAD YOU
ARE NOT ALONE STOP BUSINESS GOING WELL STOP LOVE TO YOU AND
CHARLIE STOP ANDREW STOP

Kitty read the telegram over breakfast and groaned. Even her husband
seemed to think it was wonderful that Drummond was staying with them.
And so far, her guest was making no move to leave. Eventually, she'd had
no choice but to accept some of the dinner invitations, and subsequently,
they'd been out to dinner three times in the past week. Much to her surprise, Drummond had behaved impeccably on each occasion, charming
the wives and telling swashbuckling stories to their husbands of his life
in the outback. And, most important, staying sober throughout the entire
evening.

"*Do* come again to visit!" Mrs. Jefford had tittered as Drummond
had kissed her hand as they had said their good-byes. "Perhaps Sunday
luncheon next week?"

"Thank you, Mrs. Jefford, I will let you know if we're free, as soon as
I've consulted my diary," Kitty had replied politely.

"Do. It must be strange for you, having Drummond to stay. So like
your husband, but so much . . . *more*." Mrs. Jefford had blushed like a
young girl. "Good night, my dear."

It had been raining incessantly, but even so, Drummond had found
ways to entertain Charlie and Cat. They played hide and seek inside the
house, which rang with shrieks of excitement as the three of them tore
around it. A miniature cricket pitch was set up along the entrance hall—
Drummond professing horror that Andrew was yet to teach his son the
basic rules of the game. Fred had been commandeered to whittle some
stumps and a bat, and had, as Drummond said, done "a bloody good
job."

As the rain continued to beat down, the front door became pockmarked
by the ball Drummond had bought as a present for Charlie from the
general store, and Cat was corralled into being wicket keeper or fielder,

with Kitty keeping count of the runs and overs. By the end of the session, despite Kitty's careful scoring, Drummond always declared it a draw.

"House happy when he around," Camira announced one afternoon as she herded the overexcited children into the kitchen for tea. "When he leave, Missus Kitty?"

"I have absolutely no idea," she replied truthfully, not knowing whether she wished him to or not.

"When the rains stop, I suppose," said Drummond after Kitty asked him over supper the following evening.

"That could be weeks," Kitty responded, toying with the overcooked chicken on her plate. Tarik could still not judge how long to roast a bird.

"Is that a problem for you? If I am unwelcome here, I will go."

"No. It's not that . . ."

"Then what is it?" Drummond eyed her.

"Nothing. Perhaps I'm just tired tonight."

"Perhaps you find my presence uncomfortable. I've never seen you so tense. There was me, believing I was doing so well to behave in front of all your friends and doing my best to amuse Charlie and Cat—what an adorable child she is. Going to grow up to be a beauty too. Never mind my helping Fred keep the path free of sludge and—"

"*Stop!* Please, just stop." Kitty put her head into her hands.

"God's oath, Kat, what is it I've done?" Drummond looked at her, genuinely shocked at her distress. "Please tell me and I'll try to rectify it. I've even laid off the grog because I know you don't like it. I—"

"Don't you understand?!"

"What?"

"I don't know why you're here, or what you want! Whatever it is, I'm simply . . . exhausted!"

"I see," he sighed. "Forgive me. I had no idea that my presence here was upsetting you so much. I'll leave first thing tomorrow morning."

"Drummond." Kitty put her hand to her brow. "I did not ask you to leave tomorrow, I asked you when you *would* be leaving. Why does everything with you have to be a drama? Do you go to your bed at night thinking how you fooled everyone? Or is this the real you and the other

Drummond a pretense? Or perhaps it's nothing to do with any of us here, and even though you protest it isn't, it's because you can never change the fact that you were born two hours later than your brother and he has everything you want!"

"Enough!" Drummond slammed his fist on the table, starting a cacophony of china, glass, and cutlery tinkling in a surreal impression of an orchestra.

"Well? Which is it? What is the real reason you are here?" Kitty asked him again.

He was silent for a long time before he looked up at her.

"Isn't it obvious?"

"Not to me, no."

Drummond stood up and left the room, slamming the door behind him. She wondered if he'd gone to pack and would leave immediately. It was just the kind of dramatic gesture he was inclined to.

Within a few seconds, he was back, not with his luggage, but with a decanter.

"I brought a glass for you, but I'm presuming you don't want it."

"No, thank you. It is at least one lesson I can thank you for teaching me."

"There are no others?"

"Not that I can think of presently. Although I have learned to score at cricket, even if you always fix the result."

He smiled at that and took a sip of brandy. "Then at least I have achieved something. You are right, of course."

"About what? Please, Drummond," she entreated him, "no more riddles."

"Then I will tell you straight. You said a few moments ago that perhaps I secretly wanted everything my brother has. Well, you were right, because there was—and is—something I want very much. When I first met you that Christmas, I admired your spirit, and, yes, I found you attractive, but what man wouldn't? You're a beautiful woman. And then I watched my brother set his cap at you, and I admit now that the fact I could see how much he wanted you added to your allure. Brothers will be brothers, Kitty, and 'twas ever thus, especially with identical twins." Drummond took another gulp of his brandy. "However, if it began as a game, I apologize, for over that Christmas, I watched how you adapted to our ways, how you were so patient with my mother and my aunt, never once complaining about missing your family, and throwing yourself wholeheartedly into all that was presented to you. I will never forget you clambering onto that elephant with no care for your appearance or modesty. It was at that moment everything changed. For I saw through to your soul; saw it was free like mine, unfettered by convention. I saw a woman I could love."

Kitty concentrated hard on the contents of her water glass, not daring to raise her eyes to his.

"When I asked you to wait for me, I was in deadly earnest, but it was too little, too late. I knew it when I walked away, and I admit, if I had been you, I would have made the same decision. Two brothers, identical looking, one a drunkard and a joker and the other . . . well . . ." He shrugged. "You know who Andrew is. When the inevitable happened and I heard you were to marry my brother, I knew I had lost. Time passed and I lived my life, as we all do. Then I got the telegram from Andrew, asking me to call in to see you in Broome. I will shock you by confessing that I deliberated for many hours. Eventually, I decided it was best I came here to lay the ghost to rest and move on. I walked in here out of the rain, depleted and exhausted, took one look at you, and immediately knew that nothing had changed. If anything, as I've witnessed your strength and determination to make a life for you and your child in a hostile environment which most men—let alone women—would find daunting, my admiration and respect for you has increased. Put simply, my darling Kat, you are by far the most courageous, stubborn, intelligent, irritating, and gorgeous female I have ever had the misfortune to come across. And for some extraordinary reason that I cannot fathom, I love every bone in your beautiful goddamned body. So"—he raised his glass to her—"there you have it."

Kitty could hardly believe what she'd just heard, or dare to trust it. Every word he'd spoken mirrored her feelings exactly. Yet she knew she must reply pragmatically.

"I am your brother's wife and you have admitted you covet what he has. Are you sure that this *feeling* you say you have for me is not to do with that?"

"Good Lord! I have just put my heart on the plate in front of you, so I'd ask you to refrain from cutting it up into small pieces with your sharp tongue. However, it matters not whether you believe me, but whether I believe myself. You asked me why I was still here and I have told you the truth: I am yours for the taking. If you wish me to leave, then I will."

"Of course you may stay. Why, my husband himself invited you. Please, ignore my strange mood tonight. It's probably something I ate."

He searched her face to find the truth, but she pushed it down deep inside.

I will not be like my father . . .

"I am tired, Drummond. If you'll excuse me, I'm retiring to bed. Good night."

She felt his eyes on her as she walked to the door.

"Good night, Mrs. Mercer," he said.

As the Big Wet took hold of Broome, the streets became flooded and impassable. The shops along Dampier Terrace were shored up with sandbags and Fred valiantly waded through the sludge to fetch provisions. Kitty looked out of a window and saw that her precious garden was now buried under a river of red mud. Tears came to her eyes as she thought of the love she had put into trying to re-create a small slice of home.

The fact they were housebound made the situation with Drummond even more tense. Even if he wished to leave, with the weather as it was, he had little choice but to stay put. After several long days, during which Kitty thought she might go mad with frustration and desire, the rains finally stopped, and all of them emerged like blinking moles into the bright sunlight. Within minutes, Charlie and Cat were knee-deep in the red soupy earth, shouting and screaming as they splattered it on each other's faces and bodies.

The air felt fresher and cooler, but an unpleasant odor of sewage hung in it like an afterthought.

"We'd better be careful, this is cholera season. Scrub the children thoroughly, won't you, Camira?" she said, hauling Charlie out of the mud.

"Yessum, Missus Kitty. Bad time for big sick after rains stop."

Sure enough, word soon came that five cases of cholera had been brought to Dr. Suzuki's hospital, and subsequently, many more were reported.

"At least it's confined to the shantytown for now," Drummond comforted her after he'd taken a stroll into town to stretch his legs. "No white cases reported so far."

But soon there were, and having escaped from their homes, the residents' doors were once again shut tight, this time against a deadly plague.

Fred was the first one down in the Mercer household, and lay delirious on his straw pallet in the stables. Kitty was surprised when Camira insisted on caring for him herself rather than allowing him to be taken to hospital.

"He bin good to me an' I dun trust those docta fellas," she said firmly.

"Of course," Kitty said, knowing that Aboriginals were the last priority for hospital care. She clasped Camira's hands. "You must let me know what I can do to help."

As she retreated to the house, Kitty's heart pounded as she thought of the amount of contact Fred had with Charlie on a daily basis.

"Try not to worry. The Aboriginals have a far lower resistance to cholera than we do. Our Western illnesses came to Australia with us and slew the natives in their thousands," Drummond said.

"As horrific as that is, it's a comfort to me for Charlie's sake." She gave him a weak smile. "I'm glad you're here."

"Well now, that's the first positive thing you've said to me in days. My pleasure, ma'am." Drummond gave a mock bow.

While Fred sweated his way through the following two nights, Camira reported that she "dun know if he make it" and scurried back to the hut with noxious-smelling concoctions from the kitchen.

"How say you we take the kids on the cart to the beach?" Drummond suggested.

"Surely not?"

"Riddell Beach is well away from the town. And I think a breath of fresh air will do us all good," he added.

Kitty was as desperate as he to leave the house, so she packed up a small picnic and they set off, Drummond taking the longer way around to avoid going through the town.

Kitty sat on the soft sand as Drummond removed his clothes and went into the water in a pair of long johns.

"Sorry, but it has to be done," he teased her. "Come on, kids, race you to the water!"

She watched Charlie and Cat shouting and screaming as Drummond played with them in the shallows. She was glad to be out of the oppressive atmosphere of the house, but was disturbed by the facsimile of a family outing with a man who was not cowed by the rules of society, who looked like Andrew, but was not Andrew. A man who knew how to laugh, and live in the moment.

And yes, Kitty confessed to herself finally, she wished with all her heart that things were different.

When they arrived back home, Camira was already in the kitchen, her face full of relief. "Fred be fine now."

"Thank God," Kitty said as she gave Camira a hug. "Right, let's get these children into the tub and think about supper."

In the small hours of the night, Kitty felt sick and feverish. Then her stomach began to cramp and she only just made it to the privy, which was where Camira found her the following morning, collapsed on the floor.

"Mister Drum! Come-a quick!"

Perhaps she dreamed Camira screaming at Drummond, "Nottum hospital, Mister Drum! Many people sick! Go gettum medicines, we takem care of Missus Kitty here."

She opened her eyes to see Andrew's face—or maybe it was Drummond's—urging her to sip some salty liquid that made her gag, then vomit, and noticed that a foul, acidic smell hung permanently in the air.

Gentle hands washed her down with cool water as her stomach contracted again and again. She dreamed then of floating off to join Camira's ancestors who lived in the sky, or maybe God himself . . . Once, she opened her eyes and there was an angel, shimmering white in front of her, offering her a hand. A beautiful high-pitched voice was singing in her ear.

It would be nice, she thought with a smile, *to be free of the pain.*

Then another figure appeared in front of the angel, telling her, "Fight, my darling Kitty. Don't leave me now, I love you, I love you . . ."

She must have slept again, for when she opened her eyes, she could see small horizontal chinks of light appearing from behind the shutters.

"Why did no one close the curtains?" she murmured. "I always close them. Helps keep out the heat . . ."

"Well, Your Majesty, please do forgive my tardiness. I've had other things on my mind just recently."

Drummond stood over her, his hands clasped to his waist. He looked dreadful: pale and haggard, with dark purple rings visible under his eyes.

"Welcome back to the land of the living," he said to her.

"I dreamed an angel came to take me up to the heavens . . ."

"I'm sure you did. We nearly lost you, Kitty. I thought you were giving up. However, it looks to me like God didn't want you yet, and sent you back."

"Perhaps there is a God after all," she whispered as she tried to sit up, but then she felt horribly dizzy and lay back down on the pillows.

"Now, *that* is a conversation we'll have another time, after I've taken a nap. You seem lucid—up to a point—and you haven't messed the bed for a whole twelve hours," Drummond declared.

"Messed the bed?!" Kitty closed her eyes and used what little energy she had to turn away from him, full of horror and embarrassment.

"Cholera is a messy disease. Don't worry, I left the room when you and the sheets were changed. Camira did all that. Although I admit that if you had died, I was about to go to the police station and insist they arrest her for the murder of her mistress. When I tried to take you to the hospital, she fought like a tiger to restrain me. She's convinced that 'whitefella' hospitals are full of disease, which, in truth, they probably are. If you don't die of your own bacteria in an epidemic, you're likely to die of your neighbor's. In the end, she wore me down and I agreed, God help me."

"An angel was in here, I swear . . ."

"Are you delirious again, Kitty? I do hope not." Drummond raised an eyebrow. "Well, I will leave you to your talk of angels and go and tell Nurse Camira that you are alive and could be very well soon."

Kitty watched him as he walked toward the door. "Thank you," she managed to utter.

"My pleasure, ma'am. Always here to serve."

"I *did* see an angel," she insisted as, exhausted from the conversation, she closed her eyes and slept again.

"Mister Drum withum you night an' day. Neva left your side. Only when I change you an' dem stinkin' sheets." Camira wrinkled her nose. "He good whitefella, he listen to me when I tellum no hospital."

Kitty, who was sitting up in bed and doing her best to sip the watery, salty soup on the tray in front of her, studied Camira's dreamy expression. She realized her nursemaid and helpmeet had completely fallen under the spell of "Mister Drum" too.

"He lovem you, Missus Kitty." She nodded firmly.

"Of course he doesn't! Or at least"—Kitty tried to soften her gut reaction to Camira's words—"he loves me like any brother-in-law should."

Camira rolled her eyes in disagreement. "You lucky woman, Missus Kitty. Most fellas not good like-a him. Now, you eat an' gettum strong for your boy."

Two days later, Kitty felt confident enough to see Charlie without the sight of her terrifying him.

"Mama! Are you better?" he said as he ran into her arms and she felt the sheer life force in him.

"Much better, Charlie darling. And oh, so very glad to see you."

"Papa said he would come home when Uncle Drum telegraphed him to say you were sick."

Instinctively, Kitty's stomach turned over, just as it had during the worst of her recent illness. "Did he? That is very kind of him."

"Yes, but then you got well, so Uncle Drum went back to the telegraph office to tell Papa, so he isn't coming back."

"You must be disappointed, Charlie."

"Yes, but we have Uncle Drum to take care of us, and he looks exactly the same, but he's funnier and plays cricket and swims with us. Why won't Papa swim with us?"

"Maybe he will if we ask him nicely."

"He won't, 'cause he's always busy with work." Charlie kissed her wetly on her cheek as his chubby hands went around her neck. "I'm glad you didn't die. Me and Cat are going to help Fred build a hut in the garden."

"What hut?"

"Our own house. We can live in it together and maybe eat our supper there sometimes." Charlie's eyes pleaded with his mother. "Can we?"

"Sometimes, maybe," Kitty agreed, too exhausted to argue.

"And one day, we'll get married like you and Papa. Good-bye, Mama. Eat your soup and get strong."

Kitty watched him as he walked stoutly across the room. Even in the past few days, he seemed to have grown, in terms of both maturity and stature.

Although there was nothing wrong with childhood games, Kitty wondered once more whether she had made a mistake by entrusting Camira with so much of Charlie's care, but all that was for another time. Kitty concentrated on finishing her soup.

The following morning, she insisted she was well enough to take a bath and dress. Food was still a problem—it made her feel nauseated every time she looked at it—but she did her best to eat. Charlie and Cat were busy in the garden with Fred, who was sawing and nailing their play hut together.

"He's a good man," Drummond commented over breakfast. "You've treated him and Camira with respect, and they've repaid you tenfold."

"You're a good man too. Thank you for caring for me while I was sick. I don't know what I'd have done if you hadn't been here."

"My pleasure, or, at least, my duty. I couldn't have you die under my watch, could I? My brother would never have forgiven me. The good news is that it seems the epidemic is over in town, though Dr. Suzuki has told me they've lost a dozen souls at the hospital and you can probably triple that in the shantytown. Sadly, Mrs. Jefford was one of them."

"How tragic. I must write immediately to her husband."

"Death makes saints of us all, doesn't it?" Drummond gave her a wry smile. "Anyway, now you're well and the weather has improved, I'll probably make tracks in the next day or so."

"Surely there's more rain to come?"

"Perhaps, but I don't want to be under your feet any longer."

"Please stay until the weather is more settled," she begged, the thought of his leaving unbearable. She was sure it was *his* voice that had called her back when she'd stood on the brink of death. "Charlie adores you."

"That's kind of you to say so. And you?"

"Mama! Uncle Drum!" Charlie burst through the door. "Our hut is finished. Will you come and see it now?"

"Of course." Kitty stood up, grateful her son had broken the moment.

They crowded into the tiny hut, drank tea, and ate the iced buns that Tarik had made. They had the texture of bullets, but nobody minded.

"Can we sleep in here tonight, Mama?" Charlie begged.

"Sorry, darling, but no. Cat sleeps with her mother, and you sleep in your bedroom."

Charlie pouted as the adults rose and crouched down to leave the claustrophobic space.

That evening, Kitty took more time than normal to perform her toilette. Whether it was the way Drummond had nursed her, his voice pulling her back toward life, or the way he played so naturally with Charlie and Cat, she could deny it no longer. Dabbing her neck with a little perfume even though she knew it attracted mosquitoes, she stared at her reflection in the looking glass.

"I love him," she told it. "God save me, I can't help it."

They ate dinner together that evening, Kitty's hands shaking as she struggled through the three courses. Whether Drummond could feel the sudden electricity in the air, she had no idea. He ate well, enjoying a bottle of wine from a case that Andrew had had sent up from Adelaide. He seemed oblivious to the seismic shift inside her.

"Might you pass me a small glass of the wine?" she asked.

"Do you think that's wise?" Drummond frowned at her request. "I hardly think it's a good idea, given the delicate state of your health."

"Maybe not, but I wish to toast to the fact that I still have health to worry about, and am not lying in the morgue like poor Mrs. Jefford."

"All right." He poured her a thimbleful.

"A little more, if you please."

"Kitty . . ."

"For God's sake, I'm a grown woman! If I wish to take a glass of wine, I shall."

"I can see you're better." He raised an eyebrow. "Back to your bossy ways."

"Am I bossy?" she asked him.

"It was a joke, Kitty. Most things I say are. What's bitten you tonight? You're as jumpy as an unbroken mare."

Kitty took a sip of her wine. "I think that almost losing my life has . . . changed me."

"I see. How?"

"I suppose I've realized how fleeting it can be."

"It can indeed. And here in this great new world of ours, more so than most other places."

"I will also confess that in the past I've doubted God's existence, but that night I felt Him. I felt His love."

"God's oath!" Drummond refilled his glass with wine. "You've had an epiphany. Will you soon be begging the local reverend to be the first female to take the cloth?"

"For once will you stop teasing me!" Kitty drained her wine, already feeling her head spinning. "The point is that I . . . that is . . ."

"For pity's sake, Kitty, spit it out."

"Just like I felt His love, I love you, Drummond. And I believe I have done so since the first moment we met."

Kitty reached for the bottle of wine but Drummond snatched it away from her. "No more of that, missy. It brings back far too many bad memories. And"—he grasped her wrist—"I want to believe you mean what you're saying."

"I mean it. Yes." Kitty laughed suddenly. "And no, I am not drunk on a thimbleful of wine, but on relief! Have you any idea how exhausting it has been to deny my feelings for the past few weeks? Please, I beg you, Drummond, can we simply celebrate the joy of being alive? In this moment? And not worry about tomorrow, or what's right or wrong . . ."

After a long silence, he finally spoke. "You have no idea how happy your confession makes me feel. However, putting aside the small glass of wine you've just drunk, I think that you are perhaps more drunk on life itself, having so recently almost lost it. As much as I am desperate to love you in all possible ways, I suggest that for your sake, a hiatus is required. Some time for you to regain your strength and contemplate what you have said to me tonight. And the ramifications it would have for both of us and our family."

Kitty stared at him in disbelief. "Here I am, wantonly offering you my body and soul, and you choose this moment to be sensible! Time is a luxury that is finite, and my God, I do not want to waste another second of it."

"And by taking some of it to think about what you have said, it will not be wasted. If you're still of the same mind in a few days, well—"

"Now *I* am speaking from my heart, you from your head . . . Good grief!" Kitty wrung her hands. "Do you always find a way to be contrary? Or is it perhaps because seeing me so sick, and my body . . . out of control, has changed your mind?"

"I have seen every inch of your body, I can assure you it is quite beautiful." Drummond reached out his hand toward her, but she refused it and stood up on her still-weak legs.

"I am retiring to bed." She walked to the door, as straight-backed as she could manage, but an arm grabbed her and pulled her to him.

"Kat, I . . ." Then he kissed her roughly and her already giddy head spun even more. When he removed his lips and released his grip, she almost sank to the floor.

"You are as insubstantial as a rag doll," he said gently as he supported her weight in his arms. "Come, I will escort you along the hall and up to your bedroom."

Outside the door, he paused. "Have you the strength to undress yourself or should I help you?" He gave her a wry smile.

"I do," she managed.

"I must know you are sure, Kitty, because I cannot come back from this once it has begun. Ever."

"I understand. Good night, Drummond."

The few days he had asked for passed as slowly as watching a large boulder become sand. Luckily the children had their hut in which to play—Kitty had little idea of what they actually did together in there, but a stream of high-pitched giggles emanated from it whenever she went to check on them.

Drummond had announced he had some business to conduct in town for his father and had absented himself from the house for most of the time, leaving Kitty to pace restlessly, mad with the oppressive heat and feverish desire. No matter how many times she told herself to "think," as he had asked her to do, her rational brain seemed to have completely deserted her. And even when a loving telegram from Andrew arrived, she could not muster the necessary guilt to dominate her treacherous thoughts.

TRULY RELIEVED YOU ARE WELL AGAIN STOP GLAD DRUMMOND WAS THERE STOP HOPE TO RETURN WITH GIFT FIT FOR A QUEEN STOP ANDREW STOP

Two days later, Kitty could stand it no longer. Lying in bed, she heard Drummond's door close. Since Andrew's departure, she had taken to lying naked with only a sheet to preserve her modesty. Waiting until the grandfather clock in the entrance hall struck midnight, she stood up and put on her robe. Closing the door gently behind her so as not to disturb Charlie, she tiptoed along the corridor. Without knocking, she entered Drummond's room. He hadn't closed the shutters, and in the moonlight glinting through the glass panes, she saw him splayed naked on the bed.

She untied her robe and let it drop to the floor. Walking toward the bed, she reached out her hand to him.

"Drummond?"

He opened his eyes and stared up at her.

"I have thought. And I am here."

18

"You well now, Missus Kitty," Camira commented a week later. "You mended good, yes?"

"I've mended good," Kitty repeated as she drank a cup of tea on the veranda, looking at her demolished rose bed and wondering whether it was actually worth the effort of planting another. She gazed dreamily at Camira, who was sloshing water onto the caked red mud and scrubbing it off with a hard brush.

"You different." Camira leaned on her brush and contemplated her mistress. "You lit up likem star!" she said, then carried on scrubbing.

"I am certainly relieved to be well again, and perhaps we have seen the last of the heavy rains for this year."

"Dem all good reason for happy, but I thinkum Mister Drum makem you happy too, Missus Kitty." Camira tapped her nose, winked, and went off to get a fresh pail of water.

Kitty's heart missed a beat at Camira's words. How did she know? Surely she could not have seen anything—they were both so careful, leaving any affectionate embraces until after Camira was in her hut with Cat, and Charlie fast asleep in his bed. Yet the sound of laughter as Drummond teased her perpetually, or tickled Charlie until he begged for mercy, *was* different. The house had a new energy and so did she. In fact, Kitty mused, she felt properly alive for the first time in her life.

Day and night, her body tingled with longing for Drummond, whether he was present in the room with her or tucked away in her imagination. Even the simplest pursuits now gave her pleasure if he was by her side. The merest touch of his hand shot a wave of electricity through her, and she'd wake up in the morning already longing for the evening to arrive so she could go to him and share their secret world of ecstasy.

After that first night, they had made a pact to simply live in the moment, not to let thoughts of the future destroy what they had found together. Kitty was amazed and ashamed at how easily she'd been able to do this. Though the rational part of her mind knew that Andrew would be returning in less than a month, its far more powerful emotional "twin" overrode it. She justified her actions with the thought that Drummond's presence during the long rainy season had not only saved her life, but been a blessing for Charlie too. Drummond's inventive mind could turn a chair into a ship filled with pirates and treasure being tossed on the sea, or a table into a hut in the jungle outside which lions and tigers roamed. It made a welcome change from the monotonous card games that Andrew always suggested when it rained.

Drummond's a child himself, Kitty thought to herself as she watched him crawl along the hall, growling fiercely. But at night, he was very much a man . . .

Since the weather had cleared, there had also been trips to Riddell Beach and in the farthest corner, shielded by the rock formations, Kitty had joined Cat, Drummond, and a now proficient Charlie in the gorgeous aquamarine waters.

"Mama! Take off your bloomers!" Charlie had shouted at her. "Uncle Drum said clothes weigh you down."

Kitty had not gone that far in front of Charlie, and had sworn him to secrecy about the swimming trips, but on a couple of occasions, she had left Charlie with Camira on the premise of business in town. She and Drummond had taken the cart to the beach and swum naked together. As he'd held her in his arms, kissing her face and her neck and licking the salty water off her breasts when they arrived back on the sands, she knew that no future moment she experienced could ever hold more happiness.

"Darling," Drummond said at the end of February as they lay together in his bed, Kitty half drugged from their lovemaking. "I have received a telegram from my father. He wishes me to join him and Andrew in Adelaide at the end of next week when they return from Europe. It's to do with the Mercer business empire. He wishes to apportion his interests to both Andrew and me so there will be no confusion in the event of his death. I must go home to Alicia Hall to sign the legal papers with the solicitor, and Andrew and I will draw up our own wills."

"I see." Kitty's heart, so recently full of love and contentment, plunged down to her stomach. "When will you leave?"

"I catch the boat in two days' time. Won't you ask what he is giving me? Find out what my prospects are?"

"You know I care not a jot about that. I'd live with you in a gum tree with nothing if necessary."

"Nevertheless I'll tell you. As you can well imagine, Andrew will have the Mercer pearling business transferred to him, which at present comprises seventy percent of the family income. I am to be endowed with a thousand square miles of arid desert and half-starved cattle—in other words, Kilgarra cattle station. Oh, and also a few acres of land some hours' journey outside of Adelaide. There's talk of some form of mining in the region, and my father has duly signed up. It may come to nothing, but knowing my father's instinctive nose when it comes to money, which is akin to a dingo catching the scent of a dead heifer, it will probably turn out to be profitable. I also inherit a bungalow in the Adelaide Hills and the vineyard that surrounds it. After my parents' deaths, my brother inherits Alicia Hall."

"Oh! But the bungalow is so much more beautiful! I have been there, and the views are spectacular!" Kitty said, remembering it vividly. "It was where Andrew proposed . . ." Her voice trailed off in embarrassment.

"Did he now? How very . . . quaint."

"Forgive me. That was tactless."

"I agree entirely." Drummond swept a tendril of hair back from her face. "Sadly, Mrs. Mercer, it seems to me that reality is encroaching on our godforsaken love nest. However much we have done our best to avoid it during these blissful few weeks, the time has come for you to make some decisions."

She knew it all too well. "And surely you too? After all, Andrew is your brother."

"Yes, a brother who had no compunction about snatching away my favorite toys when we were younger."

"I pray that I am not any form of retribution for his past misdemeanors," Kitty countered.

"If you are, then all to the good," Drummond chuckled. Then, seeing her expression, he relented. "Kitty . . . my Kat, I am, as always, teasing you. Although it concerns me that I have never yet won any battle Andrew has cared to wage."

"Oh yes, you have." Kitty reached up and kissed him gently on the cheek. "You know how to be happy. And because of that, so do I."

"I'm likely to become extremely *un*happy if we do not talk about our future, my love." Drummond cupped her face in the palms of his hands. "When I leave for Adelaide, do you wish it to be forever?"

"Oh, Drummond." She shook her head despairingly. "I do not know."

"I am sure you don't. Good God, what a mess we find ourselves in. Perhaps it might help for me to tell you what I have been thinking."

"Please do."

"It's very simple: I can't bear the thought of leaving you. I may cry like a girl in front of you if you insist on staying with my brother." Drummond gave her a weak smile.

"So what do you suggest?"

"That, together with Charlie, we elope."

"Where to?"

"The moon would be preferable, but given that's even farther than my cattle station and we'd have to grow wings to get there, Kilgarra is probably the best option."

"You want me to come with you?"

"Yes, although I warn you, Kat, life out there is harsh and brutal. It makes Broome seem like the very epicenter of civilized society. The Ghan camel train passes but twice a year with supplies and the nearest settlement, Alice Springs, is a two-day ride away. There is no doctor or hospital, and only the outside dunny for necessities. There is one benefit, mind you."

"What's that?"

"The nearest neighbor's a day's ride away, so there'll be no more interminable dinner parties to face."

Kitty managed a smile, knowing Drummond was doing his best to lighten the atmosphere.

"What about Andrew? How can *we* do this to him? It would devastate him. Losing his wife, let alone his beloved son . . ." She shook her head. "He doesn't deserve it."

"No, he doesn't, and yes, it will hurt him deeply, particularly given that

Andrew has never lost anything in his life. He was always the blighter at school that scored the final try to save the day."

"I am hardly a rugby ball and neither is Charlie." She eyed him. "Are you absolutely certain that this isn't about you winning?"

"Under the circumstances, absolutely not. I swear to you, Kat, despite my jesting, I love him. He's my twin and I'd walk a thousand miles not to hurt him, but this is life and death and it can't be helped."

"What do you mean?"

"I physically can't live without you. It's unfortunate, but there we have it. So, that's where I stand. And now, my Kitty-Kat, to use the rugby analogy, the ball is firmly in your hands. It's up to you to decide."

Once again, Kitty found herself in an agony of indecision, because it was not just *her* future she had to consider. If she left with Drummond, she knew that she would be denying Charlie the right to grow up with his father. Even more troubling was the thought that Andrew might try to fight her to claim Charlie back. At least there was no doubt that he adored his Uncle Drum and would have a loving uncle and father figure there to steer him as he grew. God only knew what she would tell Charlie when he was older; Kitty was well aware of the shock of discovering the bleak truth about a parent one had idolized.

Back and forth she went, even visiting the local church and kneeling to ask for guidance.

"Please, Lord, I have always been taught that God is love. And I love Drummond with every inch of my soul, but I love Charlie too . . ."

As she knelt, once more she saw her father clasping Annie's hands on the doorstep. And her poor innocent mother, also pregnant and unaware of her husband's duplicity.

"I am not a hypocrite and I cannot be a liar," she whispered to a mournful painting of angels flying the dead up to heaven. *Though even now,* she thought as she stood up, *I am no better than my father, lying in my husband's brother's bed night after night . . .*

"Lord, I may have had an epiphany," she sighed, "but I seem to have broken most of Your commandments since I did."

Outside in the sunshine, Kitty went to study the graves of the departed.

"Did you ever love like me before you left the earth?" she whispered to Isobel Dowd's remains. The poor thing had died at the age of twenty-three—the same age she was now.

Kitty closed her eyes, a deep sigh emanating from inside her. "It has gone too far already and I will not deceive my husband for the rest of our lives. Therefore"—she swallowed hard—"the Lord help me, but I must take the consequences."

"I have decided we will come with you to Kilgarra when you return from your meeting in Adelaide," Kitty said calmly as she sat with Drummond over dinner that evening.

He stared at her in surprise. "Good grief, woman! We were just discussing whether we should take Charlie to the beach for a last swim and you drop *that* into the conversation!"

"I thought you should know," she said, at least enjoying the stunned expression on Drummond's face.

"Yes, you're right, I should." He cleared his throat. "Well then. We'd better make a plan."

"I have also decided I shall tell Andrew myself when he returns home. I will not behave like a coward, Drummond. Camira will take Charlie out beforehand and I shall have a trunk packed and ready. I will leave immediately, collect Charlie from Camira, and we will travel to meet you, wherever that may be."

"It seems you already have it all worked out."

"I have a practical nature and I have found that in difficult situations, it helps to be organized." Kitty did not wish him to see the gamut of emotions that were swirling beneath her calm exterior.

"Am I allowed to express my complete and utter joy at your decision?" he asked her.

"You are, but I also wish to know where we should meet after I have . . . done the deed."

"Well now." Drummond snaked a hand to her across the table. "Kitty, are you sure you don't wish for me to be there with you when you tell Andrew?"

"Completely. I fear he may shoot you on the spot."

"He may well shoot you too."

"And it would be no less than I deserve." Kitty swallowed hard. "But I doubt it. Shooting his wife would certainly damage his reputation in Broome society."

They both allowed themselves a hollow smile.

"Are you sure about this, my Kat?"

"I have no choice because Andrew deserves far better than an unfaithful wife who can never love him."

"If it's any comfort, I am sure it won't be long before the pearling mothers of Broome have their dutiful daughters lined up along the path to his front door. Now, enough of that. I suggest that I still travel on to Darwin by ship, as I've already told both my father and Andrew I plan to do. Then you and Charlie make your escape on the next boat out to Darwin and meet me there."

"Andrew may come after us."

"He may, and if he does, we shall deal with it." Drummond squeezed her hand. "By then I shall be by your side."

"Must you go to Adelaide? Surely this business meeting with your father can be conducted on another suitable date?" Kitty could feel her resolve to remain unemotional slowly melting away.

"The last thing in the world I want to do is to leave you here; above all, I fear that you might change your mind while I'm gone." He gave her a grim smile. "However, in order for the three of us to have any kind of future, I must go and put my signature on the deeds to Kilgarra station and the other assets. I doubt my father will be keen to transfer them once he knows the truth."

"And what about Charlie?" Kitty felt tears pricking her eyes. "How do I explain all this to him?"

"Just tell him he is going on a trip to the outback to visit Uncle Drum and his thousands of cows. I have told him many stories about Kilgarra, and I know he is eager to see it for himself. Then"—Drummond shrugged his broad shoulders—"time passes and you simply don't return home." He paused then. "Are you sure about all this, Kat?"

"No." Kitty gave a small shake of her head as he raised her hand to his lips and kissed it tenderly.

"Of course not. Why should you be?"

Kitty wept softly against Drummond's shoulder the night before he left, then, as he slept, took in every inch of him and consigned it to memory. The awfulness of what she had to face between now and the next time she would see him was simply too huge to contemplate.

Their public parting on the quay the next morning was as it should have been—she kissed him chastely on both cheeks and wished him well. Any emotion she felt was subsumed by an inconsolable Charlie.

"Come and visit me soon," Drummond called as he walked up the gangplank.

"I will, Uncle Drum, I promise." Charlie was crying openly.

"I love you," he shouted back, though his eyes fell on Kitty. "I'll see you sooner than you think."

And with a last wave, Drummond disappeared from sight.

Kitty did her best to keep busy, spring-cleaning the house and even insisting Fred help her plant some rose cuttings. She had no idea whether they would take, and even if they did, she wouldn't be there to see the result.

Yet there was no doubt of her resolve. She could not continue to live a lie. It was as if her life with Andrew had been like a blister pearl—so bright and large on the surface, but at its core, nothing but dull mud. Now she and Drummond had created their own perfect pearl, its edges smooth with joy, and impenetrable love at its very center.

She received two telegrams a few days later, one from her husband, telling her he had docked safely in Adelaide and that Stefan would be returning to Broome with him and Drummond on the *Koombana* to see his grandson.

The other telegram was from Drummond saying the same, and adding that the "legalities" were progressing nicely. The Mercer men were due in Broome on March 22—*Only ten days away*, Kitty thought.

That night, she began to pack her trunk, needing to make what currently felt surreal, real.

"Whattum doing, Missus Kitty?" a voice came from behind her.

She jumped a mile in the air and wished for once that Camira did not move around with the silence of a cat.

"I'm packing away some of Charlie's baby clothes," she improvised, and let the lid of the trunk fall closed.

"But that shirt, it still fittum him good."

Kitty felt Camira watching her as she stood up. "Isn't it time the children were in bed?"

"Yessum." Camira made to walk away, then turned back toward Kitty. "I see every little thing, I knowa why you packum dat trunk. Jus' don't forget us. We come alonga you, an' Fred protect you from bad blackfellas." With that, she left the room.

Kitty shook her head in wonder and irritation. Camira seemed to intuit her inner emotional machinations by an invisible osmosis.

At night, her head spun with feverish plans as she tried to think of everything that could go wrong and factor it in. The one thing she knew for certain was that Drummond would never let her down, and once she was safely in his arms in Darwin, all would be well.

She wrote heartfelt letters to her mother and Mrs. McCrombie, asking for their forgiveness and understanding, then secreted them in the lining of the trunk. She then began a letter to Edith, but decided against it, as there was simply nothing she could say to make the situation better. Edith would at least have the comfort of knowing she'd been right all along. Kitty was her father's daughter through and through.

"I could not be more prepared," she whispered.

Another telegram arrived for her the next morning from Andrew.

WILL SURPRISE YOU ON ARRIVAL IN ALL SORTS OF WAYS STOP FATHER
CAN EXPLAIN STOP LAST-MINUTE ERRAND BUT WILL BE HOME SAFE
AND SOUND STOP LOVE TO YOU AND CHARLIE STOP

Kitty frowned, wondering what on earth Andrew meant, but then Charlie came in for a cuddle and a story and she thought no more about it.

The night before her planned escape, the weather was in sympathy with Kitty's roiling emotions. The clouds hung black and foreboding in the sky and thunder shook the earth, bolts of lightning tearing the sky like a ripping seam. Kitty paced the house, the shuttered windows rattling with the effort of keeping out the elements.

She rose along with the rest of the town the next day, and stepped outside in relief to see that the storm had been all bark but no bite. Her roses were still standing, and Fred commented that the winds had exhausted themselves over the Pindan sands in the south. Not that she had slept a wink—the *Koombana* was due to arrive in Broome that evening, and she knew that even after she had told Andrew she was leaving, there was a long and arduous journey ahead of her to Darwin. And she still felt occasionally nauseated, her stomach unsettled, which Dr. Suzuki had assured her was the aftermath of her illness.

Should I tell Andrew tonight, or perhaps tomorrow morning? Kitty asked herself for the umpteenth time. It hardly made things easier that Stefan would be here in Broome too, and she would have to wait until he was out of the way. Kitty's hands shook visibly as she washed and dressed. She found Camira in the kitchen, making eggs for Charlie's breakfast.

"You look white, like-a dem spirits up in the sky, Missus Kitty," she commented, then patted her shoulder. "Dun worry, me an' Fred, we takem care of Charlie on beach when you wanta talk to Mister Boss."

"Thank you." Kitty covered Camira's hand with her own. "And I promise to send word to you and Fred once we are safely out at Kilgarra."

"We come wid you," Camira said with a nod. "We-a here for you, Missus Kitty."

"Thank you, Camira. Truly, I do not know what I would do without you."

The *Koombana* was due to dock with the evening tide, but when Kitty—by now in such a state of agitation she'd had to resort to a nip of brandy to calm her nerves—reached the harbor there was no sign of the ship out in the bay.

"There's been a cyclone," the harbormaster was telling those already gathered there. "We think she might have taken shelter in Derby to wait out the storm. No point hanging around here, ladies and gents. Go to your homes and come back later."

Kitty cursed the bad weather for striking on the very day she had so carefully prepared herself for. On the train back along the jetty neighbors greeted her, making small talk about the storm the night before and how many of the boats had taken shelter. Mr. Pigott, one of Andrew's fellow pearling masters, sat down next to her.

"Hope that ship comes in soon. It's got half my family upon it. Yours too, I hear."

"Yes. You think the *Koombana* is safe? After all, she's the newest in the fleet."

"I'm sure she is," Mr. Pigott replied, "but it was one hell of a storm last night, Mrs. Mercer, and I've known bigger ships than the *Koombana* to go down before. Well, all we can do is hope for the best. And pray." He patted her hand and got up as the train came to a halt. Kitty felt the first tingle of fear creep like a silken thread up her spine.

Back at home, she paced the drawing room as Camira tried to convince her to eat, but she refused. Fred, whom she'd sent to wait on the dock and alert her to any sighting of the ship, returned home at midnight.

"No-a boat, Missus Boss."

Kitty retired to bed, but sleep refused to take her, as her mind turned over in anxiety.

The next morning, as Fred drove her toward the dock, she was swept up in crowds of people gathered in the town who were discussing the fate of the *Koombana* in hushed whispers. Kitty decided to follow them up the hill at the end of Dampier Terrace, where the residents peered out over Roebuck Bay.

"We don't know where she is, Mrs. Mercer," said Mr. Rubin, another pearling master. "The postmaster says he thinks the telegraph lines at Derby blew down, which is why they're not replying. There'll be news soon, I'm sure."

Beneath her, the treacherous ocean was now like a millpond, and those with binoculars reported that they could see no sign of any vessel. A number of pearl luggers were missing too, and as the heat of the day grew stronger, more friends and relatives joined the throng on the top of the hill. Kitty found herself pulled along with the crowd back down the hill to the telegraph office to question the postmaster. He told the crowd that he was continuing to send messages to the Derby office, but silence was the only response.

Finally, at sunset, a hush fell over the crowd outside the hut as the telegraph machine came to life. All that could be heard was the buzzing of insects in the dusk and the tapping of the machine.

The postmaster emerged from the hut, his face somber. He hung a notice on the board outside, then retreated.

Koombana not at Derby, said the words on the black-bordered page.

The harbormaster, Captain Dalziel, called on all the men to join in the search for the ship, and Kitty overheard Noel Donovan, the Mercer Pearling Company manager, pledging their luggers' help. Back at home, her mind fogged with terror and exhaustion, Kitty was settled into bed by Camira, who smoothed her hair back from her damp forehead.

"I stay withum you, singa to sleep," Camira soothed her as Kitty held tight to her hand, unable to voice the unbearable thoughts running through her head.

Over the next few days, as there was no further news, Kitty listened numbly to all those who came to her door to update her on the situation. Issues of the *Northern Times* piled up on the front doorstep as she refused to so much as look at the headlines.

Nearly two weeks after the *Koombana* should have docked in Broome, Kitty made her way into the kitchen. Her face fell as she saw Camira crying on Fred's shoulder.

"What is it?"

"The *Koombana*, Missus Kitty. It sink. Everyone lost. Everyone gone."

In retrospect, Kitty could not remember much of the rest of that day; perhaps shock had wiped her memory. She vaguely recalled Fred driving her in the cart to the harbormaster's office, where a weeping crowd was gathered. Calling for silence, Captain Dalziel read out the telegram from the Adelaide Steamship Company:

"*With profound regret the company have to announce that they consider the discovery of wreckage by the SS* Gorgon *and SS* Minderoo, *which has been identified as belonging to the SS* Koombana, *is evidence that the* Koombana *was lost with all hands in the vicinity of Bedout Island, during the cyclone which raged on the twentieth and twenty-first of March . . .*"

He read out the passenger list to his devastated audience.

"...*McSwain, Donald; Mercer, Andrew; Mercer, Drummond; Mercer, Stefan...*"

Some deck chairs were found so that the women could sit. Many among the crowd had already dropped to the ground where they stood.

Mr. Pigott had been one of the first to collapse and was sobbing loudly. Unable to process any of her own thoughts or feelings, Kitty at least thanked God for the small mercy of not losing a child. Mr. Pigott had lost his wife and two daughters.

Eventually, the devastated townspeople began to stagger home to tell their relatives that there were no survivors. Captain Dalziel had mentioned that the victims' nearest and dearest were being contacted by telegram as he spoke. As Fred helped her onto the cart, Kitty mused that the only person she had to tell was her son. Nevertheless, when she arrived home, she automatically took up her fountain pen and wrote a short note of sympathy to Edith, understanding there were no words of comfort she could give to a woman who had lost her husband and two sons in one cruel twist of fate. She asked Fred to take it to the telegraph office, then went to her bedroom, closed the door behind her, and sat staring into space.

Andrew has gone.

Drummond has gone . . .

The words were meaningless. Kitty lay down fully clothed on the bed she had shared with both of them, closed her eyes, and slept.

"Charlie, darling, I need to talk to you about something."

"What is it, Mama? When is Papa coming home?"

"Well, Charlie, the thing is, Papa isn't coming home. At least, not to us anyway."

"Then where is he going?"

"Your papa, Uncle Drum, and Grandfather Mercer have been called up to heaven to be with the angels." Kitty felt the first pricking of tears behind her eyes. Having been unable to shed a tear since she'd heard the news, she knew she absolutely mustn't and couldn't cry now in front of her son. "They're special, you see, and God wanted them up there with Him."

"You mean, to be with their ancestors? With the rest of dem spirits? Mama"—Charlie wagged a finger at her—"Cat says that when someone goes up to the skies, we mustn't speak their name." He put his finger to his lips. "Shh."

"Charlie, it is perfectly all right for us to speak their names. And remember them."

"Cat says it's not—"

"I don't care what Cat says!" All of Kitty's suppressed tension bubbled over at his words. "I am your mother, Charlie, and you will listen to me!"

"Sorry, Mama." Charlie's bottom lip trembled. "So they are gone up to heaven? And we will never see them again?"

"I'm afraid not, darling. But we will always remember them," Kitty replied more gently, feeling dreadful for shouting at him at such a moment. "And they will watch over us from the skies."

"Can I go and visit them, sometimes?"

"No, darling, not yet, although one day, you will see them again."

"Maybe they'll come down here. Cat says her ancestors do that sometimes in her dreams."

"Perhaps, but you and she are different, Charlie, and . . ." Kitty shook her head. "Oh, it doesn't matter now. I am so very sorry, darling." She took Charlie in her arms and hugged him to her.

"I will miss them, 'specially Uncle Drum. He played such good games." Charlie pulled away from her and laid a hand on his mother's arm. "Remember, they are watching over us. Cat says—" Charlie stopped himself and said no more.

"Perhaps we will go and stay in Adelaide with Grandmother Edith?" Kitty tried desperately to recover her equilibrium. It seemed that her four-year-old child was comforting *her*.

"No." Charlie wrinkled his nose. "I like it here with Cat and Camira. They're our family."

"Yes, my brave boy." She gave him a weak smile. "They are."

Drummond is gone!

Kitty sat bolt upright, relieved to emerge from a terrible nightmare. Then, as her senses returned to her, she realized it wasn't a nightmare. Or, at least, it *was*, but not one that would dissipate as she was pulled back into consciousness, because Drummond would never be conscious again.

Or Andrew. Spare a thought for your husband. He is dead too . . .

Or maybe, she thought, it was *her* that was dead; perhaps she had been sent to hell to suffer for what she had done.

"Please, Lord, don't let this be. It can't *be* . . ." She buried her face in the pillow to drown tearless sobs that felt like great gulps of unendurable pain.

And Andrew—what had he ever done to deserve her deception? He had loved her in the only way he knew how. Excitement? No, but did that matter? Did *anything* matter anymore?

"Nothing matters, nothing matters. I . . ." Kitty stuffed a handful of sheet into her mouth, realizing she was about to scream. "I am a whore, a jezebel! No better than my father! I cannot live with this, I cannot live with myself! Oh God!"

She stood up then, pacing the floor and shaking her head from side to side. "I cannot live. I cannot live!"

"Missus Kitty, come outside an' walk wid me."

Her vision was full of purple and red lights and she was dizzy but she felt an arm go around her shoulder and guide her to the front door. And then across the garden, the fresh red soil that Fred had spread feeling damp like drying blood beneath her feet.

"I'm going to scream, I *must* scream!"

"Missus Kitty, we will walk, wid the earth beneath us, an' we will lookum up an' we will see dem fellas lookin' down."

"I killed both of them, in different ways. I lay with a man who was not my husband, but his twin brother. I loved him! God help me, I loved him so much. I love him *now* . . ." Kitty sank to her knees in the earth.

Camira gently tugged her chin upward. "Understand not for you to makem destiny. Dem makem it up there." Camira pointed. "I know you lovem dat fella. Me, I lovem him too. But we not kill him, Missus Kitty. Bad things, they happen. I see-a lotta bad things. Dem fellas, they have good life. Life, it begin an' end. No one change dat."

"No one can change that." Kitty put her head on her knees and wept. "No one can change that . . ."

Eventually, when it felt as if every single drop of fluid in her body had drained out of her eyes, Camira helped her to standing.

"I take you sleepa now, Missus Kitty. The young fella needum you tomorrow. An' next day after dat."

"Yes, you're right, Camira, forgive me for my behavior. I just . . ." Kitty shook her head. There were no more words.

"In big desert, we go an' howl loud as you like at moon an' stars. Good for you, gettum bad things out. Then feel better."

Camira helped Kitty into bed, then sat next to her holding her hand. "Dunna you worry. I singa dem fellas home."

As Kitty closed her exhausted eyes, she heard Camira's high sweet voice humming a soft monotonous tune.

"God forgive me for what I have done," she murmured, before sleep finally overtook her.

CeCe

Broome, Western Australia

January 2008

Aboriginal symbol for a meeting place

19

I wiped the tears from my eyes and sat up, trying to still my heartbeat.

I thought about the grief I had felt for Pa when he had died and tried to multiply that by all the people that Kitty had lost on the *Koombana*. All the people that this town had lost . . .

I took off the headphones and rubbed my sore ears, then went to open the window for some fresh air. I tried to imagine everyone in this town assembled up on the hill at the end of Dampier Terrace, a street I had walked down, all waiting to hear the worst news of their lives.

I shut the window to block out the nighttime wildlife choir. Despite the air-conditioning being on full blast, I still felt hot and sweaty. I couldn't even begin to think how Kitty had coped here in Broome a century ago, especially in a corset, bloomers, and Christ knew how many petticoats. Never mind having to give birth in the heat—which was surely just about the sweatiest process anyone could go through.

Even if I hadn't really thought through what Kitty was to me before I arrived, there was now a bit of me that would have loved to be related to her. Not just because of her bravery in going to Australia in the first place, but also because of how she'd handled what she'd faced when she got there. Her experiences made my own problems feel like diddly-squat. To do what she'd done by living in Broome a hundred years ago took real balls. *And* she'd followed her heart, wherever it might have led her.

Glancing at her picture on the front of the CD cover, I couldn't imagine I *was* related to her, even though the solicitor had indicated my legacy had come from her originally. It was much more likely that I was related to the maid, Camira. Especially as her daughter, Alkina, apparently had the eyes of her father, who was Japanese. They sounded similar to mine.

Camira and her daughter had come from here—their footsteps had once passed along the streets I'd been walking. Tomorrow I'd try to find out more. As I lay down, I thought how this quiet little town on the edge of the earth had been brought to life for me as I listened to Kitty's story. Once upon a time, when she'd been here, it had teemed with people. I wanted to see the things she'd seen, though how much was actually left of them, I didn't know.

I was woken by the phone ringing early the next morning. It was the hotel receptionist.

"Miss D'Aplièse? There's a man waiting for you in the residents' lounge. He says he's from the *Australian*."

"Right, er . . . thanks. Tell him I'll be down in five."

My hand trembled as I replaced the receiver. So the press had tracked me down. Knowing there wasn't a moment to lose, I scrambled out of bed, dressed hastily, then packed the rest of my stuff into my rucksack and hoisted it onto my back. Counting out the dollars I owed for my stay, I left them with the key on the nightstand by the bed so I wouldn't be arrested for not paying my bill. Then I ran along the corridor to the emergency exit I had noticed last night when I'd seen someone having a cigarette beyond it. I gave the door bar a push, and to my relief, it opened without an alarm going off. I saw a set of basic iron steps leading down into a yard at the back of the hotel. I ran down them as quietly as I could in my heavy boots. The yard wall was low, so I threw my rucksack over it and followed suit. A few backyards later, I found myself out on the street at the other end.

Okay, what do I do now?

I called Chrissie, who answered after the first ring.

"Where are you?" I asked her, still panting hard.

"At my desk in the airport. What's up?"

"Is it easy to book a flight out of here?"

"It is if you work on the tourist info desk opposite the airline sales counter, yes. Where d'ya need to go?"

"Alice Springs. What's the best way of getting there?"

"You'll have to catch a flight up to Darwin, and connect from there to the Alice."

"Can you get me on those flights today?"

"I know there's a flight from here to Darwin in a couple of hours or so. I'll go and ask the guys if there are any seats left."

"If there are, book me on it. I'll be there as soon as I can find a taxi."

"I'll send one for you now. Walk to the bronze statues at the end of the road and he'll be there in ten."

"Thanks, Chrissie."

"No worries."

At the airport, Chrissie was hovering by the entrance doors waiting for me.

"You can tell me what's up after we've confirmed your bookings," she said as she put her arm through mine and marched me over to the Qantas check-in desk. "This is my mate Zab." Chrissie indicated the guy standing behind it. "The bookings are all ready to go. You just need to pay."

I pulled out my credit card and slapped it on the counter. Zab took the payment, then handed me my boarding passes and a receipt.

"Thanks a mill, Chrissie."

"I'll come through security with ya," she said. "We can hang out at the café and you can tell me all about Thailand."

Shit! So Chrissie knew too, which was hardly a surprise as her desk faced a kiosk. She'd probably sat there for days staring at my face on the front of all the newspapers. Yet she'd never said a word.

We went through security together to a tiny café and Chrissie came back with two bottles of water and a sandwich each. I'd chosen to sit facing a wall in the corner, just in case.

"So, why d'ya need to leave so fast?"

"A reporter from the *Australian* turned up at my hotel this morning. You probably know why he wanted to interview me." I eyed her.

"Yeah, I do. I recognized you the first moment you swung by my desk. And . . . ?"

"I met this guy on a beach in Thailand and hung out with him for a bit. Turns out he's wanted for some kind of bank fraud."

"Anand Changrok?"

"Or 'Ace,' as I knew him." I then told Chrissie the story of how I'd met him.

"What was he like?" she asked when I'd finished.

"Great. He helped me when I needed it."

"Were the two of you together?"

"Yeah. I really liked him, and even if I hadn't, I'd never have done something as low as that. Even if I had known who he was."

"I know you wouldn't, Cee." Chrissie's eyes were full of sympathy rather than suspicion. "So he thinks it was you who told the newspapers."

"He sent me a text saying he'd thought he could trust me. I felt like a complete lowlife, still do, but there's no way he'd ever believe me, even if I could explain. I think that this guy Jay bribed our security guard to get a photograph, and I gave him the perfect opportunity."

"You could always write to him in jail."

"Not well enough for what I'd need to say." I gave her a weak grin. "I'm dyslexic, remember?"

"I could write it for you."

"Maybe. Thanks."

"Do you think he did it?"

"How should I know? The rest of the world seems to think so. I don't know, Chrissie, there's just something that doesn't fit. Little things he said to me . . . It's only an instinct, but I think there's more to his story than he's telling."

"Maybe you should try to find out what it is."

"How would I do that? I'm not a detective and I know nothing about banks."

"You're smart, you'll find a way," she said with a smile.

I blushed, as no one had ever called me smart. "Anyway, I'm going to concentrate on finding out more about my family."

"Hey, if you need a fellow detective to help you out in the Alice, I'm your gal," Chrissie said suddenly. "I'm due some hols anyway, and it's a quiet time of year here, so how about I meet up with ya there?"

"Really? I mean, I don't want to take up your time, but if you can manage it, it would be amazing to have your help," I said, genuinely excited at the thought. "You've seen how clueless I am about all things Australia."

"Nah, mate, you just need someone to show you the ropes. It'll be bonza and I've always wanted to go to the Alice." Chrissie glanced up at the board. "Time ta go."

"I hate planes," I said as she walked with me over to the departure gate.

"Do ya? I've always wanted to go and see the rest of the world. I'll text you once I know for sure I can come and meet you." She put her arms around me. "Safe journey."

"Thanks for everything."

Boarding the plane, I felt suddenly lost, because I had made a friend in Chrissie. I just had to make sure I didn't muck it up like I had with Ace.

As we began our descent toward Alice Springs, I saw a marked change in the landscape below me. From the sky, it looked like a green oasis in the desert—which I supposed it was—but far more dramatic in color. I saw a range of mountains that glinted purple in the hazy light, their irregular crowns like a massive set of teeth sticking up from the ground. The plane screeched to a fast and jerky halt on the short runway and all us passengers trooped off down the steps onto the tarmac.

"Wow!" I muttered as a wave of burning heat that I could probably have lit a match with just by sticking it in the air hit me. It burned my nostrils as I breathed in and I was actually glad to get inside the air-conditioned terminal.

The airport wasn't much bigger than the one in Broome, but it was buzzing with tourists. After grabbing a bottle of water and a few leaflets for hotels and places of interest, I sat down on a plastic chair to try to read them before I decided where to stay. I realized all the tourists were here because Alice Springs was the gateway to Ayers Rock—or Uluru, as Chrissie had said it was called by the Aboriginal people. The leaflet said it was one of their most sacred sites and "only" a six-hour drive away.

I then read about Alice Springs—or "the Alice," as it was affectionately called. Indigenous art was obviously a very big deal here. There were several galleries both inside and outside town, ranging from the Many Hands Art Centre, run by Aboriginal artists, to the Araluen Arts Centre—so modern it looked like a spaceship that had crash-landed in the middle of the desert.

Another tremor of excitement ran through me and some instinct told me that if I was going to find answers anywhere, it was going to be here.

"My *kantri*," I murmured, remembering Chrissie's granny saying the word. I then opened the leaflet on the Hermannsburg mission, which told me it was now a museum and a good couple of hours' drive out of town.

It also said Albert Namatjira had been born there. I had never even heard of him until yesterday, but I'd seen from the leaflets that his name was used for galleries, streets, and buildings here. I tried to read more, but the words were doing a polka on the page, especially as most of them were Aboriginal names.

I then remembered I should turn my phone back on, and two messages pinged through, both from Chrissie.

Hi! Sorted you a hotel—just ask Keith at the tourist info desk at ASP airport and he'll give you the deets! C x

Just spoke to the Qantas desk. The staff r giving me a trip for free as a pressie for all the flights I've sorted for tourists. STOKED!! Land tomorrow arvo.
See you then!! x

I was amazed that this girl I hardly knew was making the effort to fly hundreds of miles to meet me. And even if I never found out who my family were, coming to Australia had been worth it, because I'd met Chrissie.

I walked across the concourse to the tourist information desk, where a tall freckled man with blond hair down to his shoulders was sitting at a computer.

"Hi, are you Keith?" I asked.

"Yeah, who's askin'?"

"I think my friend Chrissie in Broome spoke to you earlier—she said you've got a hotel reservation for me?"

"Ah, Chrissie's mate, CeCe! I've got youse a special deal. Here we go." He handed me the booking sheet. "Just take a taxi to Leichhardt Terrace, next to the Todd River."

"Thanks for all your help."

"Any friend of Chrissie's," he said with a friendly grin. "Have a good un!"

In the taxi, I marveled at the easy way Chrissie had with everyone she met. She seemed totally comfortable in her own skin, with who she was.

By the grace of God, I am who I am . . .

For the first time, Pa Salt's quotation on the armillary sphere began to make sense, because that was how I wanted to be too.

Half an hour later, I was installed in a "deluxe room," which at least had a decent shower *and* a kettle. I looked out of the window expecting to see a river, like Keith had said, but was surprised to find only a dry, sandy riverbed with a few gnarled trees dotted around. It suddenly struck me that I was in the middle of the desert.

Dusk was falling when I ventured outside, and I realized the air smelled different here—dry and fragrant, rather than the soupy humidity of Broome. I walked along a bridge that crossed the Todd riverbed and had a solitary pizza in a restaurant full of families chatting and laughing. I missed Chrissie's company and felt really happy she was joining me tomorrow.

I wandered back to the hotel and spotted a newspaper on a coffee table in the reception area. I picked it up and saw it was a day-old English *Times* and wondered if there were any more developments on the Ace situation. The story had been demoted to a much smaller headline on the front page:

CHANGROK PLEADS GUILTY TO FRAUD

There was a photograph of Ace—or at least the back of his head and shoulders—entering court and surrounded by an angry crowd. I could read the "full story on page 7," so I took the newspaper up to my room and tried to decipher the words.

> Anand Changrok appeared at Woolwich Crown Court today, charged with fraud. Looking thin and haggard, Mr. Changrok pleaded guilty to all charges. Bail was not granted by the judge and Mr. Changrok is being remanded in custody until his sentencing hearing, expected to take place in May. Outside the court, hundreds of Berners Bank customers threw eggs at him, waving banners demanding for their losses to be compensated.
>
> The chief executive of Berners, Mr. David Rutter, has sought to allay their fears.
>
> "We are aware of the sad and difficult situation our customers find themselves in. We continue to do everything in our power to compensate those affected."
>
> Asked how Mr. Changrok could cover up the losses for so long and about his subsequent plea of guilty today, Mr. Rutter declined to comment.

I climbed into bed and eventually fell into a troubled sleep, picturing Ace curled up on a thin prison-issue mattress.

I woke with a jolt to the sound of the telephone ringing, and answered it blearily.

"'Lo?"

"Cee!"

"Chrissie?"

"Yeah, I'm here! Come on, sleepyhead, it's half three in the afternoon already! I'll be up in a sec."

There was a click as she hung up and I rolled out of bed to get dressed. A few minutes later, I heard her put the key in the lock, and the door opened.

"Hi, darl'. Good ta see you." Chrissie greeted me with a bright smile and dropped her rucksack on the other twin bed.

"You're cool bunking in with me, right? Keith said there weren't any other rooms available."

"No problem, I've shared a room with my sister my whole life."

"Lucky you. I had to share with my two brothers." Chrissie laughed, then wrinkled her nose. "It always stank of 'boy,' y'know?"

"I have five sisters, remember? Our corridor stank of perfume."

"That's almost as bad," she said with a grin. "Here, I brought some snacks as well."

She handed me a plastic box and I opened it to find square-shaped chocolate-covered cakes doused in coconut sprinkles. They smelled heavenly.

"Go on," she urged. "They're lamingtons, I made them myself. Have one for brekky, then we can go out and explore."

With my mouth full of delicious cake, which tasted like a Victoria sponge with bells on, we went outside, where the late afternoon sun was overpowering, beating fire down onto the top of my head. From the map, it looked as if Alice Springs was easy to navigate, being so small. We walked down Todd Street, lined with one-story art galleries, nail salons, and cafés with chairs set out under the palm trees. We stopped for a drink and a bite to eat at one of them, and I noticed a huge dot painting hanging in the window of the gallery opposite.

"Wow, look, Chrissie! It's the Seven Sisters!"

"They're big around here," she said with a grin. "Better not mention you're named after one of them, or you'll get the locals coming to build a shrine around you!"

After reassurance from Chrissie, I tried my first plate of kangaroo meat, thinking that Tiggy would never forgive me if she ever found out. She'd had a real thing about "Baby Roo" in the *Winnie the Pooh* stories Pa used to read us, and it had been around that time she'd decided to become a vegetarian.

"What do ya think of the 'roo?" Chrissie nudged me.

"It's good, a bit like venison. Aren't they an endangered species?"

"Strewth, no, there's thousands of 'em bouncing all over Australia."

"I've never seen one."

"You're sure to see 'em around here, there's loads in the outback. So, have you had a chance to find out more about Albert Namatjira yet?" Chrissie looked at me, her bright eyes expectant.

"No, I only got here yesterday, remember? And I don't really know where to start."

"Well, I'd reckon it's a trip out to the Hermannsburg mission tomorrow. It's some miles out of town, though, so we'll have to drive."

"I don't drive," I admitted.

"I do, as long as it's an automatic. If you have the dollars to hire the transport, I'll be your chauffeur. Deal?"

"Deal. Thanks, Chrissie," I said gratefully.

"Y'know, if you are really related to Namatjira, they'll *defo* be making a shrine to you around here, and I'll help them! I can't wait to see your stuff, Cee. You oughtta get yourself some canvas and brushes, have a go at painting the scenery around here, like Namatjira did."

"Maybe, but my artwork has been crap for the past six months."

"Get over yourself, Cee. No one gets into one of the top art colleges in London painting crap," retorted Chrissie, forking up the last of her kangaroo.

"Well, the paintings I did at college were. The lecturers mucked with my head somehow. Now I'm not sure what I should be painting," I admitted.

"I get it." Chrissie put a warm hand on mine. "Maybe you need ta know who you are before you find out what you want to paint."

After our meal, Chrissie waved a tourist leaflet in my face.

"How about we go up to Anzac Hill?" she suggested. "It's just a short hike, and it's meant to have the best view of Alice Springs and the sunset."

I didn't tell her that I'd already had my fill of sunsets on this trip, but her energy was infectious, so we trooped out into the heat and began to scale the hill at an easy pace.

Up at the top, photographers were already fiddling about with tripods ready to capture the sunset and we found a quiet spot facing west to sit down. I looked at Chrissie as she watched the sunset, her expression one of contentment as soft hues of gold and purple light tinged her face. Below us, Alice Springs lit up with twinkling streetlights, and the sun settled behind the mountains, leaving only a dark red line against the indigo sky.

After a pit stop for a Coke in town on the way back, we returned to the hotel and Chrissie offered me the first shower. As I felt the cool stream of water drenching my sweaty skin, I tipped my face up into it and smiled. It was great to have Chrissie with me because she was so enthusiastic about everything. Wrapping a towel around me, I padded back into the bedroom and did a double take. Somehow, in the ten minutes I'd been gone, Chrissie's right leg seemed to have fallen off, leaving her with only a tiny piece of it below the knee. The rest of the leg sat a few inches away from her.

"Yeah, I've got a 'falsie,'" she said casually as I gawked at it.

"How? When?"

"Since I was fifteen. I got really crook one night, but my mum didn't trust the whitefella doctor, so she just gave me a couple of Tylenol for my fever. The next morning, she found me unconscious in bed. I don't remember anything about it, but I was airlifted to Darwin by the Flying Doctor Service, and diagnosed with meningitis in the hospital there. It was too late to save my leg 'cause septicemia had started to set in, but at least I came out with my life. I'd reckon that was a pretty good swap, wouldn't you?"

"I . . . yes, if you look at it that way," I agreed, still in shock.

"No point in looking at it any other way, is there? And I get about pretty well. You didn't notice, did ya?"

"No, though I did wonder why you always wear jeans when I sweat like a pig in a pair of shorts."

"Only bummer is that I used to be the best swimmer in Western Australia. Won the junior championships a coupla times and was gonna try out for the 2000 Olympic squad in Sydney. Me and Cathy Freeman showing the world what us Aboriginals could do." Chrissie gave a tight smile. "Anyway, that's in the past," she said as she pulled herself to standing without a single wobble, as though she had just planted both feet firmly on the ground to take her weight. "Right, my turn to take a shower." She deftly used both of her strong arms to grasp furniture and swung herself toward the bathroom, closing the door behind her.

I sank down onto the bed, feeling as though my *own* legs had turned to puddles of porridge. My brain—and heart—raced at a million thoughts and beats per second as I ran through a gamut of emotions: guilt, for *ever* feeling sorry for myself when not only was I incredibly privileged but also able-bodied; anger that this woman hadn't received the kind of immediate medical care she'd needed. And, most of all, sheer awe for the way Chrissie accepted her lot, and her courage and bravery in getting on with her life, when she could have spent the rest of it feeling sorry for herself. As I had done recently . . .

The door to the bathroom opened and Chrissie, wrapped in a towel, made her way back effortlessly to her bed and dug in her overnight bag for a pair of pants and a T-shirt.

"What?" She turned around and saw my eyes on her. "Why ya staring at me like that?"

"I just want to say that I think you're incredible. The way you came through . . . that." I tentatively pointed to the missing limb.

"I just never wanted it to define me, y'know? Didn't want the missing bit to be who I was. Mind you, it did have some benefits." She laughed as she climbed into bed.

"Like what?"

"When I applied for uni, I got a full house of offers."

"You probably deserved them."

"Whether I did or didn't, I could take my pick. A disabled Aboriginal person manages to tick two boxes on the government quota forms. The unis were fighting over me."

"That sounds seriously cynical," I responded as I too got into bed.

"Maybe, but it was me who got the chance of a great education, and I made the most of it. So who's the winner here?" she asked as she reached to switch off the bedside light.

"You," I replied.

You . . . with all your positivity and strength and zest for life.

I lay there in the darkness, feeling her alien but familiar energy only a few feet away.

"Night, Cee," she said. "I'm glad I'm here."

I smiled. "So am I."

20

Y ou gonna wake up or what?"

I felt someone's breath on my face and struggled to rise to consciousness through the deep fug of my usual late-morning sleep.

"Christ, Cee, we've wasted half the morning already!"

"Sorry." I opened my eyes and saw Chrissie sitting on the bed opposite me, a hint of irritation on her face. "I'm a late sleeper by nature."

"Well, in the past three hours, I've eaten brekky, taken a wander around the town, and hired us a car that you need to pay for at reception. We need to leave for Hermannsburg, like, pronto."

"Okay, sorry again." I threw back the sheet and staggered upright. Chrissie watched me quizzically as I pulled on my shorts and rooted in my rucksack for a clean T-shirt.

"What's up?" I asked her as her eyes followed me to the mirror, where I ran a hand through my hair.

"Do you often have nightmares?" she asked.

"Yeah, sometimes. My sister told me I did anyway," I said casually. "Sorry if I disturbed you."

"You don't remember them?"

"Some of them, yes. Right," I said, shoving my wallet into my shorts pocket, "let's go to Hermannsburg."

As we drove out of town onto a wide, straight road surrounded by red earth on either side, the sun beat down on our tiny tin-can car. I was amazed it didn't explode from the heat it was enduring.

"What are they called?" I asked, pointing to the jagged mountains in the distance.

"The MacDonnell Ranges," said Chrissie without missing a beat. "Namatjira did lotsa paintings of them."

"They look purple."

"That's the color he painted them."

"Oh, right." Then I wondered if *I* could ever paint a realistic representation of what I saw in the world. "How does anyone ever survive out here?" I mused, looking out of the window at the vast open landscape. "Like, there's nothing for miles and miles."

"They adapt, simple as that. Did you ever read Darwin?"

"*Read* it? I thought Darwin was a city."

"It is, idiot, but a bloke called Darwin also wrote books—the most famous was called *On the Origin of Species*. He talks about how all the plants and flowers and animals *and* humans have adapted to their surroundings over millennia."

I turned to look at Chrissie. "You're a secret science nerd, aren't you?"

"Nope." Chrissie shook her head firmly. "I'm just interested in what made us, that's all. Aren't you?"

"Yeah, that's why I'm here in Australia."

"I'm not talking about our families. I mean, what *really* made us. And why."

"You're sounding like my sister Tiggy. She goes on about a higher power."

"I'd like to meet your sister. She sounds cool. What does she do?"

"She works up in Scotland at a deer sanctuary."

"That sounds worthwhile."

"She thinks so."

"It's good for the soul to be responsible for something or someone. Like, when our Aboriginal boys have their initiation, they're circumcised and then given a stone—it's called a *tjurunga*—and on it is a special marking showing them what they need to look after in the bush. Could be a water hole or a sacred cave, or maybe a plant or an animal. Whatever it is, it's their responsibility to protect and care for it. There used to be a human chain all the way across the outback that had a responsibility to look after the necessities. The system kept our tribes alive as they crossed the desert."

"That sounds incredible," I breathed. "Like the traditions actually have a point. So, do only boys get one of those *tju*—"

"*Tjurunga* stones. Yeah, only men get one—women and children aren't allowed to touch them."

"That's a bit unfair."

"It is," she said with a shrug, "but we women have our own sacred traditions too, that we keep separate from the men. My grandma took me out bush when I was thirteen, and I'm not joking, I was scared shitless, but actually, it was really cool. I learned some useful stuff, like how to use my digging stick to find water or insects, which plants are edible and how to use them. And"—Chrissie tugged at her ears—"by the time I came back, I could hear someone sneeze from halfway down the street and tell ya exactly who it was. Out there, we were listening for danger, or the trickle of water nearby, or voices in the distance that would guide us back to our family."

"It sounds amazing. I've always loved that sort of stuff."

"Look!" Chrissie shouted suddenly. "There's a buncha 'roos!"

Chrissie steered the car onto the dusty verge of the road and slammed on the brakes, flinging our heads backward into their rests.

"Sorry, but I didn't want ya to miss them. Gotta camera?"

"Yup."

The kangaroos were much larger than I'd been expecting and Chrissie encouraged me into silly poses in front of them. As we walked back to the car, swatting away the interminable flies that investigated our skin, I couldn't help remembering the last time I'd used my camera and what had happened to the roll of film inside it. Standing in the middle of nowhere with a bunch of kangaroos and Chrissie, Thailand seemed a world away.

"How far now?" I asked as we set off again.

"Forty minutes, tops, I reckon."

And it was at least that before we finally turned off a dirt track and saw a cluster of whitewashed buildings. There was a hand-painted wooden sign telling us we'd arrived at Hermannsburg mission.

As we climbed out, I saw that we—and the occupants of a pickup truck parked close to the entrance—were the only humans who had arrived by car. I wasn't surprised. The small cluster of huts was surrounded by miles and miles of nothingness, like the surface of Mars. I noticed it was almost completely silent, not a whisper of a breeze, just the occasional buzzing of insects. Even I, who liked peace and wide open spaces, felt isolated there.

We walked toward the entrance and ducked inside the tin-roofed bungalow, our eyes slowly adjusting after the blinding sunshine.

"G'day," said Chrissie to the man standing behind the counter.

"G'day. Just the two of youse?"

"Yeah."

"That'll be nine dollars each."

"Quiet here today," Chrissie commented as I paid him.

"Don't get many tourists out here in the heat this time-a year."

"I bet. This is my friend Celaeno. She's got a pic she wants to show you." Chrissie nudged me and I pulled out the photograph and gave it to the man. He glanced at it, then his eyes swept over me.

"Namatjira. How did you come by this pic?"

"It was sent to me."

"Who from?"

"A lawyer's office in Adelaide. They're in the process of tracing the original sender for me as I'm trying to find my birth family."

"I see. So, what ya wanna know?"

"I'm not sure," I said, feeling like I was a fraud or something. Maybe the guy faced possible "relatives" of Namatjira here every day.

"She was adopted when she was a baby," put in Chrissie.

"Right."

"My dad died a few months ago, and he told me I'd been left some money," I explained. "When I went to see his Swiss lawyer, that photograph was in the envelope he gave me. I decided I should come here to Australia and find out who'd sent me the picture. I spoke to the lawyer in Adelaide, but I'd no idea who Namatjira was, hadn't ever even heard of him before, and—" I rambled on until Chrissie put a hand on my arm and took over.

"CeCe's basically come here 'cause I recognized Namatjira in the picture. She thinks it might be a clue to who her parents originally were."

The man studied the photograph again.

"It's definitely Namatjira, and I'd say the pic was taken at Heavitree Gap, sometime in the mid-1940s, when Albert got his pickup truck. As ta who the boy is standing next to him, I dunno."

"Well, why don't me and Cee take a look around the place?" suggested Chrissie. "Maybe you could have a think. D'you have archives here?"

"We have ledgers of every baby that was born here or brought to us at the mission. And a crate-load of black-an'-white pictures like that." The man pointed to my photo. "It would take me days ta go through them, though."

"No pressure, mister. We'll just go take a look around." Chrissie shepherded me past a postcard stack and a fridge full of cold drinks to the sign that proclaimed the entrance to the museum. We walked down another dusty path and found ourselves out in a large open space, surrounded by what was a vague L shape of white huts.

"Right, let's start in the chapel." Chrissie pointed to the building.

We wandered across the red earth and stepped inside the tiny chapel with rickety benches acting as pews, and a large picture of Christ on the cross hanging over the pulpit.

"So, this guy called Carl Strehlow came to this mission to try to get the Aboriginals to turn to Christianity." Chrissie paraphrased for me as she read the words on the information board. "He arrived from Germany with his family in 1894. It started out just like a regular Christian mission, but then he and the next pastor became fascinated with the local Arrernte culture and traditions," Chrissie explained while I stared at rows of dark faces in the pictures, all dressed in white.

"Who are the Arrernte?"

"The local Aboriginal mob."

"Do they still live around here?" I queried.

"Yeah, in fact, it says that in 1982 the land was officially returned to them, so Hermannsburg now belongs to the traditional owners."

"That's good, isn't it?"

"Yeah, it's awesome. Come on, let's go see the rest."

A long building with a tin roof turned out to be a schoolhouse that still had words and pictures scrawled on the blackboard. "It also says here that no half-caste Aboriginal was ever brought here by force by the Protectorate. Everyone came and went of their own free will."

"But were they actually made to become Christians?"

"It doesn't exactly say that because they'd all have had to attend services and Bible readings, but apparently the pastors turned a blind eye if they wanted to celebrate their own culture."

"So actually, they believed—or pretended to—in two different religions?"

"Yup. A bit like me," said Chrissie, grinning. "And all the rest of our mob in Oz. Come on, let's go and have a sticky-beak at Namatjira's hut."

The hut was comprised of a few basic concrete rooms, and I recognized Namatjira's face in a picture on the mantelpiece. He was a big man with strong, heavy features, grinning and squinting in the sun, standing next to a demure woman in a head scarf.

"'Albert and Rosie,'" I read. "Who was Rosie?"

"His wife. Her given name was Rubina. They had nine children, although four of them died before Albert did."

"I can't believe they needed a fire in this heat," I said, pointing at the fireplace in the photo.

"Trust me, it gets pretty cold at night in the Never Never."

A painting on the wall caught my eye and I went to study it.

"Is this by Namatjira himself?" I asked Chrissie.

"It says it is, yeah."

I stared at it, fascinated, for, rather than looking like a typical Aboriginal painting, this was a beautifully formed watercolor landscape with a white ghost gum tree to one side of it, then gorgeously soft colors depicting a vista that was backed by the purple MacDonnell Ranges. It reminded me of an Impressionist painting and I wondered how and where this man who had grown up in the middle of nowhere—Aboriginal by birth, Christian in life—had found his particular style.

"Not what you were expecting?" Chrissie stood next to me.

"No, because most of the Aboriginal art we saw in town was traditional dot paintings."

"Namatjira was taught by a white painter called Rex Battarbee, who was influenced by the Impressionists and came out here to paint the scenery. Albert learned how to paint watercolors from him."

"Wow, I'm impressed. You know your stuff, don't you?"

"Only 'cause I'm interested. I told you that art—especially Namatjira's—is a passion of mine."

As I followed her out of the hut, I thought how art had been a passion of mine too, but recently it had got lost somewhere along the way. I realized that I *really* wanted it back.

"I need the toilet," I said as we went back out into the glaring heat of the day.

"The dunny's over there." Chrissie pointed. I walked across the courtyard toward it and saw an illustrated sign hung outside on the door.

SNAKES LIKE WATER! KEEP THE LIDS DOWN!

I had the quickest pee of my life and bolted back outside, feeling sweatier than when I'd gone in.

"We should make a move," said Chrissie. "Let's go and grab some water for the journey back."

Inside the hut that comprised the ticket office and gift shop, Chrissie and I went to the till to pay.

"You got that photo, miss?" said the man we'd met on the way in. "Reckon I could show it to one of the elders. They're due here for our monthly meeting tomorra night. They might recognize the boy Namatjira's standing next ta. The eldest is ninety-six and as sharp as a tack. Brought up here, he was."

"Er . . ." I looked at Chrissie uncertainly. "Would we have to drive back out here to get it?"

"I'll be in the Alice on Saturday, so I can always drop it back to ya if ya give me your mobile number and the address of where you're staying."

"Okay," I said, seeing Chrissie nod at me in encouragement, so I handed it to him, then scribbled down the details he'd requested.

"Don't worry, love, I'll keep it safe for ya," the man said with a smile.

"Thanks."

"Safe drive home," he called as we left.

"So, did you feel anything?" Chrissie asked as we set off along the wide, deserted road back to civilization.

"What do you mean?"

"Did any instinct tell ya that ya might have come from Hermannsburg?"

"I'm not sure I 'do' instincts, Chrissie."

"Sure you do, Cee. We all do. You just gotta trust 'em a bit more, y'know?"

As we drew near Alice Springs, the sun was doing the perfect curtsy, bowing down at the end of the MacDonnell Ranges, casting shards of light onto the red desert beneath it.

"Stop here!" I ordered suddenly.

Chrissie did one of her sharp brakes and pulled the car over to the side of the road.

"Sorry, but I just need to take a photo."

"No worries, Cee."

I grabbed my camera, opened the door, and crossed the road.

"Oh my God! It's glorious," I said as I snapped away, and out of the blue I felt my fingers begin to tingle, which was the signal my body gave me when I needed to paint something. It was a sensation I hadn't had for a very long time.

"You look happy," Chrissie commented as I climbed back in.

"I am," I said, "very."

And I meant it.

The next morning, I woke up when I heard Chrissie tiptoeing around the room. Normally, I'd have dozed off again, but today, some kind of weird anticipation forced me out of bed.

"Sorry I woke you. I was just going down to get some brekky."

"It's okay, I'll come with you."

Over a strong cup of coffee and bacon and eggs, with a side of fruit to salve my conscience, we discussed what we would do for the rest of the day. Chrissie wanted to go and see the permanent Namatjira exhibition at the Araluen Arts Centre, but I had other ideas because I'd realized what it was that had woken me up so early.

"The thing is . . . well, I got inspired on the drive home yesterday. I was wondering if you'd mind taking me back to that spot where I took the pics of the sun setting last night? I'd like to have a go at painting it."

Chrissie's face lit up. "That's fantastic news. Course I'll drive ya there."

"Thanks, though I need to find some paper and paints."

"You're in luck here," Chrissie said, pointing out of the window and indicating the number of galleries along the street. "We'll pop into one of them and find out where they get their gear."

After breakfast, we walked along the street and into the first gallery we came to. Inside, Chrissie asked the woman on reception where I could find paper and paints, adding that I was a student from the Royal College of Art in London.

"D'you wanna stay here an' paint?" The woman pointed to a large room to the side of the gallery, where a number of Aboriginal artists were working at tables or on the floor. Light spilled in from the many windows, and there was a small kitchenette area where someone was making a round of coffee. It looked far more cozy than the shared workrooms at my old art college.

"No, she's planning to go bush, aren't you, Cee?" Chrissie winked at me. "Her real name's Celaeno," Chrissie added for good measure.

"Righto." The receptionist gave me a smile. "I have some oils and canvases, or does she paint with watercolors?" she asked, glancing over me to Chrissie as though they were discussing a four-year-old child.

"Both," I said, interrupting, "but I'd really like to try watercolors today."

"Okay, I'll see what I can find."

The woman stepped out from behind the counter, and I saw a sizeable bump under her yellow kaftan. While she was away, I wandered around the gallery, looking at the traditional Aboriginal works.

The walls were bursting with different depictions of the Seven Sisters. Dots, slashes, strange-looking shapes that the artists had used to depict the girls and their "old man"—Orion, who chased them through the skies. I'd always felt embarrassed about being named after a weird Greek myth and a set of stars a few million light-years away, but today it made me feel special and proud. Like I was part of them, had a special connection. And here in the Alice, I felt like I was in their high temple.

I also loved the fact that I was standing among a bunch of artists whom I'd have bet my posh riverside apartment in London hadn't attended art school. Yet here they all were, painting what they felt. And doing a good trade too, judging by the number of tourists milling around the gallery and watching them at work.

"Here ya go, Celaeno." The woman handed me an old tin of watercolors, a couple of used brushes, some tape, a sheaf of paper, and a wooden-backed canvas. "You any good?" she asked me as I fumbled for my wallet to pay.

"She's brilliant," chirped Chrissie before I'd opened my mouth to speak, just like she was my agent. "You should see some of her work."

I blushed red under my sweaty skin. "How much for the paints and paper?" I asked her.

"How about a swap? You bring me a painting, and if it's good, I'll hang it in the gallery and share the profits. My name's Mirrin, and I run the gallery for the bossman."

"Really? That's kind of you but—"

"Thanks a mill, Mirrin," interrupted Chrissie again. "We'll do that, won't we, Cee?"

"I . . . yeah, thanks."

In the blinding sunlight outside the gallery, I rounded on her. "Jesus, Chrissie, you've never seen anything that I've painted! I've always been rubbish at watercolors, and this was just an experiment, like a bit of fun and—"

"Shut up, Cee. I *know* you're great already." She tapped where her heart was. "You just need to get yer confidence back."

"But that woman," I panted from agitation and heat, "she's going to be expecting me to bring something to her and—"

"Listen, if it's crap, we'll just return the paints and pay for the paper, okay? But it won't be, Cee, I know it won't."

On the drive out of town, Chrissie decided to give me a lecture on how Namatjira approached his painting.

"You said yesterday that you were surprised that he painted landscapes, 'cause most Aboriginal artists paint using symbols to depict Dreamtime stories."

"Yeah, I was," I said.

"Well, look closer, because Namatjira does the same, just in a different form. I need ta show you what I mean exactly, but when you look at the ghost gums he paints, they're never just a tree. There's all kinds of symbolism painted into them. He tells the Dreamtime stories in his landscapes. Understand?"

"I think so."

"He drew the human form into nature, so if you look closely, the knots in a mulga tree are eyes, and there's one of his paintings where the composition of the landscape—the sky, the hills and trees—all shift and morph, so you're suddenly looking at the figure of a woman lying on the earth."

"Wow!" I tried to picture this. "Ever thought of doing something with your art knowledge, Chrissie?"

"Like, on a quiz show with 'Australian artists of the twentieth century' as my pet subject?" she chuckled.

"No, I mean, professionally."

"Are you kidding me? The guys that run the art world have studied for years to be curators or agents. Who'd want me?"

"I would," I said. "You did a great selling job today. Besides, that woman in the gallery didn't look as if she had a million degrees in art, yet she was running the joint."

"True enough. Right, we're here. Where d'you want to set up?"

Chrissie helped me spread out the blanket and cushions we'd sneaked out of the hotel room. We sat down in the shade of a ghost gum and drank some water.

"I'll take a wander for a while, shall I? Leave you be?"

"Yeah, thanks." Unlike the artists in that gallery, I wasn't anywhere near the stage of being able to paint while someone else watched. I sat cross-legged, with the sheet of paper taped onto the wooden-backed canvas. Panic clutched at me, just as it had every time I'd tried to pick up a paintbrush in the past few months.

I closed my eyes and breathed in the hot air, vaguely scented by a minty, almost medicinal, smell that was coming from the gum tree I was leaning against. I thought of who I was—Pa Salt's daughter, one of the Seven Sisters themselves—and imagined that I had flown down to earth from the heavens and stepped out of the cave into this magnificent, sunlit landscape . . .

I opened my eyes, dipped my brush into the water bottle, mixed it with some color, and began to paint.

"How ya doing?"

I jumped, nearly spilling the sludge-colored water in the bottle all over the painting.

"Sorry, Cee. You were lost in your own little world, weren't ya?" Chrissie apologized as she bent to stand the water bottle back upright. "You hungry yet? You've been painting for a good coupla hours."

"Have I?" I felt drowsy, as though I'd just woken up from a deep sleep.

"Yeah. I've been sitting in the car with the air-con on full blast for the past forty minutes. Strewth, it's hot out here. I brought ya a bottle of cold water from the car." Chrissie handed it to me, and I gulped back the liquid, feeling disoriented. "Well?" Chrissie regarded me quizzically.

"Well what?"

"How'd it go?"

"Er . . ."

I couldn't answer, because I didn't know. I looked down at the paper resting on my knees and was amazed to see that what looked like a fully formed painting had somehow arrived onto it.

"Wow, Cee . . ." Chrissie peered over my shoulder before I had time to stop her. "Just . . . wow! Oh my God!" She clasped her hands together in delight. "I knew it! That's bloody amazing! Especially considering you've only got that crappy little tin of watercolors to work with."

"I wouldn't go that far," I said as I studied the picture. "I haven't got the perspective of the MacDonnell Ranges quite right, and the sky is a bit of a muddy blue because I must have run out of clean water at some point."

But even as I looked at it, I knew that it was far and away the best watercolor I'd ever painted.

"Is that a cave?" Chrissie had crouched down next to me. "It looks like there's a shadowy figure standing in the entrance."

I looked closer and saw she was right. There was a blurry cloud of white, like a wisp of smoke coming out of a chimney. "Yeah," I said, though I couldn't really remember painting it.

"And those two gnarly bits on the ghost gum's bark—they look like eyes secretly watching the figure. Cee! You only went and did it!" Chrissie threw her arms around me and hugged me tightly.

"Did I? I've no idea how."

"That doesn't matter. The point is, you *did* do it."

"Well, it *does* matter if I ever want to do it again. And it's definitely not perfect." As always when people told me I was good at something, my critical eye began to examine it more closely and see its faults. "Look, the gum tree branches are unbalanced, and the leaves are really splodgy and not quite the right green. And—"

"Whoa!" Chrissie drew the painting from my knee and out of my reach as if she was afraid I was about to rip it to shreds. "I know artists are their own worst critics, but it's down to the audience ta decide whether it's good or bad. And as I'm the audience and a secret art nerd, especially on paintings like this, I am telling you that you just painted something great. I gotta take a piccie of this, have you got your camera?"

"Yeah, in the car."

After taking a number of photographs, we packed up and headed back to town. All the way to the Alice, Chrissie talked about the painting. In fact, she didn't just talk about it, she analyzed it to death.

"The most exciting thing of all is that ya took Namatjira's style and made it your own. That little wisp coming outta the cave; the eyes hidden in the tree, watching it; the six clouds sailing off into the sky . . ."

"I was thinking about when your granny told me the Dreamtime story of the Seven Sisters just before I started to paint," I admitted.

"I knew it! But I didn't want to say so until you did. Somehow, just like Namatjira, you managed to paint another layer into a gorgeous landscape. But in your own way, Cee. He used symbols, and you've used a story. It's awesome! I'm rapt!"

I sat there next to her, half enjoying her praise and half wishing she'd shut up. I understood she was trying to be supportive, but my cynical voice told me that however knowledgeable she seemed to be on Namatjira, she was hardly an art expert. And beyond that, if the painting did show promise, could I ever replicate it again?

She parked the car along the main street, and we went back to the café where we'd had the good kangaroo. I ordered burgers for us as I listened to her rabbit on.

"You're gonna have ta learn to drive, because you need ta go out there again. And I've got to fly back to Broome early tomorrow morning." Her eyes darkened. "I really don't wanna. I love the Alice. So many people told me bad stories about it, about the problems between us lot and the whites. And yeah, I'm sure some of them are true, but the art movement here is just amazing, and we haven't even started on Papunya Tula yet."

"What's that?"

"Another school of art that came just after Namatjira's time. Like, most of the dot paintings you saw in the gallery earlier."

I tried to suppress an almighty yawn, but failed miserably. I didn't understand why I felt so exhausted.

"Listen, why don't you go back to the hotel and grab a kip?" she suggested.

"Yeah, I might," I said, too sleepy to object. "You coming with me?"

"Nah, I thought I might take a wander to see the Namatjiras in the Araluen Arts Centre."

"Okay." I put the necessary dollars to cover the lunch on the table and stood up. "See you back at the ranch."

I came to a couple of hours later and sat bolt upright.

Where's the painting? I thought immediately as I shook myself into wakefulness. My mind searched its memory files, and I realized that we'd left it in the boot of the car when we'd gone to find lunch.

And the car was due back to the rental company at six this evening . . .

"Shit!" I swore as I looked at the time on the clock and saw it was nearing half past seven. What if Chrissie had forgotten about it? I pulled on my boots and ran down the stairs, which probably took me far longer than spending a few seconds patiently waiting for the lift. I reached reception and saw her through the glass doors, sitting on a sofa in the little residents' lounge. She was reading a book on Namatjira and as I pushed open the doors and walked toward her, my panic increased. There was no sign of the painting beside her.

"Sleeping Beauty awakes." She looked up and grinned at me. The grin faded as she saw my face. "What's up?"

"The painting," I panted. "Where is it? It was in the boot, remember? And the car was going back at six and it's half past seven now and—"

"Strewth, Cee! D'ya really think I'd have *forgotten* about it?"

"No, but where is it?" As I put my hands on my hips combatively, I realized just how much that painting meant to me. Brilliant or rubbish— or more likely somewhere in between—that wasn't the point. The point *was*, it was a start.

"Don't worry, it's perfectly safe, promise."

"Where?" I asked again.

"I said it's safe." She stood up, glaring at me now. "You really have a problem with trust, don't ya? I'm going out for a walk."

"Okay, sorry, but could you just tell me where it is?"

She shrugged silently and walked out of the lounge. By the time my legs had galvanized themselves into action and followed her into reception, she had left the hotel. I went outside and looked up and down the street, but she had vanished.

I went back upstairs to the room and lay on my bed, my heart beating like a tom-tom. Eventually, I calmed down and told myself that I'd overreacted, but surely it had been fair enough to expect a straightforward reply from her as to where my painting was? Because it signaled the return of something I'd seriously thought I might have lost forever. Something that was *mine*, that belonged to *me*, that no one could ever take away, *except* me.

Having given it away, both metaphorically and in real life, I needed it back. It wasn't "safe" unless it was with me. Couldn't she understand that? I took a long hot shower to drown out my thoughts, then lay down on my bed to wait for her to come back.

"Hi," she said as she walked into the room two hours later and threw her key down onto the desk.

"Hi," I replied.

I watched her as she sat down and undid her boots, then stripped off her trousers to begin taking off half of her right leg. She didn't speak to me, giving me the silent treatment like Star used to when I'd said or done something wrong. I lay back on my bed and closed my eyes.

"Did you hear what I said when I left the hotel earlier?" she asked me eventually.

"Yeah, I might be stupid and dyslexic, but I'm not deaf," I said, my eyes still shut.

"Jesus!" Chrissie gave a long sigh of frustration, and I heard her maneuvering herself toward the bathroom. The door slammed behind her and I heard the shower being turned on.

I *hated* these moments, the ones when everyone seemed to know what it was I'd done wrong, except for me. Like I was some alien who'd fallen to earth and didn't get the rules of the game. It was really irritating and, after all the euphoria I'd felt earlier, a total downer.

Eventually, I heard Chrissie come out of the bathroom and the creak of the bed as she sat down on it.

"Shall I turn out the light, or are you going to need clothes?" she asked me coldly.

"Whatever you want. I'm fine either way."

"Okay. Night." She turned out the light.

I managed approximately five minutes—actually, probably less—before I had to speak.

"What is your problem? I was just asking you where my painting was."

There was silence from the bed next to me. Again, I held it as long as I could, but then blurted out, "Why is it such a big deal?"

The light was switched on and Chrissie glared down at me from her sitting position on the side of her bed.

"All right! I'll tell you where the friggin' painting is! At the moment, it's probably in the store at the back of the Tangetyele Gallery waiting to be framed, which by tomorrow, Mirrin has promised me it will be. And maybe by the day after, it'll be hung on the wall of the gallery, with a selling price of six hundred dollars, which I negotiated. Okay?"

The light was snapped off again, and me and my agitation—with added astonishment—were plunged back into darkness.

"You took it to the gallery?" I said slowly, trying to breathe.

"Yup. That was the deal, wasn't it? I knew you'd never value my humble opinion on the work, so I took it to a professional. FYI," she spelled out through gritted teeth, "Mirrin loved it. Almost grabbed it outta my hand. Wants ta know when more are on the way."

There was too much in those sentences for my brain to take in, so I said nothing. Just breathed as best I could.

"She bought my painting?" I managed eventually.

"I wouldn't say that—she didn't hand over any money—but if some punter does buy it, then ya get three hundred an' fifty dollars, and the gallery two hundred an' fifty. She wanted to make it fifty-fifty, but I beat her down on the promise of more Celaeno D'Aplièses."

Celaeno D'Aplièse . . . how many times had I dreamed about that name becoming famous in the art world? It certainly wasn't a name anyone could forget, being such a mouthful.

"Oh. Thanks."

"That's okay."

"I mean," I added, beginning to see why she was so upset, "really, thanks."

"I said it's okay," came the terse response from the blackness.

I closed my eyes and tried to think of sleep but it was impossible. I sat upright, feeling it was my turn to exit stage left. Groping for my shorts, and being as clumsy as I was, I tripped over Chrissie's false leg, which stood like a booby trap between the beds.

"Sorry," I said, fumbling for it in the darkness to stand it back upright.

The light was switched on again.

"Thanks," I repeated as I looked for my shoes.

"You running out on me?" she asked.

"No, I'm just not tired. I slept for ages this afternoon."

"Yeah, while I was off doing you a deal." Chrissie regarded me with her head propped up on her elbow. "Look, Cee, it's my last night here and I don't want us ta fall out. I was just gutted that you didn't trust me to take care of that painting after all I'd said and done. And then today, I saw what kind of artist you could be, and I was so excited. But ya didn't see any of that when you marched into the lounge demanding to know where your painting was. It just . . . shook me. I really thought you'd started to trust me. I was rapt when Mirrin loved it and I couldn't wait ta tell you about it and go out an' celebrate. But you came in so angry with me that the moment was ruined."

"I'm really sorry, Chrissie. I didn't mean to upset you."

"Don't you see? I came here to the Alice because I wanted ta be with you. I missed you when ya left Broome."

"Did you?"

"Yeah. A lot," she added shyly.

"And I'm really happy you came," I said blandly, wondering whether my mind was correctly processing what I was hearing. Or, more important, its undercurrent. "I'm really sorry again," I said, wanting to blank the whole thing out, because I really couldn't deal with it right now. "I'm such an idiot sometimes."

"Look, you've told me about Star and the relationship you had with her, and how she let ya down."

"She didn't really, she just needed to move on," I said loyally.

"Whatever. I know you find it difficult to trust, especially in love when it's . . ." I heard Chrissie sigh heavily. "I suppose I just want you to know before I leave that I . . . well, I think I love you, Cee. Don't ask me how or why, but it's just the way it is. I know you had a boyfriend in Thailand and . . ." I watched tears come to Chrissie's eyes. "But I'm just being honest, okay?"

"Okay, I understand," I said, averting my eyes. "You've been fantastic, Chrissie, and—"

"No need ta say anything else. I understand too. At least we can be friends before we go to sleep."

"Yes."

"Night then." She reached to switch off the light again.

"Night." I lay back down on my bed, suddenly too exhausted to move as my brain took in the implications of what Chrissie had said.

Apparently, she *loved* me. And even I wasn't going to be as naive as to think she meant it just as a friend.

The question was, did I *love* her? I mean, only a few weeks ago, I'd been with Ace. It struck me that now Star was gone, I seemed to be forming attachments to all sorts of people, male *and* female . . .

21

I felt a gentle hand on my shoulder. "Wake up, Cee, I gotta leave for the airport right now. I overslept."

I pulled myself out of sleep immediately and sat upright.

"You're leaving? Now?"

"Yeah, that's what I just said."

"But . . ." I climbed out of bed and looked for my shorts. "I'll come with you."

"No. I'm not good at that kinda stuff." Then she pulled me to her and hugged me. "Good luck with finding out who you are," she said as she released me and walked toward the door. I didn't miss the double meaning behind her words.

"I'll keep in touch, promise," I said.

"Yeah, I'd like that. Whatever happens," she said, then reached out for the door handle.

The sight galvanized me into action and I walked toward her. "Look, I've really enjoyed being with you, Chrissie. These past few days have been, like, well, the best of my life really."

"Thanks. Sorry about last night and all. I shouldn't have . . . well." She smiled bleakly. "I gotta go."

Then she reached for me, her warm lips brushing against my mouth as she kissed me. We stood like that for a few seconds before she pulled away. "Bye, Cee."

The door slammed behind her and I stood in a room that suddenly felt lonely and sad, as if Chrissie had taken all the warmth and love and laughter with her. I sank down onto the bed, not really equipped to know what to think or feel. I lay back, but the silence pounded in my ears. I felt just like I had when Star had left to go down to Kent to be with her new family: abandoned.

Except, I thought, I wasn't. Even if what had just happened had been a shock, Chrissie had told me she loved me.

Now, *that* really was a revelation. So few people in my life had said those words to me before. Was that the reason why I was feeling all gooey inside about her? Or was it . . . ? Was *I* . . . ?

"Shit!" I shook my head in complete confusion. I'd never been good at working out my emotions—I literally needed a Sherpa and a flaming torch to walk me through my psychological paces. I was just thinking about the fact that maybe I should join most of the Western world and offload everything to a professional when the phone by my bed rang.

"Hi, Miss D'Aplièse. I've gotta guy down here who wants to see ya."

"What's his name?"

"A Mr. Drury. He said he met you at Hermannsburg mission."

"Tell him I'll be down in a tick." I slammed down the receiver, put on my boots, and left the room.

I found the man from Hermannsburg wandering around reception, reminding me of a large wild animal who'd just been put in a small cage and didn't like it one bit. He towered over everything, his dusty clothes and sun-worn face out of place among the modern plastic furniture.

"Hi, Mr. Drury. Thanks for coming," I said, defaulting to the politeness that Ma had always drummed into us as children and holding out my hand.

"Hi, Celaeno. Call me Phil. Is there somewhere we can go to have a yak?"

"I think breakfast is still probably on the go." I looked at the receptionist, who nodded.

"The buffet closes in twenty minutes," she told us, and we wandered through.

"Here?" I indicated a table by the window in the half-empty dining room.

"Suits me," he said, and sat down.

"Want anything from the buffet?"

"I'll grab a coffee if there is one. You go ahead with the tucker."

Having ordered two coffees—both strong and black—I dashed over to the food and piled up a plate with cholesterol.

"I like a woman who enjoys her grub," Phil commented as I put the plate down opposite him.

"Oh, I do," I said as I ate. Judging by the way he was staring at me, I reckoned I might be in need of brain food.

"We had our meeting with the elders last night at Hermannsburg," he said, having downed the dainty cup of coffee in a single gulp.

"Yeah, you mentioned you were going to," I said.

"Right at the enda the meeting, I handed around your photograph."

"Did anyone recognize the young guy in it?"

"Yeah." Phil signaled for the waitress to pour him another coffee. "Ya could say that."

"What do you mean?"

"Well, I couldn't understand why all of them were looking at it and pointing, then having a right old laugh."

"Why were they?" I asked, anxious to cut to the chase.

"Because, Celaeno, the bloke in the photo was present at the meeting. He's one of the elders. The others were all giving him gyp about the pic."

I took a deep breath and then a sip of coffee, wondering whether I was going to scream, jump for joy, or throw up the enormous breakfast I'd just stuffed down myself. I wasn't used to this much excitement in the space of twenty-four hours.

"Right," I said, knowing he was waiting to continue.

"The laughter eventually died down, and the fella who's in that photograph came to talk ta me afterward when the others had left."

"What did he say?"

"Want me to be honest?"

"Yeah."

"Well." Phil swallowed. "I've never seen an elder cry before. Last night, I did."

"Oh," I said, for some reason swallowing a massive lump in my own throat.

"They're big, strong men, y'see. Don't have none of those girly emotions. Put it like this, he knew exactly who you were. And he wants to meet you."

"Oh," I said again. "Er, who does he think he is? I mean . . ." I shook my head at my crap use of language. "Who is he to me?"

"He thinks he's your grandfather."

"Right."

This time, I couldn't stop the tears or I really would have thrown up my breakfast. So I let them pour out of my eyes in front of this man that I didn't even know. I watched him dig in his pocket and pass me a spotless white handkerchief across the table.

"Thanks," I said as I blew my nose. "It's the shock, I mean . . . I've come a long way and I never really expected to find my . . . family."

"No, I'm sure." He waited patiently until I'd pulled myself together.

"Sorry," I offered, and he shook his head.

"I understand."

I held his soggy hanky in my hand, reluctant to let it go. "So, why does he think that he might be my . . . grandfather?"

"I think it's his place to tell you that."

"But what if he's got it wrong?"

"Then he has"—Phil shrugged—"but I doubt it. These men, they don't just work on fact, y'see. They have an instinct that goes far beyond what I could even begin to explain ta ya. And Francis, of all the elders, is not one to muck around. If he knows, he knows, and that's that."

"Right." The hanky was so wet now that I resorted to wiping the back of my hand across my still-dripping nose. "When does he want to meet me?"

"As soon as possible. I said I'd ask you if you'd be able to spare the time ta come back with me to Hermannsburg now."

"Now?"

"Yeah, if it suits ya. He's going bush soon, so I'd suggest there's no time like the present."

"Okay," I said, "but I don't have any transport to get back here."

"You can kip at my place tonight if necessary, and I'll drop ya back in town whenever ya want," he replied.

"Right. Er, then I need to get my stuff together."

"Sure." He nodded. "Take your time. I got some errands ta run in town anyway. How about I see you back here in half an hour?"

"Okay, thanks."

We parted in reception and I ran up the stairs to my room. To say my head was spinning doesn't even begin to describe it. As I packed my stuff into my rucksack, I felt as if I'd been trapped in a film that had gone on for hours—i.e., my life before this morning. And then, it had suddenly been fast-forwarded so that lots of things all happened at once. That was the way my life felt right now.

Australia, Chrissie, my grandfather . . .

I stood up and felt so woozy that I had to steady myself by leaning against the wall. I shook my head but that only made it worse, so I lay down instead, feeling like a wimp.

"Too much excitement," I muttered, trying to breathe deeply to calm myself. Eventually, I stood up again, seeing I only had ten minutes left before I had to meet Phil downstairs.

Go with the flow, Cee, I thought as I brushed my teeth viciously and looked at my reflection in the mirror. *Just go with the flow.*

The receptionist told me there was nothing to pay, and I realized that Chrissie must have used the little money she earned to clear the bill. I felt terrible that I hadn't thought about it and got there first. She was obviously proud, like me, and didn't want to feel as though she was taking advantage.

The dusty, battered pickup truck I'd seen in the car park at Hermannsburg was outside the hotel.

"Throw your pack in the back of the ute an' climb aboard," Phil instructed me.

We set off, and I studied him slyly as he drove. From the tips of his huge dirt-spattered boots, to his brawny well-muscled arms and the Akubra hat atop his head, he was the archetypal Australian bushman.

"So, quite a moment for ya coming up, young lady," he commented.

"Yeah. If this guy really is my grandfather . . . I just don't understand how he could know it's definitely me. I mean, he's not seen a picture of me or anything, and I know it was my adoptive dad that named me."

"Well, I've known Francis half my life, and he's not someone who'd normally react the way he did when I mentioned you ta him yesterday. Besides, you had that piccie of him, remember?"

"Yeah, maybe he was the one who sent it and gave me the inheritance?"

"Maybe."

"What's he like? As a person, I mean?"

"Francis?" Phil chuckled. "He's pretty hard to describe. 'Unique' would be the word. He's getting on now a-course—he was born in the early thirties, I think, so he's well inta his seventies, and his painting has slowed down a bit recently . . ."

"He's an artist?"

"Yeah, and pretty well-known around here. He lived at the mission as a child. And from the way the elders were teasing him last night, he followed Namatjira around like a pet dingo."

"I'm an artist too." I bit my lip as I felt the swell of tears again.

"Well, there y'go. Talent runs in families, doesn't it? Not sure what my old dad passed down ta me, apart from a hatred of towns and people . . . No offense to you, miss, but I'm far more comfortable with my chooks an' dogs than I am with humans."

"So I'm definitely not related to Namatjira?" I thought how disappointed Chrissie would be.

"Doesn't look like it, no, but Francis Abraham is still a decent rellie to have in ya closet."

"'Abraham'?" I questioned.

"Yeah, they gave him a surname at the mission, like with all the orphaned babies."

"He was an orphan?"

"It's best he tells ya. I only know the basics. All you need ta know is that he's a good, solid bloke, not like some-a the rubble around these parts. I'll miss him when he retires from the committee. He keeps the resta them in line, if ya know what I mean. They respect him."

My heart rate began to rise as we finally pulled into the Hermannsburg car park and I wished Chrissie were by my side to calm me.

"Righto, let's go an' get ourselves a cool drink while we wait for him," Phil said, springing out of the truck. "Best leave yer stuff where it is—you don't want any unwelcome visitors climbing inta that rucksack, do ya?"

I shuddered and my heart rate went up by another ninety thousand beats as panic rose through me. What if I actually had to stay the night here? In the outback, surrounded by my worst eight-legged nightmares?

Come on, Cee, be brave. You've just got to face your fears, I told myself as I tramped across the hard red ground behind Phil.

"Coke?" He reached into the chiller cabinet.

"Thanks." As I pulled off the top, Phil went to the rack of books, searching for something.

"Here we go."

I watched him leaf through a big hardback entitled *Aboriginal Art of the Twentieth Century*, and I only hoped he wasn't going to give me an enormous essay to read.

"Knew he was in here." He pointed a finger to a page and tapped it.

"That's one of Francis's. They got it in the National Gallery of Australia now."

I looked down at the glossy picture and couldn't help but smile. Given that my possible grandfather had learned from Namatjira, I'd been expecting a watercolor landscape. Instead, my senses were blown away by a vibrant dot painting—what looked like a round swirl of fiery red, orange, and yellow—which reminded me of the Catherine wheel that Pa had set off in the garden at Atlantis for my eighteenth birthday.

As I looked closer, I began to make out shapes within the perfect spiral. A rabbit perhaps, and maybe that was a snake weaving its way through the circle to the center . . .

"It's amazing," I said, for the first time understanding what a talented artist could do with dots.

"It's called *Wheel of Fire*," commented Phil from behind the counter. "What d'ya think?"

"I love it, but it wasn't what I was expecting because you said he learned from Namatjira."

"Yeah, but Francis also went up ta Papunya with Clifford Possum long before Geoffrey Bardon came on the scene. The two-a them helped start the Papunya movement. Here, I'll show you Clifford Possum's work."

I was embarrassed that this man was talking a whole new language to me. I'd no idea who Geoffrey Bardon or Clifford Possum was, or where Papunya was. *Some art scholar I am*, I thought.

"Here." Phil tapped a page and another glorious painting appeared before my eyes. The artist had created a picture in soft pastels, the shapes formed by thousands of the tiniest and most delicate dots. I was reminded a little of Monet's *Water Lilies*, although it was as if the painter had taken the two different schools of painting and mixed them together to produce something unique.

"That's called *Warlugulong*. It sold for over two million dollars last year." Phil raised an eyebrow. "Serious moolah. Now, 'scuse me, Celaeno, I need to check out the dunny—found a Western brown in there yesterday."

"Right. Did he . . . my, er, grandfather, say when he might arrive?"

"Sometime today," Phil said vaguely. "Take what you need from the fridge, love, and I'll see ya in a bit."

Armed with a bottle of water, I picked up the book and looked for somewhere to sit and flick through it. There was only the high stool behind the counter, so I perched myself on that and opened the book at the beginning.

I was actually so engrossed, not only in the amazing paintings, but in trying to decipher the Aboriginal titles of the paintings and their meanings, that I only looked up when I heard the door to the hut open, having obviously missed the sound of a car.

"Hello," said the figure standing in the doorway.

"Hi."

At first, I thought he was a tourist come to visit Hermannsburg, because he couldn't be my grandfather—all the old Aboriginal men I'd seen in photos were small and very dark, their skin parched by the sun into wrinkles and crevices like dried-up prunes. Besides the fact that this man looked far too young to be him, he was tall and thin, with skin the same shade as my own. As he removed his Akubra hat and walked toward me, I saw he had the most incredible pair of eyes. They were bright blue with flecks of gold and amber, so that the irises appeared rather like the dot paintings I had just been looking at. Then I realized he was staring at me as hard as I was at him, and I felt the color rise to my cheeks under the intensity of his gaze.

"Celaeno?" His voice was deep and measured, like honey. "I'm Francis Abraham."

My eyes locked with his in a moment of recognition.

"Yes."

There were more pauses and staring, and I realized he didn't know how to play this moment any more than I did, because we both knew it was BIG.

"Can I take some water?" he asked me, indicating the fridge. I was thankful that he'd broken the moment, but also wondered why he was asking *me*. After all, he was an "elder," whatever that meant, so I was pretty certain that he could take as much water as he wanted.

I watched him stride over to the chiller cabinet. The way he walked and then stretched out a muscled arm to pull open the glass door belied how old Phil had told me he was. How could this strong, vital man be in his seventies? He was far more Crocodile Dundee than OAP, which he confirmed as he used the lightest touch of his thumb and forefinger to screw off the bottle cap. I watched as he drank deeply, perhaps using the gesture to play for time and think what to say.

Having drained the bottle, he threw it in the bin, then turned to me once more.

"I sent you that photograph," he said. "I hoped you'd come."

"Oh, thanks."

A long silence ensued, before he gave a deep sigh and a small shake of his head, then walked around the counter to me.

"Celaeno . . . come and give your grandfather a hug."

As there wasn't room to actually go anywhere in the tiny, confined space behind the counter, I just reached forward to him and he took me in his arms. My head lay against his heart and I heard it thumping steadily in his chest, feeling his life force. And his love.

We both wiped away a surreptitious tear when we eventually parted. He whispered something in a language I didn't understand, then looked heavenward. As he was closer now, I could see fine wrinkles crisscrossing his skin and ropes of sinew in his neck, which revealed that he was older than my first impression had suggested.

"I'm sure you have a lot of questions," he said.

"Yes, I do."

"Where's Phil?"

"Gone off to look for snakes in the . . . dunny."

"Well, I'm sure he won't mind if we use his sleeping hut to chat." He held out his arm. "Come, we've got lots to talk about."

Phil's sleeping hut was just as it said on the tin: a small, low-ceilinged room with an ancient fan dangling above a rough wooden bed that boasted only a sleeping bag on top of the stained mattress. Francis opened the door that led from the bedroom onto a shady veranda beyond it. He pulled out an old wooden chair for me, which wobbled as he placed it down.

"Sit?" he asked.

"Thanks." As I sat down, I saw the view in front of me immediately made up for any lack of facilities inside. Uninterrupted red desert in the foreground rolled down to a creek. On the other side of it, a small line of silver-green shrubs that depended on sucking out the limited water supply to stay alive grew along the edges. And beyond that . . . well, there was nothing until the red land met the blue horizon.

"I lived along that creek for a while. Many of us did. In, but out, if you understand what I mean."

I didn't, but I nodded anyway. It dawned on me then that I stood at the junction of two cultures which were still struggling to come to terms with each other two hundred years on. Australia—and I—were only young and trying to work ourselves out. We were making progress, but then making mistakes, because we didn't have centuries of wisdom and the experience of age to guide us.

I felt instinctively that the man sitting opposite me had more wisdom than most. I raised my eyes to meet his again.

"Ah, Celaeno, where should we begin?" He steepled his fingers and looked at that distant horizon.

"You tell me."

"Y'know," he said, turning his gaze back to me, "I never imagined this day would come. So many moments that one wishes for don't."

"I know," I agreed, wishing I could place his strange accent, because it was a mixture of so many different intonations that every time I thought I'd cracked it, I knew I was wrong. There was Australian, English, and I even thought I recognized a hint of German.

"So, you received the letter and the photograph from the solicitor in Adelaide?" he prompted.

"I did, yes."

"And the amount that went with it?"

"Yes. Thank you, it was really kind of you, if it was you that sent it."

"I arranged for it to be sent, yes, but I didn't use these hands to earn it. Nevertheless, it is yours by rights. Through my . . . *our* family." His eyes crinkled into a warm smile. "You look like your great-grandmother. Just like her . . ."

"Was that the daughter of Camira? The baby with the amber eyes?" I hazarded a guess from what I had listened to so far on the CD.

"Yes. Alkina was my mother. I . . . well." He looked as if he might cry.

"Oh," I said.

"So." Francis visibly pulled himself together. "Tell me what you have discovered so far about your kin?"

I told him what I knew, feeling shy and uncertain because this man had such *presence*, an aura of calm and charisma, that made me feel even more tongue-tied than I usually did.

"I only got up to where the *Koombana* had sunk. And the dad and both brothers had been lost at sea. The person who wrote the book seemed to be saying that there'd been a really close relationship between Kitty's husband's brother—Drummond, was it?—and her."

"I have read it. It suggests that they had an affair," he agreed.

"I know how people just write stuff to sell books, so I didn't necessarily believe it or anything," I babbled, feeling terrible that I might be slandering a close member of his—*our* family.

"Celaeno, are you telling me you feel this biographer may have sensationalized Kitty Mercer's life?"

"Perhaps, yes," I hedged nervously.

"Celaeno."

"Yes?"

"When you hear what I have to tell you, you will know that she didn't sensationalize it enough!"

I watched in amazement as Francis put his head back and laughed. When his eyes turned back to me, they were full of amusement. "Now, I will tell you the real story. A truth that was only told to me on my grandmother's deathbed. And we are not laughing about that, because she was one of the most dear, precious human beings I ever knew."

"I understand, and please, don't tell me if you don't want to. Maybe we should get to know each other better, so you know you can trust me?"

"I have felt you since you were a seed in my daughter's womb. It is you I worry for, Celaeno. To never know your roots, where you came from . . ." Francis gave a deep sigh. "And you must know the story of your relatives. You are kin. Blood of their—and my—blood."

"How did you find me?" I asked. "After all these years?"

"It was my late wife's—your grandmother's—last wish that I look once more for our daughter. I didn't find her, but instead I found you. To help you understand more, I must take you back. You know the story up until the *Koombana* sank, taking all the Mercer men with it?"

"Yes. But how do I fit in?"

"I understand your impatience, but first you must listen carefully to understand. So, I shall tell you what happened to Kitty after that . . ."

KITTY

Broome, Western Australia

April 1912

22

Kitty had often wondered how humans made it through the darkest moments of loss. In Leith she had visited families in the tenements, only to discover that they had been decimated by an influenza or measles epidemic. They had put their faith in the Lord, simply because there was nowhere else to put it.

And I'm surely on my way to hell, she thought constantly.

In the week that followed, though outwardly her daily routine didn't alter, Kitty walked through it like a wraith, as though she too had departed this world. The windows of the stores along Dampier Terrace were hung with black cloth and there was barely a family in town that had not been touched by the disaster. To add to their shock, news reached them that the "unsinkable" *Titanic* had also been swallowed by the ocean, with few survivors.

No one had any idea how the *Koombana* had gone down, taking her precious cargo to the bottom of the sea. A cabin door, a Moroccan-leather settee cushion . . . these were the scant remains that had drifted to the surface. No bodies had yet been found, and Kitty knew they never would be. Hungry sharks would have feasted on their flesh within hours.

For once, Kitty was glad of her small community and its shared grief. The usual social rules were ignored as people met in the street and held each other, allowing tears to fall unchecked. Kitty was humbled by the kindness she received, and by the condolence cards pushed through the letter box so as not to disturb her.

Charlie, whose initial reaction had been so calm, had cried on his mother's knee a few days after she'd told him.

"I know they've gone to heaven, Mama, but I miss 'em. I want to see Papa and Uncle Drum . . ."

Her son's suffering at least gave Kitty something to focus on and she spent as much time as she could with him. With the loss of his father, grandfather, and uncle, the male Mercer line had been wiped out in one fell swoop and Charlie was now the sole heir. Kitty feared what a burden it might prove to be for him in the future.

After she had tucked Charlie into his bed for the night, gently stroking his hair to send him to sleep, Kitty fingered the growing stack of unopened letters and telegrams on her writing bureau. She could not bear to open them, accept the writers' sympathies, for she knew she deserved none of it. Despite trying to rein in her duplicitous heart and focus her sorrow on Andrew, she continued to mourn incessantly for Drummond.

She went out onto the veranda and looked up at the vast expanse of stars, searching for an answer.

As always, there was none.

Since there were no bodies to be buried, Bishop Riley announced that there would be a memorial service held in the Church of the Annunciation at the end of April. Kitty went to Wing Hing Loong, the local tailor, to purchase mourning attire, only to discover that they had already sold out of black dress fabric.

"Dun worry, Missus Mercer," said the diminutive Chinaman. "Wear what you have, no one care what you look like." Kitty left the crowded shop with a grim smile, seeing for herself that it was an ill wind that blew nobody good.

Although most of the luggers in the pearling fleet had been hauled in for the lay-up season, a few had been caught in the cyclone. Noel Donovan, the gentle Irish manager of the Mercer Pearling Company, came to the house to give her the details of the losses.

"Twenty men," she sighed. "Do you have their addresses so I can write to their families? Do any of them have relatives in Broome? If so, I'd like to visit them personally."

"I'll get what addresses I can from the office, Mrs. Mercer. I'd be reckoning that the twentieth of March, the day the mighty *Koombana* sank, will go down in history. Teaches us never to become complacent, doesn't it now? Man's arrogance lets him believe he can command the oceans. Nature knows better."

"Sadly, for all us souls left behind, you are indeed right, Mr. Donovan."

"Well now, I'll be leaving ye to it." He rose from his chair, then clasped his hands nervously together. "Pardon me mentioning it at such a time, but have you heard from Mrs. Mercer Senior at all?"

"I'm afraid I have not yet found the courage to open all the telegrams I have been sent. Or the cards and letters." Kitty indicated the growing pile on her desk.

"Well now, I haven't heard from her either and I hardly like to bother her, but I wondered whether ye had an idea of what's to become of the pearling business. What with all three Mercer men gone . . ." Noel shook his head.

"I confess that I have no idea, but with no one left to run it, and Charlie still so young, I can only imagine it will be sold."

"I thought as much, and I should warn you, Mrs. Mercer, that the vultures are circling already. I'd reckon 'tis ye they'll come to first, so I'd be advising you to contact the family lawyer in Adelaide. There is one particular gentleman, Japanese I believe, who is most interested. Mr. Pigott is also planning on selling everything. 'Tis a mighty blow to our industry indeed. Well now, good day, Mrs. Mercer, and I will see ye at the memorial."

The morning of the service, Kitty tried to persuade Camira and Fred to accompany her and Charlie. Camira looked horrified.

"No, Missus Kitty, dat whitefella place. Not for us."

"But you deserve to be there, Camira. You and Fred . . . you loved them too."

Camira stoically refused, so Kitty set off with Charlie on the cart. In the tiny church, people moved aside to allow her to sit with Charlie near the front. The congregation overflowed into the garden and many peered through the louvered windows to hear the bishop's sermon. Throughout the ceremony and amid the sound of pitiful sobbing, Kitty sat dry-eyed. She prayed for the many souls lost but would not cry tears for herself. She knew she deserved every second of the pain and guilt she was suffering.

Afterward, there was a wake in the Roebuck Bay Hotel. Some of the men drowned their sorrows in the alcohol that the pearling masters had provided and began singing Scottish and Irish sea shanties, which took Kitty spinning back to the day she had stumbled into the Edinburgh Castle Hotel.

Back at home later, she sat down in the drawing room and, out of habit, picked up her embroidery. As she sewed, she pondered her own and Charlie's future. No doubt what she'd said to Noel Donovan was correct and the businesses would be sold, with the funds put in trust for Charlie. She wondered whether she should return to Edinburgh, yet she doubted Edith would be happy about her only grandson leaving Australia. Perhaps she would insist they both come back to live in Adelaide, and if Kitty refused, might even hold Charlie's future fortune to ransom . . .

Kitty rose from her chair and walked across to her desk. Now that the memorial service was over, she had to begin to face the future. She separated the letters from the unopened telegrams, sat down, and started to read.

Tears began to stream down her face at the generosity and thoughtfulness of the Broome townspeople.

. . . *And Drummond, what a delightful breath of fresh air he was. Lighting up our dinner table with his wit and humor* . . .

Kitty jumped as she heard the front door slam. Heavy footsteps sounded along the entrance hall, and the drawing room door creaked open. Kitty held her breath, realizing too late that she was now a woman alone in a dangerous town. She turned around from her desk and saw a figure standing there, a figure that was all too familiar, even covered as he was in filth and red dust. Kitty wondered if she was hallucinating, because this *could not be* . . .

She closed her eyes, then reopened them. And he was still there, staring at her.

"Drummond?" she whispered.

His eyes narrowed but he did not reply.

"Oh my God, Drummond, you're alive! You're *here!*" She ran to him, but was startled when he pushed her away harshly. His blue eyes were steely and red rimmed.

"Kitty, it is not Drummond, but Andrew, your husband!"

"I . . ." Her head spun and she fought off the urge to vomit, but some deep instinct told her she must dredge her mind to produce an explanation.

"I have been so lost in grief, I can hardly remember my own name. Of course it is you, Andrew, yes, now I see it is." She urged her hand to caress his cheek, his hair. "How can this be? How can my husband return to me from the dead?"

"I hardly know . . . oh, Kitty . . ." His face crumpled and he fell back against the wall. She caught him by the arm and led him to a chair, where his head dropped into his hands and his shoulders shook with heavy sobs.

"Oh my darling," she whispered, tears coming to her own eyes. She went to the sideboard, poured him a measure of brandy, then thrust it into his trembling fingers. Eventually, he took a sip.

"I can't bear it," he murmured. "My brother and father . . . gone. But I am still here. *How* can God be so cruel?" He looked up at her, his eyes desolate. "I should have been on the *Koombana*. I should have died with them . . ."

"Hush, my darling, it is a miracle to have you back with us. Please, how did you survive?"

Andrew took another sip of brandy and gathered his strength. Pain seemed to have deepened the lines on his young face, and beneath the red streaks of mud, his skin was gray with exhaustion and shock.

"I left the ship shortly after Fremantle. I had some . . . business to attend to. I traveled overland, and it was not until I reached Port Hedland two days ago that I heard the news. I have not slept since . . ." His voice broke then, and he hid his face from her.

"It has all been a grave shock for you, my love," she said, trying to collect herself, "and you have not had time to process it. Let me fetch you something to eat. And you must take off your wet clothes. I shall lay out some dry ones for you." Her body was eager to have some occupation, as her mind could not be still. He caught her hand.

"Did you not get my telegram? I told you I had a last-minute errand to attend to."

"Yes, I did. You said your father would tell me what you meant, but, Andrew, he didn't arrive . . ." Kitty's voice trailed off.

He winced. "Of course. How is my mother? She must be devastated."

"I . . . do not know. I did write to her straight after it happened, but . . ." Guiltily, Kitty pointed to the pile of still unopened telegrams. "Noel Donovan came to see me only yesterday and said that he had not heard from her either."

"For God's sake, Kitty!" Andrew stood up, shaking with anger. "Noel Donovan is merely a member of my staff. At a time like this, she would hardly respond to such a man. You are her daughter-in-law! Did you not think that she might need to have a further response from you?" He began to tear open the telegrams, read them briefly, then shook one in her face.

COME TO ADELAIDE AT ONCE STOP I CANNOT TRAVEL THERE FOR I AM UNDONE STOP MUST KNOW WHAT HAPPENED STOP REPLY BY RETURN STOP EDITH STOP

Andrew threw it on the floor. "So, while you have been comforted by the local townsfolk, attending memorial services and receiving letters of condolence, my mother has been alone in her grief, thousands of miles away."

"You are right, and I am so very sorry. Forgive me, Andrew."

"And forgive *me* for coming home in anticipation of seeing my wife, having discovered that my father and brother are dead. And yet you have sat here for these past weeks without even having the foresight to think of my poor mother."

They didn't speak much after that. As Andrew wolfed down the plate of bread and cold meats she brought him, Kitty watched his expressions carefully as a variety of emotions passed across his eyes, but he didn't share them with her.

"Andrew, will you come to bed?" Kitty asked him eventually. "You must be exhausted." She reached a hand out but he snatched his away.

"No. I will take a bath. Go and sleep."

"I will draw one for you."

"No! I will do it. Good night, Kitty. I will see you in the morning."

"Good night." Kitty left the room, and upon reaching her bedroom, closed the door behind her, biting her lip to stop the sobs that were building up inside her chest.

I can't bear it . . .

After undressing, she lay down and buried her face in the pillow.

I called him Drummond . . . my God! How could I have done that?

"Does he know?" she whispered to herself. "Is that why he's so angry? Lord, what have I done?"

Eventually, she sat up, and took some deep breaths. "Andrew is alive," she said out loud. "And it is wonderful news. Charlie, Edith . . . they will be so very happy. Everyone will tell me how lucky I am. Yes. I *am* lucky."

Andrew did not come to her bed that night. She found him at breakfast the next morning, with Charlie sitting on the chair next to him.

"Papa came back from heaven," her son said, smiling happily. "He's an angel now, an' flew back wiv wings."

"And I am glad to be home," said Andrew.

As Camira served them, Kitty saw the confused look in her eyes.

"Isn't it wonderful? Andrew is home!"

"Yessum, Missus Kitty," she said with a hurried nod, then left the room.

"Your little black doesn't seem herself," Andrew commented as he munched his way through three slices of toast and bacon.

"She is probably amazed and overwhelmed at your miraculous return, as we all are."

"I'd like you to accompany me into town, Kitty. I think it is important that people see us reunited."

"Yes, of course, Andrew."

"I shall then go to the office, as I can imagine there will be much to do there. I will send a telegram to Mother on the way and tell her we shall all go to Alicia Hall for a visit soon."

Once Camira had taken Charlie off to the kitchen, Andrew stood up and studied Kitty.

"I read the condolence letters from the townsfolk after my bath last night. They were very kind about Father and myself, and poor old Drummond. He in particular was obviously very popular here."

"He was, yes."

"The two of you seemed to do rather a lot of socializing together while I was gone."

"Invitations came and I felt I should accept them. You always tell me how important it is."

"And I remember how many times you came up with an excuse to turn them down in the past. With me, anyway."

"I . . . that is, the rains were worse than usual this year. I think we all suffered from cabin fever and needed to get out once they'd stopped," Kitty improvised.

"Well, now that I am returned from the dead, we are able to celebrate. And I hope I will not disappoint our neighbors by being myself rather than my brother, God rest his soul."

"Andrew, please don't talk like that."

"Even my own son says nothing but 'Uncle Drum' this and 'Uncle Drum' that. It seems he has endeared himself to everyone. Does that include you, my dear?"

"Andrew, please, your brother is dead! He is gone forever! Surely you cannot resent the fact that he enjoyed the last few weeks of his life here with family and new friends?"

"Of course not. What do you take me for? However, even though he is dead, it feels rather as if he walked into my house and my life and took both over while I was away."

"And thank God he *was* here, especially when I was sick."

"Yes, of course." Andrew nodded, chastened. "Forgive me, Kitty, it has all been rather overwhelming. Now, I would like to leave for town at ten o'clock. Can you be ready?"

"Of course. Will we take Charlie?"

"Best leave him here," Andrew decreed.

As they drove along Dampier Terrace, Kitty could only assume that Andrew wished as many residents as possible to see he had returned. She watched the reactions of the shopkeepers and passersby who crowded around him, desperate to know how he'd managed to escape from his watery grave. Andrew told the same story a number of times, and people hugged Kitty and told her how lucky she was.

I am, she reiterated silently as they set off for the office close to the harbor.

Again, Kitty witnessed astonishment, then joy as an emotional Noel Donovan embraced his boss. A bottle of champagne was procured and an impromptu party ensued. It seemed that everyone in town wanted to celebrate the miracle of Andrew's survival and Kitty fixed a tight smile on her face as people hugged her, crying with happiness at her husband's return. Andrew too was constantly surrounded by people, all slapping him on the back, as if testing to see if he was real.

"Perhaps they should rename me Lazarus," Andrew jested that evening, as the party moved to the Roebuck Bay Hotel. It was a rare moment of humor from him, and Kitty was glad of it.

Over the following week, they welcomed a constant stream of visitors to their home, as people crowded in to hear Andrew repeat the tale of his decision to leave the ship at Geraldton.

"Did you have a vision?" asked Mrs. Rubin. "Did you know what was to occur?"

"Of course not," Andrew said, "or I would never have let the ship continue. It was nothing but coincidence."

But it seemed no one wanted to believe that it had been. Andrew had taken on the role of Messiah, his survival a sign that good fortunes were in store for the town of Broome. It invigorated the lugger captains and divers, who had been despondent since the recent losses. Even the fellow pearling masters, who had almost certainly been eager to see the fall of the Mercer Pearling Company, embraced Andrew at the head of the table as the weekly dinner meeting was resumed.

Among this whirlwind, Kitty found herself moving through the days like a puppet, her arms and legs feeling as if they were operated by outside forces, her mind trapped as a witness to a life she was not meant to have. Guilt plagued her waking and sleeping thoughts constantly. By day, Andrew was courteous, kind, and grateful to those who surrounded him, but at night over dinner, he barely spoke to her. Afterward, he would retire to bed, now favoring the single cot in his dressing room.

"Wouldn't you be more comfortable back in our bedroom?" Kitty had asked him tentatively one night.

"I find myself restless and would only disturb you, my dear," he'd replied coldly in return.

By the end of the week, Kitty was a nervous wreck. She sat with Andrew and Charlie over breakfast, noticing that even her son was subdued in the presence of his father. Perhaps it was simply the dreadful loss that Andrew was struggling to come to terms with that had affected his attitude toward her, or . . . she couldn't bear to think of the other reason.

"Kitty, I wish you to accompany me on some errands today," Andrew broke in on her thoughts without so much as looking at her.

"Of course," she agreed.

After breakfast, he helped her onto the cart, then sat stiffly beside her as he steered it out of the drive. But instead of taking the road into town, Andrew took the road toward Riddell Beach.

"Where are we going?" she asked.

"I thought that you and I should have a talk. Alone."

Kitty's heart thudded in her chest, but she remained silent.

"Charlie tells me you went to the beach often while I was gone," Andrew continued. "Apparently you went swimming. In your pantaloons."

"Yes, I . . . well, it was very hot and . . ." Kitty blinked the tears away.

"Good God! What is the world coming to? My wife swimming in her pantaloons like a native." Andrew pulled the cart to a halt and tethered the pony to a post. "Shall we walk?" He indicated the beach below them.

"As you wish," she said, musing that if Andrew was going to tell her he knew about her affair, he had chosen the very spot where only weeks ago she'd lain with his brother and made love. Never before had Andrew suggested a walk on the beach; he'd always hated the feeling of sand in his shoes.

A pleasant breeze blew gently, and the same sea that had robbed Kitty of her love was now as calm as a sleeping baby. Andrew walked ahead toward the ocean as Kitty—who dared not remove her boots and face Andrew's disapproval—stumbled along behind him. They reached the rocky inlet where she had so recently climbed onto a boulder and dived off. Andrew stood inches from the water, the waves frothing close to his shoes.

"My father and brother lie somewhere out there." Andrew pointed to the ocean. "Gone forever, while I live."

Kitty watched him slump onto a rock as his head bowed and he put his hands to his face. "I'm so very sorry, darling." She understood now why he'd come here: to cry and mourn in private for his father and brother. She saw his shoulders shaking and her heart went out to him.

"Andrew, you still have Charlie and me, and your mother, and . . ." She knelt down and tried to hold him, but he broke away from her, stood up, and staggered along the beach.

"Oh, forgive me, please forgive me, God, but . . ."

Kitty stood watching him, confused. He almost seemed to be laughing, rather than crying.

"Andrew, please!" She hurried after him as the waves started to lap over his highly polished shoes and he collapsed onto the sand, his shoulders shaking, his eyes still hidden behind his large brown hands. Finally, his head came up, and he removed his hands from his eyes. They were streaming with tears.

"God forgive me," he said eventually, "but it had to be done. For me and for you and Charlie. My Kitty. My Kat . . ."

"Andrew, I don't understand . . ." She stared at him and realized that indeed the tears were not of sorrow, but of mirth. "Why on earth are you laughing?"

"I know it isn't funny, quite the opposite, but . . ." He drew in a few deep breaths and gazed at her. "Kitty, do you really not know me?"

"Of course I do, darling." Kitty was already wondering how she could get Andrew back to the cart and take him straight to Dr. Suzuki. It was obvious he had quite lost his mind. "You're my husband and the father of our child, Charlie."

"Then I have truly done it!" he cried, punching the air. "For God's sake, Kitty, it's *me*!"

He pulled her to him then and kissed her hungrily, passionately. And as her body melted into his, she knew exactly who he was.

"*No!*"

She wrenched herself away from his grasp, sobbing with shock and confusion. "Stop it! Please, stop it! You're Andrew, my husband . . . my *husband*!" She sank to her knees. "Please, stop playing games," she begged him. "Whatever it is you want me to admit, I'll admit it. Just please, stop!"

A pair of strong arms came around her shoulders. "Forgive me, Kitty, but I had to do this to ensure that everyone believed I *was* your husband, including you. If I was convincing enough to fool the person who knows us best, then I could fool anyone. If you had known, then the merest look or touch could have given us away. Now even Charlie is convinced I'm his father. Oh, my darling girl . . ." His fingers skimmed down her arms and he kissed her sweating neck gently.

"No!" Kitty pulled away. "How could you do this to me?! How could you? Impersonating your own brother back from the dead! It's . . . outrageous."

"Kitty, can't you understand? It's love!"

"I understand nothing! All I know is that you have fooled us all! You have masqueraded as my dead husband, allowed my child to believe his father is back from the grave, shown yourself to the townsfolk, and presented yourself as Andrew at his office!"

"And they believe me, Kitty. They believed I was Andrew, as you did. The idea came to me when I thought of the last time I'd come to visit, and the townsfolk—and you initially—believed I was Andrew. Yes." His arms dropped away from her shoulders. "I have lied—a terrible lie—but I had to take this opportunity. So, when I heard what had happened and made my way overland, I formulated my plan."

"So you knew before Port Hedland?"

"Of course I *knew*! Good God, even the kookaburras hundreds of miles from here were shouting the news from the trees. It is the biggest tragedy to hit the region in decades."

"So, you decided to impersonate your brother?"

"There has to be some advantage to having an identical twin. I've certainly never seen one before, but then I realized that perhaps it had all been for a reason. I consulted the heavens for advice as I sat alone by my campfire in the desert. They told me that life is very short on this earth. And although I may have been able to marry you one day when it was seemly to do so, the thought of wasting perhaps years being apart from you seemed pointless when I could come back and claim you as mine now. We could be together as man and wife, and everyone would rejoice that I was saved and—"

"Drummond." Kitty used his name for the first time. "I think you must be mad. Do you not understand the implications of what you have done?"

"Perhaps not all, but most of them, yes. I just wished to be with you. Is that so wrong?"

"So you are prepared to change your identity and lie to every single person other than me about who you really are?"

"If that's what this takes, then yes. To be honest, I'm still stunned that my impression of Andrew was so excellent that no one questioned it!"

"You have been far too fierce with me. In fact, you have been perfectly horrible."

"Then I shall tone down my behavior toward you from now on."

"Drummond . . ." Kitty was lost for words at his grotesque disregard for the gravity of his charade.

"From now on you must call me Andrew," he replied.

"I will call you what I choose to. Good God! This is not a game, Drummond. What you have done is completely immoral, even illegal! How can you wear your deception so lightly?"

"I don't know, but I look out there and picture my father and brother dead at the bottom of the ocean, already picked to nothing by sharks. And I think of you, Kitty, who almost left me too when you were so sick.

I simply understand now how precious life is. So yes," he agreed, "I wear it lightly."

Kitty turned away from him, trying to process the ramifications of what he had done.

To be with her . . .

"I must admit that I am surprised you didn't guess, even though I did my best to remain distanced from you physically." Drummond had removed his shoes and socks and was stepping out of his trousers. "For a start, surely you knew Andrew well enough to realize that he would never travel overland by horse and cart? In fact, I traveled to Broome by camel as usual, but I decided a cart sounded more realistic."

"Yes, I did think it strange, but at the time I had no reason to believe my husband would lie," she replied coldly. "Perhaps now you can tell me how you came to be saved."

"It was Andrew who asked me to leave the *Koombana* at Geraldton. He gave me a briefcase of money and told me where I must meet his contact and he showed me a photograph of what I was to collect in return. In short, he confessed himself too frightened to make the journey himself, and knew I had far more experience navigating Australia's hinterland. Given that I was about to elope with his wife and son on my return, I felt it was the least I could do. A last good deed, if you will."

"And what was it you had to collect?"

"Kitty, that is a story for another time. Suffice it to say that Andrew's last-minute cowardice saved my life, and out of it, he lost *his*. If you had opened your telegrams, you would have found one from me warning you I was to meet Andrew here in Broome with his . . . prize, before sailing on to Darwin as I had planned. I wrote that I would be delayed by a few days and you were to wait for me there until I arrived. Now excuse me, but I need a swim to cool off."

Kitty sat on the beach, her head not so much spinning as swirling. She watched as he dived into the waves in such an un-Andrew-like way, she could hardly believe that she'd been fooled. But fooled she had been, along with the rest of the town.

The implications of what he'd done and the risk he had taken hung over her like a curse. And yet, she could not help but imagine the happiness they could now share—legally—as a married couple.

How can you think like that, Kitty? Her conscience nudged her and she ground her palms onto the sand to bring herself back to reality.

What angered her most was the fact he hadn't shared his plan with her, taking it for granted that she would want the same.

And she did. God help her, she did . . .

But what was the price?

Kitty knew it was a high one, but after the carnage of the past few weeks, what did it matter? If living in Australia had taught her anything, it was that human life was fragile; nature was in charge and cared not a jot for the havoc it wreaked on those who populated its earth.

Besides, she mused, her family had never even met Andrew; it was entirely possible that she could waltz home to Edinburgh with Drummond on her arm and they would be none the wiser. Australia was still a young country, and those brave enough to inhabit it had the gift of making up the rules themselves—and that was exactly what Drummond had done.

As he walked out of the sea toward her, shaking the drops off him like the dog that he was—a chancer and a charmer who, it seemed, would do anything to get what he wanted—Kitty finally glimpsed the reality of her future:

To be with Drummond, she would live a lie for the rest of her life, betraying two dead men and a grieving wife and mother. Let alone her precious son—an innocent in all this—who would grow up believing his uncle was his father . . .

No! No! This is wrong, it is wrong . . .

As Drummond approached her, Kitty stood up. She walked off along the beach, suddenly unable to contain her fury.

"How dare you!" she screamed to the sea and the clouds gently scudding above her head. "How dare you implicate *me* in your disgusting charade! Can't you see, Drummond, that this isn't one of your little games? What you've done is no less than"—Kitty searched for the word—"obscene! And I shall have no part in it."

"Kitty, my darling Kat, I thought that you wanted to have a life with me. I did it for us—"

"No, you did not! You did it for *yourself*!" Kitty paced backward and forward on the sand. "You did not even have the grace to ask me what I thought beforehand! If anyone discovers the truth, there's no doubt you would go to jail!"

"Surely you wouldn't wish that on me?"

"It's no less than you deserve. Dear Lord, what a mess. What a mess! And I cannot see a way out."

"Does there have to be one?" Drummond approached her as though she were a cornered scorpion that might attack at any minute. "Does it matter what my name is, or yours? This way, we can be together, always. Forgive me, Kitty, if I acted in haste." He took a step closer to her. "Please?"

There was a loud *thwack* as Kitty slapped him hard across his cheek for the second time in her life, only just restraining herself from launching at him and punching him to the ground.

"Do you not see? If you'd only waited, had some patience, not acted in your usual impetuous manner, then perhaps one day we *could* have been together. Legally, in the sight of God. Everyone would have thought it natural for a widow to grow close to her brother-in-law. But no, Drummond, you had to take the law into your own hands, and present yourself as Andrew to everyone in town!"

"Then I will tell them I had a knock on the head, or—"

"Don't be ridiculous! No one would give that credence for an instant, and it would only implicate me in your disgusting lie. Are people really to believe that I didn't know my own husband?"

"Then perhaps we stick to the original plan," Drummond offered, desperate now. "You and Charlie come with me to the cattle station. No one would know who you were there . . ."

"No! My husband is dead and I must honor his memory. Oh, Drummond, can't you see that you've made a pact with the devil, and now nothing can ever be right between us again?" Kitty sank to her knees on the sand and rested her head in her hands. Silence lay between them for a long time. Eventually, Drummond spoke.

"You are right, of course, Kitty. I was impetuous. I saw a chance to claim you, and I didn't stop to think. It is a huge fault of mine, I admit. I am so eager to live in the moment, I do not address the future consequences. So, what would you have me do?"

Kitty closed her eyes and drew in a breath, garnering the courage to say the words she needed to.

"You must leave. As soon as possible."

"To go where?"

"That cannot be my concern. You didn't ask my opinion on your rash decision, and I cannot be party to others you make in the future."

"Then perhaps I will go and see my mother. Let the dust settle. Whichever son I am, it will bring her comfort that she has one left. Who should I be?"

"I have just told you, I want nothing more to do with it." Kitty wrung her hands.

"And what of the people here in Broome? Will they not wonder why your husband has arrived and departed again so swiftly?"

"I am sure they will understand that after the death of a father and a brother, there is much to attend to elsewhere."

"Kitty . . ." His hand reached out to her and she flinched, knowing his touch would break her resolve.

Drummond withdrew his hand. "Can you ever forgive me?"

"I forgive you now, Drummond, for I know that despite your utter stupidity, you did not mean harm. Nor can I say I no longer love you, because I always will. But I can never condone what you have done, or live the lie that you have forged not just for us, but for Charlie too."

"I understand." Drummond stood up, and this time Kitty saw there were tears of utter devastation in his eyes. "I will leave as you have asked. And try—though at present I hardly know how—to put right the wrongs my selfish behavior has inflicted upon you and Charlie. He will grow up without a father—"

"Or an uncle."

"Is this forever?"

"I can never lie to my son. He must hold his father's memory sacred."

"But he saw me only this morning . . ."

"Time heals, Drummond, and if you go away, it will not be so difficult to one day tell him that his father died."

"You would have me dead again?"

"It is the only way."

"Then"—Drummond took a deep, wrenching breath—"I will leave tonight. And however much I want to beg you—*beseech* you—to change your mind, to take the chance for happiness that stands now within our grasp, I won't. Kitty, never look back on this moment and wonder if you were in any way to blame. You are not. It was I who ruined our future."

"We should be getting back. It's growing dark." Kitty rose, her limbs hanging limply, as though she were a stuffed toy plucked of its innards.

"Can I at least hold you one last time? To say good-bye?"

Kitty had no energy to answer yes or no. She let him take her in his arms and they stood close together for the last time.

Eventually he released her and offered her his hand, and they walked back together across the sand.

Kitty was only glad that Charlie was already in bed by the time they arrived home. She fled to her bedroom and shut the door, then sat in a chair like a condemned woman, waiting for the sound of Drummond's feet along the hall, and the click of the front door that would tell her he was gone. Instead, she saw shadows outside her window, and the sound of voices. Rising from her bed and peering out, she saw Drummond talking to Camira in the garden. Five minutes later, there was a knock on Kitty's door.

"Forgive me for disturbing you, Kitty, but I must give you something before I leave." Drummond proffered a small leather box to her. "It is the reason why I am still alive today. Andrew received a telegram as we were sailing up from Fremantle. He told me that there was a pearl—a very famous pearl—that he'd heard through his contacts was for sale. He'd done much detective work to confirm its provenance, and had contacted the third party acting for the seller. The telegram he received in return said he was to bring the cash to the appointed place, some hours' journey from Geraldton. As you know, I agreed to be his messenger, left the ship, and went to collect the pearl. With Andrew advising me of what to look for when I saw it, I knew it was genuine. So," he sighed, "my last gesture to my brother is to deliver the Roseate Pearl into his wife's hands as he wished. It is worth a king's ransom—almost two hundred grains heavy— and Andrew could hardly wait to see it around your neck, to show both his love for you and his success to the whole of Broome."

"I—"

"Wait, Kitty. There is more. You must know that legend has it that the pearl is cursed. Every legal owner has allegedly died a sudden, shocking death. Andrew was the current owner of the pearl, and he lies at the bottom of the sea. Kitty, even though I must do as my brother asked, I entreat you to rid yourself of it as soon as you can. Never own it. In fact, I shall not put it into your hands, but leave it wherever you deem a safe place. I beg you not to touch it."

Kitty studied the box, then Drummond's face, and saw not one hint of mirth in his eyes. He was deadly serious.

"Can I at least see it?"

Drummond opened the box and Kitty looked down at the pearl. It was the size of a large marble, with a rose-gold hue of utter perfection. Its magnificent opalescence gave off its own light and pulled one's eyes toward it.

Kitty drew in her breath. "Why, it is beautiful, the most exquisite pearl I have ever seen . . ." She reached her fingers toward it but Drummond drew the box from her reach.

"Do not touch it! I do not want your death on my conscience along with the other dreadful things I have done." He closed the box. "Where should I put it for safekeeping?"

"In there." Kitty went to her writing bureau and unlocked the secret drawer that lay beneath it. Drummond slid the box inside and locked it firmly away.

"Swear to me you will not touch it," he begged her as he pressed the key into her hand.

"Drummond, surely you of all people cannot believe such a story? There are many that circulate about certain pearls in Broome. They're all fantasy."

"Sadly, after the past few weeks, I *do* believe it. While I carried that pearl, I believed it had saved my life. And it was while it was in my possession that I came up with my plan. I felt . . . invincible, as though the impossible was possible. I was euphoric. And now, I have lost everything that matters. My soul is as dead as my father and brother. So, I must say good-bye. And if we ever meet again, I hope I will be able to show you that I have learned from my dreadful mistake. Please try to forgive me. I love you, my Kat. Forever." Drummond turned and headed for the door.

Every instinct in Kitty begged her feet to go the few yards toward him, to drag him back to her, to *live* and take the chance he had created for them to walk to the bedroom now as man and wife. But she stood firm.

"Good-bye." He smiled at her one last time. And then he left.

23

Alicia Hall
Victoria Avenue
Adelaide
5th June 1912

My dear Kitty,

    It is with a heavy heart that I write to you, because you alone can imagine the joy I felt when I received Andrew's telegram from Broome telling me the miraculous news of his survival.

    My dear, you are the only other soul I know who truly understands what it is like to go through the gamut of emotions I have suffered in the past few weeks. In truth, for days after the tragedy, I struggled to find a reason to go on. My entire world was lost to me in the space of a few hours, but thankfully I had the Lord.

    To have Andrew return to us was a miracle that we could hardly have hoped to receive. But receive it we did, although, as I said above, it will not be on a happy note that I end this letter.

    I was fully expecting Andrew to visit me here in Adelaide so that I could see my precious son with my own eyes. Yet, yesterday I received a visit from Mr. Angus, the family solicitor, to say that Andrew had been to see him and had asked him to pass on a letter he had written to me. According to Mr. Angus, it seems that the blow of losing both his father and brother on a voyage that Andrew himself was meant to take has affected him deeply. He carries dreadful guilt that he still walks the earth while they have been taken. Dear Kitty, perhaps the shock has been simply too much for him, for Mr. Angus inferred that he did not seem to have his full faculties and seemed quite unlike himself.

    Andrew asked Mr. Angus to tell me—and you—that he has decided to go away to recover. To put himself back together, if you will. I only wish he had come to me in person as I would have entreated him to stay. There are many good doctors who can help with a nervous collapse—he always was highly strung as a child—but Andrew apparently insisted he needed to do it alone. He also asked Mr. Angus to beg your forgiveness for deserting you so soon after he was returned, but he did not wish to inflict his confused state of mind on you.

I wish I could provide comfort by telling you when he will return to us, but he gave Mr. Angus no indication. He also—although I believe it was madness to do so—insisted on putting all the Mercer business interests into a trust for Charlie. Mr. Angus brought the documents around to show me and it was quite dreadful to see that the signature hardly resembled Andrew's at all. If Andrew has not returned, the businesses will pass to Charlie when he is twenty-one.

In Andrew's letter, he tells me he visited Noel Donovan before he left Broome and told him of his decision. Mr. Donovan is a capable man and will no doubt run the business efficiently. Andrew has also made you, Kitty, the sole executor of Charlie's trust. Again, I queried his decision—the responsibility places a heavy burden upon you—but Andrew tells me he trusts your judgment implicitly.

I should also mention that when Mr. Angus read out the wills of my beloved husband and Drummond, made only a few weeks previously when they were here in Adelaide, Charlie's dear uncle had also endowed his nephew with all his worldly goods, which means that our beloved boy is the sole heir to the Mercer fortune. What a weight lies on his young shoulders, but as it stands, there is nothing we women can do to alter Andrew's wishes. His letter asked me to assure you that a sizeable monthly sum will be deposited into your Broome account from the trust, which will amply cover your living costs. I realize, however, that it is but cold comfort in the face of—for now at least—losing your husband once more.

Dear Kitty, I am sure that this will come as another shock to your already battered nerves. I beg you to consider bringing yourself and my grandson back to live at Alicia Hall, so we can take comfort and strength from each other as we ride out this new storm.

All we can do is pray for Andrew and his swift return.

Please let me know of your decision forthwith.
Edith

Kitty put down the letter, feeling cold beads of sweat break out over her body and bile rise to her throat, before running to the basin in her bedroom and vomiting into it. Wiping her mouth and face with a towel, she carried the basin to the privy and emptied it into the bowl, as if she were discarding the last, poisonous entrails of Drummond's deception. Camira found her washing out the bowl in the kitchen.

"You bin sick again, Missus Kitty? You ill? I gettum doctor fella come an' see you. Skin an' bone, that what you are," she clucked as she filled a cup from a pitcher of water and handed it to Kitty.

"Thank you. I am fine, really."

"You look in dat mirror lately, Missus Kitty? You like-a spirit."

"Camira, where is Charlie?"

"In hut with Cat."

"Then I must tell you that Mister Boss has gone away for a while."

Camira eyed her suspiciously. "Which 'Mister Boss'?"

"Andrew—my husband, of course."

"Maybe for best." Camira nodded knowingly. "Me an' Fred takem care of you an' Charlie. Dem men"—Camira's eyebrows drew together—"makem big trouble."

"They certainly do." Kitty smiled weakly at Camira's understatement.

"Missus Kitty, I—"

Charlie and Cat arrived at the kitchen door, and Camira sighed and said no more.

That afternoon, Kitty sat on the veranda and reread her mother-in-law's letter. Given that Drummond had sent a telegram to say that "Andrew" had survived, Kitty supposed Drummond had had little alternative but to carry his charade through until the end. At least he had kept his promise to her and disappeared. She was particularly moved by the fact that, before any of this had happened, Drummond had already left all that was his to Charlie in his will.

Now that her initial horror had abated, Kitty knew she was in danger of wishing she had never acted in such haste. First had come anger, then sorrow, and finally regret. During the long, achingly lonely nights, Kitty agonized over whether she should have allowed some time to let the dust settle. Now it was too late—Drummond had gone forever as she had asked him to.

Having mourned him once, she now had to mourn him again.

Charlie hardly raised a glance when he was told "Papa" had gone away again on business. Having become used to Andrew's absences, and involved as he was in his own childish world of make-believe with Cat, he accepted it without rancor. Heartbreakingly, Charlie talked far more of "Uncle Drum."

"I know he went up to heaven 'cause God wanted him, but we miss his games, don't we, Cat?"

"Yes, we do." Cat nodded solemnly.

Kitty smiled at the little girl's speech. Kitty had spoken to her in English from birth and she even knew a little German too. She was a lovely child: polite, well mannered, and the apple of her mother's eye. Yet Kitty wondered what Cat's future could hold. For, despite her beauty and intelligence, she was a half-caste child: an outcast to both her parents' cultures, and therefore at the mercy of the society that currently ruled them.

Kitty slid open the drawer in her writing desk to write to Edith and refuse her offer of a home for her and Charlie at Alicia Hall. Even though she was aware of how challenging it would be to stay in Broome as a widow, at least she had her independence here. Perhaps, she thought, she might take Charlie to Scotland in the next few weeks to meet his family and decide whether to return there permanently.

Her fingers felt the coolness of the brass key that unlocked the secret drawer. Amid the chaos of her emotions, she had forgotten about the pearl that Drummond had given her just before he'd left. She unlocked the drawer, pulled out the box, and opened its lid. And there it sat, shining in the light, its magnificent pink sheen and size marking it out as a pearl of great worth. Any malevolence it was reputed to hold was deeply hidden in the grain of sand that had given birth to its luminous beauty. Like the evil but beautiful queen of childhood fairy tales, its outer shell gave no hint of what it hid at its core.

Heeding Drummond's warning not to touch it and never to "own" it, Kitty put it down and paced the room. In one sense, it was Andrew's last gift to her and should be put on display around her neck and treasured. On the other hand, if Drummond was right, a deadly curse was attached to it.

There was a knock on the door.

"Come," called Kitty, still thinking.

"Missus Kitty, dem children, they restless an' say to me an' Fred they want to run on beach. I—" Camira's glance fell on the pearl and her black eyebrows drew together. "Missus Kitty, you nottum touch that!" Camira mumbled some words to herself and dragged her eyes away as a shaft of sunlight sent sparkles reflecting off the pearl. "Closem box! Now! Do not look, Missus Kitty! Closem box!"

Automatically, Kitty did as she was bid as Camira unfastened the window behind the desk.

"Dun worry, Missus Kitty, I savem you." Muttering further incomprehensible words as Kitty looked on in astonishment, Camira drew a handful of her muslin skirt into her palm, swiped at the box, and hurled it through the open window.

"What on earth are you doing?! That pearl is valuable, Camira! Extremely valuable. What if we cannot find it?" Kitty craned her neck out of the window.

"I see it," Camira said, pointing to where the box had fallen. "Missus Kitty, you no sella dat pearl. No takem money for it. Understand?"

"My . . . husband mentioned the curse that was attached to it, but surely that's just an old wives' tale?"

"Then you tellum me why Mister Boss now dead? And many before him."

"You mean, Mister Drum, Camira," she corrected sharply.

"Missus Kitty," she said with a sigh, "I knowum dem fellas from each other, even if you don't."

"I . . ." Kitty realized there was no point attempting to keep up the charade as far as Camira was concerned. "You believe in the curse?"

"The spirits find greedy men and killem them. I can feel dem bad spirits around that box. I tellum Mister Drum no good."

"What do you suggest I do with it, if I can't sell it, Camira? Apart from the fact it was my last present from Andrew, it is worth a fortune. I can hardly just throw it into the rubbish."

"You give to me. I takem box away so no harm comin'."

"Where?" Kitty's eyes narrowed for a second, thinking that, however much she loved and trusted Camira, the girl was poor and the pearl was worth a whole new life to her and her child.

Camira studied her expression and, as usual, read her thoughts. "You keepum that bad cursed pearl, an' you sell for money from the big rich fella, an' Charlie orphan in three months." She crossed her arms and looked away.

"All right," Kitty agreed. After all, she hardly needed the money and nor did her son. "It's brought the most dreadful luck to all of us. If I was

to believe in the curse myself, I might say that it has destroyed our family."
Kitty swallowed hard and eyed Camira. "Maybe the sooner it's gone, the
sooner we can all begin to breathe again."

"Fred takem me to place he know. Me an' Cat go for one day with
him." Camira walked toward the door. "Best thing, Missus Kitty. Putta
bad thing where it can't do no harm."

"You make sure it doesn't. Thank you, Camira."

A few days later, Kitty had a visit from Noel Donovan.

"Forgive me for intruding again, Mrs. Mercer, and at such a difficult
time for your family, but I am sure ye'll be knowing that your husband has
placed the running of the Mercer Pearling Company into my hands until
either he returns, or little Charlie comes of age."

"Let us pray it will be the former," Kitty replied.

"Of course, and I'll not be doubting it. Such a difficult time for ye,
Mrs. Mercer. Me own family lost ten in the potato famine last century.
That's what brought what was left of us here. There's many a man and
woman who's arrived on these shores through tragedy."

"I did not arrive with it, but it seems to have followed me here," Kitty
said brusquely. "Now, Mr. Donovan, what can I do for you?"

"Well, the thing is that you'd be the closest to knowing what was going
through Andrew's mind. And I'm wondering if ye know exactly when
he'll be back."

"He gave me no indication, Mr. Donovan."

"Did he not talk over your supper table as my missus and I tend to?"
Noel continued to press her. "If anyone knows his thoughts on the future
of the business, 'twould be you."

"Yes, of course." Some deeper instinct in Kitty told her to answer in
the affirmative. "Before his departure, we spoke of many things."

"Then ye'll be aware that your husband removed twenty thousand
pounds from the company bank account only a few days before the
Koombana went down?"

Kitty's stomach plummeted as she realized what Andrew had almost
certainly used the money for. "Yes. What of it?"

"Perhaps 'twas for a new lugger?"

"Yes, that's right."

"And would ye be knowing who was building it? There seems to be no record in the ledgers."

"I'm afraid not, although I believe it was a company in England."

"Could well be. The fact remains, Mrs. Mercer, that we lost three luggers in the cyclone. I'm thanking God 'twas the lay-up season, or 'twould surely have been more. The problem is that, combined with the deficit of twenty thousand pounds, it means that we're running a substantial overdraft with the bank."

"Are we really?" Although Kitty was shocked, she did not show her surprise. "Surely the debt can be repaid over an agreed period of time, while the company recovers from its loss?"

"Twenty thousand pounds and three luggers down is a lot to recover from, Mrs. Mercer. Even with a good haul in the coming months, I'd say 'twould take us a good three years to pay it off before we're back into profit. Unless, of course, we strike lucky . . ." Noel's voice trailed off and she read the concern on his normally placid features.

"I see."

"And the other problem we have, if ye don't mind me saying so, is that morale among the crew's low. 'Tis the double loss, see. However hard your husband worked, many of them would still be seeing Mr. Stefan as the boss. As it is, with Mr. Andrew absent, some of our best men are being lured into taking offers from other companies. Only yesterday, Ichitaro, our most experienced diver, told me that he and his tender were off to work for the Rubin company. 'Tis a huge blow, and will only encourage other men to do the same."

"I understand completely, Mr. Donovan. It is indeed a very concerning situation."

"Well now." Noel stood up. "Here's me bothering you about business at a time when ye yerself have lost so much. I'll be on me way."

"Mr. Donovan." Kitty also stood. "It seems to me that, as you say, the men are dispirited and without a leader. Perhaps it might be a good idea if I came down to the office and spoke to them? Explained that the Mercer Pearling Company is still very much a going concern, and that there is no cause for alarm?"

Noel looked doubtful. "I'd say that—without wishing to offend you, Mrs. Mercer—I'm not sure they'd be listening to a woman."

"Do men not listen to their wives or take comfort from them at home?" Kitty retorted, and Noel blushed.

"Well now, maybe ye are right. And I can't say as 'twould do harm. Our luggers are due out the day after tomorrow. We've been delayed by trying to find replacement crew."

"Have you yet paid those men who have said they are leaving?"

"No. They'll be coming in for their final wages in the morning."

"Then please gather together as many crew as you can drag out of the bars and whorehouses and tell them that the new boss of the Mercer Pearling Company wishes to address them all at eleven o'clock tomorrow."

Noel raised an eyebrow. "Are ye telling me, Mrs. Mercer, that Andrew has handed the business over to you?"

"In essence, yes. I am executor of the trust in which the business is currently held, so I am the closest thing to a 'boss' there is."

"Well now, there's a thing. I warn ye, Mrs. Mercer, they're a motley crew, so they are, and they'll all be expecting a man."

"I have lived in Broome for five years, Mr. Donovan, and I am hardly unaware of that. I will see you tomorrow at eleven o'clock sharp." Kitty went to the drawer in her writing bureau and counted out a stack of Australian pound notes. "Go to Yamasaki and Mise and buy twenty-four bottles of their best champagne."

"Are you sure 'tis sensible, Mrs. Mercer, given the company's finances?"

"This is not the company's money, Mr. Donovan. It is mine."

"Well now." Noel pocketed the money and offered her a smile. "I'd say that one way or another, our employees are in for a grand shock altogether."

When Noel had left, Kitty called for Fred to take her into town. She walked into Wing Hing Loong's tailoring shop and asked whether he could run her up a long-sleeved bodice and skirt in the white cotton drill used for the pearling masters' suits. The bodice was to have five large pearl buttons, which fastened at the front, and a mandarin collar. Having offered double the normal cost to make sure that the garments would be ready for collection at nine the following morning, she returned home and spent the afternoon pacing the drawing room to think what she would say when she addressed the men. At a loss, and wondering if she was completely mad to do this, she remembered her father standing in the pulpit each Sunday. She had often watched the crowd mesmerized, not by his words, but by the sheer strength of his belief in them, and his undoubted charisma.

It's worth a try for Andrew, for Charlie, and for Drummond, she told herself, as an idea suddenly came to her.

Kitty studied her image in the looking glass the following morning. She fastened on the small gold chain taken from Andrew's pristine white jacket, which was the symbol of a master pearler. She picked up the white pith helmet, put it on her head, and chuckled at her reflection. Maybe it was a little too much, but nevertheless, she stowed it by Andrew's leather case, which he had used to transfer his papers between office and home.

Taking one last glance at her reflection, she drew in a deep breath.

"Kitty McBride, you were not born your father's daughter for nothing . . ."

"Gentlemen," Kitty began as she looked down at the sea of male faces below her, wondering briefly how many different nationalities she was addressing. Japanese, Malay, Koepanger, and a slew of whiter faces peppered among them. She could see some of them were already sniggering and whispering to each other.

"First of all, I wish to introduce myself to those of you who do not know me. My name is Katherine Mercer, and I am the wife of Mr. Andrew Mercer. Due to the recent loss of his father and brother, Mr. Mercer has been forced to take a leave of absence from Broome to deal with our family's affairs. I hope we would all wish him well on his travels, and pray for him to find the strength to deal with such matters at a difficult time for him personally."

Kitty heard a slight quaver in her voice as she repeated the lie.

No sign of weakness, Kitty, they'll smell it a mile off . . .

"While he is absent, he has asked me to act in his stead, ably assisted by Mr. Noel Donovan, who will continue to run the business day to day."

She saw a number of raised eyebrows and heard whispers of protest from the audience. She garnered every ounce of strength she possessed to carry on.

"Gentlemen, I have recently heard rumors in the town that the Mercer Pearling Company is struggling financially, due to the loss of three of our luggers in the cyclone. Some have claimed we may well go out of business. I am sure it is none of you here today who would have been so heartless as to spread such rumors given the tragedy that has beset not just our family, but the entire town of Broome. And that each and every one of you remembers fondly the man who began all this originally, Mr. Stefan Mercer. The Mercer Pearling Company is one of the oldest and most well established in our town and has provided many of you with an income for yourselves, your wives, and your children.

"I am here to tell you that the rumors of financial trouble are completely unfounded. They have been put about by those who are jealous of our heritage and would wish us to fail. The Mercer empire is one of the wealthiest and most successful in Australia and I can assure every man here that there is no shortage of cash, either in the pearling company, or on a wider scale. As of this morning, Mr. Donovan and I have signed a contract for three new luggers to be built. We hope to add a further two by the end of the year."

Kitty took a breath and gauged the pulse of her audience. Some men had turned to a neighbor to translate what she was saying. Many were nodding in surprise.

I nearly have them . . .

"Rather than the business collapsing, on the contrary, we will be looking to recruit the best men in Broome to join us in the next few months. My own and my husband's wish is to continue to make the Mercer Pearling Company the greatest in the world."

At this, a few cheers came up from the men, which gave Kitty the courage to continue.

"I accept that some of you here today have already decided to move on. You shall of course be paid whatever is due to you. If you wish to reconsider and stay, you will receive the ten percent bonus on your wages that Mr. Stefan Mercer requested for all his staff in his will.

"Gentlemen, on behalf of the Mercer family, I beg your forgiveness for the uncertainty that has beset you in the past few weeks. And your understanding that we, among so many families here in Broome, have struggled with the loss we have been dealt. Some of you will also doubt the capabilities of a female caretaker. Yet, I beg you to look to the women in your own family and admit their strengths. They run your households, no doubt the family accounts, and juggle the needs of many. I may not outwardly show the strength or the courage to ride the ocean that every one of you displays day after day, but I have a heart full of both. And the blessing of my dear departed father-in-law and my husband to steer the Mercer Pearling Company into the future."

Trying not to pant with emotion and stress, Kitty looked down at her audience and saw they were silent now, straining to catch every word she spoke. As per her request, trays of glasses containing champagne were being distributed around the room. Noel appeared beside her and offered her a glass, which she took.

"Tomorrow, I will be on the dock to wave those of you who are still with us off to sea. To wish you good fortune and pray for a safe harbor on your return. Finally, I would like us all to raise our glasses to all the men who were lost to us in the recent cyclone. And particularly to our founder, Mr. Stefan Mercer." Kitty raised her glass. "To Stefan!"

"To Stefan," the men chorused as Kitty took a gulp of champagne with them.

Another silence, then someone from the audience shouted, "Three cheers for Mrs. Mercer. Hip hip!"

"*Hooray!*"

"Hip hip!"

"*Hooray!*"

"Hip hip!"

"*Hooray!*"

Kitty staggered slightly and felt a strong arm go about her as Noel helped her into a chair to the side of the warehouse and she sat down gratefully.

"That was some speech ye gave there," he said as they watched the men having their glasses refilled and beginning to talk among themselves. "Even I was convinced," he whispered to her with a smile. "I'd doubt there was a man among them that wasn't. Though the Lord alone knows how we'll pay for the promises ye've just made."

"We have to find a way, Noel," she told him, "and find a way we will."

"Ye look exhausted, Mrs. Mercer. Why don't ye be off home now and rest? Ye've done your bit here, and that's for sure. Now they'll be wanting to drain their glasses and get their money, including the bonus you offered them, and, Mrs. Mercer, the accounts are drained already . . ."

"I have the extra amount with me," Kitty said firmly. "Now, if you have no objection, I would like to greet each of the men personally and pay them what they are due."

"I'd have no objection, of course." Noel looked at her in awe, gave her a small bow, and hurried away to the clerk in the back office to retrieve the wages.

At four o'clock that afternoon, Kitty was helped down from the cart by Fred. She staggered through the front door of the house.

"I'm taking a rest," she said to Camira as she passed her in the entrance hall. "Could you bring a fresh pitcher of water to my room?"

"Yessum, Missus Kitty." Camira bobbed her habitual curtsy, then studied her mistress. "You sick again?"

"No, just very, very tired."

Kitty lay on her bed and enjoyed the fresh breeze coming through the open window. In the three hours it had taken to greet each man and ask after him and his family, not a single one had requested his final wages. They had come to her instead with an embarrassed smile, told her of their belief in the Mercer Pearling Company, and offered their sympathy—sometimes through a translator—for her recent loss.

The company now had an even larger deficit in the bank, but a full crew and divers and tenders that would set sail tomorrow to restore the fortunes of the ailing company.

Kitty closed her eyes and thanked God for the Wednesday breakfasts her father had insisted on when she was a child. His potted biography of Elizabeth Tudor—even if she had put her Scottish cousin Mary to death—had inspired her speech today.

Though I have the body of a weak and feeble woman . . . , Elizabeth had said as she'd addressed her armies at Tilbury Docks, ready to defeat the Spanish Armada.

Forgive me, Andrew, I have done my best for you today . . .

For the following two weeks, Kitty rose early and was at the office before Noel. She studied the ledgers with a careful eye, using the basic experience she had gleaned from totting up her father's parish accounts. There were various inconsistencies—amounts of cash withdrawn that she queried with the clerk.

"Ask Mr. Noel. He authorized them," the man told her.

"Well now, there's sometimes an occasion when a diver has a snide pearl—that is, one that he has smuggled off the lugger. If he believes it might be valuable . . ." Noel looked down at his hands, which were clasping and unclasping nervously. "Rather than having the diver steal it and keep the value totally for himself, Mr. Andrew—and Mr. Stefan before him—would offer an amount in cash for any man who would bring what they believed to be a particularly special pearl to them. Some of them turned out to be nothing more than blister pearls, but this way, the risk was shared. Do ye see?"

"Yes, I understand completely."

Kitty made an appointment at the bank for that afternoon, and sat across the desk from Mr. Harris. His face looked pained as she explained the situation to him.

"I assure you that there is no shortage of funds, Mr. Harris. The Mercer empire is worth a fortune."

"That may be, Mrs. Mercer, but I'm afraid the bank needs immediate surety. Perhaps you can transfer such funds from another part of the Mercer empire." The bank manager remained stony-faced, used to living in a town full of souls who would blag their way into gaining further months of credit.

Given the fact that Kitty had no idea what was in the Mercer bank accounts and knowing she would need to take a trip to Adelaide to visit the family lawyer to find out, she nodded.

"I am aware of that. Could you perhaps give me a month's leeway?"

"I'm afraid not, Mrs. Mercer. The overdraft is currently running at twenty-three thousand pounds."

"Perhaps our house could provide temporary surety for you?" she suggested. "It is in the best part of Broome, and sumptuously furnished. Will you accept that until I can arrange further funds?"

"Mrs. Mercer," the bank manager said with a frown, "far be it from me to advise you, but are you sure this is wise? Perhaps you do not realize just how capricious the pearling industry can be. I would be most distressed to find you and your son without a roof over your heads in the future."

"It is indeed a capricious business, Mr. Harris, and if one was a gambler, one might also bet on the fact that the Mercer family is due a run of good luck after such a difficult time. I will bring the deeds to you tomorrow."

"As you wish, Mrs. Mercer. And the bank will require the rest of the funds to be replaced within the next six months."

"Agreed. However," Kitty said as she rose, "if I even hear a whisper about this transaction from any quarter of this town, all our business with you will be withdrawn forthwith. Is that understood?"

"It is."

"Good. I will be back tomorrow to complete the paperwork."

Kitty left his office with her head held high, fully aware that she didn't need to put herself through this—she and Charlie could scuttle back to Alicia Hall and live in luxury with Edith if she chose to.

"A fate worse than death." She repeated Drummond's words as she left the bank and walked out into the burning midday sun. Living a lie *here* alone was one thing, but to live it every day under the roof of a woman who believed her eldest son was alive and would one day return was another.

Back at home, Kitty's head swam once more and she cursed her skin and bones, knowing she needed to show nothing but strength if the business was to survive. Sitting at her desk, she drew out the ledgers she had brought home with her in Andrew's leather case and studied them again.

"Good Lord." Kitty rested her head on the desk. "What have I begun?"

There was a knock on the door and Camira came in with a tray holding the pot of tea she had requested.

"Thank you," she said, rising from her desk to take it from her.

"Missus Kitty, you look like you dead too. Rest, you needum rest."

"It is merely the heat, and I . . ."

Camira watched in horror as her beloved mistress collapsed on the floor.

"Madam, when was your last course?"

Kitty looked up into the intelligent dark eyes of Dr. Suzuki. She frowned as she tried to remember, wondering why he wished to know this when it was obvious she was still suffering from exhaustion, plus the remnants of her recent bout of cholera.

"Perhaps two months ago. I really do not know, Dr. Suzuki."

"You have not bled since?"

Kitty shuddered at his lack of delicacy. Even though she knew he was the better physician, Dr. Blick would never have talked in such graphic terms. She thought quickly. "It was the middle of April," Kitty lied. "Now I remember."

"Really? Well now, that surprises me. I would say that your baby is around four months in gestation."

"I am pregnant? Are you sure?"

"Quite sure."

It can't be true . . .

"Apart from your condition, I can pronounce that you are in perfect health. May I offer my congratulations, madam, and hope your husband returns to you soon so you can share the happy news with him."

"Thank you," said Kitty numbly.

"You have endured terrible loss, but what God takes away, he returns. Now, I can only prescribe as much rest as possible. You are far too thin and the baby is obviously large. Stay in bed for the next month and preserve the life that is growing inside you."

Kitty watched in shocked silence as Dr. Suzuki packed away his instruments.

"Good day to you, Mrs. Mercer. I am at your service, should you need me." He gave her a small bow and left her bedroom.

"No, please . . . ," Kitty gasped as a small tear dribbled from her eye in protest. "I have so much to do."

She looked up at the ceiling and saw a large spider making its way across it. And remembered how Drummond had appeared in her bedroom to save her all those years ago.

"I am pregnant with your child . . . ," she breathed, then thanked the stars in the sky that at least his recent deception would allow everyone to believe it was her husband's baby. From what she remembered, her last bleed had been in mid-February . . .

"Oh Lord." Kitty bit her lip. "What a mess," she whispered.

Tentatively, she touched her stomach.

"Forgive me," she begged this new life that was innocent of all sin. "For you will never be able to know the truth of who your father is."

Broome

January 1929

17 YEARS LATER

24

The sun had long since set when Kitty raised her tired eyes from the ledger in front of her. Taking off her reading glasses, she rested an elbow on her desk and rubbed the bridge of her nose wearily. Glancing at the clock on the office wall, she saw it was well past eight. The staff would all have left the building by now and she knew she probably should too, but if she was honest, it was quite normal for her to sit here burning the midnight oil.

She let out a sigh as she thought of Charlie, her darling son. She had meant to meet him off the boat earlier, but a lugger had arrived unexpectedly with a rich haul of shell and she had become distracted and missed him.

On the one hand, she was extremely proud that all her hard work and her canny nose for business had not only restored but grown the Mercer empire over the past seventeen years. And that Charlie would inherit the fruits of her labor lock, stock, and barrel when he turned twenty-one in just two days' time. On the other hand, she felt guilty that he'd been made a virtual orphan by the business and her dedication to it.

At least her guilt was partially salved by knowing that while she'd been toiling at the office, he'd been nurtured at home under Camira's protective wing, with Cat always close by as a playmate. The special bond that had continued to flourish between them over the years had not escaped Kitty's notice. Even when he'd left for boarding school in Adelaide, a wish of Andrew's that she'd honored and, under the circumstances, the best solution, the two of them had spent his holidays together.

It was perhaps just as well that Elise Forsythe, an extraordinarily pretty and well-bred young lady, newly arrived in Broome with her family, would be joining the company as Charlie's secretary when he took over the business full-time. Kitty had handpicked Elise for the position. Although she mentally chided herself for her matchmaking, it was vital that Charlie choose a suitable wife who could love and support him as he took on the role of head of the Mercer empire.

As for herself, she'd told no one of her own plans yet, but she had a clear idea of what she would do once she finally handed over the reins to her son. She worried about not having the distraction of work in the future, since it had given her mind somewhere else to go whenever it began to wander in the direction of Drummond and all that had happened seventeen years ago . . . The devastation she had felt at his loss, doubled by an equally painful loss five months later, had almost destroyed her.

There had been no one else since, although there had been any number of suitors willing to put their hats in the ring to wed the young, beautiful, and very wealthy owner of the most successful pearling business in Broome. When she'd promised herself never to love again after Drummond had left, she had kept to her word. Her lover had been her business, her bedtime companions the accounts ledgers.

"Good grief! I've become a man," she said with a grim chuckle. Then, putting her glasses back on, she returned her attention to the ledger.

"Thank you, Alkina." Charlie gave her a surreptitious wink as she served both him and his mother breakfast. As usual, Alkina ignored it for fear of his mother noticing, but given that Kitty's nose was buried as usual in the pages of the *Northern Times*, it was unlikely she'd notice if the ceiling fell upon her head.

"My goodness," Kitty said with a sigh as she turned the page of her newspaper. "There's been a riot at Port Adelaide. It's lucky you left in time." She shook her head and put the paper down to speak to Charlie. "Have you had a chance yet to peruse the guest list for your birthday dinner on Thursday evening? I've invited the usual clutch of the great and the good in Broome. I can hardly believe that in a few days you'll be taking your rightful place among them. How time flies," Kitty sighed. "It seems only yesterday that you were a babe in my arms."

Charlie wanted to retort that the past twenty-one years felt as if they had gone excruciatingly slowly; he'd waited for this moment for so long. "No, not yet, but I'm sure you will have left no one out, Mother."

"This afternoon, Mr. Soi is coming with your pearling master's uniforms. I've ordered a dozen, although it looks to me as though you have lost weight since I last saw you. What have you been eating in Adelaide, I wonder. And this morning I wish for you to accompany me to the office. I have employed a very efficient young lady called Miss Forsythe to be your secretary. She comes highly recommended and is from one of the best families in Broome."

"Yes, Mother," Charlie responded, used to her irritating habit of trying to set him up with any female under the age of twenty-five who came to town. Surely, he thought, as his gaze followed Alkina's lithe body out of the room, his mother knew that he only had eyes for one woman? What a relief it would be when he made his announcement and the whole charade would be over.

"So, we shall meet by the car in thirty minutes?"

"Yes, Mother," he said as he watched her rise from her chair. He knew the locals wondered if she was happy, commenting on how, after almost seventeen years since her husband's disappearance, it must be possible to apply for an annulment on the grounds of desertion. After all, she was just into her forties. He had tentatively raised the subject with her a couple of years ago, emphasizing that she shouldn't feel guilty if she wished to officially end her marriage to his father.

"I really wouldn't mind. I just want you to be happy, Mother," he'd finished lamely.

"I appreciate your sentiments and thank you for them, but I shall never marry again." Seeing the look on his mother's face as she had swept from the room, Charlie had never taken the subject farther.

As his mother went to her study to collect her business ledgers for the day, Charlie went in search of Alkina. He came upon Camira in the kitchen.

"Cat gone out, Mister Charlie," she said before he could even ask. "She gottum errands. Dun worry, she back later. You get outta here." She shooed him out of the kitchen, and Charlie trudged despondently to his bedroom to get ready for the office.

It was four months since he'd last been home from Adelaide, the longest time he and Alkina had ever been separated, and he was desperate to hold her in his arms. When he'd finished his final university exams at the end of November, he'd already packed to return to Broome. But he was literally stopped at the door by a telegram from his mother telling him that his grandmother Edith had died the night before. Instead of boarding the ship, he'd been ordered to wait for his mother in Adelaide to make the necessary arrangements.

They had buried Edith and subsequently spent Christmas at Alicia Hall. Kitty had then taken Charlie to the vineyards in the Adelaide Hills, where she had encouraged him to engage with the manager there, in preparation for taking over the business. Then they had traveled to Coober Pedy so that his mother could show him the opal mine. She had insisted he stay there for two weeks to get to know the workings of the industry while she traveled back to Broome.

At least his extended time in Adelaide had given him a chance to meet up regularly with his oldest friend, Ted Strehlow. He had known Ted since the age of eleven when they had slept next to each other in a dormitory at Immanuel College. Both had continued to the University of Adelaide, and whereas Charlie had slogged away at his economics degree, Ted had read classics and English, but was determined to become an anthropologist and go on to study the history of the Aboriginals. It was a world away from the business of making money from the labor of others, and Charlie couldn't help but envy him for it. He'd have done anything to be free of the responsibilities that lay ahead.

"Charlie, are you nearly ready to leave?" Kitty called to him.

"Yes, Mother," he sighed, "coming right away."

Charlie went through the day trying hard to be mentally present with a tailor who was proud to have the honor of making his first pearling master's suits. Then it was off to the office by the harbor to meet his new secretary, Elise Forsythe. She was indeed pretty, in an insipid English way that Charlie thought could not hold a candle to the dark, exotic beauty of Cat. Afterward, he attended a meeting with Noel Donovan and the rest of the senior staff. He sat at the mahogany table in the boardroom, listening to the conversation about the Japanese competitors.

"They call it a 'cultured' pearl, but how can they possibly believe that the word 'culture' can be attached to something that is a crude copy, as opposed to being fashioned by nature alone?" His mother gave a disparaging snort of laughter.

"I hear, ma'am, that Mikimoto is flooding the markets," said the company accountant. "His spherical pearls are almost indistinguishable from the natural, and he has recently opened another store in Paris. They are called South Sea pearls and—"

"If people wish to buy cheap imitations of the real thing, let them get on with it," Kitty retorted. "I'm sure such a thing would never be countenanced here. Now, gentlemen, if there's no more business, I shall take my son to see his new office." She stood up and the men followed, their chair legs scraping against the wooden floor. She swept out of the room and Charlie followed her down the hallway, along which were offices piled high with paper trays. The clerks within them gave servile nods as Kitty and Charlie passed by. His mother unlocked a door at the end of a corridor and ushered him inside.

"Now, darling, what do you think of this? I've had it fitted out for you as a surprise."

Charlie stood looking at a gleaming partners desk, a beautiful antique globe, and an exquisite black lacquered sideboard painted delicately with gold butterflies.

"Goodness, Mother, it's wonderful, thank you. I only hope I can live up to everyone's expectations." Charlie walked to the window and gazed out at the dock, seeing the small train that ran the mile down to the town chugging steadily on its way.

"Of course you will. The pearling business is in your blood."

"Mother." Charlie sat down heavily in the high-backed leather chair. "I don't know if I am ready for all this. You have run the business so magnificently for all these years."

"My darling, all I have been is a caretaker for the Mercer empire, bequeathed to you by both your father and your uncle. In the twenty-one years I have watched you grow, you have never given me cause to doubt your suitability. You will make a worthy successor to your father."

"Thank you, Mother." Charlie couldn't help but note that his mother took no credit for herself.

Her bright blue eyes studied him intently. "You have been everything that I, your grandmother, and your father could ever have wished for as an heir. I am so proud of you, Charlie. Just one word of caution . . ." His mother's glance moved away to the window and the sea beyond it.

"Yes, Mother?"

"Don't ever let love blind you. It is the downfall of us all. Now"—
she forced a smile onto her face and stood up—"the crews have been
prepping the luggers during the lay-up season. Come down to the docks
and inspect their work with me."

"Of course, Mother."

As he stood up and followed her out of the office, Charlie felt his
stomach turn at her words.

That night, at eleven precisely, having seen the light in his mother's bedroom
go out, Charlie left the house as stealthily as the cat he was going to meet,
and crossed the terrace into the garden. The grass was springy beneath
his feet—the result of Fred's constant ministrations and his mother's
continual optimism that one day she would be able to create a garden
that would not succumb to the red mud that streamed across it during the
Big Wet. She had given up on the rose beds, however, and these days the
roses were planted in large pots around the terrace and carried to shelter
the moment a storm threatened. Unbeknownst to her, the rose shed had
provided a dry and private area for the two young people to meet. It was
locked assiduously every night by Fred, but Cat had managed to "borrow"
the key, and Charlie had taken it to the locksmith and had a copy made.

He'd turned the rock that sat outside from the red side to the green
side earlier. This was the signal they both used to indicate they would meet
later that evening when everyone was in bed. They had weathered many
storms inside the shed, the roses forming a scented bower as they had lain
between them on a rough blanket on the floor and declared their love for
each other. And tonight, he had something very special to give her.

He'd spotted it in Ted's apartment when they'd been knocking back
some beers to celebrate the New Year. An obsessive collector, Ted's
rooms were filled with all manner of stones, shells, and tribal artifacts
that he had amassed on his travels. This piece was a small, gleaming amber
stone, with what appeared to be a minuscule ant caught inside it, trapped
there for millennia. Ted had given it to him when he'd seen Charlie's avid
interest, and the very next day he'd taken it to a jeweler on King William
Street to have it fashioned into an engagement ring for Cat. The color of
the stone would match her eyes perfectly.

Charlie smiled as he remembered when he had first asked Cat to marry him. It had been the evening before he was to leave for boarding school in Adelaide. He had been eleven years old and she had held him as he wept out of fear and loss onto her small, soft shoulder.

"One day, I won't have to do as Mother says, and I'll come back here and we will be married. What am I to do without you?" he'd moaned. "Wait for me, won't you, my Cat?"

"I will wait for you, Charlie. I will wait."

And she *had* waited, for ten long years, as he had waited for her. He'd written to her from boarding school every Sunday, pouring out his heart as the other boys around him dashed off a quick few words to their parents. He knew she found it difficult to read because she'd had no formal education, but just the process of writing to her comforted him. In return, having issued her with a large supply of stamped and addressed envelopes, he'd receive short and appallingly spelled missives, but she illustrated each letter with carefully drawn pictures of flowers she'd seen, or of the moon hanging low over the sea, with a chain of hearts held together with ivy edging the pages. If she could not speak her love for him, she could draw it.

And tonight—finally—he would ask her to marry him for real.

Charlie looked up to the skies as he heard a faint rumble of thunder. The heat was stifling, and no doubt within the hour there would be a downpour. As he reached for the handle to open the door to the shed, expecting to find it unlocked, trepidation clutched at his heart when it didn't open. Cat was always there first, as she held the key. He tried it again, but it didn't budge. He searched the blackness and listened for her light footsteps across the garden. Perhaps it was simply his imagination, but when she'd looked at him at breakfast that morning, the usual warmth had been missing from her amber eyes. His greatest fear had always been that she would tire of waiting for him and find someone else. But now, he was only hours away from declaring his intentions to the world and their both being free to love each other publicly . . .

His mind flew back to Cat and that last night when he'd been inside the shed with her, just over four months ago. Having grown up together, they hadn't felt the usual embarrassment at each other's bodies as they had matured. Charlie chuckled as he remembered her, age six, sitting in their play hut stark naked and serving him a cup of tea in a miniature china cup.

He'd known every inch of her since she was tiny and could only marvel as she blossomed from an arresting child into a beautiful young woman.

They'd had their first adult kiss on his sixteenth birthday, which had been the most wonderful yet frustrating moment of his life, for he had wanted to kiss her not merely on the lips, but all over her perfect body. However, they both knew where such intimate activity could lead, and Charlie blushed at the memory of her slapping his face once when his hand had wandered in the direction of her breast.

"I cannot," she'd wailed. "Don't make me."

Chastened, Charlie had done his best to control his natural physical urges, constantly reminding himself that once they were married, her body would be his by rights.

And then . . . that September night before he was due to return to Adelaide for his last few weeks at university, he'd stolen a bottle of champagne from the drinks cabinet and opened it with her in the hut. She'd eyed it suspiciously after he'd popped the cork and poured out two glasses.

"My mother says this stuff no good for us."

"Just try a glass, you'll love the way the bubbles tickle your tongue," Charlie had urged her. "I swear, it will do you no harm."

She'd taken a sip, just to please him, and closed her eyes to assimilate the new taste.

"I like it!" she'd said eventually as her eyes had opened and she smiled at him. She'd finished that glass, and he'd poured her another. The rest he'd finished off himself, and they'd lain there on the rough blanket, talking of the future.

It had been she who had turned to kiss him, she who had rolled on top of him and led his hand to undo the buttons of her blouse. After that, the bliss of feeling her naked skin against his own had prevented any rational thought from stopping their loving each other. Cat had fallen asleep immediately after, but Charlie had lain awake, capturing every glorious inch of her lying naked next to him. He'd consoled himself with the thought that in a few months' time, they would be man and wife, and even if the event had been premature, he was sure that all of their different gods would forgive them. After all, they were adults, and the act of love was completely natural . . .

Another twenty minutes passed outside the shed, with no sign of Cat.

Charlie stood up and paced across the lawn. He entered the house and checked the kitchen to see if she had been delayed there, but the whole house was in darkness. Walking across to the hut that Cat and her mother shared, he saw Fred asleep on his pallet in the stable and felt a pinprick of rain upon his hand. Fred always slept outside unless he'd seen the sign of a storm on its way, when he'd retreat inside for cover. Arriving at the door to the hut, he listened but could hear no sound from within. Clutching the handle, he turned it as quietly as he could. Inside, he saw the moonlight streaming through the shuttered window, illuminating only Camira asleep in the double bed.

As he closed the door, a surge of panic filled him. Where *was* she? Having made a sweep of the rest of their land, he returned to the rose shed, wondering if they had missed each other while he'd been away. He tried the door, but it was still locked. Charlie sank down onto his haunches, wondering why, so close now to what he had dreamed of for years, she wasn't here.

Perhaps she has met someone else . . . some diver off the luggers, he thought.

Charlie felt his stomach turn, then wondered if he should take the pony and cart and drive into town to search for her. Perhaps Mother had sent her out on a late-night errand, and in going about her business, she'd been accosted, or even raped . . .

The air became still with the complete silence of a pregnant storm before its waters finally broke, and he heard a sudden sound from inside the shed. A small cough, or maybe a hiccup, or a cry . . . he didn't know for sure, but it was enough to spur him to action.

The thunder rumbled above him as he slammed his fist onto the door. "Cat, I know you're there. Let me in now!"

Another burst of thunder came overhead, and he slammed the door once again. "I will break it down if you don't!"

Finally, the key was turned and Charlie entered to find Cat staring at him with fear accentuating her beautiful eyes.

"For God's sake!" Charlie fell through the door, panting. "Have you been there all the time? Did you not hear me try the lock?"

She lowered her eyes from his gaze.

Charlie closed the door behind him, locked it, then went toward her to take her in his arms. She did not yield to him; it felt akin to holding a plank of wood.

"What is it, my darling? What has happened?"

She pulled away from him, then turned and sat down on the blanket. She said something, but he couldn't hear because the thunder was right above them now, drowning out her low voice.

"I'm sorry, what did you say?"

"I said that I am pregnant. I am having a baby. *Jahygurr.*"

Charlie watched as Cat stuffed her fist into her mouth to stop herself screaming. She was shaking from head to foot. There was yet another crash of thunder and the rain began to pelt down onto the tin roof above them.

"I . . ." He went toward her to embrace her, but she backed away, terrified. "Cat, my darling Cat . . . please, don't be frightened of me. I'm not the enemy, really, I—"

"If my mother finds out, she beat me, throw me out on the street! I promised her, I *promised* . . ."

"My love." Charlie took a couple of tentative steps toward her. "I can understand why you're so distressed, and yes, it is a little premature, but—"

"I promised her, I promised not to do same thing she did," Cat wailed, backing away further. "Never trust them whitefellas, never trust 'em, never trust 'em . . ."

Charlie watched her bring her knees up protectively in front of her. "And your mother was right," he said, taking another step toward her. "But I'm not just any old 'whitefella.' I'm your Charlie, and you're my Cat. Just think of the times we've imagined we would be married and have a family."

"Yes! But we were children, Charlie. It was playing games. Not real life. And now it is. I wanta get rid of it, drown it as soon as it born. Then I won't have this big problem."

Charlie was horrified at her words. "Please, Cat." He took the last two steps toward her. Thunder continued to crash directly above their heads as though the full force of the heavens were voicing its displeasure. "Here in my pocket I have something for you." He crouched down next to her and drew out the amber ring. "Everything is all right, my love. Listen to me." Charlie took her small hand in his. "My darling Cat"—he reached for her fourth finger—"will you marry me?" He slipped the ring onto her finger, then watched her eyes move to the ring and study it silently.

"It's made of amber, and there is some kind of insect caught inside it. I thought it would match your eyes. Do you like it?"

"I . . ." Cat bit her lip. "It a beautiful gift, Charlie."

"See? Everything will be all right. We will be married as soon as possible, my love."

"No." Cat looked up at him. "I can't marry you, Charlie. I am your maid."

"You know I don't care about that! I love you. I've wanted to marry you since I was a small boy."

Cat tipped her eyes up to the heavens. When her gaze returned to him, it was full of sorrow. "Charlie, in twenty-four hours you become most important whitefella in Broome. You inherit the Mercer Pearling Company and become the big bossman. You know lotsa things I don't know, because you had good education. You belong to the whitefellas' world, but I don't."

"I can teach you, Cat, just as I've taught you in the past."

"No! No one would come ta eat at our table with me being your missus. You will be . . ." Cat's eyebrows drew together as she searched for the words. "A laughing pot."

"Stock," Charlie corrected automatically.

"Stock, yes. And our stock is not the same. No." Alkina shook her head firmly. "You needa white woman, not me. I cannot make you proud, be something I not. I don't want dem whitefellas laughing at me behind my back, saying I'm stupid. And they *would* laugh at me. I'm good person, just different."

"I know, but . . ." Again Charlie dug deep to find the words. "Inside there"—he pointed to her stomach—"is something that both of us made with our love. Surely, we must put that first? If we marry quickly, no one would even know, because the baby would just come early, and—"

"You dreamin' again. Everyone would know why you marry me. It's been four months already." Alkina withdrew her hand and rested her head back on her knees. "They would never believe in our love."

"But I do," Charlie said, his voice strong and clear above the thunder. "I understand that you're all that's kept me going for the last ten years. That there haven't been more than a few minutes—not even during my final exams—when I've not thought of you. Do not . . ." He cupped his palms to her cheeks and lifted her head from her knees. "I repeat, *do not* ever put me in the same category as other men. I love you with all my heart. You are my *jarndu nilbanjun*—we are promised to each other. My life would be nothing without you and our baby to come." He reached for her, drew her into his arms, and kissed her roughly, passionately, but she pulled away from him.

"*Marlu!* No! Stop it! Please stop! For all education, you don't understand! I cannot be your wife. There *is* no future for us."

"There is, my darling. And yes, you're right, perhaps it will be difficult, and perhaps everyone will be shocked by our union, but surely we owe it to future generations of men and women in this country to make a stand? And I am perfectly placed to do so. In twenty-four hours I will inherit huge wealth. Money talks—especially in this town." Charlie reached for her again and held her taut body against his. "My darling, we're a family already, don't you see? It was meant to be."

"No! I . . . you, an' this"—Cat patted her stomach—"are not experiment. We are human, and dis is our life, Charlie. We have lived side by side, yes? So close together, always, but truth is, we far apart. You walka the world as a whitefella with a veil over your eyes. You do not see how the rest of the world sees me, how they treatem me because of the color of my skin. You do not see how so much of the world is closed to me, because you are free, and I not. An' our baby will not be free."

"Cat, we would be man and wife and the law would allow it! And I will do *everything* I can to make sure you and our baby are safe, just as my mother did for Camira, for *you!*" Charlie wrung his hands as he tried to make her understand. "I have nothing without you."

There was silence as they both listened to the rain drumming on the roof.

A long sigh escaped Cat's lips. "Charlie, I thinkum you not live here in Broome for long time now. You don't understand how it is."

"I don't care how it is! We will baptize the baby in front of the entire town! I've been discussing this with Ted—the friend I have told you about whose father ran the Hermannsburg mission near Alice Springs. Ted has taught me so much, he even speaks Arrernte, and tells me that the Aboriginals in the mission are free to come and go as they please. The whitefellas respect your culture, and—"

"Does he knowa 'bout me?"

"Of course he does."

"Would *he* ever marry a 'creamy' like me?"

"Goodness, I don't know, I've never asked him . . ."

"Hah! Things other fellas tell you but wouldn't do themselves . . ."

"No! That's not right. Ted Strehlow is a good man, a man who means to make a change in Australia."

"He be dead long before it made." Cat tore off the amber ring and offered it to him. "I cannot take this. You have it back, please, Charlie." She pressed it into the palm of his hand. He was just about to entreat her to keep it when there was a sudden loud banging on the door. Both of them nearly jumped out of their skins.

"Is someone in there? Good God, I'm being drowned out here, and so are my roses! Why won't my key fit into the lock?"

"*Jidu!* Hide!" Charlie hissed to Cat.

Already Cat had stood up and was blowing out candles before removing the blanket from the center of the floor.

"Sorry, Mother, it's me," Charlie called cheerily through the door. "I heard the storm and I've already begun to gather your roses together." Making sure Cat was well hidden in the shadows, he turned the key in the door as quietly as he could and threw it into Cat's hands, as he made a façade of turning the handle numerous times. "Good grief, this lock is sticky, we need to have Fred oil it," he said loudly.

Turning back to the figure in the shadows, he mouthed, "*I love you.*" Then, with an exaggerated jerk, he pulled open the door.

"Mother! You're positively drenched!"

"I am indeed, but I shall dry off soon enough." Kitty stepped into the shed, dragging a tub of roses in behind her. "I've never known that door to jam before. One would almost think that you had locked it from the inside."

"Why would I do that? Right, I'll dive out and try and save the rest of the tubs from imminent death," Charlie chuckled, then stepped out of the shed into the pelting rain.

"Thank you," Kitty said a few minutes later as the last of the roses had been brought in to their safe haven. "I pride myself on knowing when a storm is coming, but tonight," she sighed, "I was so very tired."

"Of course, Mother. You work too hard."

"And I will indeed be relieved to hand over the burden," Kitty replied. "By the way, I have invited Elise Forsythe to come to your birthday

celebration. She is such a nice young woman. She told me today after
you'd left that her grandfather hails from Scotland."

"What a coincidence. Now, Mother, shall we go to the house and get
ourselves dry?"

"Yes. Thank you, my darling. I know I can always depend on you."

"Always, Mother," Charlie said as he closed the door behind them and
Kitty locked it.

Once the footsteps had retreated, a figure emerged from the shadows
inside the shed. After tiptoeing to the door and unlocking it with the key
Charlie had thrown her, she opened it and made her way out into the
night.

The storm had abated, at least for a while. Leaning back against the
shed, Cat looked up to the heavens, her hands held protectively around
her belly.

"Hermannsburg," she breathed as a tear fell down her cheek. "Sanctuary."

Slipping into bed next to her mother as quietly as the cat she was
nicknamed after, Alkina tried to still her breathing.

Helpum me . . . please, ancestors, help me, she pleaded.

That night, she dreamed that the Gumanyba had come down to their
cave. She watched them as they went through the forest and the old man
appeared. They ran off back to their cave, but the youngest was left
behind. Suddenly, the old man was pursuing *her*, but when she arrived in
the cave, she knew she had to find something that was buried deep down
under the red soil. Her sisters were calling to her, telling her to hurry, that
the old man was almost upon her and would take her for his own. Yet still,
even though she could hear his feet thundering across the ground, she
kept digging because she could not leave the earth without it . . .

Alkina opened her eyes just as the dream version of herself had clutched
at a tin and pulled it out of the ground. A memory came flooding back
to her of her mother leading her into the bush when she was fourteen to
initiate her into the ways of their ancestors. On the way to the corroboree,
her mother had said she must stop and check on something. They had
arrived at a cave just like the one she'd seen in her dream, and her mother
had bent down and begun scrabbling in the earth before drawing out a
tin box.

"Step back," she'd told her daughter, as she'd sat cross-legged and opened it. Curious, Alkina had done as she was told, but had watched as her mother had opened the small leather box that lay inside the tin. At that moment, the sun had caught the object inside, which seemed to shimmer with a pink opalescence, the likes of which Alkina had never seen before. It shone like the moon itself, and she had been transfixed by its beauty.

Then the box had been snapped shut, returned to the tin, and buried back in the earth. Her mother had stood, mumbling some words under her breath, then had walked back toward her.

"Bibi, what is that?" Alkina had asked Camira.

"You nottum need know. It safe where it is, and so is Missus Kitty. Now, we go on our way."

As Alkina watched the dawn beginning to break through the wooden shutters of the hut, she knew what she had to do.

25

Charlie too had a sleepless night. He tossed and turned, trying to think of what was best to do, and berating himself for having triggered all of this to begin with—after all, it had been he who had given Cat the champagne.

He understood her fear, and there was no doubt it would be hard for them initially. Yet given there *were* mixed-race unions in the town these days, surely theirs would be accepted too?

There was only one other option, and Charlie had considered it many times in the past year as he'd sweated over his future as a pearling master. No one had ever asked him if it was what he *wanted* to do. As if he were the son of a king, it was taken for granted he would don the mantle when the time came—no matter if he was even suited to the task. Charlie had known for a while now that he was not. He'd hated every second of his economics course at university. Even his professors had said he did not have an aptitude for numbers, but when he had tentatively raised this with his mother, she had brushed away his doubts.

"My dear Charlie, you are not there to add and subtract, you have plenty of clerks to do that for you. You are there to lead, to inspire, and to make decisions on where the businesses should head in the future."

It was cold comfort, as he was completely uninspired by all facets of the business empire, whether it be pearls, opals, or cattle. They all seemed to involve deprivation and sometimes death for those who worked for the companies, while the "bossmen," as Cat called them, became rich on their employees' toil.

So . . . if Cat refused to marry him in Broome, Charlie was prepared to give up everything and go away with her wherever she wished.

His mother was already at the table when he walked in to breakfast, reading her habitual newspaper.

"Good morning, Charlie. How did you sleep?"

"Well, thank you, Mother. You?"

"Far better after I knew my precious roses were safe from the rains. Thank you for being so thoughtful."

"Coffee, Mister Charlie?"

"Thank you." He looked up, ready to give Cat a smile, but was instead greeted by Camira's eyes looking down at him. A sudden tightness clutched at his chest. Cat always served breakfast.

"Is Cat unwell?"

"She well, Mister Charlie. She go visit cousin," Camira replied calmly.

"I see. When will she be back?"

"When cousin baby born. Maybe one week, maybe two."

Camira's inscrutable eyes bored into him and he broke into a cold sweat, even though the heat of the day was already overpowering. Was she giving him some secret message? Surely Cat would not have told her mother of her condition?

"Right," he managed, trying to still his breathing and keep control in front of his mother—in front of *both* mothers—when all he wanted to do was jump up from the breakfast table and go and find her.

"Did you say Cat is away?" Kitty removed her reading glasses to look at Camira.

"Yes, Missus Kitty. I take over while she nottum here." Camira replaced the coffeepot on the sideboard and left the room.

"A euphemism that she's gone walkabout," Kitty sighed. "Anyway, the most important thing is you, my dear Charlie. At midnight tonight, you turn twenty-one and become the rightful owner of all the Mercer business interests. How do you feel?"

"A little daunted, Mother."

"There is no need to be, although I cannot say you're taking over at the perfect moment, as shell orders have decreased recently . . ."

Charlie didn't hear what she said, just nodded and smiled appropriately whenever she paused to gauge his reaction.

Cat, where are you?

Eventually, to Charlie's relief, his mother stopped talking and stood up. "So, I suggest you enjoy your last day of freedom before you shoulder your responsibilities. Tomorrow will be a busy day. There is a lunch at the office to welcome you, then, of course, the dinner and dance at the

Roebuck Bay Hotel in the evening. Let us pray the storm has passed us by for now, or half the great and the good of Broome will arrive with red dirt soaking the bottom of their trousers and skirts," she chuckled. "I will see you tonight."

"Yes, Mother." Charlie nodded courteously as she left the room.

He waited until he'd seen Fred pull the car out of the drive before he went in search of Camira. He found her in the kitchen, plucking a duck and tutting. These days, Cat was the cook, well taught by his mother in the ways of British food.

"Where has she gone?" he asked, not caring if she did or didn't know about the baby.

A slight shrug came from Camira's shoulders. "Gone to help cousin."

"You believe that?"

"She my daughter. She nottum lie to me."

Charlie slumped into one of the wooden chairs that surrounded the kitchen table. He knew he was very close to tears. "She is my special friend. You know that. We grew up together and . . . why would she leave on the eve of my twenty-first birthday?"

Camira turned around and studied him, her glance unwavering. "Thinka you know why, Mister Charlie. So do I, but we not talk 'bout it. Maybe for best, yes?"

"*No!*" He slammed his fist on the table. "I . . ." He shook his head, knowing the golden rule of never divulging information, let alone feelings, to a servant, but all bets were off. "I love her; she is everything to me. I asked her to marry me last night! I wanted to tell the world tomorrow that she would become my wife! Why has she gone? I just don't understand!"

Then he did cry, and the pair of arms that came gently around him were not his mother's, but those of her surrogate, who came from another world.

"Oh God, Camira . . . you don't know how much I love her, how much I need her. Why has she gone?"

"She thinkum she do best for you, Mister Charlie. She don't wanta hold you back. You musta be part of whitefella world."

"We've talked about it since we were children! I told her last night we would be married and live together for the rest of our lives!" Charlie slammed the table again. "All the letters I wrote her over the last ten years, telling her how much I miss her, how much I love her . . . I could not have given her any more. Believe me"—Charlie shook his head in devastation—"I would give up all I have willingly. It means nothing to me, I have no interest in becoming rich, only living with her, lovingly, eagerly in the sight of God."

Camira's face softened. "You whitefellas the bossmen. Maybe she wanta be her *own* bosswoman. Nottum live in your world."

"Camira, where is she? Where has she gone? For God's sake, tell me!"

"I notta know, swear, Mister Charlie. She tellum me she leave, an' I understand. I *see* an' I understand. You get me?"

She eyed him, and Charlie nodded. "She would have been safe with me. I could have protected her."

"She fulla fear. She takem time to think."

"For how long? If she returns in a couple of months, the evidence will be obvious! It's now or never. Tell me where she has gone! You must, you have to!"

Camira walked to the back door of the kitchen. She opened it and then stood outside for a while, her head tipped upward as if she was asking for guidance. When she reentered the kitchen, she shook her head. "Mister Charlie, even ancestors not tellum me where my daughter go. Believe me."

"Did she give you a message? For me, I mean?"

"Yessum, she ask me to give-a you somethin' tomorrow."

"If it will give some clue as to where she is, you must fetch it for me now!"

"I do-a like Cat say. Tomorrow."

Charlie knew better than to argue. "Then I will come to your hut at midnight."

Camira nodded. "Now, I mustum cook duck."

Charlie walked toward the hut just before midnight and put out a hand to tap on it gently, but before his skin touched wood, Camira opened the door.

"Here." She passed Charlie a brown paper package tied with a ribbon he'd once seen in Cat's hair. "Happy birthday. Congratulation! You-a man now, no longer littun boy." Camira smiled at him tenderly. "I helpum you grow."

"You did, Camira, and I am grateful for it." He stared down at the package in his hands, then up at her once more. "You are not worried about your daughter?"

"I trust, Mister Charlie, she too grown now. What choice I have? Please." She placed her hand on his, and her palm was warm. "Dis your day. You-a earn it. Please, enjoy. Me an' Cat wanta you to."

"I will try, but you have to know—"

Camira put her finger to her lips. "Dun be sayin' those words. I know 'em already." Camira stood on her tiptoes and kissed his forehead. "You my boy too. I your *bibi*. I proud o' you. *Galiya*."

She closed the door, and Charlie walked back to the house. Sitting on his bed, he tore off the brown paper, all his hopes pinned on what he would find inside. A clue, a trail he could follow, *anything* to lead him to her.

Having unwrapped the many layers that held the present within, he sat with a small painting framed in driftwood that had been carved with delicate lines to shape roses. Holding it to the light, he saw that she had painted the two of them sitting together in the rose shed, his lighter head bent toward her dark one. Their hands were entwined in such a way that he could barely distinguish their individual fingers.

He closed his eyes, the painting still in his hand. And as the night wore on until morning—twenty-one years since he'd uttered his first cry—he slept.

Charlie would always look back and try to remember the day of his twenty-first birthday, but it passed in a blur of faces, presents, and champagne, which he accepted far too freely to drown his agony. He went through the motions, acting as if he was a fully formed human being, even though every part of him cried out for Cat.

There was dancing after dinner at the Roebuck Bay Hotel and Elise Forsythe partnered him often, showing her perfect dimples as she giggled at everything he said, even if it wasn't remotely funny. She told him she was an "Hon," which was English-speak for being of aristocratic breeding, and he could see she wore it well. Charlie accepted she looked lovely in her midnight-blue evening gown, with her blond hair and pale complexion like creamy milk. When it was time to blow out the candles on his extravagant three-tiered birthday cake, the crowd burst into applause, and Kitty glowed with pride. Charlie listened to her generous speech, his eyes downcast in embarrassment and despair. Three cheers went up for him and everyone raised their glasses in a toast.

Alone in his bedroom later, after thanking his mother profusely for such a wonderful party and for the watch by an expensive Swiss jeweler, Charlie thought he'd never been so grateful to get to the end of a day. He was due in the office at nine the next morning, as he would be every day for the rest of his life.

"How can I bear this without you?" he murmured, and fell asleep with Cat's ribbon clasped in his hand.

"I have made a decision, Charlie," Kitty announced at breakfast the following morning. "In a month's time, I will be taking a trip to Europe."

"For work?"

"No, that is your job now. I wish to see my family back in Edinburgh. It is five years since I last traveled there, and even then it was only a brief visit. I shall stay with them for a few months—I have nephews and nieces I haven't even met. I also feel it is important that I leave you to find your own feet here, make a clean break, so that everyone knows you are in charge."

"Mother"—a surge of panic ran through Charlie—"do you think that's wise? I barely know what I'm doing. I need you here with me."

"We will have a month together, which is plenty of time for you to learn. Don't you see, my dear boy? If I stay, all the employees will continue to come to me rather than you and they have to understand that you are the boss. There are changes you might wish to make—ones that may not be popular with our employees. I do not wish to be the listening ear for a stream of disgruntled staff who believe I have some sway over you. No, it is far better that I go. And besides," Kitty said, letting out a sigh, "I am not getting any younger and I am tired. I need a holiday."

"You are not sick, Mother?"

"No. It seems God gave me the constitution of an ox, but I wish to keep it that way."

"You will come back?"

"Of course—the freezing Scottish winter will provide the spur." Kitty shivered at the thought. "I will sail back to Adelaide before Christmas and celebrate the festive season at Alicia Hall. I hope you can join me and we can pay a visit to the opal mine and the vineyard to make sure the mice aren't playing while the cat's away."

The Cat's away . . .

"Even though I understand you wish to take a break, I'm very concerned I don't have the wherewithal to run the business alone."

"And I am perfectly sure you do. When your father left, I had no choice but to plunge in headfirst. I was completely alone with no one to ask for advice, except dear Mr. Donovan, who will be there for you too. He knows everything there is to know, although he will reach his sixtieth birthday this year and I am aware he eventually wishes to retire. He already has someone in mind to take over from him—a bright young Japanese man who can speak fluent English. With the number of Japanese we employ, he will be able to communicate with our crews better and will be an enormous asset." Kitty rose from the table. "Right, let's get to work, shall we?"

Over the next month, even though Charlie lay in bed every night promising himself that tomorrow he'd tell his mother the reason why Cat had left and that he was going in search of her, the business be damned, he never managed to utter a word. He knew his mother had spent the past seventeen years of her life running herself ragged to grow his inheritance, and all she wanted now was to take a well-earned break. How could he deny her that?

His admiration of her grew apace as he noted her voice of authority and the way she handled her staff and any problems with the lightest of touches. He also saw how the worry lines on her face had smoothed and how relaxed she seemed compared to the past.

How could he walk out on her after all she had done for him? Yet how could he not go and search for Cat and bring her back? Torn between loyalty for the two women he loved, Charlie felt often that his head and heart might explode. On Sundays—his one day off if there wasn't a lugger coming in—he drove to Riddell Beach and swam hard to calm his tortured mind. He floated there, the waves lapping in his ears, trying to find the peace and resolution he needed. It didn't come, and as the day approached when his mother would leave for Europe, his panic increased. He wondered if he should simply plunge his head under the waves for good to find blissful release.

Besides everything else, he didn't feel he was cut out for the job. He had none of his mother's air of natural authority, or the ease with which she talked to the other pearling masters at their regular dinners. Being half the age of most of them, Charlie knew they were almost certainly laughing at him behind his back and probably already planning their bids as they watched him and the company fail. His only other thought was to sell the company to one of the local pearling masters, but he knew that his mother would see it as a betrayal of his father and grandfather. The Mercer Pearling Company was one of the oldest in town, run by a family member since it began.

In short, Charlie had never been as miserable, desolate, and lonely in his life.

Kitty had invited Elise around for Sunday lunch on a couple of occasions. There was no doubt that she was an efficient secretary and possibly more capable than he, as she covered up his mistakes where she could. She was bright, witty, and pretty, and it was obvious his mother thought Elise the perfect future wife. There were constant mutterings about marriage and an heir to the empire.

"You'd better snap her up before someone else does. Women like her don't come along often in this town," she had said pointedly.

But there is already an heir out there, growing by the day in its mother's stomach. God only knows how she is surviving . . .

"Wait for me, Cat," he'd whisper to her ancestors. "I will find you . . ."

"So, this is good-bye, at least for now." Kitty smiled at her son as they stood in the luxurious suite aboard the ship that would take her down to Fremantle and then on the long voyage across the seas to her homeland.

Charlie thought how carefree she looked today—almost like a young girl, her eyes full of excitement.

"I will do my best not to let you down."

"I know you will." Kitty reached out her hand to touch her son's face. "Take care of yourself, darling boy."

"I will."

The ship's bell rang out to tell all those not traveling to disembark.

"Write to me, won't you? Let me know how you're getting on?" Kitty asked him.

"Of course. Safe travels, Mother." Charlie gave her a last hug before leaving the suite to make his way down the gangplank. He waved until the ship was just a speck on the ocean. Then he took the little train back down the pier, where Fred was waiting in the car to return him home.

That evening, Charlie dined alone. The silence in the house was eerie and after he'd finished eating, he went to see Camira in the kitchen. In the past month, with Kitty in residence, it had been hard to pin her down alone, but she couldn't avoid him now.

"Dinna okay, Mister Charlie?"

"Yes," he replied. "Have you heard from her?"

"No."

"She has not contacted you at all? Please, I beg you, tell me the truth."

"Mister Charlie, you nottum understand. Out there"—Camira waved her arm around vaguely—"no paper and stamp."

"Maybe others have seen her? I know how the bush telegraph works and messages are delivered by word of mouth."

"No, I hear-a nothin', honest, Mister Charlie."

"I am amazed you are not beside yourself with worry."

"Yessum, I worry, but I think she okay. I feel her, and ancestors look after her."

"Has she gone to live with your people, you think?"

"Maybe."

"Will she be coming back?"

"Maybe."

"Christ!" Charlie had the urge to shake her. "Do you not see that I am going mad with worry?"

"Yessum, I see-a gray hair on you this morning."

"If she doesn't come back in the next few weeks, I will go and find her myself." Charlie paced the kitchen.

"She nottum want be found." Camira continued calmly with the washing-up.

"We both know why she left, so at least it is my responsibility to try, whether she wishes it or not. After all, she is carrying my—"

Charlie restrained himself, knowing the actual words must remain unspoken between them. Yet again, he found himself close to tears.

"Mister Charlie, you good man, I know you lovem my daughter. And she love you. She think what she do is for best. She wanta you have happy life. Too difficult for you with her. Accept things you cannot change."

"I cannot, Camira, I cannot." Charlie sank down into a chair, put his arms on the table, and rested his head upon them. To his shame, he began to sob again. "I can't live without her, I simply can't."

"Mister Charlie." Camira left the washing-up, dried her hands, and came to put her arms around his heaving shoulders. "I see-a you two for many year. I thinkum maybe it disappear, but it not."

"Exactly, so I can't just give up on her, Camira, leave her out there . . . you know what can happen to half-caste children if the mother is unwed . . . I could at least have offered her some protection! And I tried, but she refused." He took the amber ring out of his pocket and brandished it at her. "My son or daughter may end up in one of those dreadful orphanages and while I have breath inside me I cannot sit here and do nothing!" He threw the ring onto the table, where it rolled and then came to rest in front of Camira.

"I understand," she said. There was silence in the room as she thought. "Mister Charlie, I makem you deal. If I nottum hear from her in next few weeks, I go walkabout an' find her."

"And I will come with you."

"No. You whitefella, you nottum survive out there. You big bossman here. Your mother, she trust you. You nottum let her down. She work hard to make big business to give you. Here, keepum this."

She picked up the ring and held it out to him, but he pushed her hand away.

"No, you take it. Find her, and bring her back, then I will put it on her finger. Until then, I can't bear to look at it."

Camira tucked the ring into her apron. "Okay, we makem deal? You work hard now at office for Missus Kitty and I go-a find my daughter if she not come home soon. Too many people in this family gettum lost. Sleep now, Mister Charlie, or more gray hairs comin'."

Left with no choice, Charlie did his best to adhere to Camira's advice. With the assurance that she would go to find Cat when the time was right, for the next four months he threw himself into the business as his mother would have wanted him to. Ledgers, legal papers, and the endless arrival of luggers into dock at least took Cat from his mind. The business—like all in Broome—was struggling. Their vast stockpiles of shell had plummeted in price, as Europe and America were demanding cheaper materials. Charlie looked carefully into the business of the cultured pearl farms run by Mr. Mikimoto. With real pearls becoming a scarce commodity in Broome due to excessive trawling off the coast, he could see that the cultured pearls were good replicas—and, in fact, far more suited to jewelry, as each was of a more standard size and therefore could easily be strung into a necklace or bracelet. Despite his mother's disparaging comments, Mikimoto thought cultured pearls were the future, and so did the great continent of America, which was buying his product by the sackload.

Charlie was also impressed that pearl farming did not put human lives at risk in the way diving did, and was moved to invite one of Mikimoto's managers over to show him how it could be done in Broome. He knew too that, after the initial setup costs, the profits would rise. It would ultimately destroy the industry that had made the town so prosperous, but just as in nature, everything had its season and Charlie felt instinctively that Broome was moving into a dark autumn.

"Everyone has to pay the piper," he muttered as he donned his master pearler's pith helmet, straightened his gold braid, and left to find Fred waiting in the car for him outside.

At least, he thought as the car drove off, he was taking his own first step into the future, however controversial.

Charlie was fast asleep when he heard a sudden keening sound fill the still air around him. He sat upright, pulling himself into consciousness.

The noise continued—a terrible high wailing, reminiscent of a sound he'd heard before. Still drowsy, he forced his mind to comprehend it . . .

"No . . . *no* . . . !"

He sprang from his bed, bolted out of the room, and ran through the house, following the sound through the kitchen and out of the back door.

He found Camira kneeling on the ground, kneading the red dust with her fingertips. She was babbling words he could not understand, but did not need to, because he knew already.

She looked up at him, her eyes full of undisguised agony.

"Mister Charlie, she is gone! I leavem it too late. I leavem it too late!"

A pall of misery hung over the house as its two occupants grieved day and night. They hardly spoke, the bond that had once tied them now disintegrating into bitterness, anger, and guilt. Charlie spent as little time at home as possible, sequestering himself in the office just as his mother had done after his father had left them. He now understood why— a broken heart ravaged and destroyed the soul, especially when it had guilt attached to it.

Elise, his secretary, seemed to sense that something was amiss, and despite himself, with her sunny smile and her calming presence, Charlie found her to be a light in the dark sea of gloom. At the same time, he resented her naïveté, her privilege, and the very fact that she was alive, when Alkina—and their child—was not.

What tortured him most was the fact he would never know how she died, perhaps out there alone in agony, giving birth to their baby.

At twenty-one years old, and one of the richest men in Australia, Charlie Mercer could have been taken for double his age.

THE NEVER NEVER

Near Alice Springs

June 1929

26

The night was still, the only sound the cry of a distant dingo. The bright white stars and the moon in the cloudless sky above him were his only light source as the horse sauntered over the rocky desert terrain, navigating the low shrubs and bushes which grew close to the ground to protect themselves from the frequent sandstorms. The drover's eyes had adjusted to the dim light and could pick out the shadows of the rugged earth around him and the dark blue veins in the cliffs. The night air carried the cool, fragrant scents of the earth recovering from the heat of the day, and the air was thick with the sounds of skittering animals and buzzing insects.

He tethered his horse to a rocky outcrop sticking up from the earth like a red stalagmite. He'd been hoping to make it to the Alice by nightfall, but there'd been a skirmish between the local Aboriginal tribe and the drovers earlier, so he'd bided his time until it was over. Pulling off one of his camel-skin water bottles, he took a bowl from his saddlebag, filled it, and put it on the ground for the exhausted mare to drink from. Swigging back the last remains of the grog from his flask and rooting in the bag for what was left of his tucker, he laid out the rough blanket and sat down to eat. He'd be in Alice Springs by sunset tomorrow. After restocking his supplies, he'd go east and work the cattle until December. And after that . . .

He sighed. What was the point in planning a future that didn't exist? Even though he did his best to live from day to day, his mind still insisted he look toward something. In reality, it was a void of his own making.

The drover settled down to sleep, hearing the hiss of a snake nearby and throwing a rock to scare it away. Even by his standards he was filthy; he could smell his own acrid sweat. The usual waterholes he normally used had been empty, the season unusually dry even for the Never Never.

He thought of her, as he did every night, then closed his eyes on the moon to sleep.

He was awoken by a strange shrieking from some distance away. After years in the outback, he knew it was human, not animal. He struggled to place the familiar sound, then realized it was a baby's cry. *Another soul born into this rotten world*, he thought before he closed his eyes and slept again.

He was up at dawn, eager to reach the Alice by nightfall, take a room in town, and have his first decent wash since he'd left Darwin. Mounting his mare, he set off and saw the camel train on the skyline. Lit by the rising sun behind it, it appeared almost biblical. He caught up to them in under an hour, where they had stopped to rest and eat. He knew one of the Afghan cameleers, who slapped him on the back and offered him a seat on his carpet and a plate of flatbreads. He ignored the mold on one corner and chewed the bread hungrily. Out of all the human life he encountered on his usual route through the Never Never, it was the cameleers he most enjoyed spending time with. The secret pioneers of the outback, the cameleers were the unsung heroes, taking much-needed supplies across the red plains to the cattle stations sprinkled sparingly across the interior. Often they were educated men, speaking good English, but as he drank their water thirstily, he heard how their trade was in danger from the new railway line that would soon open between Port Augusta and Alice Springs. The plan was to continue it as far north as Darwin.

"We are some of the last left. All the others have gone back home across the sea," said Moustafa listlessly.

"I'm sure there will still be a place for you, Moustafa. The train line cannot reach the outlying villages."

"No, but the motorcar can."

The drover was just bidding them farewell when the strange shriek he'd heard last night started up again, coming from a basket tied to one side of a camel.

"Is that a baby?" he asked.

"Yes. It was brought into the world five days ago. The mother died last night. We buried her well and good so the dingoes wouldn't get her," Moustafa added.

"A black baby?"

"From the color of the skin, a half caste, or maybe a quadroon. The girl hitched a ride with us two weeks ago. She said she was heading for the Hermannsburg mission," Moustafa recounted. "The others did not want to take her given her condition, but she was desperate, and I said yes. Now we have a motherless babe screaming day and night for its milk with none to give. Maybe it will die before we reach the Alice. It was small to begin with."

"Can I see it?"

"If you wish."

Moustafa stood up and led him over toward the screeching. He unhooked the basket and handed it to his friend.

Inside, all the drover could see were moving folds of material. Setting the basket onto the ground, he knelt next to it and removed the muslin cloths that covered the baby. The smell of feces and urine hit him as he uncovered the rest of the tiny, skinny body, with its layer of smooth, butterscotch skin.

The baby kicked and squalled, its tiny fists punching the air fiercely. Even though he'd seen many things in his time in the outback, this half-starved motherless child produced an emotion inside him he had not experienced for many years. He felt the sting of a tear in his eye. Wrapping the sheets of muslin around the baby so he did not touch its excretions for fear of disease, he lifted it out of the basket. As he did so, he heard something drop back inside.

"It's a boy," Moustafa commented as he stood well away because of the stench. "What life can he hope for even if he does survive?"

At the drover's touch, the baby had ceased its caterwauling. It put a fist into its mouth, opened its eyes, and gazed up at him quizzically. Drummond started at the sight of them. They were blue, the irises flecked with amber, but it wasn't the unusual color that held his attention, rather the shape and the expression in them. He'd seen those eyes before, but he couldn't think where.

"Did the mother name the baby before she died?" he asked Moustafa.

"No, she did not say much at all."

"Do you know where the father might be?"

"She never said, and perhaps she didn't wish to tell. You know how it is." Moustafa gave an elegant shrug.

The drover looked down at the baby, still sucking his fist, and something in him stirred again.

"I could take him with me to the Alice, and then on to Hermannsburg."

"You could, but I think he is done for, my friend, and maybe it's for the best."

"Or maybe I am his chance." The drover's words were driven purely by instinct. "I'll take him. If I leave him with you, he'll certainly die like his mother."

"True, true," Moustafa answered solemnly, relief flooding his honest features.

"Have you a little water to spare at least?"

"I will go and find some," Moustafa agreed.

The baby had now closed its eyes, too exhausted to recommence its wailing. Its breathing was ragged, and as he held it to him, the drover knew that time was running out.

"Here." Moustafa proffered a flask. "You are doing a good thing, my friend, and I bless you and the infant. *Kha safer walare.*" He laid a gnarled hand on the baby's sweaty forehead.

After carrying the basket back to his horse, the drover fashioned a sling out of the blanket he lay on at night and tied it around himself before lifting the baby into it. As he did so, he saw a dirty tin box lying beneath the muslin and tucked it into his saddlebag. Taking a little water from the flask, he dribbled it onto the baby's lips and was relieved to see it sucking weakly at the fluid. Then he fastened the empty basket to the back of his saddle, mounted the horse, and set off at a gallop across the plain.

As he rode, the sun searing his skin, he wondered what on earth had possessed him to do such a thing. He'd probably arrive in the Alice and find a dead baby strapped to him. Yet, whatever it was, something drove him forward through the white-hot heat of the afternoon, knowing that if it stayed another night out in the desert, the tiny heart that lay against his would cease to beat.

At six o'clock that night, his valiant mare staggered into the dusty yard outside his usual lodgings. Still astride, the drover tentatively placed a hand on the baby's chest and felt a reassuring if weak flutter beneath it. After dismounting and filling a bucket with water from the pump for the thirsty horse, he unstrapped the sling and placed the baby back in its basket, covering it loosely with the muslin.

"I'll be back out to give you some decent tucker later," he promised the mare before he stepped inside to be greeted with delight by Mrs. Randall, the landlady.

"Good to see ya back around these parts. The usual room?"

"If it's available, yes. How's it going with you?"

"Ya know how it is here, though it'll be a lot better once the train is up and running. Anything I can get you, Mr. D? The usual?" She winked. "There's a couple o' new girls in town."

"Not tonight, it's been a long journey here. I was wondering, do you by any chance have some milk?"

"Milk?" Mrs. Randall looked surprised at his request. "Course we do. How many heads of cattle are there around these parts?" she chuckled. "Not your usual tipple, Mr. D."

"You're right, maybe add a beaker of some good Scotch whiskey to that order as well."

"I might have a bottle specially for you. Anything to eat?"

"Whatever's on the boil, Mrs. R." He gave her a grin. "I'm dehydrated, so I'd like a saltcellar on the side."

"Righto." She handed him a key. "I'll bring it all up to your room in a jiffy."

"Cheers, Mrs. R."

The drover picked up the basket and saddlebag and tramped up the rough wooden stairs. Entering the room, he closed the door and locked it firmly behind him. Placing the basket on the bed, he removed the muslin shroud from the baby's face. Now, even though he placed his ear next to the tiny nose, he could hardly hear it breathe.

Grabbing the flask Moustafa had given him, he sprinkled the last drops of water onto the baby's lips, but it did not respond.

"Strewth! Don't die on me now, baby! I'll be done for murder," he entreated the tiny being. Placing the basket at the side of the bed, he paced the room, waiting for Mrs. Randall to arrive. Eventually, out of frustration, and also because of the pungent smell inside the room, he ran back downstairs.

"Nearly ready?" he asked her.

"I was just going to bring it up ta you," the woman said, placing the tray on the narrow reception desk.

He looked at its contents and realized the one thing he needed was missing. "You got that saltcellar for me, Mrs. R?"

"Sorry, I'll go and get it." She returned with it in her sun-freckled hand. "It's silver plated, got it as one of my wedding presents when I married Mr. R. Make sure ya return it to me, or there'll be hell to pay."

"You can count on me," he said, the contents of the tray wobbling as he picked it up. "I'll be down later to take a wash."

Reentering his room, he took his shirt off, then unscrewed the silver top of the saltcellar and poured the contents into the fabric. Then he took the glass of milk and made a funnel with a page torn out of the Bible on the nightstand, and poured the milk into the empty saltcellar. Gathering up the baby, and breathing through his mouth to avoid the stink that came from it, he gently poked the tip of the saltcellar between the rosebud lips.

At first, there was no response, and his own heart beat rapidly enough for both of them. He removed the tiny silver teat, then dribbled a little milk from the holes in the top of the cellar onto his finger. Working on instinct alone, he smeared it around the baby's lips. After an agonizing few seconds, the lips moved. He then placed the tip of the saltcellar into the baby's mouth again and sent up a prayer for the first time in seventeen years. A few seconds later, he felt a tiny exploratory tug on the makeshift bottle. There was an agonizing pause and then a firmer tug as the baby began to suck.

The drover lifted his eyes to the ceiling above him. "Thank you."

When the child had taken its fill, he poured water from the jug into the basin, stripped off the stinking muslin cloths, and did his best to wash the encrusted muck from its body. Forming a makeshift napkin with two of his handkerchiefs, and praying there wouldn't be another explosion, he wrapped the tiny backside as best he could. He hid the soiled muslin cloths in one of the bedsheets, and stuffed the stinking parcel into a drawer. He wrapped the other sheet around the baby, noticing the engorged stomach and emaciated legs that looked as if they belonged to a frog rather than a human being. The baby had fallen asleep, so he downed the now cold and congealing beef stew in a few gulps and washed it down with some hefty slugs of whiskey. Then he left the room to feed his horse and scrub himself clean in the water barrel in the backyard.

Feeling refreshed, the drover ran back upstairs and saw the baby had not moved. Putting his ear to the tiny chest, he heard the flutter of a heartbeat and the sound of steady breathing. Climbing onto his own mattress, he remembered the tin he'd stored in his saddlebag.

The tin was encrusted in rust and red dirt as if it had long been buried. He prised it open to find a small leather box inside. Unfastening the clasp and lifting the lid, his breathing became ragged as his own heart missed a beat.

The Roseate Pearl . . . the pearl that had ended his brother's life, yet saved his own.

"How can it be . . . ?" he murmured, his eyes drawn to its mesmeric beauty, as they'd been so many years before. What he could do with that cash . . . He knew its value—he had handed over the twenty thousand pounds himself.

Banished from Broome and unable to return to Kilgarra, his beloved cattle station, he traveled across the Never Never, picking up work where he found it. He kept himself to himself, trusting no one. He was a different person now, a human void with a heart that had turned to ice. And he had only himself—and perhaps the pearl—to blame. Yet, from the moment he'd seen this baby, something had thawed within him.

He snapped the box shut and placed it back in the tin before it hypnotized him again.

How was this child connected to the Roseate Pearl? Last time he had seen it, he had locked it away in Kitty's writing desk. Camira had pleaded with him not to present it to her mistress and . . .

"God's oath!"

He knew now where he'd seen the baby's eyes before. "Alkina . . ."

He stood up and went to study the sleeping infant once more. And for the first time in many years, acknowledged the existence of fate and destiny. He'd instinctively known that this baby with the cursed pearl secreted in its basket was connected to him.

"Good night, little one. Tomorrow I will take you to Hermannsburg." He stroked the soft cheek, then went to lie back on his mattress. "And then I will journey to Broome to find out who you are to me."

Pastor Albrecht looked up from his Bible at the sound of hooves clopping into the mission. Through the window, he watched the man draw to a halt, then climb off his horse and look around him, uncertain of where to go. Pastor Albrecht stood up and walked toward the door and out into the glaring sun.

"*Guten Tag*, or should I say good morning?"

"I speak both languages," the man answered. Around the courtyard, a number of the pastor's flock, clad in white, paused to look at the handsome man. Any stranger who came here was a welcome sight.

"Back to your business," he directed them, and they returned to their work.

"Is there somewhere we might talk, Pastor?"

"Come into my study." The pastor indicated the room behind him as he heard a mewling cry emanate from the sling around the man's chest. "Please, sit down," he said, closing the door behind him, then snapping the shutters closed against prying eyes.

"I will, once I have given you this."

The man untied the sling from around him and laid its contents on the table. There, among the stinking cloths, was a tiny newborn baby boy, his lungs singing to the heavens for nourishment.

"What have we here?"

"His mother died some hours outside Alice Springs. The cameleers told me she was on her way to Hermannsburg. I offered to bring the baby here faster. I commandeered a saltcellar in my lodging house last night and it has taken some milk from that."

"How very inventive of you, sir."

"Perhaps the salt traces left inside helped too, because he seems stronger today."

"He is very small." Pastor Albrecht examined the baby, testing his limbs and his grip. "And weak from malnourishment."

"He has survived at least."

"And I commend you and bless you, sir. There are not many drovers about these parts who would do the same. I presume the mother was Aboriginal?"

"I could not say, as she had died and been buried before I arrived. Although by chance, I might know who her family is."

The pastor looked at the man suspiciously. "Are you this baby's father, sir?"

"No, not at all, but with the baby was something I recognized." He pulled the tin out of his pocket. "I will be traveling to Broome to confirm my suspicions."

"I see." Pastor Albrecht picked up the tin and cradled it in his hands.

"Then you must let me know of your findings, but for now, if he lives, the child will have a home here at Hermannsburg."

"Please retain that tin for safekeeping until I return. And for your own sake, do not look inside."

"What do you take me for, sir?" The pastor frowned. "I am a man of God. And trustworthy."

"Of course."

The pastor watched the man dig in his pocket and produce some notes. "Here is a donation toward your mission and the feeding of the child."

"Thank you."

"I'll return as soon as I can."

"One last question, sir: Did the mother name him?"

"No."

"Then I shall call him Francis, for Francis of Assisi, the patron saint of animals. From what you have told me, it was a camel who helped save his life." The pastor gave him a wry smile.

"An apt name."

"And your name, sir?" Pastor Albrecht asked.

"They know me as Mr. D around these parts. Good-bye, Pastor."

The door slammed shut behind him. Pastor Albrecht went to the window and opened the shutters to watch the drover mount his horse and leave. Even though the man was obviously in full health and strength, there was something oddly vulnerable about him.

"Another lost soul," he murmured as he regarded the baby on the table in front of him. The baby stared back, blinking his large blue eyes slowly. "You have survived a long journey, little one," he said as he picked up his ink pen, opened a ledger, and scrawled the name *Francis* and the date of his arrival on a fresh page. As an afterthought, he added, *Mr. D—drover, Alice Springs*.

A month later, the drover tethered the horse on a patch of land half a mile or so from the house, and walked the rest of the way. It was a dark night, the stars hidden by swaths of clouds, and he was glad of it. Arriving at the front gate, he took off his boots and tucked them into the hedge. The house was in complete darkness, and only an occasional rustle came from the stables. He sighed, thinking that the best and worst times of his life had been spent under this roof—once tin, but now immaculately tiled. Seeing Fred asleep in his usual spot outside the stables, he walked across to the hut. Praying that she hadn't locked it, he tried the handle and it opened easily. Closing the door behind him, he waited until his eyes adjusted to the darkness. She was there, one hand flung back behind her head. He walked closer to her, knowing that to startle her would alert the occupants of the neighboring house.

He knelt down at the side of the bed and lit the candle on the nightstand so that she would recognize him immediately.

He shook her gently and she stirred.

"Camira, it is I, Mister Drum. I have come back to see you. I really am here, but you mustn't make a sound." He put a hand over her mouth, as she stared at him, fully awake now. "Please don't scream."

The terror in her eyes began to abate and she struggled to remove his hand from her mouth.

"Promise?"

She nodded and he removed it, putting a finger to his lips instead. "We don't want to wake up anyone else, do we?"

She shook her head mutely, then wriggled to sit upright.

"What you doing here, Mister Drum? You-a dead for years!" she hissed.

"We both know that I was not, don't we?"

"So, why you-a come back now?"

"Because I have something to tell you."

"That my daughter is dead?" Camira's eyes filled with tears. "I know already. My soul tellum me."

"Sadly your soul tells you right. I'm so very sorry, Camira. Was she . . . with child?"

"Yessum." Camira hung her head. "You tellum no one. Baby now dead too."

He now knew for certain that what he had surmised was true.

"Well now, there is something you don't know," he whispered.

"What is dat?"

He placed a gentle hand on her arm. "Cat's baby survived. You have a grandson."

Then he told her the story of how he'd found the child and Camira's eyes filled with wonder and astonishment.

"Them ancestors, they make-a clever plan. Where is he?" Camira peered around the room as if the baby were there somewhere, hidden.

"He was far too weak to make the journey here. I left him in good hands at Hermannsburg mission. And I must also tell you that the bad pearl was in his basket. Alkina must have found it and—"

"No! Bad pearl is cursed. Don't wantum near my grandson!" Camira raised her voice and Drummond put a warning finger to his lips.

"I swear that it is being kept in a safe place away from him until you decide what to do with it and the baby. I thought perhaps you might want to bring him here once he has recovered."

"He nottum come here," Camira said vehemently.

"Why not? I thought at the very least, he would be a comfort to you." It was Camira's turn to tell him what had happened.

"So that baby is my nephew's son? And therefore related to me by blood?" Drummond said in astonishment.

"Yessum. Our blood mix inside, so he belonga both of us," she said solemnly.

"But most of all, Camira, to my nephew, Charlie, now that his mother is with the ancestors."

"*No!* Best for all Mister Charlie thinkum baby dead too."

"Why on earth would you of all people say that?"

"You not bin around here for long time, Mister Drum. You not understand. Missus Kitty, she workum so hard, do everything for her son after you gone."

Drummond raised an eyebrow.

"She get sick, very sick," Camira continued. "An' sad."

"Is she well now? Is she here?" He turned his head toward the house.

"She in Europe for holiday. She leavem Mister Charlie in charge. Even though he sad too 'bout my daughter, he young and gettum better soon. Maybe marry nice secretary woman. Best for him he nottum know, you see?"

"And what about Kitty? She is a grandmother like you, Camira. Surely both she and Charlie have a right to know of the baby's existence? And what of the baby himself? I for one could not just abandon my great-nephew to a mission."

Camira scrambled out of bed. "I come-a with you. You take-a me to mission. Then I care for my grandson there."

"You would leave everything you have here? What about Kitty? I know how much she depends on you."

Camira was already pulling out a hessian sack, obviously once used for vegetables by the smell of old cabbage. "I sortum my family, she sortum hers. It for best."

"I think you underestimate your mistress. After all, she brought you into her household against my brother's wishes. She has a loving heart and she would wish to be included in this decision. And I'm certain she would welcome her grandson into her home."

"Yessum, but now she take rest and needum peace. Don't wanta bring shame on her or Charlie, see? Best I go to grandson. Keep secret."

Drummond realized then that Camira would do everything she could to protect the mistress who'd saved her and the boy she'd brought into the world. Even if it meant deserting them to do it. However, it was her decision to make, whether he agreed with it or not.

"What about Fred? Surely you will tell him?"

"He no good at keepin' secrets, Mister Drum. Maybe one day." Camira looked at him expectantly, all her worldly goods now thrown into the hessian sack. "You takem me to grandson now, yes?"

Drummond nodded in resignation, and opened the door of the hut.

CeCe

Hermannsburg, Northern Territory

January 2008

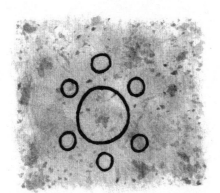

Aboriginal symbol for star or sun

27

The sun sank lower in the sky as I looked at my grandfather. At Francis, once a baby boy who had been rescued from the desert by a man who had not even known they were related.

"How could it be?" I murmured, and brushed a fly away from my face, only to find my cheek damp with tears.

"I am living proof that kin finds kin, that miracles occur." He gave me a weak smile and I could see that the telling of the story had both exhausted and shaken him. "We can't ask what the reasons are for the extraordinary things that happen to us. They up there—the ancestors, or God—are the only ones that know the answers. And we won't have those until we too go upward."

"What happened to Kitty and Drummond?"

"Ah, Celaeno, that is quite a question. If only he'd had the patience and fortitude to wait, they could have eventually shared a happy life together after Andrew's death. But he was impetuous, lived for the moment. There is some of my great-uncle Drummond in me, I confess," he admitted with a smile.

"Me too," I said, wondering if I'd have done the same as Kitty and sent the man—*or woman*, as Chrissie jumped into my thoughts—that I loved away. "Did you ever meet him?"

"That is the next part of the story, but we shall have to save it for another time. I suddenly feel as old as I am. Are you hungry?"

"I could eat, yes," I said. My stomach was rumbling like a train on a track, but it wasn't like we could just pop around the corner for a burger here.

There was a pause as he gazed across at the creek in the distance. "Then why don't I take you back to my place? I have plenty of food, and it's not far."

377

"Er . . ." The sky was beginning to turn to delicate shades of pink and peach, the precursor of nightfall. "I was planning to go back to Alice Springs tonight."

"It is your choice, of course. But if you come with me, we could talk more. And if you want, I have a bed for you."

"Okay, I will," I replied, remembering this man was my grandfather. He'd trusted me enough to share the secrets of his—and my—family, and I had to trust *him*.

We stood up and walked back through Phil's bedroom and out into the courtyard, where we found Phil himself leaning against a wall.

"Ya ready to go, Celaeno?"

I explained the change of plan and he ambled over to shake my hand. "It's been a pleasure. Don't be a stranger, now, will ya?"

"She can take my place on the committee when I retire," my grandfather joked.

"The ute's not locked by the way," Phil called as we walked away from him.

I opened the rear door of the truck and went to pull out my rucksack, but my grandfather's strong brown hands were there before me. They lifted the rucksack out as if it weighed nothing.

"This way." He beckoned me to follow as he set off.

Maybe he's parked his car somewhere else, I thought. But as we walked away from the mission entrance, the only vehicle I could see was a pony and cart waiting on a patch of grass.

"Climb aboard," he said, throwing my rucksack up onto the rough wooden bench. "Can you ride?" he asked me as he clicked the reins.

"I took lessons as a kid, but my sister Star didn't like it, so we stopped."

"Did you like it?"

"I loved it."

He proceeded to ignore the road and steered the cart onto the rough earth, the pony taking us up a gentle slope.

"I can teach you to ride if you'd like. As you've heard, your great-great-uncle Drummond spent much of his life on horseback."

"And on camels," I added as the pony picked its way confidently over the bumpy ground. My grandfather was gazing at me, his hands loose around the reins.

"If your mother and grandmother could see us now. Together, here."

He shook his head and reached out to touch the side of my face. I felt the roughness of his hand, like sandpaper, yet it was a gesture full of love.

A question floated to the front of my mind.

"Can I ask you what the Dreamtime is?" I began. "I mean, I've heard some Dreamtime stories, and about the Ancestors, but what actually *is* it?"

He gave a chuckle. "Ah, Celaeno, to us, the Dreamtime is everything. It is how the world was created—where everything originated."

"But how?"

"I will tell it the way my grandmother Camira told me when I was a young boy. In the Dreaming world, the earth was empty when it all began—a flat desert, in darkness. No sounds, no life, nothing. Then the Ancestors came and as they moved across the earth they cared for it and loved it. They created all that was—the ants, the kangaroos, the wallabies, the snakes—"

"The spiders?" I interrupted.

"Yes, even those, Celaeno. Everything is connected and important, no matter how ugly or frightening. The Ancestors also made the moon, and the sun, the humans and our tribes."

"Are the Ancestors still here?"

"Well, after doing all that creating, they retired. They went into the sky, the earth, the clouds, the rain . . . and into all the creatures they had formed. Then they gave us humans the task of protecting everything and nurturing it."

"Do all Aboriginal tribes have the Dreamtime?"

"Yes, although the individual stories vary here and there. I remember how annoyed Grandmother Camira would get when one of our Arrernte stories would disagree with one she'd been raised with. She was Yawuru, you see."

"So do you speak Yawuru too?" I asked, thinking of Chrissie.

"A little, but at Hermannsburg I learned to speak German, Arrernte, and English, and that was more than enough languages to fill one head."

Half an hour later, we arrived at what looked to me like a large garden shed that was placed on concrete stilts over the red earth. Behind it was a small stable that my grandfather steered the pony and cart toward. There was a veranda at the front, shielded from the burning sun by a tin roof. It was dotted with bits of furniture which looked like they belonged inside, reminding me of Chrissie's grandmother's house. I hauled my rucksack up the steps and turned to admire the view.

"Look at that," he said, placing a hand gently on my shoulder as the two of us stared at the landscape in front of us. The fast-sinking sun was seeping its last rays across an outcrop of rock, and beyond that snaked the line of a creek, glistening in the red sand. In the distance I could see the white huts of Hermannsburg, suffused with a deep orange glow behind them.

"To the northwest of us is Haasts Bluff, near Papunya," he said, gesturing behind us. "And to the northeast are the MacDonnell Ranges— Heavitree Gap was always my favorite place to paint."

"That's where the photograph of you and Namatjira was taken?"

"Yes. You've done your homework," he said approvingly.

"Phil did it for me. He recognized it."

"He would, we've been there together many times."

"The view's amazing," I replied as my fingers started to tingle. I wanted to paint it immediately.

"Let's go inside."

The hut smelled of turpentine and paint. The room we were in was small, with an old sofa placed in front of an open fireplace. I saw the rest of the space was taken up with a trestle table splodged with paint and littered with jars full of brushes. A number of canvases were propped against the walls.

"Let's go and see what we have for supper."

I followed him into an adjoining room that contained an old and noisy fridge, a gas stove, and a sink that didn't have any taps.

"I have some steak if you're interested. I can prepare it with a few vegetables on the side."

"Sounds great."

"The plates and cutlery are in that cupboard. There's a frying pan and a saucepan in there too."

I rooted through the cupboard and set the required items on the little wooden table in the center of the room. Meanwhile, he took some carrots, onions, and potatoes from the fridge and began to peel and chop them deftly. I sat down and watched him, my brain trying to fathom out the genetic pathways that linked us. I would have to draw myself a family tree at some point.

"Are you a cook, Celaeno?" he asked me as he worked.

"No," I admitted. "My sister Star did all that stuff."

"You live together?"

"We used to, up until a couple of months ago."

"What happened? You fell out?"

"No . . . it's a long story."

"Well," he said as he lit the flame on the gas ring and tossed the vegetables into a pan, together with some unfamiliar herbs, "after dinner, you can tell me all about your life."

We sat out on the veranda eating what tasted like the best steak ever, but maybe it was just because I was starving. I realized it was my first meal with a blood relative of mine, and I marveled at how people could do this every day without even thinking how special it was.

Once we'd finished eating, my grandfather showed me the barrel of rainwater at the back of the hut. I used a pitcher to take some to the sink and washed up the plates while he brewed some coffee on the gas ring. He lit an oil lamp on the veranda and we leaned back in the wooden chairs, sipping the coffee.

"Just in case you doubt me, I want to show you this."

It was another black-and-white photo, this time of two women standing on either side of a man. One of the women, although darker skinned than me, could have been my double. It was the eyes that clinched it— they had the same almond shape as mine.

"See the likeness?"

"Yeah, I do. Your eyes are the same shape too. She was your mother?"

"Yes, that was Alkina, or 'Cat' as everyone called her. As you've heard, I never got to meet her."

"And who is that?" I pointed to the handsome blond man who towered over the two women. He had an arm around both of them.

"That's Charlie Mercer. Your great-grandfather and my father."

"And the other woman?"

"Camira, my grandmother. Apart from my Sarah, she was the most wonderful, kind, and brave human being I have ever known . . ."

His eyes moved to the horizon and I saw they were filled with sadness.

"So she came to look after you at Hermannsburg?"

"Oh yes, she came. I grew up thinking she was my mother, and she could have been. She was only in her early forties when I was born, you see."

"Did Charlie Mercer ever know about you? Like, did you meet him?"

"Celaeno," he sighed, "let's leave the past for now. I want to hear about you. How has your life been?"

"That's a big question."

"Then let me help you. When I began to search for my daughter and eventually found you, I was told that you had been adopted by a rich man from Switzerland. You lived there in your childhood?"

"Yes, in Geneva."

"You have brothers and sisters?"

"Only sisters. And all six of us are adopted."

"What are your sisters' names? How old are they?"

"You're probably gonna find this weird, but we're *all* named after the Seven Sisters."

His eyes widened with interest and I thought that at least I could cut out explaining who we were and what the myth was. This man would have been taught about them from birth. They were *his* Ancestors too.

"You say there are six of you?"

"Uh-huh."

"Like in the legend," we both said together, then laughed.

"Merope is there, even though she hides sometimes. Perhaps one day she will be found."

"Well, it's too late now, for Pa at least. He died last June."

"I am sorry, Celaeno. He was a good man?"

"Yes, very, although sometimes I felt he loved my other sisters more than me. They're all so talented and beautiful."

"As are you. And remember, nothing happens by chance. It is all planned out for us before we even take our first breath."

"Do you really believe that?"

"I think I must, given the way I was found as a baby by my blood relative, who then brought my grandmother to care for me as I grew. I don't know of your religious beliefs, but surely no man or woman can deny that there must be something bigger than us? I put my trust in the universe, even though sometimes I feel as though it has let me down, as I did when I lost my own daughter. But that was her path to follow, and I must accept the pain."

I thought how wise and dignified this man was, and, with a pang, how much he reminded me of Pa Salt.

"Again, we have strayed away from the track of your life. Please, tell me about your sisters."

I did so, reeling off the potted biographies of each of them as I had done so many times before.

"I see. But it seems you have left one sister out."

I counted them up in my head. "No, I've told you a little about all of them."

"You still haven't told me about you."

"Oh, right, well." I cleared my throat. "There's not really much to tell. I live in London with Star, though I think she's probably moved out permanently while I've been gone. I was a dunce at school because I have dyslexia. It's—"

"I know what that is, because I have it too. And so did your mother."

The word "mother" sent a funny shiver through me. Even though from what he'd said so far I had to guess that she was dead, at least he'd be able to tell me about her. "It must be genetic then. The trouble was, Star—or Asterope—was the one I was always closest to because we were in the middle and only a few months apart in age. She's really clever, and the worst thing is that me being stupid academically held *her* back. She won a place at Cambridge, but didn't take it. She came to uni in Sussex with me instead. I know I put pressure on her to do it. I feel really guilty about that."

"Perhaps she didn't want to be without you either, Celaeno."

"Yeah, but sometimes in life you should try to be the bigger person, shouldn't you? I should have persuaded her to go, told her not to worry about me, if I'd really loved her, which I did. And still do," I gulped.

"Love is both the most selfish and unselfish emotion in the world, Celaeno, and its two facets cannot be separated. The need in oneself battles against the wish for the loved one to be happy. So unfortunately, love is not something to be rationalized and no human being escapes its grip, believe me. What did you study at university?"

"History of art. It was a disaster and I left after a couple of terms. I just couldn't hack the essays because of my dyslexia."

"I understand. But you were interested in the subject?"

"Oh God, yes, I mean, art is the only thing I'm any good at."

"You are an artist?"

"I wouldn't say that. I mean, I got a place at the Royal College in

London, which was cool, but then . . ." Shame at my failure poured through me. This man had gone to so much trouble to find me and wanted to hear what a success I was making of my life, but on paper I'd achieved absolutely nothing in the past twenty-seven years. "It didn't work out either. I left after three months and came here. Sorry," I added as an afterthought.

"There's no need to apologize to me, or to yourself," my grandfather said, only out of kindness, I was sure. "I will let you into a secret: I won a place at art school in Melbourne. It was organized for me by a man called Rex Battarbee, who was the person responsible for teaching Namatjira. I lasted less than four days, then ran away and came back to my home in Hermannsburg."

"You did?"

"I did. And it was a nerve-racking moment, having to face my grandmother Camira when I eventually arrived home after a month's journey back here. She'd been so proud when I'd got the place. I thought she might beat me, but she was just happy to see me safe and well. The only punishment she gave me was to lock me in the shed with a barrel of water, until I'd scrubbed myself from head to foot with carbolic soap!"

"And you still went on to be a famous artist?"

"I went on to be an artist, yes, but I did it my own way, just as you are doing. Are you painting again now?"

"I've really been struggling, to be honest. I lost all my confidence after I left college in November."

"Of course you did, but it will come back, and it will happen in a moment when something—a landscape or an idea—strikes you. And that feeling in your gut will make your hand itch to paint it and—"

"I know that feeling!" I butted in excitedly. "That's exactly what happens to me!"

Out of everything my grandfather had said to me so far, this was the moment when I really, truly believed we must be blood. "And," I added, "that feeling happened to me a couple of days ago when I was driving back with my friend Chrissie from Hermannsburg and saw the sun setting behind the MacDonnell Ranges. The next day, I borrowed some watercolors, and I sat under a gum tree and I . . . painted! And she said, my friend Chrissie, I mean"—my words were tripping over each other now—

"she said it was great, and then she took it to a gallery in Alice Springs without me knowing, and it's being framed, and they're going to put it up for sale for six hundred dollars!"

"Wonderful!" My grandfather slapped his knees. "If I were still a drinker, I would make a toast to you. I look forward very much to seeing the painting."

"Oh, I don't really think it's anything special and I only had an old tin of children's watercolors to work with . . ."

"But at least it was a start," he finished for me, his eyes shining with what looked like genuine happiness. "I'm sure it's far better than you think."

"I saw your *Wheel of Fire* in a book. It was amazing."

"Thank you. Interestingly, it is not my favorite, but then often the artist's preference for one particular work does not match the critical or public view."

"I painted a mural of the Seven Sisters out of dots when I was younger," I told him. "I didn't even know why I was doing it."

"The Ancestors were guiding you back to your country," Francis replied.

"I've always struggled to find my style . . ."

"As any painter of note does."

"This morning, when I saw the way that you and that Clifford Possum guy had mixed two styles together to create something new, I wondered about trying something like that too."

He didn't ask me what, just fixed his extraordinary eyes upon me. "Then you must try it. And soon. Don't let the moment of inspiration pass."

"I won't."

"And never *ever* compare yourself to other artists. Whether they are better, or worse, it only leads to despair . . ."

I waited, for I knew he had more to say.

"I fell into that trap when Cliff's paintings began to gain national recognition. He was a genius and I miss him to this day—we were great friends. But jealousy ate into me as I watched him rise to fame and receive the adulation that I knew I would never get. There is only one seminal artist from the first generation of a new school of painting. Once it was him, it could never be me."

"Did you lose confidence?" I asked.

"Worse than that. Not only did I stop painting, but I started drinking. I left my poor wife and went walkabout for over three months. I cannot tell you the jealousy I felt, or how my art seemed pointless at that moment. It took me all that time out there alone to understand that success and fame for any true artist is a mirage. The true joy is in the creative process itself. You will always be a slave to it, and, yes, it will dominate your life, control you like a lover. But unlike a lover, it will never leave you," he said solemnly. "It's inside you forever."

"When you accepted that, were you able to paint again?" I asked.

"I came home, drunk and broken, and my wife put me to bed and cared for me until I was physically better. The mental recovery had already begun while I was out bush, but it took a long time for me to gather the courage to sit in front of a canvas and hold a brush again. I will never forget how my hand shook as I first picked one up again. And then finally, the freedom of knowing that I was not painting for anyone except myself, that I would probably never achieve my original goal of world domination, gave me a sense of peace and freedom I cannot describe. Since then— over the past thirty years or so—my paintings have got better and, in fact, now command huge prices, simply because I only paint when my fingers itch. Well, there we are."

We sat in silence for a while, but it was comfortable. I was learning already that—like his painting—my grandfather would only speak when he had something to say. I also felt I'd had a massive info-dump over the past couple of days, and, a bit like a kid holding a box of sweets, I wanted to store it all in my mind-cupboard and unwrap the facts sweet by sweet. I was sure there were a lot of hungry days alone to come . . .

"Look!"

I jumped about six inches in the air at the sound of his voice, my immediate reaction one of panic in case he was pointing out a snake or a spider.

"Up there." He pointed and I followed his finger to the familiar milky cluster hanging low in the sky and as close to me as I'd ever seen it. "There you are." He walked toward me and draped his arm around my shoulder. "There's your mother, Pleione, and your father, Atlas. Look, even your little sister is showing herself to us tonight."

"Oh my God! She's there! I can see her!"

And I *could*. Merope was as vivid as the rest of us—out here, we seemed to shine so much brighter than anywhere else.

"She's coming to join you all soon, Celaeno. She has finally caught up with her sisters . . ."

His hand dropped heavily to his side. Then he turned to me, reached out his arms, and pulled me to him tightly. I tentatively wound my arms around his sinewy waist, then heard a strange guttural sound erupting and realized he was crying. Which then made me well up, especially as we were standing right under my sisters and Pa Salt in this incredible place. And I decided it was okay to join him in his tears.

Eventually, he drew away from me and cupped my face in his hands. "Can you believe it? You and me, two survivors of a powerful bloodline, standing together here, under the stars?"

"I can't take it in," I said, wiping my nose.

"No. I just did and look what happened." He smiled down at me. "Best not to do that again. Now, are you happy to stay here with me tonight? There's a nice bed and I'll sleep on the couch outside."

"Yes," I said, astonishing myself, yet I had never felt so protected. "Er, where's the dunny?"

"Around the back. I'll come with you to make sure it's free from visitors, if you know what I mean."

I did my business, then bolted back to the hut, where I saw that a door that led from the sitting room was ajar.

"Just changing the sheets—Sarah would be angry if I wasn't using clean linen for our granddaughter," my grandfather said as he placed a couple of spotless pillows with a pat onto the mattress.

"Sarah was your wife?"

"She was."

"Where did she come from?"

"London, where you said you live now. There." He drew a top sheet out of the trunk and threw it over the mattress. "I'll leave you a blanket in case it gets chilly in the early hours, and here's a fan if it gets too hot. There's a towel on the chair if you want to take a wash. Perhaps best tomorrow morning."

"Thanks, but are you sure about this? I'm used to bunking down anywhere."

"No problem for me. I often sleep outside anyway."

I wanted to tell him that so did I, but it was becoming a bit corny.

"Good night." He came to me and kissed me on the cheek.

"Er, by the way, what should I call you?"

"I think Francis will do, don't you? Sleep well," he added, then closed the door behind him.

I saw that he'd placed my rucksack on the floor next to the bed. I stripped off and climbed onto the mattress, which was one of those old-fashioned horsehair ones with a crevasse made by bodies before you, all ready to sink into. It felt wonderful. I scanned the ceiling and the rough timber walls for many-legged creatures, but I could see none in the soft light of the lamp that sat on the nightstand. I felt as safe as I had ever felt, as if before today I'd been like a moth hovering near the flame that mesmerized it. And now I'd arrived.

Maybe I would crash and burn, but before I could worry about that further, I fell asleep.

28

I woke the following morning and watched the sun starting to appear over the top of Mount Hermannsburg like a shy toddler hiding behind its mother's legs. I checked my watch and saw it wasn't even six o'clock yet, but I felt full of excitement for the new day. I noticed my calves had been turned into dot paintings by mosquitoes, and I pulled on a pair of trousers, not wanting the critters to eat any more of me before I'd had my own breakfast.

As I opened the door of my bedroom, a smell of freshly baked bread wafted from the kitchen. Sure enough, my grandfather was placing a loaf on the table outside, along with butter, jam, and a coffeepot.

"Good morning, Celaeno. Did you sleep well?"

"Really well, thanks. You?"

"I'm a night owl. I have my best thoughts after midnight."

"Same here," I said as he sat down. "Wow, that bread smells amazing. Didn't know there was a bakery around here," I said.

"I bake it myself. My wife bought me the machine ten years ago. Often, I'll be out here for some time, and she wanted to make sure I had something to eat in case I was unable to shoot a passing kangaroo."

"Have you ever shot one?"

"Many times, but that was long ago. Now I prefer the easier option of the supermarket."

He placed a slice of warm bread onto a tin plate for me. I smeared butter and jam on top and watched as it melted into the soft dough.

"This is delicious," I said, taking wolf-size bites. He cut another slice for me. "So you've really lived out in the bush? With no hut to come back to?"

"Yes," he said. "I first went, as all Aboriginal boys do, when I reached manhood, around the age of fourteen."

"But I thought you were brought up as a Christian."

"I was, but the pastor respected our traditions and made no move to stop them. We at Hermannsburg were luckier than most. Pastor Albrecht even learned to speak Arrernte and had a Bible commissioned in the language, so that those who did not speak English or German could read it and enjoy it too. He was a good man, and it was a good place. We came and went as we chose, but most of us always returned. After twenty years in Papunya, so have I. It's home. Now, what are your plans?"

"I came out here to find my family, and I found you." I offered him a smile. "I haven't thought beyond that yet."

"Good. I mean, I was wondering if you'd like to stay with me for a while. Take the time to really get to know each other. And paint, of course. I was thinking that perhaps I could act as a gentle guide, maybe help you discover where your medium of art really lies. I taught at Papunya for many years."

"Er . . ."

He must have seen the expression of fear on my face, because he said, "Really, don't worry about it. It was just an idea."

"No! It's a fantastic idea! I mean, wow, yes! It's just that, well, you're so famous and everything, and I'm just worried you'll think I'm rubbish."

"I would never think that, Celaeno, you're my granddaughter for a start! Perhaps, having made no contribution to your life so far, I can make one now and help you find your way forward."

"Maybe you should see my work before you agree to help me."

"If it'll make you feel happier, then I will. If we're to stay here for a few days, we should drive to the Alice and purchase supplies and while we're there, we can drop into the gallery that has your painting on the wall."

"Okay," I agreed, "although you'll probably think it's rubb—"

"Hush, Celaeno." Francis put a finger to his lips. "Negative thought brings negative action."

We cleared away the breakfast, sweeping every crumb from the table until it was spotless. My grandfather told me that even a sniff of the tiniest morsel would bring in an army of ants before we returned. Then we headed to the back of the stable, where an old pickup truck sat in the shade of a mulga tree.

We arrived in town three hours later, and my grandfather led the way to a supermarket so we could stock up. It was a slow process, as time and again someone came to slap him on the shoulder and say "g'day." One woman even asked to take a photo with him and he stood awkwardly in front of the meat counter, looking embarrassed. As this continued through the town, I began to realize that my grandfather—even if he wasn't Clifford Possum—was certainly a major celebrity here. This was confirmed as I trailed after him into the gallery and every artist inside stopped what they were doing and stared at him openmouthed. They clustered around him, speaking in another language, and Francis answered them fluently. After more photos and a few signed slips of paper, my heart pounded as he asked Mirrin on reception where she had hung his granddaughter's painting.

"Your granddaughter?" Mirrin gazed at me, looking flustered, then shook her head. "Sorry, it isn't here anymore."

"Then where is it?" I asked, panic surging through me.

"It was only hanging up for an hour yesterday before a couple came in and bought it."

I stared at Mirrin, wondering if she was just covering her tracks because she hadn't got around to having it framed yet.

"So, now I owe ya three hundred and fifty dollars!"

"Well now, that's the best reason I ever heard for not being able to see your work," my grandfather said, with what sounded like pride in his voice.

"Celaeno's got talent, Mr. Abraham. I'll buy anything else she paints, okay?"

A few minutes later, with the first cash I had ever made from my painting stuffed into my back pocket, we left the gallery. As I walked down the street next to Francis Abraham, renowned artist, and my grandfather, I felt genuine elation.

"Right, I'll leave you to it," my grandfather said, as he tightened the last nut on the easel that I'd bought out of the proceeds of the sale. "You have everything you need?"

"Yeah, and the rest." I raised an eyebrow. On the fold-out table next to me sat a new selection of watercolors, oils, and acrylics, along with a range of brushes.

"You'll know which to use," he said, placing a hand on my shoulder. "Remember that panic stifles your instincts and makes you blind."

He lit an insect repellent coil next to my legs to ward off the flies, then he left and I stared at the blank canvas in front of me. I'd never felt such intense pressure to perform. I opened tubes of orange and brown oils and mixed them together on the pallet. "Here goes," I breathed. Then I picked up a shiny new brush and started to paint.

Forty-five minutes later, I'd torn the canvas from the easel and thrown it to the floor because it was terrible. Next, I tried paper and watercolors, using Mount Hermannsburg as my subject in an attempt to replicate the painting I'd done a few days ago, but that was even worse than the canvas so I discarded that one too.

"It's lunch!" Francis called out from the hut.

"Not hungry," I called back, hiding the first canvas under my chair and hoping he wouldn't notice.

"It's only a ham and cheese sandwich," he said, coming onto the veranda and plopping the plate onto my lap. "Your grandmother always said that an artist needs brain food. Don't worry, I'm not going to look at anything you paint until the end of the week. So you've got plenty of time."

His words—and a really great sandwich—temporarily calmed me down, but by the end of the day I was ready to collect my rucksack and hike back to the Alice to drown my sorrows in a few stubbies. It didn't help that when I walked inside to cool down by the fan, I glanced at my grandfather sitting on a stool with a huge canvas in front of him. I watched as he mixed colors on his palette, then took a brush and filled in another section of intricate dots. Somewhere in the gorgeous mix of delicate pinks, purples, and greens, I could see the shape of a dove, barely visible and made up only of a series of tiny white flecks.

He's a bloody genius, and I can't paint the wall of a kitchen, I thought as I put my face close to the fan to cool down, then got my hair entangled in the blades and nearly scalped myself.

"Your painting's brilliant. Just awesome—ouch!" I said as Francis worked to extract my now considerable head of hair from the fan blades.

"Thank you, Celaeno. I hadn't worked on it for weeks, wasn't sure where I was going with it, but seeing you sitting there outside gave me an idea."

"You mean the dove?"

"You saw it." Even though I couldn't look at him because he was still wrestling with my hair, I knew he was pleased I'd noticed. "I think I might have to cut the last shreds out."

"Okay, do it," I encouraged him, as my neck was really beginning to crick badly.

"Right." He came back brandishing a large pair of kitchen scissors. "You know what it is that holds every human being back from fulfilling their full potential?"

"What?" I felt his hand tug gently at the clump of hair and then wield the scissors very close to my right ear. Van Gogh came to mind, but I put the thought away.

"Fear. You have to cut out the fear."

With a snip, the scissors closed in on my hair.

I didn't know if it was some kind of weird voodoo my grandfather had performed on me, but I woke at sunrise feeling calmer.

"I'm heading out to Jay Creek," he told me as we cleared away the remains of breakfast. "I'll be back late. Any problem, I've left my mobile number on the fireplace, okay?"

"Is there any signal here?"

"No," he said with a smile. "You can get a couple of bars down by the creek sometimes." He pointed below us. "See you later."

I watched him drive off in his pickup truck until he became a speck in the distance. "Right, Cee," I told myself firmly as I placed the biggest canvas I had on the easel and screwed it into place. "It might be a disaster, but we're going to be brave and have a go." Then I angled the easel away from the view of Mount Hermannsburg, because I was going to work from memory . . .

Much later, I came to and saw the sun was setting and the pickup was making its way up the slope. I looked at what I had done so far—I only had an outline and a small painted corner, but instinct told me I was on the right track. As the pickup drew nearer, I unscrewed the canvas from the easel and hurried it into my bedroom, because I really did not want my grandfather to see it yet. Then I closed the door behind me and went to put the kettle on.

"How did it go?" he asked me when he arrived on the veranda.

"Oh, okay," I said, pouring him a cup of coffee.

"Good." He nodded but said no more.

The following morning, I was up at the crack of dawn, simply because I couldn't wait to get started. And so it was for the next few days. Francis would often be out during the day, but would return at sunset with something good to eat. After supper, I'd disappear into my room to study my painting and think about where I should head with it the next day. I lost track of time as one day fed into the next, helped by the fact that my mobile had zero signal up here.

It did cross my mind that Chrissie might be thinking I'd been eaten by a dingo or, more logically, didn't want to know her after what had happened that fateful morning, and that Star might be worried about me too. So I wandered down to the creek in search of a signal, found a couple of bars, and texted them both.

Painting in outback. All fine.

My fingers hovered as I wondered whether to add *PS Staying with my grandfather*, but I decided against it and just wrote:

Speek when Im bak. No signal heer.x

Then before my mind could go wandering off to reality, I went back to my painting.

I put my brush down for the final time and stretched, feeling my right arm pulse with indignation over the way I had abused its muscles. I stared at what was in front of me, tempted to pick the brush up again and add a little dab here or there, but I knew I was hovering in the dangerous territory of over-painting something that was as near perfect as I could get it. I dragged my eyes and body away from it and went inside to make myself a strong cup of coffee, then lay down on my bed in the cool of the fan, feeling totally out of it.

"Celaeno, can you hear me?"

"Yup," I croaked.

"It's half past eleven and you haven't moved since last night when I came in and found you asleep."

I looked at the bright sun pouring in through the window and wondered why it was still shining at eleven o'clock at night.

"You've slept for almost fifteen hours." My grandfather smiled down at me. "Here, I've brought you some coffee."

"Jesus! The painting! Is it still outside?" I jumped out of bed, almost knocking the mug of coffee to the floor.

"I brought it in for you—good job I did, as we had some rain in the early hours. Don't worry, I averted my eyes and put a sheet over it as I carried it in." He put a warm hand on my shoulder. "Dr. Abraham diagnoses post-painting exhaustion. I got it too after I went on a 'painting bender,' as Sarah used to call it."

"Yeah, well, I've no idea what I've produced, whether it's good or bad or—"

"Whatever it is, it's a week of your life that will not have been wasted. If you feel like it, we'll take a look together after you have had something to eat. I'll leave you to have a wash and get dressed."

"Can we look at it now? I can't take the stress!" I explained as I followed him into the sitting room.

"Of course." He indicated the easel with a white sheet thrown over the canvas upon it. "Don't worry, I checked that it was dry first. Please, unveil it."

"You'll probably hate it, and . . . I don't know if it's good or what, and—"

"Celaeno, please, may I just see it?"

"Okay." I walked over to it, and with a big intake of breath, I pulled off the sheet. My grandfather took a few steps back—it was a big canvas—

and folded his arms across his chest as he studied it. I went to stand next to him and did the same. He then took a step closer and I followed behind him like a shadow.

"Well?" He turned to look at me, his expression telling me nothing. "What do you think of it?"

"I thought you were the one meant to be telling me," I replied.

"First, I want to hear what you have to say about it."

His words immediately reminded me of being back in art class, when a teacher would employ this method of self-criticism before he or she then tore the entire painting to shreds.

"I . . . like it. For a first try, anyway."

"That's a good start. Please, carry on. Explain it to me."

"Well, I had this idea about taking the landscape I painted a couple of weeks ago, but instead of using watercolors, using acrylics and dots."

"Right." I watched as my grandfather moved closer to it and pointed to the ghost gum and the piece of gnarled bark. "That looks like two eyes to me, and up there, in the cave, is a tiny cirrus of white, like a spirit entering it."

"Yup," I said, delighted that he'd noticed. "The idea came from Merope—the seventh sister; when the old man's eyes are watching her as she enters the cave."

"I guessed it was something like that."

"Good." I couldn't stand it any longer. "What do *you* think?"

"I think, Celaeno, that you have created something unique. It's also beautiful to look at and it's actually—for a first go with dots—very well executed. Especially the ghost gum, which even though it's made up of dots and painted in acrylic, definitely has 'luminosity.' It shines out of the painting, as does the cirrus of white."

"You like it?"

"I don't just like it, Celaeno, I love it. Yes, the technical side of the dots where they fade from one color to the next could be improved, but I can show you the best technique to do that. The point is, I've never seen anything quite like this before. And if this is a first try, I can only imagine what you could do in the future. Do you realize that you have spent six days painting?"

"To be honest, I've lost all track of time . . ."

"'In six days, the Lord made the heavens and the earth, but on the seventh day, he rested.' Celaeno, you've found your own unique 'world' this week, and I'm so very proud of you. Now come here and let me give you a hug."

After that, and a few tears shed by me, Francis disappeared outside and came back with two beers. He handed one to me. "I keep a few at the bottom of the water barrel for really special occasions. And this is definitely one of them. Cheers."

"Cheers!" We bashed our bottles together and took a sip.

"Jesus! I'm drinking before breakfast!" I exclaimed with a grin.

"You forget that it's almost lunchtime."

"And I am starving," I said, casting another glance at my painting and feeling a serious surge of pride.

Over lunch, my grandfather and I discussed it in more depth, and after we'd eaten, we sat side by side in front of a fresh canvas as he showed me his technique for painting the dots and then softening their edges so that from a distance, they didn't look like dots at all.

"Everyone has their own personal way of painting, and their own techniques," he said as I gave it a go, "and I'm sure you will develop yours. It really is a case of trial and error, and there'll be a lot of the latter. It's a part of the process as we improve." Then he turned and stared at me. "The most important question to ask is whether the painting style itself—never mind the result—felt right."

"Oh, it did, definitely. I mean, I really enjoyed it."

"Then you have found your métier. For now, at least, because an artist's life is all about finding new ways of expressing themselves."

"You mean, I might have a weird Picasso moment at some point?" I chuckled.

"Most painters do—including me—but I always came back to the style I felt most comfortable with."

"Well, I've certainly had a few of those moments in the past," I said, and told him about my weird installation last year.

"Don't you see that you were just using real objects to study shape and form? You were learning how to position the components on a canvas. All experimentation teaches you something."

"I've never looked at it like that before, but yeah, you're right."

"You're a natural-born artist, Celaeno, and now you have taken all those important first steps toward finding your own style, the sky is the limit. Just one thing, I noticed you haven't signed the painting yet."

"I never do usually 'cause I don't want anyone to know it was painted by me."

"Do you with this?"

"Yeah. I do."

"Then you'd better get practicing your signature," Francis advised me. "I promise that it'll be the first of many."

Later that afternoon, I took a thin brush and a tube of black paint and stood in front of the painting, readying myself to sign it.

Celaeno D'Aplièse?

CeCe D'Aplièse?

C. D'Aplièse . . . ?

Then a thought struck me and I wandered over to my grandfather, who was sitting on the veranda, whittling at a piece of wood.

"What are you doing?"

"Having a 'Picasso moment.'" He smiled at me. "Seeing what shapes I can create. It's not going well. Signed your picture yet?"

"No, 'cause the thing is that 'Celaeno D'Aplièse' is a bit of a mouthful and I get really irritated when everyone pronounces the 'D'Aplièse' wrong."

"You're asking me if you should have a nom de plume?"

"Yeah, but I don't know what."

"I wouldn't mind at all if you took my surname, even though that was a made-up one."

"Thanks, but then I'd be trading on your name and being your granddaughter and all and . . ."

"You want to do it by your talent alone. I understand."

"So, I was thinking that, if your biological father had married your mum like he wanted to, your surname would have been Mercer?"

"Yes, it would have been."

"And my mum's, at least until she got married."

"Correct."

"So what do you think of 'Celaeno Mercer'?"

My grandfather stared into the distance, as though his thoughts were flying back across all the generations of our family. Then he raised his eyes to mine.

"Celaeno, I think it is perfect."

When I woke up the next morning, I felt really odd. Like my time out there was over—for now—and there was somewhere else I needed to be, but I couldn't think where. And having that thought meant I had to let reality begin flooding back in to help me decide on what exactly I was going to do with my life from here. I didn't even know what day it was, let alone the date, so I walked into breakfast and asked Francis, feeling really embarrassed.

"Don't worry, losing track of time simply means you're fully engaged in what you're doing. It's the twenty-fifth of January."

"Wow," I said, feeling amazed that less than a month had passed since I'd left Thailand, and at the same time wondering where the time had gone.

He stared at me quizzically. "You're thinking where do you go from here, aren't you?"

"Yeah, I am a bit."

"I don't need to tell you how much I'd like it if you stayed for a while. Not in this hut, of course—I have a very comfortable house in the Alice with plenty of room for the two of us. But maybe you have other places to go, other people to see . . ."

"The thing is . . ." I rubbed my palms on the top of my trousers, feeling agitated. "I'm just not sure. There's a couple of situations that are a . . . bit confusing."

"I find in life that there always are. Do you want to talk about them?"

I thought about Star, then Ace and Chrissie, and shook my head. "Not right now."

"Fine. Well, I was thinking that I'd probably head back to the Alice later today, as long as you don't want to stay here any longer. Even I'm looking forward to a decent bath!"

"Yeah, that sounds really good," I agreed, trying to force a smile.

"I also have some photograph albums there which I could show you."

"I'd love to see them," I said.

"For now, why don't you take a walk? That's what I always do when I'm having to make decisions."

"Okay, I will."

So off I headed, and as I walked, I imagined going back to London and, with my newfound style, standing in my beautiful apartment and painting every day all by myself. Granted, Star would be only a train journey away, not living on the other side of the world, but I knew she would never be coming back for longer than maybe an overnight stay, so we could catch up on each other's lives. Ace was also in London, locked up in some scummy prison among murderers and sexual deviants. At the very least, I felt I owed him an explanation, and a show of support. Whether he believed me or not, it didn't really matter. It was just the right thing to do.

Then there was *home-home*—Atlantis, and Ma, both of whom I hadn't visited for almost seven months, but I couldn't imagine my future there. Even though one day, I did want to paint the view across Lake Geneva with the mountains behind it.

That was Europe. So, what about Australia, the country I'd always been too terrified to visit? Yet, the past weeks had been the most amazing of my whole life. It was cheesy to even think it, but it felt like I'd been reborn. Like all the bits of me that hadn't fit in Europe had been stripped down and rearranged so that they—I—was a better "whole." Just like my installation. I'd never managed to get it perfect, but then *I'd* never be perfect either. But I knew I was better, and that was good enough.

My grandfather, Chrissie . . . they were here too. So far, I hadn't had to earn their love, because it had been offered to me unconditionally, but I knew I wanted to in the future.

And as I stood in the middle of this huge, open space with the sun beating down far too hard on my tender head, I realized there wasn't a decision to be made.

I turned tail and walked back to the hut.

"I belong here," I told my grandfather as we sat in a restaurant in the Alice a few hours later, eating my new favorite—kangaroo. "It's as simple as that."

"I'm glad," he said, the inherent joy in his eyes telling me just how much he was.

"Although I do have to go back to England to sort out some stuff, you know?"

"I do know. You need to tie up loose ends," he agreed. "Maybe it's the streak of German in us that makes us want to put our house in order before we can move on," he said with a smile.

"Well, talking of putting houses in order, I'm planning to sell mine. I think I told you I bought an apartment overlooking the River Thames in London with my inheritance. It's all been a bit of a disaster."

"Everyone makes mistakes, it's part of the human learning curve, as long as you *do* learn from them," he added with a sigh. "If you want to come back here, my home is yours for as long as you need it."

"Thanks." I hadn't seen his house there in the Alice yet. After arriving, we'd gone straight to eat. "As well as putting my apartment on the market, I also need to see my sister to make things right there."

"Now, that really is a reason to go back," he agreed. "People are more important than possessions, I always think."

We finished our food, then got into the truck to drive to his house. It turned out to be just on the perimeter of the town, in a line of pretty white chalet-style houses with big verandas at ground and roof level.

"Ignore the garden. Keeping plants in order really isn't an interest of mine," he remarked as we walked to the front door.

"Star could sort that lot out in a few days," I said as he put the key in the lock and opened up.

Inside, I immediately got the impression that whoever had designed the interior had wanted to bring a little piece of England to the outback. It was definitely very feminine, with pretty flower-sprigged curtains hanging at the windows, hand-embroidered scatter cushions adorning an old but comfortable sofa, and scores of photographs lining the two bookshelves that sat on either side of the fireplace. The lighting was soft too, the golden glow emanating from lampshades set on brass stands.

All in all, despite the fact it had that musty smell that houses get when they're not properly lived in, I felt cocooned and comfortable there.

"I put the water heater on a timer last time I was here, so it should be piping hot. I'm off to run a bath for you," said my grandfather.

"That's great, thanks," I said, thinking of the last time I was in a bath, covered in rose petals, with a pair of gentle hands wrapped around my waist. How far I had come since then . . .

After a long and seriously fantastic soak in the tub, I stepped out and saw the water was mud colored, with all sorts of small insects that must have embedded themselves in the crevices of my body and hair while I was out at the hut. It felt good to be clean, except I only had dirty clothes to put back on. I padded back to the sitting room in a towel.

"Do you have an old T-shirt I could borrow? My clothes stink."

"I can do better than that. Your grandmother was not far off your size, and there's a wardrobe-ful in our bedroom."

"Are you sure you don't mind?" I asked him as I followed him along the corridor and he turned on a light in the room, before pulling an old cedar-wood wardrobe open.

"Of course not, I can't think of a better use for them. I was only going to give them away to the charity shop anyway. Take your pick."

Feeling a bit weird about raiding my dead granny's wardrobe, I looked through the rack of stuff. Most of it was paisley-patterned cotton dresses, dirndl skirts, and blouses featuring lace collars, but there were also a couple of long linen shirts. I put one on and walked back to the sitting room. My mobile phone had found a signal again, and there was a message from Talitha Myers, the solicitor in Adelaide. I listened to her telling me that she'd discovered the name "Francis Abraham" in the ledgers and I felt proud that I'd got there before her.

Francis was now in the bath himself, so I amused myself by looking at the silver-framed photographs. Most were of him and a woman, who I had to presume was my grandmother. She was small and pale and neat, with her dark hair fastened in a coil on top of her head.

Another was of a bright-faced little girl of about three, grinning cheekily at the camera, then another of the same child at maybe eleven or twelve, sitting between my granny and grandpa. "My mother." I swallowed hard. I couldn't see any of her older than fifteen or so, and was just wondering about this when Francis appeared in the room.

"You've seen the photographs of your mother?"

"Yes. What was her name?"

"Elizabeth. She was a lovely little girl, always laughing. Looked just like her mother."

"I saw. And as a grown-up?" I probed.

Francis sighed. "It's a long story, Celaeno."

"Sorry, it's just that there's still so much I don't know or understand."

"Yes. Well, why don't I go and make us both some coffee? Then we can talk."

"Okay."

He was back within a few minutes, and as we sipped our coffees in silence, I could feel he was garnering the strength to tell me.

"Perhaps it's easier to go back to where we left off," he said eventually.

"Whatever you feel is best. I'd love to know what happened to Kitty, and Charlie and Drummond."

"Of course you would, and it was through Kitty that I met my wife, Sarah . . ."

KITTY

Tilbury Port, England

January 1949

29

"Good-bye, dearest sister. I can't tell you what a joy it's been having you here with us," Miriam said as they stood by the gangplank that would soon separate them once more. "Promise to come back as soon as you can, won't you?"

"You know I certainly intend to, God willing," Kitty said. "Good-bye, darling, and thank you for everything."

With a final wave, Miriam made her way down the gangplank.

Milling around Kitty were relatives reluctant to let go of their loved ones who were departing for Australia. Even though she had made this journey many times over the past forty years, witnessing the human pain of separation still affected her deeply.

She felt as if she were drowning in a storm of tears as the ship's engines roared into life and the horn hooted a final warning. Amid the crowd, a few faces stood out, despair clear on their features: a woman weeping inconsolably and hugging her infant to her, and a gaunt, gray-haired man, panic clear on his face as he watched the gangplank being hauled up.

"Where is she? She was meant to meet me here on the ship! Excuse me, madam," the man said, turning to her. "Have you by any chance seen a blond-haired woman boarding the ship in the last few minutes?"

"I couldn't say," Kitty replied honestly. "There were so many people coming and going, but I'm sure she's on board somewhere."

There was a second hoot of the horn as the boat edged away from the dock and the man looked over the side as though he might jump.

"Oh God, where *are* you . . . ?!" he screamed to the wind, the sound of his voice drowned out by the engines and the screeching of the seagulls.

Another human being trounced by love, Kitty thought as she watched the man stagger away. He looked like an army boy, with his prematurely gray hair and haunted eyes. She'd seen many of them in England during her

407

extended stay. Those who had survived six years of fighting may have been termed "lucky" to have come back—she had sat next to an army captain at dinner who had laughed it off by telling stories of the fun they'd all had—yet Kitty knew it was all a façade. These men would never fully recover, and neither would the loved ones they'd left behind.

Kitty shivered in the brisk breeze that was whipping up as they eased out of Tilbury Port and along the Thames Estuary. Inside, she made her way along a thickly carpeted corridor to her cabin. Opening the door, she found a steward setting up afternoon tea on the table in the drawing room.

"Good afternoon, ma'am. My name is James McDowell and I'll be attending to your needs on the voyage. I thought you could do with something to eat, but I wasn't sure what you like."

"Thank you, James," Kitty replied, soothed by the young man's soft voice. "Have you traveled to Australia before?"

"Me? No, it's a real adventure, isn't it? I used to be a valet to a wealthy gentleman over in Hampshire, but then he died, and since the war ended folk have no need of a valet, so I thought I'd try my luck in Australia. Have you traveled there before?"

"It's my home. I've lived there for over forty years."

"Then I might be picking your brains on what to do when I get there. It's the land of opportunity, so they tell me."

And the land of broken dreams, thought Kitty. "Yes." She forced a smile. "It is."

"Well now, I'll leave you to it, ma'am. I've unpacked your trunk, but you'll have to tell me what you wish to wear this evening. You have an invitation to dine at the captain's table, so I'll be back at six to draw your bath. Just press the bell if you need me sooner."

"Thank you, James," she said as he shut the cabin door behind him. His strong features and blue eyes had reminded her so of Charlie.

During those dark days at the outbreak of war in Europe ten years ago, her son had been busy in Broome, working with the Australian navy to fit out the requisitioned luggers that would transport the soldiers to fields of battle in Africa and Europe. Soon after, the Japanese crews had been interned and with no luggers to sail, Charlie had written to tell her it felt as if the town was slowly and quietly dying.

At least Charlie's safe in Broome, she had thought at the time. She herself had already moved to live at Alicia Hall in Adelaide, so that her son—and Elise, his wife—would not feel as though a shadow were following them on their every business and domestic move.

Then, in March of 1942, Kitty had opened her newspaper to headlines of an unexpected attack on the northwest coast of Australia. Casualties were recorded in Broome. When she finally managed to get through by telephone, she was not even surprised to hear that Charlie had been one of them.

"Are you determined to take everything I love from me?!" she had railed at the gods above her, walking the gardens at Alicia Hall in her nightdress as the servants looked on at their hysterical mistress. There had been no Camira beside her to comfort her, for she had left Kitty too.

Elise had survived the air raid and it had taken only six months for Kitty to receive a letter from her daughter-in-law announcing that she was marrying a mining magnate and moving to the town of Perth. There had been no children in the marriage and Kitty had felt curiously empty at the news. She knew she had thrust Elise under her son's nose twenty years ago, wishing to take his mind from Alkina. She doubted Charlie had ever loved his wife; he had simply gone through the motions.

Kitty sipped her tea as the ship sailed her and her dark thoughts farther from England. She had had almost twenty years to ponder the mystery of how Camira and her daughter had disappeared from Broome within a few months of each other. And plenty of time to berate herself for never confronting the situation. She'd ignored Charlie's obvious devastation when Alkina had disappeared the night before his twenty-first birthday and instinct told her the two events were connected. To this day, she missed Camira, who had stood by her side and kept secrets that were beyond keeping.

Kitty took a bite of a sandwich that tasted as bland and as empty as her life had been since everyone she loved had left her. Yet—she cautioned herself against falling into self-pity—there had been one bright light that had arrived out of the blue four long years after Charlie's death.

In the immediate aftermath, she had once more by default become the caretaker of the Mercer empire. Beside herself with grief, she had been unable to rouse herself to visit the opal mines, drive up to the vineyards, or glance at the figures from the cattle station. Nor had she read the company bank statements that piled up unopened on her desk. She had— as they termed it in Victorian novels—gone into a decline and become a virtual recluse, the guilt of all she had done and not done beating down on her day and night.

During those years of darkness, she'd longed for death but had been too cowardly to approach it.

Then, one evening in 1946, her maid had knocked on her bedroom door.

"Mrs. Mercer, there's a gentleman downstairs who says it's urgent he speaks to you."

"Please, you know I do not receive visitors. Send him away."

"I have tried to, ma'am, but he refuses to go. He says he will sit outside the gate until you receive him. Do I call the police?"

"What is his name?"

"He's a Mr. Ralph Mackenzie. He claims he's your brother."

Kitty had cast her mind back across the years to think who this man might be. A man with the same name as her father . . .

And then it had come to her.

Kitty rose from the elegant silk-covered sofa and walked to one of the large picture windows, the ship now gliding gently out on the open sea. Ralph Mackenzie had arrived in her life at just the right moment, a reminder of at least one *good* deed she'd accomplished.

She remembered descending the sweeping staircase, stopping halfway down to view a tall man, clutching his hat anxiously. He'd raised his head as he'd heard her footsteps, and in the shadowy gloom of dusk, Kitty had wondered if she was seeing a replica of her father in his younger days. This man bore the same charismatic blue eyes, strong jaw, and thick auburn hair.

"Mr. Mackenzie. Please come through."

In the drawing room, he'd sat nervously on the edge of the sofa as the maid had poured their tea.

Ralph had cleared his throat. "Ma told me about you. She always said how kind you'd been to her when she was . . . encumbered with me. When I told her I was coming to seek out a new life here in Australia, she gave me your address. She'd kept it for all these years, you see. I never thought that you would still be here, but . . . you are."

Then he'd taken out the silver cross Kitty had handed all those years ago to Annie. She had stared at it, remembering her white-hot anger at her father's duplicity.

They'd talked then, and Ralph had told her how he'd been a junior accountant at a shipyard in Leith. Then she'd invited him to stay for dinner as he recounted how difficult things had become since the war had ended. She'd heard how hard his wife had taken it when he'd had to tell her he'd been laid off due to the order books being empty.

"It was Ruth, my wife, who encouraged me to come over here and see for myself what Australia could offer a man like me."

Kitty had asked a question she had been holding back since the beginning of the evening.

"Did you ever speak to my . . . *our* father?"

"I didn't know he *was* my father until Ma, God bless her soul, died. I'd seen the Reverend McBride when Ma took me to church, where we'd sit in the back pew. Now I understand why she was always so very angry after the service. She'd been using me to remind him of the sin he'd committed." He'd glanced up apologetically at Kitty, but she had only nodded grimly.

"When I was thirteen," he'd continued, "I was sent on a scholarship to Fettes College. It was the best chance I got to improve my circumstances and make a life for myself. I didn't know until much later that he—my father—had arranged it for me. Despite everything, I'm grateful to him for that."

By the end of the evening, she had offered him a job as accountant to the Mercer companies. Six months later, his wife, Ruth, had sailed over to join him.

Kitty moved away from the view of the gray waves beyond the private deck area outside the picture window, pondering on the fact that Ralph's arrival in Adelaide had undoubtedly saved her. After the unbearable loss of Charlie, Kitty had found herself stirred to focus her energy on this amiable man—her half brother and over eighteen years her junior—who had appeared so unexpectedly in her life.

And over the past few years, Ralph had proved himself bright and eager to learn, and had subsequently become her right-hand man. Even though the pearling business in Broome had never recovered after the war, just as Charlie had foreseen, the profits of the opal mine and the vineyard were growing by the day. Between the two of them—brother and sister—the Mercer finances were slowly being restored again. The only sadness was that Ruth, after years of trying, had recently been told she would never have children. Ralph had written to Kitty in Scotland to tell her that they had bought a puppy, which was currently soaking up Ruth's thwarted maternal urges.

Due to the excellent capabilities of her half brother, Kitty was sailing back to Australia for the final time. Unbeknownst to Ralph, she would be handing over the business in its entirety to him on her return, knowing that the company's future was in safe hands.

She had returned to Leith six months ago for her father's memorial service. He had died of old age, nothing more; she and Ralph had greeted the news with an uneasy mixture of sadness and guilty relief. During her time staying with her mother, Kitty had not mentioned a word about Ralph Mackenzie to her family. She'd also traveled to Italy with her sister Miriam, to take a short cultural tour of its ancient cities, and had fallen head over heels in love with Florence. There she had purchased a small but elegant apartment, from which she could see the roof of the great Duomo. Her intention was to winter there and spend the summers with her family in Scotland.

The fact she had just reached her sixtieth birthday had provided a spur; there was little left for her in Australia other than painful memories. And, having tried for years of her life to move on from the Mercer family and the silken threads it seemed to have trapped her in for most of her adult life, she was now determined to finally do it.

Kitty walked to the wardrobe to choose what she would wear to the captain's table this evening. When she arrived in Adelaide, she would spend the next few weeks putting her affairs in order. This included seeing a solicitor to legally register her "husband" as deceased. The idea of revisiting the deceit that had been wrought by Drummond sent a chill up her spine, but it had to be done so she could at last walk away and begin again.

As she held up an evening gown to her still-slim body, she pondered on whether Drummond actually *was* dead. Often during long, lonely nights when she had yearned for his touch, she'd imagined every creak of a door, or an animal rustling through foliage in the garden, to be the sound of his return. Yet how could she have ever expected him to come back? It had been she who had sent him away.

Perhaps, she thought, returning to her homeland would allow the steel box in which she'd placed her heart to finally be wedged back open.

As the voyage got under way, Kitty slipped easily into her usual onboard routine. Uninterested in socializing with her fellow first-class guests, she took bracing walks along the deck and, as they sailed south, enjoyed the warm prickle of sunshine on her skin. Sometimes at night, she'd hear the sound of music and laughter coming from the third-class deck below her, an impromptu sing-along to a penny whistle or an accordion. She remembered how she had once danced jigs on the lower deck, the air thick with cigarette smoke. The camaraderie had been infectious; her friends may not have had wealth, but they had the true riches of their hopes and dreams.

Kitty had realized a long time ago that privilege had isolated her. Even though part of her longed to run downstairs and join in, she realized that now, she could never be accepted among them.

"And there they all are, dreaming that one day they might be up here where I am," she sighed as James arrived to draw her bath.

"Are you going out today when we dock at Port Said?" asked James as he poured out her cup of English breakfast tea.

"I haven't really thought about it," she said. "Are you?"

"I am indeed! I can hardly believe we're nearing Egypt—the land of the pharaohs. To be honest, Mrs. Mercer, I'm eager to get my feet back on dry land. I'm feeling cooped up on board and my friend Stella says there's things to see, though we must be careful not to stray too far. I'm taking some of the orphans off with me to cheer them up a bit."

"Orphans?"

"Yes, I'd reckon going on a hundred of them are down in third class. They've been shipped out from England to find new families in Australia."

"I see." Kitty took a sip of her tea. "Then perhaps I will join you all."

"Really?" James eyed her incredulously. "Some of them stink, Mrs. Mercer, there's no proper facilities for washing in their quarters."

"I am sure I will cope," she replied briskly. "So, I shall meet you by the bottom of the gangplank when the ship docks at ten tomorrow."

"All right," he said, "but don't say I didn't warn you."

The following day, Kitty walked down the gangplank into Port Said. The smell of rotting fruit and unwashed bodies accosted her nose as she heard shouts ringing out along the busy port. A steady stream of crates, animals, and human beings was moving to and from the steamships.

James was waiting for her, along with a tall redheaded girl and a ragtag collection of children.

"This is Stella." James introduced the redheaded girl, her sunbonnet pulled low to protect her white skin. "She's been doing her best to take care of some of the younger ones downstairs," he said, turning to her with what Kitty recognized as utter adoration in his eyes.

"A pleasure to meet you, Stella. And what are all your names?" Kitty bent down to speak to the youngest, who could have been no more than five.

"Eddie," another boy with a strong Cockney accent answered for him. "'E don't speak much."

"And that's Johnny, Davy, and Jimmy, then there's Mabel and Edna and Susie . . . and I'm Sarah," said a bright-eyed, painfully thin young girl with sallow skin and lank brown hair, who Kitty hazarded a guess was around fourteen or fifteen. "We've all adopted each other, 'aven't we?"

"Yes!" chorused the grimy set of faces.

"Well now, I am Mrs. Mercer, and I know somewhere nearby that sells all sorts of different kinds of sweetmeats," Kitty announced. "Shall we go and take a look?"

"Yes!" the children cheered.

"Come along then," Kitty ordered as, on instinct, she swept little Eddie up in her arms.

"Glad you know your way around, Mrs. Mercer. I've never seen anything like it in my life," James said to her as they made their way through the clamor of street hawkers. Kitty looked behind her and saw Sarah and Stella holding tightly to the hands of the others.

"Lots of darkies around here, in't there, Davy?" Kitty heard Johnny whisper to his friend as the local residents swirled around them in their bright-colored robes and fez hats.

She led the party beyond the docks and into the town itself. There, she knew a vast street market which sold delicious-smelling spices, fruit, and flatbreads baking in scorching-hot ovens, the air around them rippling with the heat.

"Ooh-er, look at those." Sarah pointed to a glistening jewel-colored pile of Turkish delight, sprinkled with icing sugar.

"Yes, it is absolutely delicious," Kitty said. "I'd like"—she counted the heads—"eight bags containing three pieces each," she instructed the vendor behind the trestle table, then mimed and gesticulated until the man understood what she required.

"Here, Eddie. Try this." Kitty held out the sweet to the little boy tucked into her shoulder. Eddie glanced at it and, with some reluctance, removed his thumb from his mouth and stuck out his little pink tongue to taste the icing sugar.

"We'll have to watch out that they're not sick, Missus M," said Sarah, who was standing at Kitty's other shoulder, doling out the paper bags. "They ain't had a treat like this in the whole of their lives."

"Good God, some of them are positively emaciated," Kitty whispered to her.

"They do feed us, missus. In fact, some o' the grub is better than wot I got in the orphanage. It's just that we all got a bit sick, wot with all the big waves. Especially the little ones. He," Sarah said, pointing at Eddie, whose face was a picture of bliss as he savored the Turkish delight, "got really bad with it."

They wandered around the market, ooh-ing and aah-ing at the roughly carved wooden replicas of the Sphinx and Tutankhamun's sarcophagus.

They stopped by another stall, where Kitty bought them each a fresh orange and they all stared at the fruit as though it was the best present they had ever received.

They returned to the gangplank just before four o'clock, the children's faces sticky with icing sugar and orange juice. Kitty lifted a sleeping Eddie into Sarah's arms.

"Thanks, Missus M, we won't forget your kindness," Sarah said. "You made everyone right 'appy today. And if you need anyone to darn your posh frocks, I'm yer girl. I don't charge a quarter as much as them as are employed on board, and I'm much better than they are!" Sarah gave her a grin and shepherded the children down the stairs.

"I thought we could possibly accommodate two of the orphans per night in my bathtub," Kitty said that evening as James laid out her dress for dinner.

"That's very kind of you," James gulped, "but I'm not sure how the purser would take to me bringing the steerage passengers up to first class."

"Then you will just have to find a way. Let me tell you, James, one of the keys to health is cleanliness. At present, those children's skins encourage a wealth of bacteria to breed. Will you be responsible for little Eddie being pronounced dead before he reaches the shores of Australia?"

"Well, no, I—"

"Then I am sure you can devise a plan. If you manage this, I can offer you a good, steady wage working for one of my companies when we arrive in Adelaide. So, will we try?"

"Yes, Mrs. Mercer," he said doubtfully.

That night, two children arrived at the door of Kitty's suite of rooms. They were hurried in by James, who then left, banging the door shut behind him. After gasps ensued from the two boys, who could not believe that such luxury and space existed on the steamship, Kitty ushered them to the bathroom and asked them to undress.

"Me mam said I was never to take off me clothes in front of a stranger." Jimmy—who was eight at the most—had crossed his arms and was shaking his head.

"And me, Missus M," added Johnny.

"Well then, why don't I leave you in here alone? Please give yourselves a good scrub using the carbolic soap." Kitty pointed to it. "There's a bath towel for each of you when you step out. When you've finished, there'll be supper waiting for you."

The boys slammed the bathroom door in her face. Kitty heard a whispered conversation, then some splashes, which eventually led to giggles of delight.

"Dry yourselves off quickly, boys, your supper's getting cold," she said through the door.

They emerged looking fresher, even if Kitty still noticed smudges on their necks. As she sat them down at the table in front of two large bowls of stew, she sniffed and realized there was still a rancid smell emanating from their unwashed clothes.

The following morning, as James was serving her breakfast, they discussed which two orphans would come up to take a bath that night.

"It's a good thing you're doing for the children, Mrs. Mercer."

"It would be even better if we could provide them with clean clothes. The weather is so much warmer now. All they will need is a shirt and a pair of shorts, then we could send their current sets of clothes to the laundry. Any ideas?"

"Sarah is a great little seamstress. She's darned all the boys' socks and made a whole wardrobe of clothes out of scraps for Mabel's doll."

"Excellent. Then we must set her to work."

"She doesn't have a sewing machine, Mrs. Mercer."

"Then we shall procure one forthwith. Tell the purser that the eccentric Mrs. Mercer has a fancy for sewing to while away the hours on board. I'm sure they have a number in the laundry department."

"Righto, I'll see what I can do, but what about material?"

"Leave that one with me." Kitty tapped her nose. "And send Sarah to see me this afternoon. We shall take tea together and discuss our project."

"There now," Kitty said, leading Sarah into her bedroom. She indicated the pile of nightgowns and skirts on the bed. "Can you do something with those?"

Sarah stared at the heap of Kitty's clothes, then turned to her, horrified.

"Missus M, this is real expensive stuff, like. I can't start cutting it apart, it would be sacrilege."

"Of course it wouldn't be, Sarah. I have more clothes than I could ever wear, and we can always steal a sheet or two from the bed if need be."

"If you say so, Missus M," Sarah said as her fingers traced the delicate lace at the neck of a nightgown.

"I do. The sewing machine will arrive later this afternoon and you can get to work tomorrow."

Sarah's blue eyes were huge in her thin, pale face. "But what will they say with me bein' up 'ere?"

"The purser will say absolutely nothing because I will tell him that I have employed you as my lady's maid and that you are mending my clothes. Now, I shall see you at nine o'clock sharp."

"Right you are, Missus M."

Sarah stood up, the dress she was wearing hanging loose on her slight frame. As James ushered her out, Kitty's heart bled at the thought of these orphans, sent across the world into the unknown with no one to care for them.

Kitty only hoped that life would be kinder to them once they reached Australia's shores.

By the end of the week, all the orphans had a new set of clothes fashioned by Sarah's nimble fingers. Kitty had also enjoyed the girl's company, as she sat at her sewing machine chattering away about the bombs that had fallen in the East End during the war as if she were recalling a walk in the park.

"The last one did fer ten of us in our street, including me mam. We was in the cellar, see, 'cause the sirens had gone off, then she realized she'd left 'er knitting upstairs and went to fetch it just as the bomb fell on our roof. I were dug outta the rubble without a scratch. I were only six years old at the time. Chap that heard me caterwauling said it was a blimmin' miracle."

"Goodness," Kitty breathed. "Where did you go after that?"

"Me auntie took me into 'er 'ouse down the road, till me dad came back from soldiering in France. Except 'e never did come back, and me auntie couldn't afford to keep me, so I was put into an orphanage, see. It were all right there, 'cause we all stuck together. It's what you 'ave to do, isn't it, Missus M?"

"Yes." Kitty struggled to swallow the lump in her throat, marveling at Sarah's bravery and positivity.

"Everyone says that you can make a new life for yerself in Australia. What's it like, Missus M?"

Vast... Heartbreaking... Extraordinary... Cruel...

"It's truly the land of possibility. I'm sure you'll do very well there, Sarah. How old are you, by the way?"

"Fifteen, Missus M, and being as I'm useful with me 'ands, I'm 'oping I'll get a job and make some money of me own. And find a fella," she giggled, the palest of blushes rising to her cheeks. "Right, those are the last o' the lot." Sarah removed a pair of shorts from under the needle of the machine and gave them a shake to straighten them out. "They should fit Jimmy good, as long as he don't go losing more weight."

"Well done. These are beautifully sewn." Kitty took them from Sarah's hands and folded them neatly onto the pile with the rest of the clothes. "You can take them all down with you and hand them out."

"Yeah, though I'll 'ave to be careful they don't get stolen. There's a lot down there would rob yer as much as look at yer. I was also wonderin' whether I could take that bit of sheet that's left over an' sew some 'ankies outta it to cheer up a friend of mine. 'E cries a lot, see," she added in explanation. "A lotta them do down below."

"Of course you may, and thank you, Sarah, for all your hard work. Now, here's your wages." Kitty picked up an embroidered blouse and skirt that, at present, would drown Sarah's slight form. "Can you do something with these to make them fit you?"

"Ooh, Missus M . . ." Her hand reached out to touch the soft fabric. "I couldn't take them, not downstairs at least. They'd be filthy in five seconds flat."

"Then we will fit them to you and they can stay up here with me until we leave the ship. You'll need to be looking your best to attract a 'fella,' after all."

"Thanks, Missus M, you're like our guardian angel," Sarah said as she collected the pile of clothes, plus the spare sheet, and headed to the door. "See yer later."

"I only wish I could be," Kitty sighed as she closed it behind her.

30

Despite the look of disapproval from the purser, Kitty insisted that her small orphan tribe come to join her as the ship approached Adelaide port, where they were all to disembark. She ordered a last feast that they devoured hungrily, their eyes searching the horizon every so often for the first sight of the place where their new life would begin. When it appeared, spotted by Jimmy with a shout, they all ran onto the terrace to hang over the railings.

"Cor!"

"Look at them 'ills! They're green, not red!"

"Where's the 'ouses and the town? Don't look like there's nothing 'ere."

Kitty lifted Eddie into her arms and stroked his fine, downy hair. "Can you see the sand, Eddie? Maybe I can take you one day to make a sand castle."

As usual, Eddie didn't reply. Kitty wrapped her arms tighter around his frail body as he snuggled into her shoulder.

James appeared on the terrace to say that the children had to go back downstairs to get ready to disembark.

"Will someone be there to greet them?" she asked him as he herded them toward the door.

"Apparently there'll be officials who'll take them to meet their new families. I've heard it's a bit of a meat market—it's the strongest boys that get picked first, and the youngest and prettiest girls."

"What happens to those who don't get picked?"

"I don't know, Mrs. Mercer," James replied.

But Kitty knew he did.

"Now then," she said, turning to the gaggle of excited faces that stared up at her so trustingly. "I'm going to give each of you a card with my name and address on it. I live very near the center of Adelaide, and if any of you need my help, you're to come and find me at Alicia Hall. Is that understood?"

"Yes, Missus M," they chorused.

"Well then, I will say good-bye." Kitty kissed their clean, shiny heads and watched as they left the cabin for the last time.

"And God bless you all," she murmured, tears filling her eyes.

Back at Alicia Hall, Kitty set about tying up all the loose ends of her life in Australia. A long afternoon was spent with her solicitor, Mr. Angus, as she explained that all of the Mercer businesses should be transferred to Ralph, and a sum of money invested in stocks and shares to support herself in old age. The money was to be passed on to charity in the event of her death.

"I also wish to officially declare my husband dead, given he has now been missing for thirty-seven years," she said, her face not betraying a single emotion.

"I see." Mr. Angus tapped his pen on his blotter. "That should not present a problem, Mrs. Mercer, but I will need some time to gather the evidence."

"What evidence do you need? No one has seen or heard from him in decades."

"Of course. It is simply the bureaucracy of declaring someone dead in absentia—we have to show the court that we have made sufficient attempts to find your husband, even though the balance of probabilities is that he is, indeed, deceased. I shall begin the process for you immediately."

"Thank you."

Her brother Ralph arrived back from the opal mine in Coober Pedy, and the two of them sat down to discuss the business.

"Given the current financial crisis in Europe, I'd say that we're holding up quite well. It's a good time to expand, Kitty. When I was in Coober Pedy, I was offered some land that's going cheap. I think it will be an excellent investment."

"I trust to your judgment, Ralph, but do we have the funds?"

"We certainly would if we sold off Kilgarra cattle station. I've been looking at the accounts—you may remember the old manager died a while back? The replacement manager does not seem to be quite as regular with his monthly reports. I think I should travel up to the north to see for myself what's going on."

"Is that really necessary?"

"I believe so, yes. I've had no reply to any of my recent telegrams."

"I've never been up there," Kitty said, knowing full well why she hadn't. "It's such a very long way away."

"Closer now that one can take the Ghan train to Alice Springs. Kilgarra station is only two days' ride away by pony and cart, but I would need to leave soon."

"Of course."

"Then there is the question of the properties in Broome. I have sold off all the luggers as we discussed, but that still leaves the office, warehouses, and, of course, the house. Do you wish to keep it? I know how many memories it holds for you."

"Yes," she said, surprising herself, "but the business premises can be sold. Now, dear Ralph, I must tell you of *my* plans for the future."

Kitty watched Ralph's expression turn to abject surprise when she told him she was handing over the entire Mercer empire to him.

"I will take a modest pension from the business, but I have other money of my own and besides, my needs will be few. And then, of course, there is Alicia Hall. I intend to pass it over to you."

"Truly, Kitty, are you sure? You have known me less than three years and—"

"Ralph." Kitty laid a gentle hand on his arm. "You are my brother, blood of my blood. I can think of no one better to care for the business in the future. You have proved yourself a talented manager, with an excellent head for business. I am sure you will be able to ride the storm of change I feel is coming to Australia. And in truth, I will be quite happy to hand over the reins. I have been an accidental caretaker for far too long."

"Then thank you, Kitty. I am honored by your trust in me."

"So, that is settled. I am thinking . . ." Kitty stared off into the distance. "I am thinking that I shall ready myself to leave by April. Although there is one more journey that I promised myself I should make when I first sailed over here as a young girl."

"And where is that?"

"To Ayers Rock. Can you believe I have never seen it still, after all these years? So," Kitty said, smiling at him, "you will have company on the Ghan. I shall come with you as far as Alice Springs."

As Kitty made her final preparations to leave Australia's shores, she realized there was little she wished to take to Europe with her—almost everything at Alicia Hall had been chosen by Edith, her mother-in-law. Papers were being drawn up ready for her to sign the business into Ralph's name when she returned from her trip to Alice Springs. Mr. Angus informed her that he was well under way with registering Andrew's death in absentia and Kitty had written a brief statement as to her "husband's" mental state after the *Koombana* had sunk, hoping it would be enough to convince a judge.

She received Andrew's death certificate in the post two weeks later, and sat staring at it with a mixture of horror and relief. Walking outside onto the veranda, she glanced at the very spot where she had first laid eyes on Drummond as an eighteen-year-old girl.

"It's over," she murmured to herself, "it's finally over."

A strange sense of peace had descended on her by the time she heard the doorbell ring as she was eating her solitary dessert. Wondering who could be calling so late at night, she heard Nora, her Aboriginal maid of all works, answer the front door.

"Scusum me, Missus Mercer," Nora said as she peeped around the dining room door a few seconds later, "there's some beggar who sayum she need see you. She say you givem her address. Her name Sarah. Shall I let her in?"

"Why yes, of course." Kitty rose from the table.

"Has young fella with her too," Nora added darkly as Kitty followed her into the hall.

"Missus M! Thank the blinkin' Lord we found yer!"

Sarah, if she had been thin before, now resembled a ghost of her former self. She launched herself into Kitty's arms. "Oh, Missus M . . ."

Then Kitty's gaze fell on Eddie, who had been hiding behind Sarah, his eyes round as saucers as he stared up at the chandelier that hung in the center of the high vaulted ceiling.

"Goodness, what on earth has happened?" She drew Eddie to her, with Sarah still attached to her. "Why don't we go and sit down and you can tell me all about it." She steered both children in the direction of the drawing room and sat them down on either side of her.

"Oh, Missus M, we've 'ad the most 'orrible time of it at the orphanage."

"Orphanage?" Kitty could see Sarah was near to tears.

"Yeah, 'cause it was all a lie, see? The others got taken by families but me an' Eddie, there weren't no one waiting for us. We was taken with a load of other kids to this 'ome run by nuns."

"Are you hungry?" Kitty asked.

"We're blinkin' starvin', Missus M!"

Kitty rang the bell for Nora and asked her to plate up some bread and cold meats for her guests. After Kitty had watched the two of them stuff the food into their mouths as though they were famished scavengers, she asked Sarah to tell her slowly what had happened.

The tale of woe at the St. Vincent de Paul orphanage spilled out of Sarah's mouth. "They worked us like slaves, Missus M, and if we refused, we'd get beatings, or we'd 'ave to stand still for hours and no one were allowed to speak to us. They wouldn't even let us get out of bed to go to the toilet after lights-out. Little Eddie 'ad no choice, 'e 'ad to wet the bed—all the little ones did—and then they'd get beaten for it. All of us old enough to carry a mop and bucket 'ad to be up before the crack o' dawn to start scrubbing, and all we got to eat was stale bread." Sarah took a moment to breathe, her face pinched with fury. "And the worst of it was, Missus M, those nuns, they called 'emselves Sisters of Mercy, but they 'ad none. One of 'em—Sister Mary—would pick on one of the little girls every night, and take 'er to a room, and . . . oh, Missus M, I can't even say it!" Sarah covered her face with her hands.

With each word she uttered, Kitty's horror grew. "Where exactly is this place?"

"It's in Goodwood. We took a few wrong turns getting 'ere to you, but I'd reckon only 'alf an hour's straight walk away. If you can't 'ave us 'ere, we understand, but neither of us are going back there. *Ever*," Sarah added firmly.

Kitty turned to see Eddie, whose head was nestled in the crook of her arm. He was fast asleep.

"I think it's high time the two of you were in bed, don't you?"

"You mean we can stay? Just for the night, o' course, but please, Missus M, don't tell no one we're 'ere if they come callin'. The nun said we'd end up in prison if we was to run away." Sarah yawned then, her tiny heart-shaped face almost disappearing behind her mouth.

"I won't call the police, Sarah, I promise. Come now, let's get you both to bed. We will talk in the morning."

Carrying Eddie up the stairs, Kitty took them to the old nursery that still contained the twin beds that Drummond and Andrew had slept in as children. Laying Eddie on one bed fully clothed and tucking a sheet across him, she indicated Sarah should sleep in the other.

"Thank you, Missus M, I'll never forget what you've done for us tonight. Ever," Sarah murmured as her eyes drew shut.

"Dear child," Kitty whispered as she closed the door behind her. "I can never have done enough."

"I can hardly believe it," said Ruth, Ralph's wife, the following afternoon, as they sat drinking lemonade on the terrace, watching Eddie play with Tinky, the King Charles spaniel. "Are you sure that this girl isn't exaggerating?"

"Quite sure. I spent a lot of time with her on my voyage over here, and I believe every word she says."

"But they're nuns . . . women who have pledged their lives to do God's work."

"In my experience, pledging one's life to God does not necessarily mean that one acts in His name," Kitty replied with feeling, as she watched Eddie reaching out to try to catch a butterfly.

"What will you do with them?" Ruth asked.

"I haven't decided yet. I certainly won't be sending them back whence they came," Kitty said as they watched Eddie run around the garden after the butterfly. His laughter stopped abruptly as he tripped over a patch of stony ground and fell.

Before he'd had time to utter a cry of pain, Ruth was on her feet and running toward him, her arms around him as she took him on her knee.

The child buried his face in her chest as she murmured words of comfort. An idea began to form in Kitty's mind.

"'Ere, Missus M, I made this for you to say thank you."

Sarah shyly handed Kitty a square of material, one edge embroidered with her initials, woven into an intricate design of pink climbing roses.

"It's beautiful, Sarah, thank you. You're a very talented young lady."

"That's not what Sister Agnes used to tell me," Sarah snorted. "She said I were a wretch of the earth, along wi' the rest o' us."

"I can assure you that you're not, Sarah," Kitty replied firmly.

"I was 'oping I could go into town today and find a job at a dressmaker's. Earn some money to support me an' Eddie. Do you know of any?"

"Perhaps, Sarah, but I think you're rather young to be in full-time employment."

"I'm not afraid of hard work, Missus M."

"Well, as a matter of fact, I wanted to ask whether you were willing to help me for a while. I have many things to organize before I leave for Europe and I'm due to take a trip up to the north of Australia. As Nora is needed here, I shall require someone to assist me with my clothes and what you will. Be warned, mind you, that it's a long journey, first by train, then by pony and cart."

"Oh, Missus M, I'd follow you to the ends of the earth, I really would. Are you serious?"

"I am never anything but, Sarah, I can assure you."

"Then I would love to, Missus M. But . . ." Sarah's face fell. "What about Eddie? 'E's not made of strong stuff like me. I'm not sure 'e'd be able to come with us."

Kitty tapped her nose and smiled. "You leave Eddie to me."

"I was wondering, Kitty, given that you are away with Ralph for the next few weeks, if you've decided what you're going to do with Eddie?" Ruth gazed down fondly at him sitting next to her, utterly enthralled by the jigsaw puzzle she'd brought for him.

"Do you know, Ruth, you've just read my mind, because I am really not at all sure what I will do," said Kitty. "I wouldn't like to return him to the orphanage . . ."

"No, you certainly must not! I was talking to Ralph only last night and we thought it would be a good idea for him to stay with us while you are both away."

"Goodness! What a clever idea! But what about the imposition on you?"

"It would be no imposition at all. He's a dear child, and I really feel he's beginning to trust me." Ruth's eyes filled with tenderness as Eddie nudged her to show her the completed jigsaw.

"Yes, I believe he is. Well now, if you're sure . . ."

"Perfectly. It would be good to have a man about the house to protect me while Ralph's away up north with you." Ruth smiled.

"If Eddie's happy, then so am I."

"What do you think, Eddie?" Ruth touched the little boy's arm. "Would you like to come and live at my house for a while?"

"Yes please!" Eddie said as he reached for Ruth and she pulled him closer to her.

"Well now, I think that's the decision taken," Kitty managed to say through the lump that had appeared in her throat.

It was the first time she had ever heard Eddie speak.

31

Five days later, Kitty and Sarah left Adelaide with Ralph at the break of dawn to travel to Port Augusta, where they boarded the Ghan train, their luggage neatly stowed in their sleepers by the porters. Over the three-day journey, they settled into a calm routine, accompanied by the rhythmic chug of the train as it pulled them through the increasingly rugged and empty red desert. Kitty was happy to have Sarah with her, not only for her practical nature, but also for her enthusiasm—her constant delight at every turn of the journey helped Kitty to see the landscape through fresh eyes.

They spent the long afternoons in the observation car, Sarah's face glued to the window as she announced each new sight and sound to her mistress.

"Camels!" she gasped, pointing to a line of them snaking through the landscape.

"Yes, the steward mentioned they're most likely traveling to meet the train at the next station," said Ralph without glancing up from his papers. And sure enough, when they stopped at Oodnadatta, Sarah watched with rapt attention as the Afghan cameleers, dressed in their white turbans and flowing robes, collected supplies from the train and packed them onto their own stalwart and elegant chauffeurs of the desert.

With Sarah by her side, Kitty too watched the changing scenery of red mountains, shining white salt flats, and azure rivers, marveling that, after all these decades in Australia, its interior had passed her by.

They arrived in Alice Springs onto a packed platform, where it seemed as if the entire town had turned out to greet the train. They squeezed through the clamoring crowd and Ralph organized a pony and cart to take them to the main street of the town.

They were deposited in front of what proudly named itself the Springs

428

Hotel. With their driver bringing up the rear carrying their cases, they stepped into a dark and dusty reception area.

"Not quite what you're used to, is it, Missus M?" Sarah whispered into her ear as Ralph asked if the proprietor, Mrs. Randall—a grizzled woman who looked as though she bathed in gin regularly—had any spare rooms. She did, and they were each given a key.

"Privy's out the back, an' there's a water barrel for washing in."

"Thank you," Kitty said, nodding at the woman as Sarah pulled a face to show what she thought of the sanitary arrangements.

"Blimey, even the orphanage 'ad an inside privy," she whispered.

"I'm sure we'll survive," said Kitty as they made their way up the wooden stairs.

All three of them were exhausted that night and ate dinner early in the tiny downstairs parlor.

"Mrs. Randall says that Kilgarra cattle station is two days' ride away. So I'll set about finding someone to take me there. Will you be accompanying me?" asked Ralph.

"No," Kitty said firmly. "We only have ten days here and I wish to see Ayers Rock. I'm sure you'll be able to report back to me on the situation, Ralph. Now, I think I will retire for the night. The journey here has quite exhausted me."

Upstairs in her basic room, she lay on the hard horsehair mattress and gazed through the pane of glass that wore its outer dust as a second skin. She knew Drummond wouldn't be at the cattle station—he couldn't have risked being recognized. Yet however much logic told her he could be anywhere in this vast landscape, being here in the outback made him feel close, somehow.

This is his *place,* his *land* . . .

"Kitty," she spoke fiercely to herself, "you have just officially had him declared dead. Besides, he is almost certainly no more than bones by now . . ."

With this stern talking-to administered, Kitty rolled over and fell asleep.

Outside the hotel the following morning Ralph looked more than a little nervous as he sat on a cart next to his Aboriginal driver.

"This'll be an adventure to tell Ruth and Eddie about, won't it?" he said, giving Kitty and Sarah a strained smile. "God willing, I'll see you both at the end of the week. Right, let's be on our way."

The driver gave the pony a tap and the cart rumbled off down the dusty street.

"Rather 'im than me, Missus M. Blimey, it's 'ot!" Sarah fanned herself. "I were thinking I should go to the draper's across the road and see if I can buy some material to make us a couple o' sunbonnets, with netting across 'em to keep these blinkin' flies out o' me face." Sarah swatted one that had landed on her cheek.

"Good idea," Kitty agreed. "I suggest we spend the day here in town and travel to Ayers Rock tomorrow."

"Right you are, Missus M. When I come back, I'll do me best to wash your smalls in that barrel outside."

Having given Sarah some coins from her purse, she watched the girl disappear into the crowded street. It was bustling with a mixture of white and Aboriginal people, the road busy with men on horseback, ponies and carts, and the odd car. The scene took her back to her early days in Broome—a multicultural mix of humanity, determined to make its way in a harsh, unforgiving environment.

Having eaten lunch and unused these days to the sweltering heat, Kitty went back inside the hotel and took refuge under the ceiling fan above her bed. As dusk fell and the heat of the day abated, she decided she would take a walk outside or she would never sleep tonight. Arriving downstairs in the tiny reception, Mrs. Randall looked up from a man she was talking to over the counter.

"Good evening, Mrs. Mercer. Marshall says he'll be here bright and early to take you out ta the rock. Best if you travel before the sun's up, so he suggests four o'clock tomorrow morning. That all right with you?"

"Thank you. That will be perfect."

Kitty had just turned the door handle when Mrs. Randall added, "Just the two of you for supper tonight, is it? Maybe Mr. D here can join you."

"I—"

The man had turned around and was now staring straight at her, his blue eyes wide in his nut-brown skin above a fuzz of gray beard.

Kitty clutched the front door for support, her gaze unable to leave his.

"O' course, if you would prefer to eat separately, I can arrange it."

Mrs. Randall looked bemused as her two guests continued to stare at each other.

"It's up to the lady," he said eventually.

Kitty tried to form a reply, but her brain was simply scrambled.

"Are you all right, Mrs. Mercer, love? You've gone ever such a funny color, you have."

"Yes . . ." She tried hard to release her hand from the doorknob, but knew she might well fall over if she did. With an almighty effort, she turned it to pull the door open. "I'm going out."

In the street, Kitty turned blindly and began to walk briskly away from the hotel.

It cannot be . . . it just cannot be *. . .*

"Kitty!"

At the sound of his voice behind her, her legs broke into a run. She turned down a narrow lane, not caring where she was going as long as *he* couldn't catch her.

"For God's sake! I could outrun you by hopping!"

"Damn you! Damn you to hell!" she swore as her chest tightened. She slowed as purple patches began to appear in front of her eyes and a firm hand gripped her arm. On the verge of fainting, she bent over, panting like an asthmatic dog and having no choice but to let him take her weight.

"Sit down. I'll go and get you some water." He gently eased her down onto a doorstep. "Wait there, I'll be back."

"I don't want you back . . . Go away, go *away* . . . ," Kitty moaned as she bent her head between her knees and tried to hold on to consciousness.

"Here, drink this."

With her eyes closed, she smelled the whiskey before she saw it.

"NO!" She swiped at the tin mug, which went sailing through the air, then bounced and rolled across the ground, spilling its contents. "How dare you!"

"How dare I *what?*"

"Bring me liquor! I need water!"

"I have that here too."

Kitty grabbed the flask he offered her and gulped the water down. She took some deep breaths while fanning herself with her bonnet, and her senses slowly returned to her.

"What are you doing here?" she gasped.

"I've been coming here for almost forty years. I rather think it's me that should ask *you* that question."

"I hardly think it's any of your business . . ."

"You are right as always, but I will warn you that our theatrics along the main street of Alice Springs will soon be everyone else's business. Could I suggest that we continue this conversation somewhere more private?"

"You will escort me back to the hotel," she said, allowing him to pull her to standing and feeling a number of eyes upon them. "And then you will leave."

"Hah! You've arrived on *my* patch. *You're* the one who should leave."

"We'll see about that," she retorted.

They said no more until they reached the hotel. He paused on the doorstep and turned to her.

"I suggest that for the sake of form, we take dinner together tonight. We happen to be sharing a roof under the watchful eye of the town gossip." He indicated Mrs. Randall, standing behind her reception desk and peering at them through the dust-coated pane of glass in the front door. "And later, when she is asleep, which is usually around nine thirty after a few bottles of grog, we will talk."

"Agreed," Kitty said as he moved to open the door.

"Everything all right, ducky?" Mrs. Randall asked her as they walked into reception.

"Yes, thank you. It must have been the heat of the day affecting me."

"For sure, dearie, it gets to all of us, don't it, Mr. D?" Mrs. Randall winked at him.

"It certainly does, Mrs. R."

"So have we decided if we're eating together?" Mrs. Randall queried.

"Of course," he answered. "Mrs. Mercer and I met many years ago. Her husband was a . . . close friend of mine. It will be a pleasure to catch up on old times, won't it, Mrs. Mercer?"

Kitty could see that at least part of him was finding this charade funny. Before she put her hands around his neck, she managed a strangled "Yes," then walked as calmly as she could up the stairs to her room.

"Good God!" she exhaled as she slammed the door, then locked it behind her for good measure. She lay down on her bed to try to still her banging heart.

You loved him once . . .

Kitty rose a few minutes later, and prowled the room like a trapped animal. She studied her face in the small looking glass, which had beveled black lines that crisscrossed it and marred her reflection.

She gave a small chuckle that fate should bring her here to a place where there was barely a feminine comfort to make herself smell nice or to look better for him. Even though, of course, she didn't want to and it shouldn't matter . . . Deriding herself for her vanity, but nevertheless, fetching Sarah from the room next door, she asked her to take out her favorite cornflower-blue muslin blouse, and do something with her mane of graying auburn hair, which had become as unruly as a spoiled child and was hanging in an unwashed mass of curls about her face.

"I think it suits you down, Missus M," commented Sarah as she attempted to twist it into combs. "Makes you look years younger."

"We're eating with a very old friend of my husband's," announced Kitty as she added a little lipstick to make her mouth seem fuller. Then, as it began to bleed into the lines that led from her lips, she rubbed it off harshly.

"Missus Randall mentioned there was a gentleman who'd be eating with us tonight. Didn't realize 'e was an old friend of yours. What's 'is name?"

Kitty swallowed hard. "Everyone here calls him Mr. D."

He was waiting for them in the parlor, and Kitty could tell from his clean skin and freshly shaved face that he too had made an effort to smarten himself up.

"Mrs. Mercer." He stood, then bent to kiss her hand. "What a coincidence this is."

"Indeed."

"And who is this?" His attention turned to Sarah.

"This is Sarah. I met her aboard ship on my journey back to Australia a few months ago. She is my lady's maid."

"'Ow do you do, sir?" Sarah dipped an unnecessary curtsy.

"Very well indeed, thank you. Shall we sit down?" he suggested.

As they did so, he reached to whisper in Kitty's ear. "You really do excel at collecting waifs and strays."

Over the rather good stew, which they were informed by "Mr. D" was kangaroo, Kitty sat back and watched as Drummond charmed Sarah. She herself was happy for another person to be present, which removed the attention from her. Her stomach was so tight that every swallow made her feel as though she would burst.

"So, where do you go from here?" he asked Sarah.

"We're off to see some big rock in the center of the desert tomorrow," Sarah informed him blithely, taking another slug of the ale Drummond had insisted she try. "Missus M wants to see it for some reason. It seems a long way to go to see a bit o' stone, if yer know wot I mean."

"I do, but trust me, once you get there, you'll understand. It's special."

"Well, if we're up at four, I'm off to me bed. What about you, Missus M?"

"She'll be up after a coffee, won't you, Mrs. Mercer?" Drummond eyed her.

"All right." Sarah gave one of her enormous yawns, and rose from the table. "See you bright and early tomorrow morning."

Kitty watched as she tottered unsteadily out of the parlor.

"Is it a habit of yours to get young women tipsy? Sarah is not yet sixteen!" she whispered.

Drummond raised his glass of ale. "To you, Kitty. I swear you haven't changed one jot since the first moment I laid eyes on you. What is it, I've often wondered, that makes you quite so angry?"

Kitty shook her head, hating how, after all these years, Drummond could reduce her to a mass of seething insecurity and fury. Again, she had a desperate urge to slap him.

"How dare you speak to me like that!"

"Like what? You mean, not like the rest of your lackeys who bow and scrape at the feet of the famous Kitty Mercer, who suffered such a huge family tragedy, but against all odds rose to be the most powerful pearling mistress in Broome? Respected and revered by all, despite the fact that her success has stripped any form of love from her life?"

"Enough!" Kitty rose instinctively from her chair, not wishing to give Mrs. Randall further gossip to spread about town and knowing she was about to explode. "I will say good night." She walked toward the door.

"I'm impressed at your self-control. I was expecting a punch at any second."

Kitty sighed deeply, too weary and confused to fight any longer. "Good night, Drummond." She walked up the stairs to her bedroom and closed the door behind her. Stripping off her cornflower-blue blouse, and berating herself for ever thinking to wear it in the first place, she climbed into bed. For the first time in as long as she could remember, she cried.

Just as she was calming down and thinking that she might actually doze off, there was a timid knock on her door. She sat up, fully awake.

"Who is it?"

"Me," a whisper came through the wood.

Kitty darted out of bed, not sure whether she had locked the door behind her when she had come in. The answer stood in front of her as Drummond entered, looking as wretched as she felt.

"Forgive me, Kitty." He closed the door behind him and locked it firmly. "I came to apologize. I don't behave like such a pig around anyone else. It was a shock to see you. I . . . didn't—*don't*," he corrected himself, "know how to handle this."

"That makes two of us. And you're right, this is your patch. It is I who should leave. I shall go to Ayers Rock tomorrow, then make plans to return to Adelaide as soon as possible."

"Really, there is no need to do that."

"I'm afraid there is. Good Lord, if anyone recognizes me, or us together . . . I just received Andrew's death certificate before I left."

"So, you have finally killed me off. Well now, there's a thing." Eventually he roused himself, looked at her, and gave her a weak smile. "No matter, Kitty. Around here I'm simply known as Mr. D: a drover who never stays in one place for longer than a few weeks. I've heard it whispered that I'm an ex-convict, escaped from Fremantle Jail."

"You could certainly be taken for one." Kitty eyed his still-thick mass of dark hair, turned gray in parts; the rugged face lined more by the sun than age; and the broadness of his chest complemented by thick, muscled arms.

"Now, now, let's not start trading insults again." He gave her a half smile. "I shall begin our new détente by telling *you* that you look hardly a day older than you did. You are still beautiful."

Kitty touched her graying hair self-consciously. "I know you're being kind, but I appreciate the gesture."

A silence hung between them as a lifetime of memories flashed before their eyes.

"So here we are," Drummond said eventually.

"Yes, here we are," she echoed.

"And I must tell you, in case I don't get another chance, that there has not been a day in almost forty years when I have not thought about you."

"In anger, probably." Kitty gave him a wry smile.

"Yes," he chuckled, "but only in connection with my own impetuous behavior, which has rendered my life since nothing but a hollow sham."

"You look very well on it, I must say. I can hardly believe that you are over sixty."

"My body knows it," he sighed. "These days I am beset with the vagaries of age. My back aches like the dickens after a night out on the ground, and my knees creak every time I climb onto my nag. This is a life for a young man, Kitty, and I'm not that any longer."

"What will you do?"

"I have absolutely no idea. What do clapped-out drovers do in their old age? Come to think of it, I hardly know a single one. We've normally all copped it by fifty. Been bitten by a snake, died of dysentery, or ended up on the end of a black man's spear. I've had the luck of the nine blind, in that regard anyway. Perhaps it's because I gave up caring if I lived or died after I last saw you, so the old bugger upstairs has kept me alive to punish me. Well." He slapped his thighs. "There we go. How about you?"

"I'm leaving Australia for good after I return to Adelaide."

"Where are you going?"

"Home, or at least, to Europe. I've bought an apartment in Italy. Like you, I feel Australia is a young man's—or woman's—game."

"Ah, Kitty, how did we grow so old?" Drummond shook his head. "I still remember you at eighteen, singing at the top of your voice in the Edinburgh Castle Hotel, as drunk as you like."

"And whose fault was that?" She eyed him.

"Mine, of course. How is Charlie? I know a fellow from the mission at Hermannsburg who said he'd been to school with him and hoped he'd come to visit him one day."

"You must be talking about Ted Strehlow."

"I am. The fella is mad as a cobra with a migraine, but I meet him occasionally on his travels in the outback. He's a self-fashioned anthropologist, studying Aboriginal culture."

"Yes, I met him once in Adelaide. Sadly, you cannot have seen Mr. Strehlow recently. Charlie died seven years ago in the Japanese attack on Roebuck Bay."

"Kitty, I didn't know!" Drummond walked toward her and sat down on the bed next to her. "Good God, I didn't know. Forgive me for my insensitivity."

"So"—Kitty was determined not to cry—"I have nothing to keep me here in Australia, which is why I'm going home." After a pause, she looked at him. "It's so very wrong, isn't it?"

"What is?"

"That you and I should still be sitting here on the earth, while my boy—and so many others we loved—are no longer with us."

"Yes." His hand reached to cover hers.

Kitty felt its warmth traveling through her skin and realized his was the last male hand that had touched her in such a gesture for almost forty years. She wound her own hand around it.

"You never remarried?" he probed.

"No."

"Surely there were plenty of suitors?"

"Some, yes, but as you can imagine, they were all fortune hunters. You?"

"Good God, no! Who would have me?"

Another long silence hung between them as they sat there, hands clasped, each contemplating the secrets they kept from each other, but cherishing the moment they were sharing.

"I really must retire, or I'll be good for nothing in the morning," Kitty said eventually. Yet her body made no move to release his hand from hers. "Do you remember Alkina?" she asked into the silence.

"I do."

"She disappeared the night before Charlie's twenty-first birthday. And then Camira did the same a few months later when I was away in Europe."

"Really?"

"Yes. Fred left too after that. He went walkabout and never returned. And I haven't had sight nor sound of any of them since. I must have done something very bad in my life. Everyone I love leaves me."

"I didn't. You sent *me* away, remember?"

"Drummond, you know that I had no choice. I—"

"Yes, and I will regret my actions until my dying day. Rest assured I've had long enough to do that already."

"We were both culpable, Drummond, make no mistake."

"It was good to feel alive, though, wasn't it?"

"It was, yes."

"Those memories have kept me going on many a long, cold night out in the Never Never. Kitty . . ."

"Yes?"

"I have to ask this." Drummond ran a hand through his hair, uncharacteristically nervous. "I . . . heard rumors that you were with child after I left."

"I . . . How did you know?"

"You know how news travels in the outback. Kitty, was the baby mine?"

"Yes." The word came out in an enormous bubble of released tension, as Kitty finally voiced the secret she'd kept for all these years.

"There is no doubt?"

"None. I had . . . bled after Andrew left." A faint blush rose to Kitty's cheeks. "Before you and I were—"

"Yes. So." Drummond swallowed hard. "What happened to our baby?"

"I lost him. For seven months, I felt him inside me, a part of you, a part of us, but I went into labor early and he was stillborn."

"It was a boy?"

"Yes. I called him Stefan, after your father. I felt that was right under the circumstances. He's buried in Broome cemetery."

Kitty sobbed then. Huge, gulping, ugly tears as her body expressed all that she'd held inside her for so long. To the only other person on the earth who could possibly understand. "Our baby son and Charlie, both gone to ashes. Good grief! Sometimes the days have seemed so dark I've wondered what the point of it all is." Kitty used the bedsheet to wipe her eyes. "There now, I'm being self-indulgent and I have no right to be living when my two sons are dead."

"My God, Kitty . . ." Drummond put his arm around her trembling shoulder. "What havoc love can wreak on us sad humans."

"A little love," Kitty murmured, her head lying against his chest, "and it destroyed us both."

"You must take comfort from the fact that nothing in life is quite that simple. If Andrew had not sent me to collect the Roseate Pearl, it would be him that had returned to you alive, and me lying at the bottom of the ocean. We must try to be responsible for our own actions, but we cannot be responsible for the actions of others. They have an insidious way of wrapping like bindweed around our own destinies. Nothing on earth is separate from the other."

"That's awfully profound," whispered Kitty with the ghost of a smile.

"And thankfully, I believe it to be true. It is all that has kept me from throwing myself off the top of Ayers Rock."

"But where has it left us? Neither of us have family to pass any of our wisdom on to. For the Mercers, it is the end of the line."

There was a long pause before he replied. "Kitty, I beg you to trust me one last time. There is somewhere I should take you before you leave. You must come with me tomorrow."

"No, Drummond, I have spent the last forty years of my life wishing to go to Ayers Rock and I will do so in a few hours' time. Nothing can dissuade me."

"What if I swear I'll take you there the day after? Besides, it will mean you don't have to rise until eight, given it is already past one in the morning. I beseech you, Kitty. You must come."

"Please, Drummond, swear to me it is not simply a wild goose chase?"

"It is not, but equally, we must go as soon as we can. Before it's too late."

Kitty looked at his grave expression. "Where are we going?"

"To Hermannsburg. There is someone you need to see."

32

"Missus M! It's past eight o'clock! Wasn't we meant to get up at four? You said you'd come and wake me."

Kitty stirred, seeing Sarah's anxious face hovering above her.

"There's been a change of plan," she said hoarsely as she came to. "Mr. D is driving us out to Hermannsburg today."

"That's good then, is it?" Sarah waited for confirmation.

"Yes, it is."

"What is Hermannsburg?" Sarah asked as she folded the clothes that Kitty had dropped on the floor last night.

"It's a Christian mission. Mr. D felt it would be too hot to take the trip out to Ayers Rock today. He says Hermannsburg is far closer."

"I don't like God-botherers," said Sarah. "They used to tell us stories of the little Lord Jesus at the orphanage, said that we should pray to him for our salvation. All I could think was that he didn't last that long, did 'e, miss? For all that he was the son of God." Sarah stood at the end of the bed with her hands on her hips. "What time are we leaving?"

"At nine o'clock."

"Then I'll go and get you a fresh basin of water so as you can have a good wash before we leave, 'cause the Lord knows when we'll get another. I like your friend, by the way. It's good we have someone protecting us out 'ere, isn't it?"

"Yes." Kitty suppressed a smile.

"D'you think he'd let me steer the cart for a bit? I've always loved 'orses, ever since the rag an' bone man came around to me auntie's and 'e gave me a ride."

"I'm sure that could be arranged," Kitty said, and fell back onto her pillow as Sarah left the room.

"What am I doing?" she moaned as the events of only a few hours ago came back to her.

You're living, Kitty, for the first time in years . . .

Downstairs, she forced down a breakfast of bread and strong coffee as Sarah chatted away opposite her.

"Mr. D said he'll meet us outside when we've finished breakfast. We're to take a change of clothes each because of the dust, but he's seeing to the supplies. I'm glad 'e's coming, Missus M, 'e looks like a man who knows 'is way around. It's a bit like the Wild West out here, in't it? I once saw a flick that showed horses galloping across the desert. Never thought I'd see it for meself."

Outside, Drummond waited with a pony and cart, and the two women clambered up onto the board bench. Kitty mentioned that Sarah wished to drive the pony at some point and put her firmly between them.

"Right. Off we go." Drummond gently snicked the pony's back and they trotted off along the high street.

Kitty was only too happy to let Drummond regale Sarah with his adventures in the outback. She took in the scenery, which, as they headed out of the town, became a vibrant red, the mountain range a hazy violet behind it. Sarah constantly questioned him, and he patiently pointed out the varieties of shrubs, trees, and animals as she sucked up information like spinifex sucking up water during a drought.

"And that over there is a ghost gum." Drummond indicated a white-barked tree in the distance. "It's sacred to the Aboriginals, and you can use the bark to treat colds . . ."

As the sun beat down, Kitty was glad of her cotton bonnet with its net veil, and eventually the rhythmic clopping of the pony's sure footsteps lulled her into a doze.

"Turn left here."

She was pulled back to consciousness by Drummond's voice.

"No, left, Sarah."

The pony lurched and Kitty roused herself to see Sarah steering the cart into a drive, beyond which stood a number of whitewashed buildings.

"Welcome to Hermannsburg, sleepyhead." Drummond grinned as he offered his hand to help her down. "Your Sarah has the makings of a fine horsewoman. You didn't even stir when I handed the reins to her."

"Oh! An' I loved it, Missus M! Wish I could sit on his back." Sarah looked plaintively up at Drummond.

"There's plenty of horses here, I'm sure someone will give you a trot around before we leave. Now, let's see if the pastor is about."

Drummond led them past a cluster of huts toward a central area which was humming with life. Most of the faces were Aboriginal, the girls of assorted ages all dressed in white, which Kitty found rather ridiculous given the red dust that had already blown up onto her own clothes. There were men sitting outside a big open shed, stretching large swaths of beige cowhide and hanging them up to dry in the sun.

"That's the tannery; the mission sells the leather on. There's the schoolhouse, the cookhouse, the chapel . . ."

"Goodness, it's a village!" Kitty followed his pointed finger around the huts, hearing the sweet sound of young voices singing a hymn inside the chapel.

"It is indeed. And a lifeline for the local Arrernte people."

"Those children," Kitty said, pointing at a group of little ones being led from the schoolroom. "Have they been brought here against their mothers' will because they are half castes?"

"No. The Protectorate is not welcome here. These people come of their own free will to learn about Jesus, but, more important, to get a good meal inside their bellies," Drummond replied with a chuckle. "Many of them have been here for years. The pastor allows them to practice their own culture alongside Christianity."

As she heard the sound of the children's laughter, Kitty was filled with emotion. "It's the most beautiful sight I've ever seen: two cultures working in harmony together. Perhaps there's hope for Australia after all."

"Yes. And look who it is over there." Drummond indicated a tall, bulky man lugging a table into a hut. "Hermannsburg's most famous son, Albert Namatjira. We're lucky to catch him. He's often out walkabout painting—but his daughter Hazel died here in childbirth some weeks ago, and he and his wife have decided to move into a hut inside the mission."

"That's Namatjira?" Kitty squinted her eyes against the sun, awed that the most famous Aboriginal artist in Australia was standing only a few feet away from her.

"It is. Interesting fella. If you're a good girl, I'll introduce you later on. Now, let's go and find the pastor."

They walked across to a low bungalow set apart from the others and Drummond knocked on the door. A short, broadly built white man opened the door and greeted them with a smile. Despite the heat, he was dressed in black robes and a white clerical collar, and a pair of round rimless glasses rested on his large nose.

"Mr. D, what an unexpected pleasure," he said, thumping Drummond on the back heartily. He spoke English with a strong German accent.

"Pastor Albrecht, this is Mrs. Kitty Mercer from Adelaide and late of Broome," said Drummond. "She was very interested to see Hermannsburg for herself, having heard of it through her son, who was at school and university with Ted."

"Indeed?" Pastor Albrecht's eyes swept over Kitty as if he was assessing her for a place in the kingdom of heaven. "I'm afraid Ted is not here. He is currently based in Canberra working on a research project at the university, but it is my pleasure to welcome you, Mrs. Mercer. And the young lady?"

"This is Sarah, a friend of Mrs. Mercer's," Drummond replied.

"How d'you do, yer honor." Sarah, looking nervously at the clerical robes, dipped a curtsy.

"Are you thirsty? My wife has just made a jug of quandong cordial." Albrecht, walking with a slight limp, led them through to a small sitting room, its Edwardian furniture looking out of place in the simple hut. Once they had all been handed a glass of sweet pink cordial, they sat down.

"So, how have things been here since my last visit?" Drummond asked.

"The usual ups and downs," said the pastor. "Thank the Lord that we have not had another drought, but Albert has had his problems, as you know. There was also a break-in some weeks ago. The robbers took everything from the safe, and I'm afraid to say that the tin box you gave me all those years ago when you brought Francis went with them. I do hope there was nothing particularly valuable in it. Francis told me his grandmother was relieved, for some reason."

Kitty watched Drummond blanch. "No, it was nothing of value," he said lightly.

"Well, you may be pleased to hear that justice was done. It was a couple of cattle rustlers who'd been robbing the safes of stations around here. They were found shot dead near Haasts Bluff. Whoever killed them made off with the stolen goods. My apologies, Mr. D."

"So, the curse continues . . . ," Drummond murmured.

There was a knock on the door. A young woman popped her head around it, and spoke in German to the pastor.

"Ah, the choir is about to sing!" said Albrecht. "Yes, we will take a walk across, thank you, Mary. And could you also find Francis for me? He was helping Albert move his furniture in earlier."

"Of course," Drummond said, smiling, "where else would Francis be?"

As the four of them walked across the courtyard toward the chapel, Drummond held the pastor back and the two men talked in low voices behind Kitty and Sarah. When they arrived on the doorstep of the chapel, Kitty noted Drummond's grave expression.

"Please." The pastor indicated a rough wooden pew at the back of the church and the four of them sat down. The chapel was basic, its only decoration a large painting of Christ on the cross. Standing in front of it were perhaps thirty immaculately dressed young girls and boys, their faces eager with expectation as they waited for their pastor to indicate they should begin.

Kitty closed her eyes as the beautiful tune of "Abide with Me" was sung in German by the Aboriginal choir. At the end, the four of them clapped enthusiastically.

"I'm not one for hymns meself, but that singing were lovely, Missus M, even if I couldn't understand a word they were saying," said Sarah.

"*Danke schön*, Mary, *Kinder*." The pastor stood up and the three of them followed suit. Kitty saw that an old woman in a wooden wheelchair had been pushed to the back of the chapel by a gray-haired man. With them was a breathtakingly handsome young man, his hair a rich mahogany, his skin the color of butterscotch, and with enormous eyes that, as Kitty drew closer, she saw were a startling and unusual blue, with flecks of amber in the irises. They were not, however, looking at her, but fixed on Sarah next to her. Sarah was staring back just as blatantly.

"What a beautiful young man," murmured Kitty as they waited for the choir to file out ahead of them.

"He is indeed. And a very talented artist too. Francis has followed Namatjira about like a puppy ever since he could toddle," Drummond said.

Kitty dragged her eyes away from Francis and glanced down at the woman in the wheelchair. The woman looked up at her and Kitty had to grasp the back of the pew to steady herself. Even though the woman was desperately thin, her skin streaked with lines of age, Kitty knew the face as well as her own.

"Good grief, it can't be!" she whispered to Drummond. Then she looked at the old man who had pushed the wheelchair in. "And that's Fred!"

"It is," he agreed, "but Camira is why I have brought you here. She doesn't have much time left. Go and say hello."

"Camira?" Kitty walked toward her, her legs trembling. "Is it really you?"

"Missus Kitty?" Camira whispered back, equally startled. Fred gawped at her from behind the wheelchair.

"Now, Francis, this is Sarah," said Drummond, watching emotion cross both women's features. "She has a passion for horses—would you take her and give her a riding lesson?"

"Of course, Mr. D." Francis spoke halting English, but his expression as he beckoned Sarah to follow him told everyone how much of a pleasure it would be.

"Mr. D and I have some business to conduct," Pastor Albrecht said. "Fred, why don't you join us? We shall leave you two ladies alone."

Once the men had gone, Kitty bent down and put her arms tenderly around her dearest friend.

"Where did you go? I missed you so terribly, I . . ."

"I missum you too, Missus Kitty, but things happen, don't they?"

Kitty released the emaciated body and took Camira's hand. "What 'things' happened?"

"First you tellum me how you here. Mister Drum come-a find you?"

"No, it seems I found him. Or we found each other."

Kitty explained how they'd met as swiftly as she could, desperate to know why Camira had left her all those years ago.

"See? Dem up in heaven wantum you two together."

"It's not like that. I leave permanently for Europe very soon," Kitty said hurriedly. "And no one must know the truth, Camira."

"Who here would I tellum?" Camira gave a hoarse laugh. "Whattum Mister Drum say to you?"

"Absolutely nothing—not even that you were here. Please, dearest Camira, tell me why you and Alkina left."

"Okay, but it longa story, Missus Kitty, so you sittum down and I tella to you."

Kitty did so. Between halting pauses for breath, Kitty learned the truth of her son's relationship with Camira's daughter.

"God, oh God." She buried her face in her hands. "Why on earth did they not come to me? I would have sanctioned their marriage."

"Yessum, but my daughter, she-a strong-willed woman. She not wanta live in whitefella world an' be treated like mangy dingo from street." Camira sighed. "She love Charlie, Missus Kitty, so much she leavem him. You understand?"

"I do, of course I do, but I could have announced their engagement and the whole town would have seen they had my backing."

There was a pause as Camira's eyes found the painting of Jesus at the front of the church. "Missus Kitty, there something else that made her run."

"What?"

Camira's expressive eyes begged Kitty to think, to say the words for her.

"No! You mean she was pregnant?"

"Yessum. Four months when she go walkabout."

"Did Charlie know?"

"Yessum, he know. He wanta go find her, beggum me to tell him where she go, but I do not know. After you went away to Europe, he feel he cannot leave. One night, I knowum she dead. Charlie and me, we cry together."

"Oh God, where did she die?"

"Out there, in Never Never." Camira rested her head on Kitty's arm. "Love, it causem the big trouble. Mister Drum, he come all the way to Broome to see me an' tell me 'bout it. An' I go with him here. Den Fred turnem up few month later." Camira rolled her eyes. "I smellum him before I see him."

"But if Alkina died, then why . . ."

"She die, yessum, but baby alive. Mister Drum, he find baby with Ghan camel men, an' bring him to Hermannsburg. He savem baby's life. He a miracle man." Camira nodded vehemently. "Ancestors helpum him find my grandson."

Kitty's head was spinning with what Camira was telling her. There were so many questions she wanted answers to, she hardly knew what to ask next.

"But how did he know the baby was Alkina's?"

"Thattum bad pearl. My daughter once see me check that it still buried where I leave it. She takem it to sell for money for her and baby. Mister Drum, he see bad pearl with baby and baby's eyes. Dey like his mum's. He comun see me an' bringum me here to care for baby."

"So you didn't tell Charlie that he was a father?" Kitty tried to control the anger rising inside her. "That my son's baby was alive? Good God, Camira, why did you not tell *me*?!"

"Maybe I makem mistake, but Charlie friend with Elise, an' I thinkum best he not know. He running big business, an' my daughter dead. How could he bringum up baby? You away in Europe. Yessum I hear later Charlie die too. So sad, but now they up there together with Ancestors. So, everything turnum out for best, yes?"

Camira's eyes begged Kitty to agree, but she stood up and began to pace up and down the narrow aisle of the chapel. "I really don't know just now, Camira. I feel as though I wasn't given any choice in the matter. I feel . . ." Kitty wrung her hands. "Totally deceived."

"Missus Kitty, we all lovem you, we wanta do best thing."

"How many wrong decisions come out of love . . . ," Kitty sighed. As she did her best to control herself in front of a woman *she* loved and who, from her obvious frailty, was facing her last few weeks on earth, another thought came to her.

"What happened to the baby?" she asked, bracing herself for more bad news.

Camira's features finally gathered themselves into a wide smile. "He sick as baby, but now he big, strong boy. I do-um best to bring him up good for both of us." She chuckled then. "Missus Kitty, you just met our grandson. His name Francis."

Drummond watched Kitty pushing Camira's wheelchair toward the stables, uncertain how she would have reacted to the news. He turned his head at the shrieks of laughter emanating from Sarah as she did her best to steer the reluctant horse around in a circle, with Francis holding the end of the rope below her.

"He keeps wanting to go straight ahead! Can we, please?"

"Only if I climb up with you," Francis called to her.

With the past and the present about to collide, Drummond pondered whether Sarah's words were an apt metaphor. So many humans wandered around in circles, wishing for a future they were too fearful to seize.

"Come on then! Jump aboard!" Sarah shouted.

Francis released the rope and swung his long body onto the horse behind her.

If nothing else, he knew those two *would* seize it.

"I tellum her, Mister Drum, I don't think she very happy," Camira murmured as Fred took the wheelchair from Kitty's shaking grasp. She greeted him, then stared at the young man on horseback.

"Maybe I diddum wrong thing," Camira continued as they watched Francis doing his best to impress a lady. With a hand tucked proprietorially around Sarah's waist, his strong thighs controlling the movements of the horse, he set it to a brisk canter. Expletives fell from Sarah's mouth, but the onlookers could all see their sheer joy in being alive, with their future ahead of them.

Kitty turned to Drummond and finally spoke. "I believe I am watching my grandson career around a field with my lady's maid?"

"You are, yes. Are you angry?"

"When a decision is taken out of your hands—when one is left completely in the dark—of course there is anger."

"Forgive her, Kitty, Camira only did what she thought best at the time." Drummond braced himself for her verbal onslaught. Yet, as her gaze fell once more onto Francis and Sarah, Kitty was silent.

Eventually she said, "Thank you."

"*What?*"

"The polite response would be 'pardon me,' as you well know, but given that you apparently saved our grandson's life ..." Kitty put her hand to Camira's shoulder. "I can overlook your appalling use of language just this once."

"Glad to hear it," he said and gave her a smile.

"I can see Charlie in him already," Kitty breathed, her blue eyes bright with unshed tears. "His energy, his kindness ..." Then she lifted a palm to Drummond's cheek. "I have made so many mistakes in my life—"

"Hush, Kitty." Drummond caught her hand and kissed it. He pressed his forehead to hers. "I love you," he whispered. "I've never stopped."

"I fear I feel the same," she whispered back.

"It's time now, isn't it? For us."

"Yes," Kitty replied. "I rather believe it is."

Camira turned her head and watched as Mister D's arms encircled Kitty tenderly and held her close to him. She looked to the field where her grandson was whooping with joy as he let the girl take the reins of the horse, holding her safe to him as she cantered them around the field.

Camira closed her eyes and smiled.

"I diddum the best I could."

CeCe

Alice Springs, Northern Territory

January 2008

Aboriginal symbol for a resting place

33

So, that's the story of how I met my Sarah. It sounds rather ridiculous, but it really was love at first sight for both of us. You could say we rode off into the sunset that very first moment we met." Francis's eyes misted at the memory.

"She didn't go back to Adelaide with Kitty?"

"No. She stayed at Hermannsburg with me. They were glad to have her, what with her sewing skills." Francis indicated the embroidered cushion covers. "And her natural way with the young ones. She was born to be a mother. The irony was, it took us years to have our own child."

"*My* mother?" I whispered.

"Yes. Sadly, the doctors told us she was the only child we could have. We both adored her." Francis struggled to suppress a yawn. "Do excuse me, it's getting late."

Before he made a move to stand up, there was one more question I had to know the answer to before I could sleep. "What about Kitty and Drummond?"

"Now, there *was* a happy ending. He went with her when she left for Europe. God knows how he acquired a passport to do it, given he'd been declared officially dead, but knowing him, he probably paid for a forged one. You could do that kind of thing in the old days." Francis smiled. "They made their home in Florence, where no one knew their past, and lived happily together for the rest of their lives. Kitty never did get to Ayers Rock, mind you. She stayed on at Hermannsburg until just before my grandmother died."

"Did Kitty tell you that day that *she* was your grandmother too? And that Drummond was your great-uncle?"

"No, she left that to Camira, who told me the whole story on her deathbed a few days later. After they went to Italy, Drummond and Kitty kept in touch regularly with Sarah and me, and in 1978, when she herself died, Kitty left us her apartment in Florence. We sold the apartment and bought this place with the proceeds, with a view to retiring here. The Broome house Kitty had left in a trust for our daughter, along with her stocks and shares, which had grown over the years to a sizeable sum."

"What happened to Ralph Jr. and his family at Alicia Hall?" I queried.

"Dear Great-Uncle Ralph," said Francis with a smile. "He was a good man; trustworthy and steadfast to the last. His family always welcomed us at Alicia Hall on the rare occasions we traveled to Adelaide. Little Eddie did rather well for himself too. He blossomed under the tender care of Ruth and Ralph, and once he knew he was safe, he began to speak. Sarah, who kept in touch with him to her dying day, always said that he hadn't shut up since! He was as bright as a button and became a very successful barrister. He only retired last year. Perhaps one day, I could take you to visit him at Alicia Hall."

"Yeah, maybe. So . . ." I needed to ask the question. "Is my birth mum dead too?"

"She is, yes. I'm sorry, Celaeno."

"Well, I suppose you can't grieve for someone you've never known, can you?" I said eventually. "And my dad? Who was he?"

"He was called Toba and your mother met him while we were still living in Papunya, when she was just sixteen. Papunya was a village full of creative types, and a hub for the local Pintupi and Luritja Aboriginal communities. Your mother fell in love with him but he was an . . . unsuitable man. He was a talented Aboriginal painter, but far too keen on his grog and other women. When she announced she was pregnant with you, we"—Francis's fingers curled around each other in tension—"suggested that she shouldn't go through with the pregnancy. I'm sorry, Celaeno, but that's the truth of it."

I swallowed hard. "I understand. I really do. It was like your history playing out all over again."

"Of course, your mother refused to listen to us. If we wouldn't give permission for her to marry her lover, she threatened that they would elope. She always was impulsive, but I suppose that trait runs in the family." He gave me a wry smile. "Sadly, neither Sarah nor I thought she would go through with it, so we stood firm. A day later, the two of them left and"—his voice broke—"we never saw her again."

"That must've been really awful for you. Was there no way of finding her?"

"As you have already learned, it's quite easy to disappear here. But everyone was on the lookout for her, and for years Sarah and I trekked all over the outback following up on possible sightings. Then one day, we simply couldn't take it any longer, and decided to finally give up."

"I understand. Too much pain when the leads came to nothing."

"Exactly, but then when Sarah became seriously ill two years ago, she begged me to have another try, so I engaged a private detective. Six months after she died, I got a call telling me he'd found a woman in Broome who claimed she'd been present at your birth. I admit to not having been enthused with hope—I'd been up too many blind alleys before. But nevertheless, this woman knew your mother's name: Elizabeth, after Sarah's beloved English queen."

"Elizabeth . . ." I tried the name out loud for the first time.

"This woman had been a nurse at the hospital in Broome and I was able to see the date that Lizzie had arrived there in the hospital records, apparently in the throes of childbirth. The dates fitted exactly."

"Right. Did this woman mention my father?"

"She said that Lizzie had been alone. Remember I told you earlier that Kitty had left the Broome house to Lizzie? Your mother had visited it with us and probably thought it was the perfect love nest for her and her waster of a boyfriend. I can only assume that he dumped her somewhere between Papunya and Broome. In her condition, and given the rift at home, your mother probably felt she had no alternative but to continue to Broome alone."

"So what happened after she gave birth to me?"

Francis stood up, walked over to a bureau, and pulled out a file. "Here is your mother's death certificate. It's dated seven days after you were born. Lizzie had a severe postpartum infection. The nurse told me she just wasn't physically strong enough to fight it. Forgive me, Celaeno, there was no easy way to tell you this."

"It's okay," I murmured as I stared at the certificate. It was past two in the morning by now, and the words were a mass of jumping squiggles. "What about me?"

"Well, that's where the story gets a little better. The nurse told me that after your mother died, they kept you for as long as they could, hoping they could find a family who would adopt you. It was obvious when I spoke to her that the nurse had a fondness for you. She said you were a very pretty baby."

"Pretty?" I blurted out. "Me?"

"Apparently so," Francis said with a smile. "However, after a couple of months they had no choice but to make preparations to hand you over to a local orphanage. Sad to say, even twenty-seven years ago, there was no one who wanted to adopt a mixed-race baby. Just as the paperwork was being processed, she said that a gentleman in expensive clothes turned up at the hospital. From what she recalls, he'd come to Broome to look for a relative, but had found the house in question empty. A neighbor had informed him that the former owner had died, but there had been a young girl living there for a few weeks. The neighbor also told him the girl had been pregnant and he should try the hospital. When the nurse met the man and told him Lizzie had died and left you behind, he offered to adopt you on the spot."

"Pa Salt," I gasped. "What was he doing in Broome? Was he looking for Kitty?"

"The woman couldn't remember his name," said Francis, "but given the circumstances, she suggested he took you back to Europe with him and completed any adoption formalities there. The man left her the name of a lawyer in Switzerland." Francis rifled through the file. "A Mr. Georg Hoffman."

"Good old Georg," I said, disappointed that Pa had managed to hide his true identity yet again.

"It was Mr. Hoffman I wrote to when I was trying to trace you. I told him you'd been left a legacy—the money and property that Kitty had put in a trust for your mum, which was rightfully yours as Lizzie's daughter. Once the Broome house was sold, combined with the proceeds from the stocks and shares, it amounted to a healthy sum, as you know. Mr. Hoffman wrote back to confirm that his client had indeed adopted you, and that you were well. He promised any funds would be passed on to you directly. I directed the Adelaide solicitor to transfer the money and I also gave him a photograph of me with Namatjira, to be sent alongside the payment."

"Why not a photo of Sarah and Lizzie?"

"Celaeno, I didn't want to disturb your life if you didn't want to be found. By the same token, I knew that if you *did* want to find me here in Australia, it wouldn't be long until someone recognized Namatjira and his name on the car in the photograph, and pointed you in the direction of Hermannsburg." Francis gave a small smile of pleasure. "My plan worked!"

"It did, but I wasn't going to come at first, you know."

"I'd already decided that if you hadn't turned up within the year, I would contact Georg Hoffman and come and find you. You saved me and my old bones the trouble. Celaeno." He took my hands and held them. "It's been so much for you to take in, and a lot of it has been upsetting. Are you all right?"

"Yeah." I took a deep breath. "I'm glad I know everything now. It means I can return to London."

"Right."

I could see he thought I meant that I'd changed my mind. "Don't worry," I added quickly, "as I said earlier, it's only loose ends that need to be tied up before I move here permanently."

The grip on my hands tightened. "You're definitely coming to live in Australia?"

"Yeah, I mean, I reckon that you and me should stick together. We're the last of the Mercer line, aren't we? The survivors."

"Yes, we are. Although I never want you to feel that you owe me—or your past—anything, Celaeno. If you have a life back in London, don't do the wrong thing out of guilt. The past is gone. It's the future that matters."

"I know, but I belong here," I said, feeling more certain than I'd ever felt about anything in my life. "The past is who I am."

I woke up the next morning feeling like I had a really bad hangover—caused by information overload, not alcohol. I lay in the room with the pretty flowered curtains under the patchwork quilt that no doubt my grandmother Sarah had sewn over many a hot and sweaty night there in the Alice.

I closed my eyes then, thinking of my momentous decision of yesterday, and the weird dream I'd just had, and my hands tingled. It felt like all the angst and pain that had made me needed to be set free so it didn't poison me from within.

And I knew how to do it.

I got out of bed and pulled on one of my grandmother's blouses and a pair of her shorts that were flared at the bottom and made my legs look like two lamp stands that were too thick for the lampshades at the top of them.

Francis was eating breakfast in the kitchen at a table that was set for two.

"Do you by any chance have a spare canvas? Like, the biggest you've got?" I asked him.

"Of course. Follow me."

I was grateful he understood my urgency without explanation and I followed him to a greenhouse that he used as a storeroom. I set up my canvas and easel in a shady part of the back garden, and Francis lent me his special sable brushes. I selected the right size and began to mix the paints. As soon as the brush touched the canvas, that strange feeling that sometimes happened when I was painting came over me, and the next time I looked up, the canvas was full and the sky was dark.

"Celaeno, it's time for you to come inside," Francis called from the back door. "The mosquitoes will eat you alive out here."

"Don't look! It's not finished yet!" I made a pathetic attempt to cover the enormous canvas with my hands, although he'd probably seen it through the sitting room window already.

He walked across the lawn to put his arms around me and hug me tight. "It's a need, isn't it?"

"Absolutely," I said with a yawn. "I couldn't stop. This is for you, by the way."

"Thank you, I will treasure it."

I'd been sitting in the same spot for a very long time and my legs weren't working properly, so Francis helped me up and let me lean on him as if I were some old person.

"It's probably terrible," I said as I slumped exhausted into an armchair in the sitting room.

"Perhaps it is, but I already know where I'm going to hang it." He pointed to the space over the mantelpiece. "You need some food?" he asked me.

"I'm too tired to eat, but I could murder a cup of tea before I go to bed."

He brought it to me, then propped up my new canvas in front of the fireplace and sat down to study it.

"Have you decided what you will call it?"

"*The Pearl Fishers*," I said, surprising myself, as I was usually crap at choosing names. "It's about, well . . . our family. I had a dream I was in Broome, swimming in the sea. There were lots of us and we were all looking for a pearl and—"

"So is that a moon in the center?" Francis broke in as he studied the painting. "You know my mother was called Alkina, which means 'moon.'"

"Maybe I did, maybe I didn't," I mused, "but the white circle represents the beauty and power of female fertility and nature, the endless cycle of life and death. In other words, it's our family history."

"I love it," said Francis, studying the big, sweeping shapes of the sea below the moon, dotted with small, pearly spots lying beneath the waves on the seabed. "And already your technique is improving. This is seriously impressive for a day's painting."

"Thanks, but it's a work in progress," I said, yawning again. "I think I'll head to bed now."

"Before you go, I wanted you to have something." He reached into his pocket and drew out a small jewelry box. "I've held on to it ever since Sarah died, but I've been waiting to give it to you."

He placed it in my hand, and I opened it nervously. Inside it was a small ring, set with a smooth amber stone. "It's the very same one my father, Charlie, gave to Alkina the night before she left him," said Francis.

I held the ring to the light and the amber gleamed a rich honey color. A tiny ant was suspended in its center, as if it had just been caught out on a stroll. I could hardly believe that it was thousands of years old. *Or* that I'd had that vivid dream about the little insect sitting in the palm of my hand. It had looked just like this one.

"Camira brought it with her to Hermannsburg after Alkina died," Francis continued. "And on the day I told her that I wanted to marry Sarah, she gave it to me."

"Wow." I took out the ring and slid it onto the fourth finger of my right hand, where it winked up at me. "Thank you, Francis."

"No need to thank me," he said, beaming at me. "Now, you'd best get to bed before you fall asleep right here. Good night, Celaeno."

"Night, Francis."

We drove into the town the next morning, as Francis had suggested I take the canvas I'd painted out bush to show Mirrin, and because I needed to go to a travel agent and book my flight home.

"Is it a return?" the woman behind the computer screen asked me.

"Yes," I said firmly.

"And the return date?"

"I need about a week there, so that would be the sixth of February," I said.

"Are you sure that's long enough?" said Francis. "You should take as much time as you need. I can cover the extra cost on a flexible ticket for you."

"I only need a week," I reassured him, and went ahead with the booking. Although, it turned out that he *did* have to pay, because my credit card had finally decided to conk out from exhaustion. It had obviously reached its limit and I couldn't pay it off until I got home and went to my bank. I could have died of shame when it was declined; I'd always made it my golden rule never to borrow money.

"It's no problem, really, Celaeno," he said as we left the travel agent with the ticket, "it's all going to come to you eventually anyway. Think of it as an advance payment."

"You've already given me so much," I moaned in embarrassment. "Maybe whatever Mirrin offers me for the painting can cover it."

"As you wish," he replied.

At the gallery, Mirrin cast her eyes over the canvas and nodded in approval. "It's very good."

"Better than good." Francis eyed her. "I'd say it was exceptional."

"We'll try it on the wall for a thousand dollars."

"Double that," Francis countered. "And my granddaughter will expect sixty-five percent of the price."

"We never give more than sixty, Mr. Abraham, you know that."

"All right then, we'll take it to the Many Hands Gallery down the road." Francis made to pick up the canvas, but Mirrin stopped him.

"As it's you, but you're not to tell the other artists." She flinched suddenly and put a hand to the large bump of her belly, covered in a luminous kaftan. "The little fella is getting ready to come," she said as she rubbed the side of her stomach. "And I still haven't found anyone to replace me. At this rate, I'll have the baby at my desk!"

A thought sprang into my head. "You need someone to cover your maternity leave?"

"Yes, but it's so hard finding the right person. The artists need to know they can trust ya, and you have to be able to understand what they're creating and encourage them. That, and you have to be able to negotiate—though, luckily, not everyone is as killer as you, Mr. Abraham." Mirrin raised an eyebrow.

"I might know someone," I said, as casually as my excitement would allow. "Do you remember the girl that came in with me a couple of weeks ago?"

"Chrissie? The lady who bargained nearly as hard as your grandfather?"

"Yes. She studied history of art at uni," I exaggerated, "and she knows everything there is to know about Aboriginal art, especially about Albert Namatjira. And loads of other art too," I added for good measure.

"Is she working in a gallery now?"

"No, she's in the tourist industry, so she's used to handling foreigners and, as you know, is from an indigenous background, so the artists would like her."

"Does she speak Arrernte?" Mirrin's face had brightened.

"You'd have to ask her," I fudged, "but she definitely speaks Yawuru. And as you saw, she wouldn't take any messing when it came to the sale."

"Is she looking for a job then?"

"Yes."

I saw Francis was watching me with amusement as I sold this person he'd only briefly heard of before.

"Not gonna lie to you, Celaeno, the money's not good," Mirrin said.

"No one's in art for the money, are they? They do it for love," I replied.

"Some of us are." She eyed my grandfather. "Well, ya tell her to come and see me. Fast," she said as she flinched again. "I'm here every day this week."

"I will. Can you write down your number for me? I'll get her to give you a call to arrange it."

She did so, and I left the gallery in high excitement.

"So, exactly who is this Chrissie?" Francis asked me as we walked back to the truck.

"A friend of mine," I said as I hopped onto the passenger seat.

"Where does she live?"

"Broome."

"Isn't that a little far to commute to work here every day?" he asked as he reversed out of our parking space and we headed home.

"Yes, but if she got the job, I'm sure she'd be prepared to move. She loved it when we were here together a couple of weeks ago. She's an absolutely brilliant person, like, she's totally inspirational and so passionate about art. You'd love her. I know you would."

"If you love her, Celaeno, I'm sure I will too."

"I'm going to ring her the minute I get home, tell her to call Mirrin. She'll have to fly down here as soon as possible. It's a shame I've just booked my flight and I leave tomorrow."

"You were the one who insisted on the nonrefundable ticket," he reminded me.

"Well, if she got the job, maybe we could share an apartment in town." My mind immediately raced forward to a future with Chrissie in it, both of us surrounded by art.

"Or you could come and live with me, and keep house for your old grandfather," Francis suggested as we pulled into the drive.

"That would be nice too," I said, grinning at him.

"Tell her there's a bed for her here. She'll need to stop over for the night when she comes to meet Mirrin. I'll give her some Arrernte lessons," he added as he unlocked the door and I ran to get my mobile from the sitting room.

"That's really great of you, thanks," I said, and dialed Chrissie's number. She answered on the second ring.

"Hello, stranger," she said. "Thought you'd disappeared off the face of the earth."

"I texted you to say I'd been out bush painting," I said, smiling into my mobile because I was so happy to hear her voice. "With my grandfather," I added for good measure.

"Strewth! So, are you related to Namatjira?"

"No, although my grandfather is an artist."

"What's his name?"

"Francis Abraham."

There was a pause on the line.

"Ya kidding me!"

"No, why? Have you heard of him?"

"Just a bit, Cee! He was in Papunya with Clifford Possum and painted *Wheel of Fire* and—"

"Yeah, that's the one." I stopped her midsentence. "Listen, can you bunk a day or two off work to come to the Alice?"

"I . . . why?"

I explained, and the frostiness that had been in her voice when she'd first answered melted away.

"That sounds beaut, though she won't offer me the job when she hears I work on the tourist information desk at Broome airport. You've made me sound as though I'm the curator of the Canberra National Gallery!"

"Where's your positivity? Of course she will!" I chided her. "It's worth a shot, anyway, and my grandfather says you can stay at his place overnight."

"The prob is, Cee, I'm not sure I've got the moolah for the ticket. I used up all my spare cash last time I was in the Alice."

"Because you paid for the hotel, silly," I reminded her. "Hold on a minute . . ."

I asked my grandfather if Chrissie could use his credit card to book the flight in exchange for the dollars that I still had from the sale of my first painting.

"Of course," he said, handing the card to me. "Tell her I'll collect her from the airport too."

"Thanks so much," I said, and reported the good news to Chrissie.

"Am I dreaming? I thought that when I didn't hear from you, I'd frightened you off . . ."

"I'm sorry I didn't call. Things were busy this end and"—I swallowed—"I just wanted some time to think stuff through."

"I understand. Never mind for now," she said after a pause. "Ya can tell me all about it when I get there."

"Actually, I can't, because I'm booked to fly back to England tomorrow."

"Oh." She fell silent.

"It's a return ticket, Chrissie. I've got to go home and sort my life out, put my apartment on the market, and see my family."

"You mean you're coming back?"

"Yeah, course I am, as soon as I can. I'm gonna live here in the Alice. And . . . it would be great if you were here too."

"You mean it?"

"I never say things I don't mean, you should know that. Anyway, you'll have my grandfather to keep you company when you arrive, and from the sounds of things, you'll be far more excited to see him than me," I teased her.

"Ya know that's not true. How soon will you be back?"

"In about ten days. Now, get off the phone to me and call Mirrin, then book a flight and I'll text you my grandfather's number so you can call him with the details."

"Okay. Honest, Cee, I dunno how to thank you."

"Then don't. Good luck and I'll see you soon."

"Yeah. Miss ya."

"I miss you too. Bye."

I clicked off the phone and thought that I really *did* miss her. There was a long way to go because I wasn't sure yet what form the relationship between us would take, but it didn't matter because I was moving forward. One way or another, during the past few weeks it had been feeling much better to be me.

"By the grace of God, I am who I am," I whispered, and out of it all, I knew I had learned something important: I was certainly bicultural, possibly bisexual, but I definitely didn't want to be *by* myself.

"All sorted?" Francis wandered into the sitting room.

"I hope so. She's gonna book the flight and let you know what time it lands."

"Perfect," he said. "I'm hungry. You?"

"Starving, as it happens."

"I'll go and do something with eggs then."

"Okay, I'm off to pack."

"Right." He paused in the hallway. "Does your Chrissie cook?"

Remembering her homemade cakes, I nodded. "Yeah, she does."

"Good. I'm glad you've found your person, Celaeno," he said as he ambled off along the corridor.

"Take care of yourself, won't you?" my grandfather said as he gave me a hug in the airport departure lounge and I thought how great it felt to have two people who really didn't want me to leave Australia.

"I will."

"Here, I've collected some documents for you." He handed me a large brown envelope. "In there is your birth certificate—I got it from the public records office in Broome when I visited the ex-nurse. If you're serious about coming to live here for good—"

"Of course I am!"

"Then I suggest that you apply for your Australian passport as soon as possible. The form is in there too, as well as your mum's birth certificate."

"Right," I said as I tucked the envelope into the front of my rucksack, trying not to crumple it up. "Say hello to Chrissie for me, won't you? I hope you like her."

"I'm sure I will."

"Thanks for everything," I added, as the boarding call was announced over the PA system. "I hate planes."

"Perhaps you'll hate them less when one is bringing you back home to me. Good-bye, Celaeno."

"Bye, Francis." With a wave, I walked toward security, bracing myself for the long journey to London.

34

When I stepped out of the doors at Heathrow, the freezing-cold air of London hit me like a block of ice. Everyone around me was bundled up to their ears in thick coats and scarves, and the cold air stung my eyes and nose. I pulled my hoodie over my head and hailed a taxi, hoping I had enough English cash in my wallet to get me to Battersea.

When the taxi driver pulled up in front of my apartment building, I handed him a crumpled note and some coins, then stepped out. The Christmas lights I'd left had been replaced by a late January gloom and I felt like I had been taken from a Technicolor film and plunged into monochrome.

The lift took me up the three floors to the door of my apartment. I unlocked it and was startled to see that all the lights were on inside. What a dunce I was that I hadn't even switched those off before I left, I thought as I slammed the door behind me, realizing the apartment felt far warmer than I had set the thermostat to. The air smelled sweet, like a yummy cake, not fusty as I'd expected. In fact, it smelled like Star.

I'd texted her from my stopover in Sydney to let her know I was flying home and would be landing today, and asking if she had time to meet up in the next week. I needed to tell her I was selling the apartment, because even though it was me who'd owned it, it had been her home too.

I grimaced at the Guy Fawkes scarecrow still in my studio, sitting on top of the oil drum as if it were a throne, then walked toward the kitchen and saw with horror that the light in the oven was on. I was just about to turn it off when I heard the front door open.

"Cee! You're here already! Oh damn! I thought it would take you ages to get through immigration and London in the traffic . . ."

I turned to see Star, her face and the top half of her torso hidden behind an enormous bunch of bell-headed lilies, which she held out to me.

"I just went out to get these to welcome you home," she said breathlessly. "They were meant to be in a vase on the table, but never mind. Oh, Cee, it's so lovely to see you."

During the ensuing embrace, some of the lilies got squished between us, but neither of us cared.

"Wow!" she said as she stepped back and laid the lilies down on the coffee table. "You look incredible. Your hair's got lighter as well as longer."

"Yeah, it's all that sunshine in Oz. You look great too. You've had your fringe cut!" I knew the long fringe had been there for her to hide behind. Now that it was chopped shorter, her beautiful blue eyes shone out of her face like sapphires.

"Yes, it was time for a change. Listen, why don't you go upstairs and take a shower? I'll get on and prepare supper."

"I will, but first, do I smell cake?"

"Yes, it's lemon drizzle. Want a slice?"

"Do I? I've been dreaming about a slice of your cake since I left."

She handed me a thick, perfect wedge, and I bit into it. I finished the whole slice off in a few seconds and with another slice in my hand, I took my rucksack upstairs, where I saw that the bedroom was as neat as a pin, the sheets freshly changed. I walked into the bathroom, stepped under the power shower, and decided it was good to be home.

When I returned downstairs, Star was waiting for me with a beer.

"Cheers," I said, and clinked my bottle against her glass of Chardonnay.

"Welcome home," she said. "I've made your favorite. It should be ready in about twenty minutes."

"Steak and kidney pudding!" I confirmed as I saw the pastry rising under the spotlight in the oven.

"Yes. So, go on, I want to hear everything that's happened to you in the past couple of months."

"Wow, that's a big ask. How long have you got?"

"All night."

"You're staying over?" I asked in surprise.

"If that's okay, yes."

"Course it is, Sia! This is—was—your home too, remember?"

"I know, but . . ." She sighed and went to put some broccoli florets on to steam.

"Look, before you say anything, I just want to apologize," I blurted out. "I was a real pain in the backside last autumn—in fact, I've probably been a pain for most of my life."

"No, you weren't, silly. It's me who needs to say sorry. I should have been there for you when you were going through that rough patch at college." Star bit her bottom lip. "I was really selfish and I feel terrible about it."

"Yeah, I was pretty hurt at the time, but it gave me the push that I needed. I see now that you had to do it, Sia. The way we were—the way I was—well, it wasn't healthy. You had to go out and get a life for yourself. If you hadn't, I wouldn't have found mine."

"You've met someone?" She turned to me. "It's Ace, isn't it? You two looked so cozy together on Phra Nang Beach."

"Er, no, it's not Ace, but . . ." I felt completely unprepared for this conversation, so I changed the subject. "How's Mouse?"

"He's good," she said as she pulled the steak and kidney pudding out of the oven and began to plate up our supper. "Let's talk as we eat, shall we?"

For a change Star did most of the talking, while I gobbled down as much food as my tummy could manage to hold. I heard all about High Weald—"the Mouse House," as I'd mentally nicknamed it—and how it was under renovation, so she, Mouse, and his son, Rory, were staying in the farmhouse opposite.

"It'll take years to restore, of course. The property is Grade I listed, and Mouse is an architect, so everything has to be perfect." Star rolled her eyes and I was glad to see the tiniest flicker of Mouse's imperfection in them. It made him more human, somehow.

"You're happy with him, though?"

"Oh yes, although he can be incredibly anal, especially over chimney stacks and architraves. Rory and I just take ourselves off for a walk and leave him to it. And when Rory's in bed and Mouse is still studying different varieties of chimney pot, I write."

"You've started your novel?"

"Yes. I mean, I'm not very far on—only eighty pages or so—but . . ." Star stood up and began to clear the plates away. "I've made sherry trifle for pudding. You look as though you need feeding up."

"Listen, mate, this is a woman who's eaten a whole 'roo in one sitting," I joked. "And what about your family? Have you heard from your mum since she left for the States?"

"Oh yes," Star said as she brought the trifle over. "But now I want to hear about your adventures. Especially with Ace. How did you meet him? What was he like?"

So I told her, and as I did, I remembered how kind he'd been to me. And felt sad all over again that he thought I'd betrayed him.

"Are you going to see him in prison?" she asked me.

"He'd probably get me thrown out," I said as I scraped the last of the trifle out of the bowl. "I suppose I could try."

"The question is, did he do it?"

"I think he did, yeah."

"Even if he did, as Mouse said, it's doubtful that he would have done it alone. Why aren't others at the bank coming forward?"

"'Cause they don't want to spend the next ten years banged up?" I rolled my eyes at her. "He did mention something about somebody called Linda knowing the truth, whoever 'Linda' is."

"Don't you think you owe it to him to find out? Perhaps he'd forgive you if you tried to help him."

"I dunno, 'cause when I think about it, it was like Ace had just accepted the situation, given up."

"If I were you, I'd put in a call to the bank and ask to speak to Linda."

"Maybe, but there might be more than one of them."

"So, it wasn't love or anything?" Star continued to probe.

"No, though I really, really liked him. He was thoughtful, you know? He was the one who sent off for the biography about Kitty Mercer—that's the person who Pa had said in his letter that I should investigate. Ace read the book to me after I told him I was dyslexic."

"Really? Wow, that doesn't sound like the Ace we've all been reading about in the papers. They've made him sound like an absolute jerk: a hard-drinking womanizer who only cared about making more millions."

"He wasn't like that at all. Not when I knew him, at least. He only had one glass of champagne the whole time I was staying with him." I smiled as I remembered that night.

"So that's Ace. Now what about your birth family? Did you find them?"

"Yeah, I did, though most of them are dead. My mother for certain—and my father, well, who knows where he is."

"I'm sorry, Cee." Star reached out her hand to grasp mine. "It's like that with my biological father too."

"It's fine, though, because the person I *did* find is fantastic. He's my grandfather. He's an artist—and a pretty famous one at that."

"Oh, Cee, I'm so happy for you!"

"Thanks. It feels good to find someone who shares the same blood, doesn't it?"

"Yes. Go on then, tell me all about how you found him, and who you are."

So I did. Star's eyes were out on stalks as I brought her up to the present day.

"So, you've got Japanese, Aboriginal, German, Scottish, and English blood in you." She counted the nationalities off on her fingers.

"Yup. No wonder I've always been confused," I said, grinning.

"I think it sounds exotic, especially compared to me, who turns out to be English through and through. So weird, isn't it, how your granny Sarah and my mum came from the East End of London? And here we are, living only a few miles along the river from where they were born."

"Yeah, I suppose it is."

"Did you bring any photos back of your paintings?"

"I forgot, but I think Chrissie took a shot of the first one I did with my camera. I'll get the roll developed."

"Who's Chrissie?"

"A friend I made in Oz." I couldn't tell her about Chrissie yet; I had no idea how to put it into words. "Actually, Sia, I think I'm gonna have to crash. It's, like, midday in Oz and I didn't sleep much on the plane."

"Of course. You go up and I'll follow you when I've put the dish-washer on."

"Thanks," I said, relieved to have escaped further conversation. Comforted by the domestic sounds of Star cleaning up below me, I slid into bed, pulling the soft duvet over me.

"It's so great to have you back, Cee," Star said when she came into the bedroom. She undressed and climbed into the bed next to mine, then switched off the light.

"Yeah, it feels great. Better than I thought it would," I said sleepily. "I just want to say sorry again if I've been, like, difficult over the years. I haven't meant to be. It's all there inside me, but it just comes out wrong sometimes, but I am learning, I really am."

"Shush, Cee, there's no need to apologize. I know who you are inside, remember? Sleep tight."

The next morning, I woke at the same time as Star, which usually never happened. I pottered around the apartment, trying to sort out what bits I would take to Australia with me, while Star stood out on the terrace, wrapped up in her dressing gown and talking on the phone. When she finally came in to make breakfast, she had a pleased look on her face, and I guessed she'd been speaking to Mouse. To make me feel better, a message from Chrissie pinged onto my phone.

> Hi Cee! Hope ur flight was good. Interview at gallery was scary. Will hear back tomorrow, fingers crossed! Miss u!

"So, have you decided what you're going to do now you're back?" Star asked me over breakfast. The eggs Benedict was so good, it almost made me want to change my mind and stay.

"Well, I was going to talk to you about that, Sia. I'm thinking of selling this apartment."

"Really, why? I thought you loved it here." Star frowned.

"I did . . . I mean, I do, but I'm moving to Australia."

"Oh my God! Are you really? Oh, Cee . . ." Star's eyes filled with tears. "It's so far away."

"Only a day away on a plane," I joked, trying to cover my shock that she seemed genuinely upset. Only a few weeks ago, I was sure she'd have been glad to see the back of me.

"But what about the spiders there? You were always terrified of them."

"I still am, but I suppose I can handle it. And the weird thing is, I didn't actually see a single one while I was there. Look, Star, it's . . . where I belong. I mean, more than anywhere else, anyway. And Francis—my grandfather—isn't getting any younger. He's been lonely since his wife died, and I want to spend as much time with him as I can."

Star nodded slowly, wiping away tears with the sleeve of her sweater. "I understand, Cee."

"There's also something about being there that inspires me to paint.

Maybe it's the Aboriginal part of me, but when I was out bush, it was like I just *knew* what to do without really thinking about it."

"You've moved closer to your muse. Now, that really *is* a reason to move to the back of beyond," she agreed sadly.

"Yeah, I mean, I was so lost when I left London, didn't know what I wanted to paint, but when Chrissie drove me out to the ghost gum with the MacDonnell Ranges behind it, something magical happened. She sold that painting two days later for six hundred dollars!"

"Wow, that's amazing, Cee! So, who is this Chrissie? Does she live where you're going?" Star eyed me.

"Er, she doesn't at the moment, but she might be moving there in the next few weeks."

"To be near you?"

"Yes, no, sort of . . . She might be offered a job in an art gallery, and, er"—I kept nodding like I was one of those dogs that sat in the back window of a car—"we're really good friends. She's great, really positive, you know? She's had a difficult life, and she's got this, like, false leg from below her knee, and . . ."

I realized I was rambling and had probably completely given myself away.

"Cee"—a gentle hand landed on my wrist—"Chrissie sounds amazing, and I really hope I'll get to meet her one day."

"I hope so too, 'cause what she's been through, well, it made me realize how spoiled I was growing up. We had this magical childhood at Atlantis, sheltered from everything, but Chrissie really had to fight to get to where she is now."

"I understand. Does she make you happy?"

"Yeah," I managed after a pause. "She does."

"So, she's your 'special' person then?"

"Maybe, but it's early days, and . . . Christ!" I hit the table with my fist. "What is it about being back here? I can't get the words right."

"Hey, Cee, it's me, Sia. We never needed words, remember?" Her hands began to move in the sign language we'd made up as children when we didn't want our other sisters to know what we were saying.

Do you love her? she signed.

Not sure yet. Maybe.

Does she love you?

Yes, I signed, without pausing to think.

"Then I'm SO happy for you!" she said out loud, and stood up from the table to give me a big hug.

"Thanks," I muttered into her hair, "though knowing me, it might all go wrong."

"That's what I think every day with Mouse. It's called trust, isn't it?"

"Yeah."

"And remember," she said, pulling back to look at me. "Whatever happens, we'll always have each other."

"Thanks." I squeezed my eyes shut to hold back the tears.

"Now," she said, sitting back down, "I've done some research on 'Linda.'"

"Have you?" I said, trying to pull myself together.

"Yes." Star placed a name and number in front of me. I squinted at what was written there. "There are three Lindas at the bank. Given one works in the catering department and the other has only been there for the past two months, the most likely candidate is Linda Potter. She was the PA to the CEO of the bank, David Rutter."

"Really? How did you find out?"

"I called the bank and asked for Linda. Each time I got through, I pretended she was the wrong Linda and they connected me to the others in their different departments. Finally, I got to the CEO's office—Linda Potter has recently retired, apparently."

"Right."

"Well?" Star eyed me.

"Well what?"

"If Ace said Linda knows and this Linda used to be the PA to the CEO, she'd be in on everything that's going on in the company. PAs always are," she said confidently.

"Okay . . ." I nodded, wondering where this was heading.

"Cee, I really think you should go and see Ace, and ask him about Linda. And besides, this isn't just about him, it's about you too! He thinks you were the one who shopped him to the press. Surely you want to put the record straight before you leave for Australia?"

"Yeah, but there's no proof, is there? The film was on *my* camera, and I gave it to the security guard to develop."

"Then you should tell him that yourself. And also ask him why he isn't making any effort to defend himself."

"Wow, you're seriously passionate about this, aren't you?"

"I just don't like people being blamed for something they haven't done. Especially when it's my sister," she said fiercely.

"I'm trying to learn to keep my mouth shut," I said with a shrug.

"Well, for once in our lives, I'm saying the words for you. And I think you should go."

I saw then that she had changed in the past few months. The old Star would have thought all of this stuff on the inside, but would never have said it out loud. Whereas I had always said too much. Perhaps we were both adjusting to being apart from each other.

"Okay, okay," I agreed. "I know he's at Wormwood Scrubs prison. I'll find out what the visiting hours are."

"Promise?" she asked me.

"Promise."

"Good. I have to leave in a bit to collect Rory from school."

"Okay, well, before you go I was wondering if you'd help me fill in my Australian passport application? My grandfather's given me all the documents I need, but you know how I am with filling in forms."

"Of course. Do you want to go and get them?"

I brought the envelope downstairs and Star went off to find a black ink pen to start filling it in. We spread the documents out on the kitchen table and had a brief glance at my mum's birth certificate, before Star reached for mine.

"So you were born in Broome on the fifth of August 1980," she read, her head bent in concentration as she read more details on the certificate. "Oh my God! Cee, have you actually looked at this yet?"

"Er, no. My grandfather just gave me the envelope before I left."

"So, you haven't seen what your original birth name was?" She pointed to it and I leaned over to take a look.

"Strewth! As they say in Oz."

"Too right, Miss Pearl Abraham!" Star said, then she began to giggle.

"*Pearl*, ugh," I groaned. "And I always complained about Celaeno . . . I'm sorry, Pa."

Then I couldn't help myself and joined Star in her laughter, trying to imagine this other *me* called Pearl. It just wasn't possible. Yet, in so many ways, it was perfect.

Once we'd calmed down, I slid the birth certificate back into its envelope.

"Speaking of birth certificates, my mum's flying over here in a few days' time. And so is Ma," said Star.

"Oh, that's fantastic!" I said, thinking it would save me the trip to Geneva. "Are they coming to meet each other?"

"Sort of," said Star. "When my birth mum found me, she got in contact with some of the other members of her family. There's a heap of them still living in the East End of London. We're all going to a surprise party there for a relative of ours. My mum said a while ago she'd like to meet the woman who brought me up and thank her in person, and this was the perfect moment to invite Ma. I'd love you to meet my mum too—I've told her everything about you."

"What's she like?"

"Lovely, really lovely. She's not bringing her other kids over with her this time, but I'm going to fly over to New England and meet my three half siblings soon. Right, you need to sign there." Star indicated the box. "You'll also have to include a copy of your official adoption papers. Just give Uncle Georg Hoffman a call," she added. "He certainly had mine."

"So, how are the rest of the sisters? I haven't heard a peep from anyone since the newspaper thing."

"Well, Maia's started teaching English to kids in a favela in Rio, and Ally told me last week her tummy is getting more enormous by the day, but she sounds good. I called Tiggy just after New Year, she's changed jobs and is working on an estate not far from the animal sanctuary. She also wants to organize us all getting together at Atlantis for the anniversary of Pa's death in June. And I haven't heard a word from Electra in weeks, *or* seen her in the newspapers, which is unusual. That badge of notoriety goes to you, little sis," she chuckled. "By the way, when are you flying to Australia?"

"Early next Wednesday morning."

"So soon?" Star looked crestfallen. "The party's on Tuesday night. Can you make it?"

"Probably not. I have to pack. And stuff," I added pointlessly.

"I understand. Then maybe we can have a little leaving celebration for you before we go to the party? Then you could meet my mum and see Ma too."

"If you could spare Ma for a night, I could collect her from Heathrow and she could stay with me on Monday night and then go to the party with you from here on Tuesday?"

"That sounds perfect! Thank you, Cee. Now, I need to go and grab my things. Why don't you call Wormwood Scrubs in the meantime and see what the process is for getting in to visit? I've put the number on the table."

Star went upstairs to pack her bag and I wandered over to the phone, knowing I'd get no peace from Star if I didn't make the call. The receptionist at the other end was friendly enough, although she gave me the third degree on what my relationship was to "the prisoner."

"A friend," I said. Then she took my date of birth and my address, and told me I'd need to present some form of ID before I'd be allowed in.

"Did you get through?" Star said when she came down the stairs with her overnight bag.

"Yeah, but I'm afraid I can't wear that pair of tight hot pants you know I like so much. It's against prison rules."

"Right." Star smiled. "When are you going to see him?"

"I'm booked in for two o'clock tomorrow afternoon. Maybe they can do the mug shots for my new passport while I'm there." I shuddered. "It feels weird thinking of Ace as a 'prisoner.'"

"I'll bet. Are you sure you're going to be okay in the apartment alone, Cee?" Star put a hand on my shoulder.

"Course I will. I'm a big girl now, remember?"

"Well, let me know what happens with Ace. Love you, Cee. See you next week."

I really did feel as though I were in a film as I traipsed through the towered gateway of "the Scrubs," as the other visitors waiting in line had called it. Inside, each one of us had our bags and ourselves thoroughly searched. Eventually, we were led into a large room full of tables and plastic chairs, and actually, it wasn't as depressing as I'd imagined it would be. Someone had obviously made an effort to stop the prisoners and their visitors from slitting their wrists by putting up bright posters on the walls. As we all sat down at separate tables, we were read a list of dos and don'ts and finally, the prisoners filed in.

My heart was beating like a tom-tom as I searched the line for Ace. By the time a familiar voice said, "Hi," in my ear, I realized I hadn't even recognized him. His hair was cut into a crop, and he was clean shaven and painfully thin.

"What are you doing here?" he asked me as he sat down.

"I . . . well, I just thought that as I was back in England, I should come and see you."

"Right. You're the first visitor I've had. Other than my lawyer, of course."

"Well, sorry that it's me."

There was silence between us, as Ace looked down at his hands, to his left, to his right, above him . . . In fact, at anything but me.

"Why did you do it, CeCe?" he said eventually.

"I didn't, honestly! That's what I've come to tell you. It was Po, the security guard, who was bribed by a guy called Jay. Someone at the Railay Beach Hotel had told me that he knew who you were. I didn't want to worry you or anything, so I didn't mention it at the time. I mean, I had no idea who you were anyway, so I didn't believe him."

"Oh, come off it, CeCe," he sneered, "that picture came straight from your camera. I allowed it to be taken because I trusted you, I thought we were mates."

"We were! You were great to me!" I insisted, then tried to keep my voice down as I saw others looking over at us. "I'd never have done anything to betray you. Po must have got a duplicate set of photos and given them to Jay. Anyway, it's the truth. It's what happened."

"Yeah, well." Ace stared off into the distance again. "It had to happen sometime, I suppose. I knew I couldn't stay hidden forever. You just hastened the inevitable."

"It matters to *me* that you believe me. I nearly had a fit when I got to Australia and all my sisters texted me to say I was on the front page of every newspaper! Do you think I wanted that?"

"What? To be involved with the most notorious criminal of the moment?"

"Exactly!"

"Lots of girls would."

"Well 'lots of girls' aren't *me*," I said firmly, trying to keep my cool.

"No," he agreed eventually. "You're right. I really thought you *were* different, that I could trust you."

"And you could—you can! Look, let's just forget it. If you don't want to believe me, that's up to you, but I'm not a liar. I'm here because I wanted to ask you if you needed any help. I could be a character witness, or something."

"Thanks, Cee, but courtesy of the media, my reputation is beyond redemption, and I deserve it. I'm sure you've read about my past antics. Not that they had anything to do with what happened at the bank, but I seem to be the most hated man in Britain just now."

"The good news is, I'm dyslexic, remember? I can't read properly."

Finally, he gave the ghost of a smile. "Yeah, okay."

"Who's Linda Potter?"

His eyes met mine for the first time. "What?"

I knew then that Star had found the right woman. "Linda Potter. You told me one night that she 'knew.' So, what does she know?"

"Nothing, she's no one."

"Well, I know she's someone, because she used to be PA to the CEO of Berners Bank."

"Just . . . don't go there, CeCe, all right?" he said through gritted teeth.

"Does she know something? Ace, why won't you let me help you?"

"Listen," he said, leaning toward me, "what's done is done, okay? Whatever happens, I'm going down. I did it, no one else."

"There must have been others that knew about it."

"I said, leave it."

I watched as he lifted his hand to alert one of the prison officers, who had the type of physique you wouldn't want to meet down an alley late at night. The man walked over to us.

"I want to go back to my cell now," said Ace.

"All right, mate. Time's up, miss," the guard added to me.

Ace stood up. "Thanks for trying to help, Cee, but really, there's nothing you can do, believe me."

Outside the prison, waiting for the bus that would take me back into central London, I realized that Star was right. Even if it got Ace nowhere in the long run, I had to show him that at least someone cared.

I knew what it felt like to be a beaten dog.

35

The jet lag didn't seem to want to leave me alone, so I was awake again early the next morning. First, I called Ma and told her I would meet her off the plane from Geneva at Heathrow on Monday afternoon. Then, at nine o'clock sharp, I called the Berners Bank number Star had left for me.

"Hello, can I speak to Linda Potter, please?"

"I'm afraid she's left," said a clipped female voice. "Are you the lady who called a couple of days ago?"

"Yes, I was just . . ."—I thought quickly—"trying to contact her because she's meant to be coming to my birthday party tonight and I, um, haven't heard from her."

"Well, you'd be best to try her at home."

"Yeah, but . . ." I paused, searching my brain cells for every thriller I'd seen to tell me what to say. "I'm at the venue now and she isn't answering her mobile. I don't have her landline number with me—have you got it at your end?"

"Yes, wait a minute."

I held my breath.

"It's . . ."

"Thanks so much," I said as I wrote the number down. "It's a really special birthday and it wouldn't be the same without her."

"I understand. It'll probably cheer her up a bit. Bye now."

"Bye."

I did a little wiggle of triumph around my vast sitting room before I collected myself and dialed Linda's number. My heart was pounding as the line rang, then finally clicked onto an answering machine and I hung up. Then I called Star, as I had no idea what my next step should be.

"Okay," she said. "You need her address. Hold on a minute."

I could hear her chatting in the background with a deep, velvety male voice.

"Cee, I'm going to pass you over to Orlando, Mouse's brother. He's fantastic at playing detective."

"Miss Celaeno?"

"Yes, but call me CeCe."

"Goodness, I do wish those blessed with unusual Christian names would actually use them. If anyone but my nephew would even dare call me 'Lando,' I should go into a funk for the rest of the year. Now then, Miss Star tells me you need the address of a person."

"I do, yes," I replied, trying to stifle a giggle at the old-fashioned way he spoke.

"Well now, I've just checked on the computer and the 01233 dialing code tells me your mystery woman hails from Kent. In fact"—there was a pause as I heard him tap the keys—"to be precise, Ashford. A quality little town, which is coincidentally very near to here. So, now I am searching the online electoral register in that area for a Linda Potter. Bear with me, please, while I scroll . . . ah, yes! Here she is. The Cottage, Chart Road, Ashford, Kent."

"I'll text it to you, Cee," said Star as she came straight back on the line. "Are you going to see her? It's only an hour's train ride from Charing Cross station."

"She might be away."

"Or lying low. Hold on . . ."

I waited as a discussion ensued between Orlando and Star.

Star came back on the line. "It's only a short drive to Ashford from High Weald. What about if we go and stake the house out for you?"

"You really don't have to, Sia, it's not like it's life or death or anything."

"It might be to Ace, Cee. We could check if there's any sign of an occupant before you traipse down here."

"Okay," I agreed, wondering whether Star's life was simply so dull that she had to fill it with weird missions to see a woman neither of us had ever met, on the off chance she could help a man who was in jail for fraud, who never wanted me to darken his doorstep again.

"We'll go during our lunch hour," said Star. "Orlando can be my lookout." The two of them giggled like kids on Halloween, so I said my thank-yous and left them to it.

Ten minutes later, the doorbell rang. It was the estate agent I'd contacted about selling the apartment.

We shook hands and he wandered around nodding and grunting. Eventually, he came to me and gave a dramatic sigh.

"What's the matter?"

"Well, you must know the state of the property market in London at the moment?"

"No, I haven't got a clue."

"To put it bluntly, it's dire."

And then, the same man who had sold me the apartment in the first place by extolling its virtues proceeded to explain to me why no one else would *ever* buy it, certainly not at the price I'd bought it for anyway.

"The market's flooded with new-build waterside apartments, a third of which are currently standing empty. It's the subprime market in America that's doing it, of course, but everything has a knock-on effect."

Christ!

"Could you just tell me in plain English what you think I should put the apartment on the market for?"

He did, and I nearly gave him a serious black eye.

"That's twenty percent less than I paid for it!"

"Sadly, Miss D'Aplièse, the property market is a law unto itself. It relies on sentiment, which, unlike waterside apartments, is in short supply at the moment. It will come back, of course, as it always does in London. If I were you and didn't need the money, I'd hedge my bets and rent it out."

We then discussed how much I could rent it out for, which actually, to someone like me, was enough money to keep me in 'roo dinners for years and years. He said his agency would handle everything, so we signed some forms and shook hands. I gave him a spare key and just as I was showing him out, my mobile rang.

"Sia?" I said breathlessly.

"We're here."

"Where's 'here'?"

"Sitting outside Linda Potter's house. She's in."

"How do you know?"

"Orlando knocked on her door, and when she opened it, he announced himself as the local Conservative candidate for the area. I said that the Monster Raving Loony Party might be more applicable . . ."

Howls of laughter ensued down the line. When the two of them had recovered, Star continued. "Anyway, I took over from Orlando and introduced myself as his secretary and her face lit up. She told me that she was 'once a private secretary to a very important man.'"

"Oh," I said. "Was that significant?"

"Hang on, Cee, let me tell you the rest. I then asked her if she was retired. She nodded and said yes. 'Put out to grass before my time,' were her words. Orlando and I think she was got rid of."

"Maybe it was just her time to retire?"

"We reckon she's not even fifty yet."

"Oh," I repeated. "What do you think I should do?"

"Come and see her. I can collect you from Ashford station tomorrow, as long as it's not after three thirty, because that's when I pick up Rory from school."

"You mean you'll be my wing gunner?"

"That's what sisters are for, aren't they?"

"Yeah. Thanks, Sia. Bye."

I started packing up my stuff in the apartment half-heartedly, and as the afternoon wore on, I began to feel that really bad sensation of being alone. Star had her people now, and so did I, except mine were on the other side of the world. I slumped down on the sofa, feeling really low. Then, as if by magic, my mobile rang.

"Hello?"

After a long crackly pause, a familiar voice said, "Cee? It's me, Chrissie."

"Hi! How are you?" I said.

"Great, I'm just great. Your grandpa sends his love."

"Send my love back. How's things?"

"Good, good. I just wanted you to be the first—or, in fact, the second person to know, as I told your grandpa—I just got offered the job at the gallery!"

Chrissie gave a squeal of joy, which made me smile.

"That's brilliant news!"

"I know! Isn't it? The money's pathetic, of course, but your sweet grandpa has said I can stay with him until I save up some moolah for my own place. Not joking, Cee, he's my new BFF, but we both really miss you."

"I miss you both too."

"So, I'm just about to phone and jack in my job in Broome. D'ya think it's the right thing to do?"

"Chrissie, I'm about to jack in my life here in England. Of course it is! It's what you want to do."

There was a pause on the line.

"So you're definitely coming back?"

"Course I am," I said firmly.

"Then I will."

"What?"

"Jack in my job, idiot! What about Ace? Have you seen him?"

"Yeah, yesterday. He's in a bad way."

"Oh, but you're definitely coming back?"

"I said so, didn't I?"

"Yeah, you did. Listen, this is costing your grandpa a fortune, so I'll say good night. Miss you."

"I miss you too."

I went around the apartment and watered Star's plants. It was one small thing I could do for her, as she did so much for me. That made me consider my dependency on her, and the way that I had already slipped back into her helping me do the stuff that I wasn't good at.

Later on in bed, I decided that if I did go and visit the now infamous Linda, I would do it by myself.

After the short train journey to Ashford the next morning, I took a taxi to the address Orlando had given me.

"We're here, miss," said the cabbie, pointing at the house. I asked him to drive past it and turn into the next side road.

"If I'm not back in ten minutes, you can leave," I said, bunging him an extra fiver. "I'll call you later."

I walked along the road and paused as nonchalantly as I could opposite the house, which stood in a row of similar houses. THE COTTAGE was written on a little wooden sign on the gate. Crossing the road, I saw that the patch of garden fronting the house was immaculate. I opened the gate and walked up the path to ring the bell, trying to work out what I would say. Before I got there, the door flew open.

"If you're here to preach to me about supporting you in the local council elections, I'm not interested."

The woman was about to slam the door but I put my palm out to hold it open.

"No, I'm CeCe D'Aplièse, Ace's friend from Thailand."

"What?" The woman peered at me. "Good grief! It's *you!*"

"Yes." The door was still partially held open by my palm, and as she stood there gaping at me, I took in her brown hair cut into a sensible and unflattering bob, a neat blouse, and what Star and I would call an old woman's skirt, because the material reached to cover just beyond her kneecaps. She was obviously still speechless, so I continued. "I just wanted to talk to you." I watched her brown eyes leave me, darting left and right outside.

"How did you find me?"

"On the electoral register. I saw Ace at the prison. He thinks it was me who gave the newspapers that photo, but it wasn't. I really believe he's a good person underneath it all. And"—I swallowed—"he helped me when I needed it, and I just feel like he's got no friends right now, and he really, really needs some," I finished, panting with the effort of trying to say the right thing.

Eventually she nodded.

"You'd better come in."

"Thanks." I stepped inside and she slammed the door firmly shut behind us, then locked it.

"No one else knows you're here, do they?"

"No one," I confirmed, as I followed her along a narrow hall and into a sitting room where I'd have been scared to even think about having a drink because some of the liquid might just spill onto the shiny varnished surface of the coffee table. Even the sofa had had its scatter cushions symmetrically positioned in sharp Vs.

"Please, sit down. Can I get you a cup of tea?" the woman asked me.

"No thanks, I'm fine," I said, sitting down gingerly. "I'm not staying long."

Linda sat down in the armchair opposite and stared at me for a bit, then looked away, her eyes suddenly blurry, like she was about to cry.

"So," she breathed, obviously trying to collect herself. "You are Anand's girlfriend?"

It took me a moment to register that she was referring to Ace by his proper name. "I wouldn't go that far, but we kept each other company, yes. By the way, why did he tell me his name was Ace?"

"It was a nickname he was given on the trading floor because he always wins. Or at least he used to . . . Why exactly are you here?"

"Look, I just care about him, okay? And one night he mentioned your name. He said, 'Linda knows.' I really didn't understand what he was talking about at the time, but now I do, and I'm about to go to live in Australia, so I thought I owed it to him to find you before I left."

"He's a lovely boy," said Linda, after a long pause.

"Yeah, he is. He let me stay with him when I had nowhere else to go. I don't even know what I'm meant to ask you, but . . ."

I realized that Linda was far away, staring off into space. So I sat and waited for her to speak.

"He came over to England when he was thirteen to go to boarding school," she said eventually. "I was the one who met him off the plane from Bangkok, and took him down to Charterhouse School, which is close to here. He was so small at the time—looked no more than nine or ten—a baby really. He'd recently lost his mother too, yet he was so very brave, didn't cry when I introduced him to the housemaster, then left him there. It must have been such a shock, leaving Bangkok and coming to boarding school in cold, gray England."

I watched as Linda paused and sighed deeply, before saying, "Young boys can be so cruel, can't they?"

"I don't really know, to be honest. I have five sisters."

"Do you indeed?" She gave me a small smile. "Lucky you. I was an only child. Anyway, I used to call him every week, just to check he was all right. He'd always sound jolly on the phone, but I knew things weren't easy for him. Occasionally, at first, I'd drive over on Sundays and take him out to lunch. We became close, and eventually, with his father's permission, he came to stay with me during exeats and holidays. However, that's all in the past." Her hands clenched together to match her knees.

We sat in silence for a while, me trying to work this plot out in my tiny mind and not managing to. I was sure Ace had made it clear he hadn't even known his father, yet Linda had just mentioned him. Was she related to Ace? Was that why she'd cared for him when he was younger?

"Weren't you the CEO's PA at Berners Bank?" I asked her.

"I was, yes. As you might already know, quite a lot's changed there in the past few months. I'm now officially retired."

"Oh, that's nice."

"No, it isn't," she hissed. "It's utterly horrendous! I hardly know what to do with myself, being at home all day. Still, I'm sure I'll get used to it eventually, but it's quite difficult when a way of life is pulled from you suddenly, isn't it?"

"Yes, it is," I said with feeling. "Is it because the bank's been bought?"

"Partly, yes, but David felt it was better if I disappeared into the background."

"David?"

"The CEO. Thirty years I worked for that man, lived for him and my job. And now . . ." She shrugged. "Well, there we are. Are you sure you wouldn't like a cup of tea?"

"I'm fine, really. Your boss is still working there, isn't he?"

"Oh yes." She nodded vehemently. "I've heard he's got a new version of me now called Deborah. She's very . . . blond, apparently. Not that it matters," Linda added hastily. "I'm sure she's very efficient."

"Linda," I said, thinking that this was really getting us nowhere, other than to make her more upset. "What is it you know about Ace? Like, is it anything useful that could help him?"

"Oh, I know everything about Anand," she said slowly. "I know exactly how he liked his hair stroked as he fell asleep, that he's a little deaf in one ear due to a rugby injury, and how he loves my homemade shortbread."

"I meant, do you know anything that might help defend him in the coming trial?" I asked. "To, um, reduce his sentence, or anything?"

She bit her lip and her eyes filled with tears once more. "Do you know, it's almost noon and I think I would like a little sherry. Would you?"

"Er, no thanks."

She stood up and went to a sideboard from which she extracted a bottle and a very tiny glass that she filled with some brown liquid. "Goodness, I haven't drunk sherry at lunchtime for years. Cheers."

"Cheers," I replied. For someone who said they didn't drink much, Linda knocked the glass back pretty quickly.

"That's better," she said. "Goodness, one can understand why people turn to alcohol, especially when they're under pressure. Was Anand drinking when you saw him in Thailand?"

"No. Nothing, apart from one glass of champagne on New Year's Eve."

"That's wonderful. He never was a drinker before he started trading. The problem is, excessive drinking is a rite of passage in the City, and he wanted to fit in with his fellow traders. No one wants to be different, do they? Especially if they are."

"No, they don't." I nodded in agreement.

"I told David right from the start that I thought it was a mistake to employ Anand at the bank after he left school, but he could see how gifted he was already. Anand didn't want to do it. He told me that, sitting right where you are now, but David ruled his world," she sighed.

"Are you saying that your boss forced Ace into being a trader?" I queried, even further confused.

"Put it this way: Anand was so in awe of him, he'd have done anything David said."

"Why?"

Linda's eyebrows knitted together in a frown. "Surely he told you? Otherwise you wouldn't be here."

"Told me what?"

"David is Anand's father."

"Oh," I gulped, trying to take in the ramifications of what she'd just said. "No, he didn't tell me."

"I, oh, dearie me, I presumed he had . . ." Linda buried her face in her hands. "No one else knows, you see, about that . . . blood tie."

"Really? Why not?"

"David was paranoid about his reputation in the City. Didn't want anyone to know he had an illegitimate son. And, of course, he was already married when Anand was born, had a young child with his wife."

"Right. Does Ace know David's his dad?"

"Of course he does, which was why he was constantly trying to please him. David did the proper thing to assuage his guilt by bringing his son over to England and educating him at a top British school when he heard Anand's mother had died. Then he offered him a job at the bank, as I said, on the condition that no one knew of their real relationship to each other."

"You mean, David was ashamed of his mixed-race child?"

"He prided himself on being the quintessential English gentleman. And he's always presented himself as the perfect family man."

"Jesus," I said under my breath, pinching myself to remember that it was 2008, and this kind of thing could still be happening. "So, Ace was desperate to impress his dad? Even to the point of trading fraudulently?"

"It was clear from the beginning that Anand was as talented as his father had once been, which was why David had employed him. Within the space of two years, he had risen through the ranks and was Berners's most successful trader. There were only three words that mattered on the trading floor: 'profit,' 'profit,' and 'profit.' And Anand was making more than any of them."

"Was his dad proud of him?"

"Yes, extremely, but then Anand had a run of bad luck and rather than taking it calmly, he panicked. And that's when I suspect he started to cheat. The problem is, even if you say you'll take a risk just once to cover your losses, and then don't get caught, you'll do it again. It becomes addictive, and Anand was also addicted to his father's praise and attention."

"Christ, it's just so sad." I shook my head, really feeling for Ace. "Linda, do you think David knew what Ace was up to? I mean, surely he must have done? He lost so much money."

Linda stood up to pour herself another glass of sherry and took a hefty gulp. "The truth is, I don't know for sure, but what I *do* know is that David should be standing by him now. It's his *son*, for crying out loud! And I wouldn't be at all surprised if David *did* know the trouble Anand was in. He is the CEO after all. I've even wondered since whether he slipped Anand some cash to help him conveniently 'disappear' to Thailand."

"Wow, what a mess," I sighed.

"It is, yes. My poor, poor boy. I . . ." Linda's eyes filled with further tears. "I never had children of my own, but I loved Anand like my own son, CeCe. I was there when his mother and father weren't, helping him through those difficult teenage years."

"Then why haven't you been to see him in prison?"

"David said I couldn't. He ordered me to keep away."

"In case someone traced your involvement with Ace and David, and discovered the truth about their relationship?"

"Yes, although there's no written proof—David's name isn't even on Anand's birth certificate."

I felt a surge of anger rise inside me. "There are genetic tests. I'm sorry to say this, but David sounds like a really serious"—I chose the most delicate word I could think of—"prat. Ace needs all the support he can get just now. He's, like, totally alone, going through this all by himself."

"You're right about David," Linda said darkly. "It's taken thirty years to remove the blinkers from my eyes. The problem was, I adored him from the first moment I started as a junior typist at the bank and when he eventually employed me as his PA, it was the happiest day of my life. I gave him everything. Wherever I was, whatever time of day or night, I was there to sort out and organize his life. And not just his, but that arrogant, patronizing woman he married and his two spoiled children who have never done a serious day's work in their lives. I was in love with him, you see," she confessed. "What a cliché I am: the secretary in love with her boss. And now, he's tossed me aside along with Anand. Do you know, he didn't even have the grace to tell me himself when the redundancies were announced after the bank was bought by Jinqian for a pound? I was sent to HR, along with the rest of the employees."

By now, I wanted to throttle this arsehole with my own bare hands. "It's because you knew too much."

"I was the shadow on his shoulder, the reminder of what he truly was. He's Anand's *father*, CeCe. He should be there for him in his hour of need, and he knows it."

"Have you ever thought about telling the media the truth?"

"Of course I have, constantly! I *dream* about the look on David's face if I did!" She gave a small chuckle and drained the rest of her sherry.

"And?"

"I . . . just *can't*. I'm simply not a spiteful person. And that's what it would be—spite, because it wouldn't achieve anything positive, apart from David's public humiliation."

"That's quite a lot in my book," I commented.

"No, CeCe. Try to understand that the one thing I have left is my integrity. And I will not allow him to compromise that as well."

"But what about Ace?" I insisted. "I understand that you're saying he did all the bad stuff of his own accord, but surely, when it comes to his court hearing, if someone could explain *why* it happened, it might help? After all, you've known him since he was a young boy, and you worked at the bank, so you could be a character witness. I'm willing to be one!"

"That's sweet of you, dear. The problem is that my redundancy payout is dependent on me keeping my mouth shut. I had to sign a clause agreeing that I wouldn't speak to either the media or the barrister defending Anand."

"That's blackmail, Linda!" I exclaimed.

"I'm aware of that, but without seeming selfish, that redundancy money is all I have to live on until I can draw my pension in seven years' time."

"Surely you can get another job? I mean, it sounds like you were a great PA."

"Oh, CeCe, you are sweet, dear, but I'm forty-eight. Bosses want young women, not middle-aged ones like me."

"Can't you, er, blackmail David back? I mean, you've worked for him for all these years. You must have some stuff on him."

"I certainly do. The things I could tell the newspapers about. For a start, his endless affairs, with me covering for him if his wife called the office. And his extravagance was breathtaking—only the best would do, and he'd move heaven and earth to get it. Do you know, even on the day that his precious bank was about to be sold for a pound, he sent me over to Hatton Garden to pick up a pearl he'd been hunting down for years. He'd finally traced it and had it sent to London by private jet. I took a million pounds in cash in a black cab to meet the middleman. David was like a child on Christmas Day when I returned to his office with it. I watched him open the box and take the pearl out. He held it up to the light, and admittedly, it was huge, and a pretty rose color, but David looked more in love with that jewel than I've ever seen him look with a human being."

I swallowed hard, then stared at Linda in shock. Surely it couldn't be what I thought it might be . . . ?

"Er, where did the pearl come from? Do you know?"

"Australia. Apparently, it had been lost for years."

"Did it . . . did David say it had a name? Like, because it was so special?"

"Yes, he called it the Roseate Pearl. Why?"

The spirits find greedy men and killem them . . .

"Oh, nothing." I had a horrible urge to giggle hysterically, but Linda wouldn't understand, so I controlled myself. "I really have to go now, but why don't I give you my number and we can keep in touch?"

"Yes, I'd like that," she said. We exchanged numbers, then I stood up and walked swiftly to the front door before the dam burst inside me.

"It's been good to talk to someone who understands, and who cares for Anand like I do," she said, laying a hand on my arm. "Thank you for coming."

"Please, Linda, even if you can't go to court to speak up for him, think about going to see Ace in prison. He needs you. You're . . . well, basically, his mum."

"Yes, you're right. I will think about it, dear. Good-bye now."

Outside, I walked along the road and down a narrow lane until I found a green. I sat down on a bench, and howled with what I knew was inappropriate laughter, but I couldn't help myself. If it *was* the cursed Roseate Pearl that Ace's dad had bought, which it definitely sounded like it was, then it could not have gone to a more deserving home.

Not that I wanted him to die, of course . . . well, not much, anyway.

I shivered in the cold and reached for my mobile to call the taxi driver. When the car arrived, I climbed inside, and called the Scrubs to book myself in for another visit.

When I arrived home, I realized I felt far calmer about the Ace situation. I had the strongest feeling that the Ancestors had everything in hand and David Rutter's destiny had already been set.

When I went to meet Ma at Heathrow, she emerged from Arrivals, looking elegant despite her long journey. I pushed through the crowd toward her and gave her a tight hug.

"*Chérie*, you look wonderful!" she said as she kissed me on both cheeks.

"Thanks, I'm feeling pretty good as it happens," I said and linked my arm through hers. We took a taxi to Battersea, and I led her into my apartment.

"*Mon dieu!* This is stunning." Ma stood in the center of the sitting room and waved her arms to indicate the enormous space.

"It's cool, isn't it?"

"Yes, but Star tells me you are selling it?"

"Not any longer, no. The estate agent tells me that property prices have tanked around here since I bought it, so I'm going to rent it out. The agent called earlier today. He's already found tenants for the apartment, so that's good. Can I take your coat?"

"Thank you." Ma removed it and handed it to me, then sat down and smoothed out her tweed skirt. She looked utterly immaculate as always and, comfortingly, exactly the same.

"Can I get you a cup of tea?" I asked her.

"I would love one. I refuse to eat or drink anything on a plane."

"I don't blame you," I said as I went to switch on the kettle. "Though I might have starved on the way to Australia and back if I hadn't."

"I still cannot believe you made all those journeys by yourself. I know how much you hate flying. I am proud of you, *chérie*."

"Well, life is all about facing your fears, isn't it?"

"It is. And you have made amazing progress."

"I'm trying." I took a cup of her favorite Darjeeling tea over to the coffee table and sat next to her on the sofa. "It's great to see you. Thanks for coming, Ma."

"Well, even if Star hadn't invited me to England previously, I would not have let you go off to Australia without visiting you. I'm so glad I have. And it's good to be away from Atlantis for a few days. So . . ." She took a sip of the tea. "Tell me everything."

"There's a lot to tell," I said.

"We have plenty of time. Just start at the beginning."

So I did, feeling embarrassed and awkward at first, because I realized that I'd never really been alone with Ma without Star beside me. But this was another step I had to take, now that I was my own person. Ma was the best listener I could have hoped for, and held my hand at the emotional bits, which was a good thing, because there were quite a few of them.

"Oh my, it is quite a journey that you have been on, *chérie*. And I would love to meet your grandfather," Ma said after I'd brought her up to date.

"He's special, yes." I paused then, because I needed to find the right words and not be clumsy with them. "You know, Ma, all this stuff—what Star, Maia, Ally, and me have been through—has really made me think."

"Has it?"

"Yes. About what being a parent actually is. Like, is the blood tie the most important thing?"

"What do you think, *chérie*?"

"That it was really, *really* great to meet my grandfather, but I've only added to the family I already have. I didn't need or want to replace you and Pa with a new version. It's a bit like my friend Ace—the one who's in prison; he had a mum in Thailand who he really loved, but she died. Then he got another mum here, just by chance, who's really rooted for him, like you do for all of us sisters."

"Thank you, *chérie*. I try my best."

"Ma . . ." This time, it was me who reached for *her* hand. "Hasn't it been really hard for you to see some of us going off and finding our other families? I mean, you've brought us up since we were babies."

"Ah, CeCe, you know that you are the only sister who has thought to ask me that question? I appreciate it, *chérie*. And yes, you are right. I watched you all grow from the babies you were, and was honored by the trust that your father had placed in me. For any parent, it is difficult to watch their young fly the nest, and perhaps find new families of their own from the past *or* in the present. But the fact that we are sitting here together tonight, that you wanted to see me, is enough for me, truly."

"I'll always want to see you, Ma. You're just . . . ace!"

We looked at each other, not sure whether to laugh or cry, so we decided to laugh. And then we hugged and I rested my head on her shoulder like I had done when I was little.

I looked at my phone and saw it was gone nine o'clock, and realized that Ma must be completely starving. I phoned for a takeaway, and we tucked into a delicious Thai green curry.

"So, you leave for Australia on Wednesday?" Ma asked.

"Yes. Ma," I blurted out suddenly, "can I ask you something?"

"Of course you can, *chérie*."

"Do you think Pa chose each of us girls specially, or was it random? I mean, like in my case, how come he happened to be in Broome not long after I'd been born and needed a home?"

Ma put down her spoon and fork. "*Chérie*, really, I would answer that question if I could. As you know, your father traveled a lot and I am not aware that there was a plan. Every baby that arrived at Atlantis was a surprise to me, especially you, CeCe. Why, only six months before, Star had joined us. Yes." She nodded, taking a sip of wine. "You were the biggest surprise of all."

"Was I?"

"You were." Ma smiled at me. "I also think that we humans wish to believe there is a plan. And perhaps there is, but in my experience, it isn't always man-made."

"What you're saying is that fate—or a higher power—leads you there?"

"Yes." Ma nodded vigorously. "I do believe it's true. It happened to me, for sure." Ma used her napkin to wipe her mouth, then surreptitiously wiped her eyes. "The kindness of strangers," she whispered, then took a deep breath. "So, would you excuse me if I retire for the night? From what Star has told me, we have a big evening tomorrow."

"You mean the party for Star's relative?"

"Yes, and of course, your leaving party," Ma reminded me.

"Oh yeah." I'd been so caught up in everything, I kept forgetting that I was flying off for good in little more than twenty-four hours' time.

"And I will meet her Mouse for the first time," Ma continued. "Have you met him yet?"

"Once, yes. He was . . . a nice guy," I managed. "I'm really happy that Star is happy."

Upstairs in the spare bedroom that had never been slept in, it felt really weird to show Ma where the towels were and how the shower worked, as if I were the grown-up and her the child.

"Thank you, CeCe. You have been a wonderful hostess, and I hope that one day, you will invite me to visit you in Australia."

"Course I will." I smiled. "Anytime, Ma."

"Good night, *chérie*." Ma kissed me on both cheeks. "Sleep well."

36

I surprised Ma the next day with my new early morning routine, and after a quick breakfast of croissants and coffee together, I left her to prepare for the drinks party and caught the bus to Wormwood Scrubs.

Ace slumped down in the plastic chair opposite me, looking irritated.

"I thought I told you to leave me alone," he said, crossing his arms defensively.

"Well, hello to you too," I responded. "Guess who I met yesterday?"

"CeCe, tell me you didn't—"

"Yes. I found Linda, and we had a chat, and she loves you so much," I blurted out, and leaned across the table toward him. "She told me the truth about your dad, and he's got to help you, and . . . did he know what you were doing? 'Cause if he did, then—"

"Stop! You don't know what you're talking about," he hissed, his eyes slits of anger. "It's all much more complicated than you can imagine."

"I know. Linda told me, but David is your dad, and that's not complicated at all. And he should be there for you, as your dad *and* your ex-boss, because I think he *did* know, and you're protecting him, and it's just not fair!"

Ace regarded me for a moment, then silently handed me a tissue from the box on the table between us. I hadn't even realized I was crying, but I supposed the guards were used to that in the visitors' center.

"CeCe," Ace said more gently. "I've had lots of time to think since I've been here, and when I was in Thailand with you. I knew that I would have to face up to what I'd done eventually, and that's what I'm doing now. Whether or not my dad knew—or even whether he *is* my dad—is irrelevant. It was *me* that pressed those keys on the computer to make the illegal trades. I've also realized that my fa—that David never loved me, or cared about me. Though to be fair, he doesn't care much for anything except money."

"Agreed," I said vehemently.

"So, he—and what I did—has made me realize exactly who I was becoming and don't want to be. In a way, this whole experience has saved me. The counselor has told me I can do a degree while I'm banged up. I think I'm going to take philosophy and theology. I'm only twenty-eight—I have plenty of time to make a different life once I get out of jail."

"Well, that's a positive attitude," I said, beginning to understand where he was coming from and admiring him big-time for it.

"And by the way, I know you didn't sell me out, CeCe. I checked up and that photo of us is copyrighted to a 'Jay.' You were right, and I apologize for thinking it was you. I have a lot of happy memories of us on Phra Nang Beach and I want to keep them like that."

"Me too," I gulped. "Listen, I'm moving to Australia, like, tomorrow. When you get out of prison, please come and visit me. Maybe that's where you could start your new life. It's the land of opportunity, remember?"

"Who knows? We'll keep in touch for sure. By the way, did you find out more about Kitty Mercer?"

"Better." I grinned. "I found my family."

"Then I'm happy for you, CeCe." For the first time, his face lit up in a full-blown smile. "You deserve it."

"Listen, I have to leave now, but I'll send you my new address once I'm settled there."

"Promise?" He grasped my hand as I stood up.

"Promise. Oh, and by the way," I whispered, "don't worry about your dad. I've got a feeling he's going to get everything he deserves."

I spent the afternoon packing the rest of my stuff into bin bags, which Star had said she would store at High Weald. Then I went out to buy all the bits I knew I couldn't get in Alice Springs, like Heinz baked beans and a gigantic bar of Cadbury's Fruit and Nut chocolate. Star, her mum, and Mouse were due to come to the apartment at six o'clock for my leaving drinks, before heading off to the East End. I splurged on three bottles of champagne and some beer to send them—and me—on our respective ways.

When I arrived home, loaded down with all my shopping bags, I saw that Ma had taken Star's place and was wearing her white apron, neatly tied around her waist. She greeted me at the door with a look of despair.

"*Mon dieu!* Is there a local patisserie nearby? The canapés I tried to make have gone wrong. See?"

She pointed to some weird—and actually quite arty—green pastry things that looked like someone had stamped on them.

"It's okay, Ma. I've got some tortilla chips and dip from the shop."

"Oh, CeCe, I'm so embarrassed! You have found me out." She sat down at the kitchen table and buried her face in her hands.

"Have I?"

"*Mais oui!* I am French, yet anything I cook is a disaster! The truth is that I have hidden behind Claudia for all these years. If it had been left to me to feed you girls, you would have been starved—or poisoned—to death!"

"Honestly, Ma, it doesn't matter. We love you anyway, even if you are a rubbish cook." I stifled a laugh at her distraught expression. "We all have strengths and weaknesses, remember? That's what you've always told us, anyway," I added as I dumped the tortilla chips into a bowl and put the champagne and beers into the fridge.

"It is, *chérie*, and you are right, I must accept my own."

"Yeah." I saw she needed a hug, so I went over to offer one.

"Oh, CeCe, I think that just now, out of all of my girls, I am proudest of you," she said as she stroked my hair.

"Why?"

"Because you know how to be yourself. Now, I will go upstairs and get ready for the party."

They all arrived just after six and I saw that Star's mum, Sylvia, was literally an older version of Star in more expensive clothes. She was really sweet, and told me she'd heard lots of good things about me, before giving me a hug.

"Thank you for looking after her when I couldn't," she whispered in my ear.

I immediately warmed to her, and was glad that Star had someone else who loved her as fiercely as I did.

Mouse was his usual gruff self, and I decided that if I were casting Mr. Darcy in that Jane Austen novel Star went on about all the time, I'd definitely pick him. I had to admit he was handsome, if you were into that sort of thing, but a bit standoffish, like most English aristocrats I'd met. Then I remembered that technically I was descended from a Scottish aristocrat too, and felt a bit more on the same level.

I watched as Sylvia approached Ma, and wondered how Ma felt about it. Then I closed my eyes and visualized a human heart beating. I watched it expand as it encompassed all the new people that I loved. And I understood that the heart had an infinite capacity to extend itself. And the fuller it was, the more healthily and happily it beat inside you. Best of all, my fingers itched, and I knew immediately what the inspiration for my next painting would be.

I came to as Ma pressed a glass of champagne into my hand. I noticed that everyone had quieted and was standing around me, watching me expectantly.

"Erm . . . ," I said stupidly, still dazed.

Ma came to my rescue. "I would just like to say," she began, "that I am so proud of you, CeCe, for how far you have come on your journey. *Chérie*, you are talented and brave, and your heart is true. I hope that Australia will give you everything you have been searching for in your life. We will all miss you, but we understand that our little dove must fly. *Bon voyage!*"

"*Bon voyage!*" everyone chorused, and clinked glasses. I stood back and watched them, this eclectic collection of people who had been knitted together by love. And I would always be a part of this patchwork quilt of humanity, even if I was flying off to the other side of the world tomorrow.

"Are you okay?" Star nudged me.

"Yeah, I'm fine." I swallowed. "Your family's great, by the way."

Mouse appeared at her elbow. "We need to leave now or we'll be late. Sorry, CeCe."

"Okay." Star looked at me miserably. "Cee, are you sure you don't want to come to the party with us?"

"Really, don't worry about me. I need to do some final clearing up and packing. It's just bad timing."

"I should stay here with you tonight." Star bit her lip as Mouse handed her her coat. "Oh, Cee, I have no idea when we'll see each other again."

Sylvia came to say good-bye to me and wish me luck, then it was Ma's turn.

"Good-bye, *chérie*, promise me you will take good care of yourself, and keep in touch?" Ma hugged me, and I saw Star shrug on her coat, then begin to walk back toward me.

"Darling, we're going to be late." Mouse took her arm and led her firmly toward the door. "Bye, CeCe."

I love you, Star signed to me from the doorway.

Love you too, I signed back.

The door swung shut with a bang behind her, and I did my best not to howl my eyes out. I hated Mouse for not even allowing us a proper good-bye.

I put the glasses and plates into the dishwasher, glad of the distraction, then I went to my studio and dismantled my installation, taking it down piece by piece to the communal rubbish container outside the building.

"You're binned," I said to Mr. Guy Fawkes as I stuffed him inside and slammed down the lid. Upstairs in the apartment, I watered Star's plants for the last time. She'd handed me her key earlier, entreating me to make sure the new tenants took care of her "babies," as she called them.

"Wow, this is seriously the end of an era," I muttered as I paced the apartment, the silence around me reminding me of why I'd gone to Australia in the first place. Putting on my hoodie, I braved the cold night air out on the terrace. I thought of Linda, and the life she'd never had; how she'd spent hers loving someone who would never love her. I felt a bit better then because, unlike her, I had a future to go to with people who *did* love me. What it might contain, I still wasn't sure, but it was there for me to write it. Or, more accurately, paint it.

I looked up and found the tiny milky cluster and I thought how much brighter the Seven Sisters shone over the Alice.

My new home.

When the taxi arrived at five the next morning, the sky was still depressingly dark. In the end, I hadn't bothered to go to bed, hoping it would help me sleep on the plane later. As we drove away from my apartment, a text pinged onto my phone.

> CeCe, this is Linda Potter. I've given it a lot of thought, and I've decided to visit Anand. You were right, he needs my help and I will do what I can. God bless you, and safe journey to Australia.

Relief and pride rose up inside me, because I had changed Linda's mind. *Me*, with my clumsy words . . . I'd actually managed to make a difference.

I checked in my three bags at Heathrow and walked to the security entrance, wondering if I'd remember this moment for the rest of my life, because it was so seminal. Then I thought how it was never the big moments I remembered; it was always the little things—picked out at random by some weird alchemy—that stuck in the photo album of my brain.

I dug in the front of my rucksack for my boarding pass, and my hand brushed against the sugary brown envelope which had once contained the clues to my past.

"Christ," I breathed as I handed my boarding pass to the woman. I felt like it was almost a rerun of two months ago.

The woman nodded at me as she took it, looking half-asleep, which was only fair because it wasn't even seven o'clock in the morning yet. I was just about to walk through when I heard a voice behind me.

"CeCe! Stop!"

I was so tired that I thought I was dreaming.

"Celaeno D'Aplièse! *Arrête!* Stop!"

I turned around and there was Star.

"Oh my God, Cee!" Star panted as she arrived beside me. "I thought I'd missed you. Why on earth weren't you answering your phone?"

"I switched it off when I got out of the taxi," I said. "What are you doing here?"

"We didn't say good-bye properly last night. And I couldn't let you leave without giving you a proper hug and telling you how much I'm going to miss you, and"—Star wiped her nose on her sleeve—"saying thank you for everything you've done for me."

She flung her arms around me and held me tighter than she ever had before, as if she couldn't bear to let me go. We stood there for a while, then I pulled away, knowing if I didn't, I'd stay forever.

"I'd better go through," I mumbled, my voice croaky with emotion. "Thanks so much for coming."

"I'll always be there for you, darling Cee."

"Me too. Bye, Sia."

"Bye. Keep in touch, won't you? And promise you'll come back to Atlantis for Pa's first anniversary in June?"

"Course I will."

I blew a final kiss to Star, then I turned away and walked through security and into my future.

TIGGY

The Highlands Scotland

January 2008

37

Y ou sure about going out again later, Tig? There's a blizzard comin' in," Cal said to me as he studied the benign blue sky through our cottage window, the midday sun sprinkling a glitter topping on the permanent layer of snow that covered the ground all winter. The view was Christmas-card perfect.

"Yes! We just can't take the chance, Cal, you know we can't."

"I doubt even the Abominable Snowman'll be out tanite," Cal muttered.

"You promised we'd keep watch," I entreated him. "Look, I'll take the radio with me and contact you if there's any trouble."

"Tig, d'you really think I'm going tae let a wee lassie like you sit alone in a snowstorm while there's a possible poacher with a rifle prowling the estate? Don't be a dafty," Cal growled at me, his ruddy features showing irritation, then finally, compliance. "No longer than a couple o' hours, mind. After that, I'm dragging you home by the hair. I'll not be responsible for you ending up with hypothermia again. Understand?"

"Thanks Cal," I replied with relief. "I know Pegasus is in danger. I just . . . know it."

The snow had fallen thickly around us in the dugout and the tarpaulin roof had buckled under the weight of it. I wondered if it would collapse altogether and we would be buried alive under the sheer weight of snow above us.

"We're leavin' now, Tig," said Cal. "I'm numb to my innards an' we'll be struggling tae drive back. The blizzard's eased for a while and we need tae get home while we can." Cal took a last slurp of lukewarm coffee from the flask then offered it to me. "Finish that. I'll go an' clear the snow off the windshield and get the heat going."

"Okay," I sighed, knowing there was no point in arguing.

We'd sat in the dugout for over two hours, watching nothing but the snow hurl itself to the ground. Cal left and headed toward the Land Rover, parked beyond a stone outcrop in the valley behind us. I peered out through the tiny window of the dugout as I sipped the coffee, then turned off the hurricane lamp and crawled outside. I didn't need my flashlight as the sky had cleared and now twinkled with thousands of stars, the Milky Way clearly visible above me. The moon, which was waxing and within two days of being full, shone down, illuminating the pristine white blanket that covered the ground.

The utter silence that came just after fresh snowfall was as deep as the sparkling carpet that claimed my feet and most of my calves.

Pegasus.

I called him silently, searching for him around the cluster of birch trees that marked our special place. He was a magnificent white stag, whom I'd first noticed when I'd joined Cal on his rounds of the estate counting the deer. Pegasus had been grazing among a cluster of red deers and at first I'd thought that perhaps he was yet to shake the snow from his body. I'd alerted Cal and pointed out the spot, but by the time he'd focused the binoculars, the herd had moved away up the hill, camouflaging the mystical and all too rare creature that ran somewhere in their midst.

Cal hadn't believed me. "White stags are akin tae the golden fleece, Tig. Everyone searches for them, but I've been on this estate for all o' my life an' I've never seen the hide o' one." Chuckling at his own joke, he'd climbed back into the Land Rover and we'd moved on.

I knew, however, that I *had* seen the stag, so I'd returned to the copse with Cal the following day, and as often as I could after that.

My patience had finally been rewarded as I'd crouched behind a thicket of gorse and trained my binoculars on the ragged birch trees. Then I'd seen him, standing away from the others just to my left, perhaps only ten feet from me.

"Pegasus," I'd whispered, the name arriving on my tongue as though it had always been there. And then, as if he knew it was his name, he'd lifted up his head and looked at me. We'd held eye contact for perhaps only five seconds before Cal had arrived beside me and sworn loudly in wonder at the fact that my "flight o' fancy" had actually been real.

That moment had been the start of a love affair, a strong, strange alchemy connecting us. I'd rise at dawn, when I knew that the herds were still taking shelter from the biting winds at the bottom of the valley, and drive to the cluster of trees that provided scant protection from the bitter cold. Within a few minutes, as if he sensed my presence, Pegasus would appear. Each time, he'd take a step closer and, following his lead, so would I. I felt he was beginning to trust me, and at night I dreamed of one day being able to touch the velvety gray-white of his neck, but . . .

At my old animal sanctuary, my natural ability to connect with the young motherless or injured deer that had been brought to us to nurse back to health had been an asset. Here at Kinnaird, the livestock were wild, living as nature had intended them to and roaming the twenty-three-thousand-acre estate with minimal interference from humans. Apart from controlling their deaths through the organized culling of both stags and hinds.

During the shooting season, wealthy businessmen arrived at the estate on corporate hospitality jaunts and paid exorbitant prices to shed their aggression through their first experience of a live kill, then returned home to hang a deer's skull on their wall as a trophy.

"There's nae natural predators left, Tig." Cal, the estate ghillie—whose gruff manner and a Scottish accent you could cut with a knife hid a genuine love for the natural wilderness he struggled to protect—had done his best to comfort me when I'd first walked into the estate larder to find four blooded and skinned hinds hanging by their hooves. "We humans have tae take their place. It's the natural order of things. Y'know their numbers have tae be kept under control."

Of course I *knew*, but that didn't make it any easier when I was faced with mutilated life, snuffed out by a man-made bullet.

"O' course, Pegasus is somethin' different, somethin' rare an' beautiful. He'll not be touched on my watch, I swear tae you."

How word had got out that a white stag had been spotted on the Kinnaird Estate and passed to the press, I didn't know, but it was only a few days later that a journalist from the local newspaper had beaten the treacherous path to our door. I'd been beside myself, entreating Cal to deny Pegasus's existence—to say it was a hoax—knowing that a white stag's head was catnip for any poacher, who would sell it on to the highest bidder.

Which was why I was standing here now at two in the morning in an eerie frozen wonderland. Cal and I had constructed a primitive dugout close to the copse of birch trees and kept watch. All land in Scotland was open to the public, and we had no idea who might be prowling around the estate in the darkness.

I walked slowly toward the trees, begging the stag to make an appearance so I'd be able to go home and sleep, knowing he was safe for one more night.

He appeared as if from nowhere, a mystical sight as he raised his head to the moon, then turned, his deep brown eyes fixed upon me. He began to walk hesitantly toward me, and I to him.

"Darling Pegasus," I whispered, then immediately saw a shadow appear on the snow from the cluster of trees. The shadow raised a rifle.

"No!" I screamed into the silence. The figure was behind the stag, his gun aimed and ready to fire. "Stop! Run Pegasus!"

The stag turned around and saw the danger, but then, rather than bolting away to safety, he began to run toward me. A shot rang out, then two more, and I felt a sudden sharp pain in my side. My heart gave a strange jolt and began to pound so fast that dizziness engulfed me. My knees turned to jelly and I sank onto the snowy blanket beneath me.

There was silence again. I tried to hold on to consciousness, but I couldn't fight the dark any longer, not even for him.

Sometime later, I opened my eyes and saw a beloved, familiar face above me.

"Tiggy, sweetheart, you're going to be all right. Stay with me now, won't you?"

"Yes, Pa, of course I will," I whispered as he stroked my hair just as he used to when I was sick as a little girl. I closed my eyes once more, knowing that I was safe in his arms.

When I woke up again, I felt someone lifting me from the ground. I searched around for Pa, but all I saw above me was Cal's panicked features as he struggled to carry me to safety. As I turned my head back toward the cluster of trees, I saw the prone body of a white stag, blood-red drops spattering the snow around him.

And I knew he had gone.

Author's Note

The joy of writing the Seven Sisters series is that each sister—and subsequently their journey—is totally different from the last. And this has never been more apparent than when I finished Star's story and began to think about CeCe's story. I realized that I was as fearful about embarking on it as she is. I too was reticent about traveling to Australia—one of the only large landmasses in the world I had never visited, mainly due to its infamous huge and dangerous spiders. However, just like CeCe and her other sisters, I had to overcome my fears, so I got on that plane and traversed Australia to find the research detail I needed. And in the process, fell in love with this incredible, complex country. Especially the "Never Never"—the vast area around Alice Springs, colloquially known as "the Alice"—which, to my utter delight, I discovered is the high temple of the Seven Sisters of the Pleiades myths and legends. Learning not only about the beauty, but also the pure practicality, of a belief system and culture that kept the indigenous Aboriginal population alive for over fifty thousand years in the unforgiving landscape was perhaps the most humbling moment of my many research journeys across the globe.

I am a fiction novelist, but I take the background research to my novels as seriously as any historian, because history—and the effect it has on the lives of not only my sisters, but *us* in the present too—is my passion. Both the stories of the sinking of the *Koombana* and the Roseate Pearl are taken from historical accounts, although the last sighting of the pearl was on the fated *Koombana*'s last journey up the coast to Broome and I added a possible fictional outcome from there.

Even though every detail in the books is checked and triple-checked, what I have come to understand is that every account of a historical event is subjective, simply because every written or spoken view is a human one. Therefore, any mistakes in my interpretation of the facts in *The Pearl Sister* are totally my own.

Acknowledgments

So many people have contributed to the research for this novel and I am hugely grateful to each and every one of them:

In Adelaide, my old friend and London lodger, Mark Angus, who was my tour guide, chauffeur, and fount of knowledge, especially on the best Aussie wine! In Broome, Jay Bichard at the Pearl Luggers Tour, the staff at the Broome Historical Society, and the Yawuru community. In Alice Springs, major thanks go to Phil Cooke and Alli Turner, who traveled from Brisbane to the Alice to accompany us on our research tour. Driving out to Hermannsburg through the "Never Never" was a journey I shall never forget. Thank you to Adam Palmer and Lehi Archibald at the Telegraph Station, and Rodney Matuschka at Hermannsburg Mission. And to a number of indigenous Australian men and women we met on our journey, who did not wish to be named, but helped me form a picture of their life and culture.

In Thailand, a big thank-you to Natty, who—when I was writing Kitty's past and the temperature soared to 113 degrees, breaking the air-conditioning—did her best to keep me sane and cool. And to Patrick at the Rayavadee Villas on Phra Nang Beach, who warded off the monkeys and kept me fed and watered.

Also a huge thank-you to Ben Brinsden, who patiently guided my writing of CeCe's texts, and helped me understand the challenges of dyslexia.

The biggest thanks of all have to go to Olivia Riley, my fantastic PA and helpmeet, who traversed Australia with me and kept me going. Nothing was too much trouble and I really couldn't have done it without you, Livi.

To all my fantastic publishers across the world, who have supported both me and the Seven Sisters series from the very beginning, even though most of them have since admitted they thought I was crazy to embark on such a huge project: Jez and Catherine at Pan Macmillan, UK; Knut, Pip, and Jorid at Cappelen Damm, Norway; Georg, Claudia, and the team at

Goldmann, Germany; Donatella, Antonio, Annalisa, and Allessandro at Giunti, Italy; Marite and Una at Zvaigzne ABC, Latvia; Jurgita at Tyto Alba, Lithuania; Fernando, Nana, and "the Brothers" at Arqueiro, Brazil; and Marie-Louise, Anne, and Jakob at Rosinante, Denmark, to name but a few. You have all become my friends and we have shared so much laughter together when I have visited for a tour. Thank you, thank you, thank you, for being such caring and wise godparents to the sisters, and to me.

I am hugely grateful to Ella Micheler, Susan Moss, Jacquelyn Heslop, Lesley Burns, and of course, Olivia Riley—more commonly known as "Team Lulu"—who have provided vital research, editorial assistance, and domestic backup behind the scenes during what has been a chaotic year. Thank you all for your patience and ability to multitask at short notice as I, and my life, become ever more busy. And to Stephen—husband, agent, adviser, and best friend—I simply couldn't do this without you.

Harry, Bella, Leonora, and Kit—I'm so proud of each one of you. You make me scream with laughter, frustration, and happiness, and never fail to bring me down to earth. I love you all.

Last, as always, to my readers around the world: You have taken my sisters to your hearts, laughed, loved, and cried with them as I have done when I am writing their stories. Simply because we—and they—are human. Thank you.

Lucinda Riley
April 2017

BIBLIOGRAPHY

The Pearl Sister is a work of fiction set against a historical background. The sources I've used to research the time period and details of my characters' lives are listed below:

Munya Andrews, *The Seven Sisters of the Pleiades* (Spinifex Press, 2004).

John Bailey, *The White Divers of Broome* (Pan Macmillan Australia, 2002).

Annie Boyd, *Koombana Days* (Fremantle Press, 2013).

Diney Costeloe, *The Throwaway Children* (Head of Zeus, 2015).

J. E. deB. Norman and G. V. Norman, *A Pearling Master's Journey* (BPA Print Group Pty Ltd, 2008).

Susanna de Vries, *Great Pioneer Women of the Outback* (Harper Collins, 2005).

Mark Dodd, *The Last Pearling Lugger* (Pan Macmillan Australia, 2011).

Martin Edmond, *Battarbee and Namatjira* (Giramondo, 2014).

Aji Ellies, *The Pearls of Broome* (CopyRight Publishing Company Pty Ltd, 2010).

Barry Hill, *Broken Song: TGH Strehlow and Aboriginal Possession* (Vintage, 2002).

Ion L. Idriess, *Forty Fathoms Deep* (Angus and Robertson Limited, 1945).

John Lamb, *Silent Pearls: Old Japanese Graves in Darwin and the History of Pearling* (Bytes On Colours, 2015).

Peter Latz, *Blind Moses* (IAD Press, 2014).

Carl Strehlow, *Die Aranda- und Loritja-Stämme in Zentral-Australien*, vols. 1–5 (Joseph Baer and Co., 1907–1920).

T. G. H. Strehlow, *Journey to Horseshoe Bend* (Giramondo, 2015).

John G. Withnell, *The Customs and Traditions of the Aboriginal Natives of North Western Australia* (Dodo Press, 1901).

ABOUT THE AUTHOR

Lucinda Riley is the *New York Times* bestselling author of *The Orchid House*, *The Girl on the Cliff*, *The Lavender Garden*, *The Midnight Rose*, *The Seven Sisters*, *The Storm Sister*, and *The Shadow Sister*. Her books have sold more than ten million copies in thirty languages globally. She was born in Ireland and divides her time between England and West Cork with her husband and four children.

www.lucindariley.com
www.thesevensisters.com
www.facebook.com/lucindarileyauthor
www.twitter.com/lucindariley

Author Q & A

1. How does the fourth sister, CeCe, relate to her mythological counterpart?

Celaeno's mythological story and personality, as CeCe points out herself, is the least-documented of all the Seven Sisters. So I took the bones of CeCe's legend, then set her free to create her own destiny in not only the land of new possibilities but, ironically, the high temple of The Seven Sisters legends themselves, where the girls are revered in Aboriginal culture.

2. CeCe is in many ways the polar opposite to her sister Star—how did you find her voice?

To begin with, CeCe was definitely the sister I was most nervous about writing. I was worried that readers would have a negative view of her before they came to read *The Pearl Sister*, as she seems controlling and abrupt. In *The Shadow Sister* we see the breakdown of Star and CeCe's relationship from Star's perspective. But as CeCe points out, there are always two sides to every story and *The Pearl Sister* is hers. Writing CeCe was a total revelation. She has such a unique and interesting perspective on life. She's always calling herself a "dunce," but that's because she struggled at school due to her dyslexia. In reality CeCe is seriously bright, funny, talented, and very, very *real*. When we meet her, she is so vulnerable and full of self-doubt and I don't think I have *ever* felt as protective about a character as I feel about CeCe.

3. You have written about Thailand before in *The Orchid House*. How did you feel about revisiting it in *The Pearl Sister*?

Thailand is one of my favorite places in the world, and I visit every year with my family. Our favourite place is Phra Nang Beach and I was walking along the shore early one morning when I came up with the character of Ace and why he is hiding out on the beach. People travel to this magical peninsula to "find themselves" and it also seemed apt for CeCe to begin her journey there while she gathers the courage to continue to Australia. I stayed on in Thailand to write the first draft of *The Pearl Sister,* with a one-legged mynah bird called Colin for company!

4. How did you approach the research for this book?

The research was like the country of Australia itself—vast! I always begin by reading everything that I can get my hands on, and while I was in Australia I found a number of out-of-print historical books, which provided the detail I needed on the pearling industry in Broome. Sadly, Aboriginal history has largely been documented by white men, from their subjective view rather than the Aboriginal people themselves. Their culture has always been passed down to the next generation by word of mouth. Luckily, I was able to find several online resources, such as a community website of the Yawuru people (whom I write about in Broome) which contained a dictionary of their language and information on their traditions and their Dreamtime stories.

The sinking of the *Koombana* was one of the greatest maritime disasters in Australia's history. I then discovered that whenever the *Koombana* or Broome are mentioned in historical texts, the Roseate Pearl makes a cameo appearance. The rumors of its curse were written down in *Forty Fathoms Deep*, a book published in 1937 about pearl divers in Broome. There are many different legends surrounding the pearl, perhaps the most well-known is this one: It was found by a white pearling master, but stolen by a diver. Two Chinese burglars then stole the pearl and it was sold to a man who then died of a heart attack. The next owner committed suicide when it was stolen from him, and in 1905, a pearl trader was murdered over it. Finally Abraham De Vahl Davis, a wealthy pearl dealer, is thought to have purchased it for £20,000 before boarding the *Koombana*, and that is the last we heard about it. Unless, of course, it wasn't on the ship at all . . .

5. What surprised you the most when you visited Australia?

One of my main source texts for the Pleiades myths has been Munya Andrews's *The Seven Sisters of the Pleiades*. Andrews herself is from the Kimberley region in Western Australia, so it was amazing to see the birthplace of these stories that have been orally passed down for thousands of years. Even though I knew how important the Seven Sisters are in Aboriginal culture, I was not expecting to see them so ingrained in everyday life. Walking through Alice Springs, I saw homages to the Sisters everywhere. It felt like a homecoming for me and, like CeCe, I totally fell in love with the Never Never.

6. You have mentioned before that there is an invisible plot thread spun throughout the books. Can you give us a hint about what is hidden in *The Pearl Sister*? What should we look out for in future books in the series?

There are hidden clues throughout the books, and every day I receive questions and theories from my readers as to #whoispasalt and where the "missing" seventh sister is. I can neither confirm nor deny any of them! The overarching plot is detailed in a file that is well hidden. Only six people on the planet know the ending. I had to write it down for the production team of the TV series of *The Seven Sisters*.

7. Yes, while you were writing *The Pearl Sister*, you made a deal with a Hollywood production company for a TV adaptation of the Seven Sisters series.

The series has been optioned by Raffaella di Laurentiis's production company, and the project is still in its early stages. The production company is very brave—they have their work cut out for them, as the story spans so many locations and time periods, but I trust them completely to translate the sisters' journey to the screen.

8. CeCe and Chrissie's relationship is very tender and complex. Can you tell us more about CeCe's journey toward discovering who she is?

When CeCe embarks on her journey to Australia, it's the first time in her life that she's taken off without Star. It was fascinating to write the development of her relationships with both Ace and Chrissie, who are very different people, but who each bring out something different in her. While Ace gives CeCe self-confidence and friendship, Chrissie helps CeCe find out who she is, what her roots are, and what a "home" truly means. Throughout the book, CeCe struggles with her identity, as we all do in our different ways at various points in our lives. CeCe is a work in progress and even by the end of *The Pearl Sister*, she is still uncertain about her sexuality, but at least she has begun her journey of self-realization and rediscovered her talent, her passion for art and found the inner confidence she so lacked.